Cry of Justice

Cry of Justice

Jason Pratt

Bittersea Publications

For further information, please contact:

AtlasBooks
30 Amberwood Parkway
Ashland, OH 44805
www.atlasbooks.com

Printed in the United States

Cry of Justice
Jason Pratt

1. Title 2. Author 3. Fantasy

ISBN: 978-0-9778884-0-5
Library of Congress Control Number: 2006902083

ACKNOWLEDGMENTS

Thank you, various readers over at critters.org, for feedback on drafts of Section One of *Cry of Justice*. I hope the rest of the story measures up to your expectations; and I'll be back someday (I hope)—this time as a publisher.

Thank you, Alex and Family, for giving me breaks from writing (and editing, and editing, and *editing* . . .) All work and no play makes Jason kind of edgy!

Thank you, Jim and Dale, for helping me save the U.T. Knoxville Fencing Team from extinction. Being a swordfighter—and a teacher—in the decades since (well, more than a decade anyway), makes a sufficiently obvious contribution to the story, I think.

Thank you, Stefan, for being the very first person to ever read the book besides myself. I hope other readers will be cheering along as loudly as you, during the Macro Fight Scene at the end (in an airport or otherwise!) Now anyone who wants to know what happens in Book 2 can go bug Stefan, who lives in a Nashville. (Ah—but *which* Nashville? Have fun . . . !)

Thank you, Bro, for helping me learn and appreciate strategies and tactics over 20 years of playing games against you.

Thank you, Mom and Dad, for being awfully patient with me over the years, what with the late nights away and missed dinners and all. Hopefully you'll have more reason to be patient with me for decades to come! This is my life—and I wouldn't be here (including at all!) without you.

Thank you, Jen, for helping to keep me sane, through the most difficult years of my life.

Thank you, Marie, for preventing the book from being *completely* unreadable. It simply would not be here without you; and (hopefully) generations of readers will owe you a debt they can never completely repay. (Although they can make a stab at that, by reading *your* books as well! Visit swantower.com to see what Marie is currently up to in fantasy writing!)

As for my highest acknowledgments . . . well, those will be in the dedication.

And then—the end begins.

(And now let us see what the future will bring . . .)

DEDICATION

yuqowç hfu yihhur mua,
lfuru paw I ko, I favu woh asruaçí kowu?
Lfuw liss ní musgimfwumm yu çumhroíquç?
Lfí lam I kivuw, lfah I lam kivuw?
Lfo lam I kivuw gor?
Lfah kooç im hfu folu iw ní fuarh,
lfipf muubm ihm sigu iw hornuwh?
Fol preyuç ho bolçur
nemh ní fuarh yuponu
yugoru I giwimf çíiwk, Sorç?
Quh, ass liss vu luss
or lo Qoe favu bronimuç.
Wuvurhfulumm:
gor hfu owum I sovu hfu nomh
hfu Owu Ayovu awç hfu owu yulol
I an brubaruç ho yuar hfu folu iw ní fuarh
goruvur
ig hfah im lfah Qoe loesç favu og nu
ashfoetf I twol hfah yoe nemh lawh monuhfiwk noru
gor nu
Ní fobu nemh woh yu gor nímusg,
yeh nemh yu gor hfu owu
gor lfon Qoe kivu Qoer vurí sigu.
awç quh
ig hfim peb
paw vu bammuç
lihfiw Qoer liss
I braí
hfah monuowu liss yu laihiwk gor nu
yuqowç hfu yihhur mua

Jason Pratt
March 27, 2006

TABLE OF CONTENTS

Section Six—WITHOUT

PREFACE

My wife, my beloved;
  I promise.
  I can explain.
  I can explain where I went. And why.
  I can explain why I didn't explain, when I returned.
  I didn't explain . . . because I was afraid.
  Our duties require us to be apart, sometimes—as you yourself are gone. Always we have kept in touch, even when apart.
  But . . . this time I could *not* do so. Not because a power prevented me; but . . . because . . .
    . . . *how can I explain . . . ?*

  I wanted to tell you. You deserve to know, because you love me. But I couldn't find the courage—and now you are gone.
  And you refuse to keep in touch this time.
  I deserve no better.

  But, how to tell you . . . how to explain . . .
  so much pain and horror and death . . .
  and I am responsible . . .

  I brought back books from that world. I tried to save something.
  I needed to find a place to begin.
  I met people there. This is their story—the story that I am responsible for destroying.
  They never knew that, of course. I never told them.

  There is one who suffered most. She *also* was responsible—for terrible things. She also wrote a confession.
  I will begin with her story. And I see another I met; who is also part of her story. Good.

I will follow their history, then; using her book and those of others to guide my search. It won't take long, by our standards—I can write it in a day; you can read it in an hour.

I am a coward. I rather would tell you a story of them—

than simply to tell you the truth.

But, I promise: you *shall* have the truth.

In this life, or in the next.

Introduction—To a World

I will tell you a story, beloved;
    a story of a cradle.

Once,
there was a world,
bobbing and spinning within the center of her space,
infused with life, alit by lights both great and small,
upon her and above her.
From the beginning, she had borne her children
—not to stay, but to leave.

But, the children did not always play well.
And, they did not always leave well.
Sometimes they pushed each other out.

Sometimes, they pushed each other hard.

On this cradle lay a vastness of mountains and forests, lakes and islands, rivers and valleys and plains. Half the cradle, the children called Mikon; the other half was water.
On the land, the children lived.
The children often grew into monsters.

Fires and floods, storms and quakes, blood and steel and wood and life, crackled and *cracked.* This happened many times in Mikon.
And monsters laughed—
while a mother cried, and a father sighed . . .

I look upon them with my power, beloved—
with the power that doomed them.
I look through their space; I see their times.
I read their words.
I read their minds.

I will allow them to tell their story, letting them lead where I will look, respecting them.

I will live within them; I will let them teach me.

I will let them speak through me, as they would have spoken.

I will tell what they would have told, had they been able.

I will do no less.

I can do no more.

no more.

❖ ❖ ❖

And so I look along the line of their time. Three sources gleam as lights to begin my hunt, through the darkness of their history—that they do not know has almost reached its end.

I see a stag, stepping cautiously through the dappled shadows of early night, cropping grass as it moved from place to place, comfortable in its confidence, instinctively trusting its nose and ears in the quiet misty dusk.

Its reactions to food, and brush, and paths of unquiet travel were largely predictable; but, the buck couldn't know this.

So, it was entirely natural for the deer to pass too close to one particular tree.

From behind that tree, now on the deer's left flank, an unnatural shriek erupted.

The deer's heart *surged!* —it leaped away in the other direction, responding precisely in line with its instincts.

Consequently, the deer leaped straight through a wall of brush.

The stag *thrashed* the entangling branches and leaves, ripping with its rack of antlers. The threatened attack had not yet come, but the stag couldn't ponder what this meant. It only struggled, eventually tearing free on the brush's farther side, bleeding from minor cuts, its right eye swollen shut from a poke by a branch.

The stag gasped for air, and gathered itself to leap again—

—one leg crumpled as weight was applied.

The deer crept through the tiny glade, regressing to cries of infancy.

But, it couldn't bear the physical stress; and so it fell, quietly.

Its ears twitched; its nostrils flared; its neck bobbed, this way and that.

All these movements made it feel more comfortable—slightly. Nothing gave it new signs to fear.

The stag began to relax. The starlight-speckled glade was swirling in the deer's euphoric relief.

The deer felt sleepy.

The deer felt a spike punch through its lungs and heart.

It jerked in response—then spiraled deeper into its relief . . . no leap could save it from such a wound.

The deer felt only its final need—as if to sleep.

The spike stabbed, twice again. The deer felt neither stab.

The dull-black spike, longer than the body of the deer, withdrew: gripped, by a black hand, of a black arm, glistening with sweat, stretching from the nearby brush. A tall, limber creature raised itself on legs with muscles taut as cables.

Unlike the deer, the only hair the creature wore was thin and close on the top of its head.

Unlike the deer, the creature wore . . . *more*—though not much more than hair: short barbadense trousers, harvested from Manavilin Island; woven in Fyzabad City; dyed—black to match the creature's skin.

The deer would have thought the creature a monster, had it been able to judge.

The creature thought of himself as a man.

But he wondered, as he laid his palm on the deer he had pierced, how close he was to being a monster.

The man did *not* gloat over his crafty slaying. He had alerted the deer, not only to make it entangle itself—but to give it a fair running start.

He would have trotted silently afterward, tracking the sounds of flight, the sight of starlight-scattering flicks in the night, even the smell of the blood.

Had it escaped detection, he would have bidden the deer goodspeed.

The deer would not, *could* not, have begun to understand fairness.

Sometimes, the man wished neither could he.

In recent weeks especially.

The man returned through the forest, bearing the body away from the quiet nightly hum, the patchy starlit glades. He returned: to the brightening fires of controlled destruction, by which his species survived—even when at peace.

His species hadn't been at peace for several seasons.

He passed pickets; then paced between the fires at night—a creature who killed: a man of the Guacu-ara . . . the Hunting Cry.

The men and women around him didn't see him, as he carried his catch to the cooks of the camp; or, if they happened to see him, they looked away.

They did not speak to him; because he never really spoke to them.

Because he never really spoke to them, words had boiled his brain for weeks. He had bought a book and pen.

So he returned, to where he had put his small, blank book; through dangerous men who shrank away if they saw him, back to each other and back to their fires, back to polishing swords and axes, back to the safety that lay in numbers.

For this man, Seifas, safety had never lain in numbers; but in movement, in striking first and striking last.

Yet, now, as he slid into his own small tent, he faced an enemy he could no longer avoid, with which he must now do battle—perhaps to the death.

He faced his own despair.

Seifas sat, knelt, lay himself down; turned up his small lantern; and started to write:

"It all has fallen apart . . ."

SECTION ONE
TURNING POINTS

CHAPTER 1

It all has fallen apart.
Again.

Sometimes at night I see the glow of another village burning.
Behind closed eyes, at night, I see that glow again: of coals that shouldn't burn.
I don't have tears enough, to wash away those fires.
Why does this always happen?
Where are the Agents?
Where is the Eye??
I don't even know why such a war is called a Culling . . .

Matron Cami might have known. But she is gone—the woman who tried so hard to teach us juacuara something other than how to hurl a javelin fifty paces or to knock out a brain with a blade.

She tried to give us poetry for our souls; to help express and judge the events of our lives; to make some sense of the hidden world behind the obvious.

My Matron is gone.

She vanished one day.

. . . perhaps that was best. Her heart would have broken, in bearing the tragedies afterward.

No . . .

No, not that. She would have led us, and we would have followed her, putting our faith in her wisdom and strength.

Was that why she was taken?

Was that why she went away?

Other klerosa than Cami have vanished: the indisputable sign of a Culling. All klerosa—the ones allotted true power, true healing—always go, and never are seen again.

Leaving us alone to put our trust in . . .

. . . what?

My weapon? My body? My peer? My commander? These shall all fail me. I know this distinctly.

Trust in the magi? They surely did *not* disappear all at once! They chose their sides and disbanded the Cadre, and scoured the skies and the lakes and the trees with their wrath!

A year they did this; then, within the slopes of a season, they also fell silent—leaving the wounds they had made.

I remember Qarfax, who claimed four faces guarded him, so that he would *never* be caught by surprise. He had hired a garrison for his private tower: I and some troops from the city of Wye.

His fear drenched the air of his tower.

Whenever a man—moreover a magus—invests his soul within a place, his presence seeps into the stones.

But when we awoke one night for our watch, I knew with some others: the feel was gone. We wouldn't find Qarfax alive.

We found some ash on the floor of his room instead, where he had watched and waited.

We never learned for what he had waited. We left his service that very moment.

We also left his regalia, on the floor, within the ash—no one would touch the remains of a magus.

The students of magic—the dabblers and the apprentices—will soon recover their masters' work. I serve one now: Portunista.

But, I don't trust her either . . .

No, nothing mortal remains to trust. Not even my brethren, destroyed by the wars of the Culling.

I have no home. No family.

No hope.

Some men say they only trust themselves.

I am not so foolish. I know my strengths; and I know my weaknesses. I might as well lift myself into the air by pulling my arms . . . !

No answers. No hope.

No justice.

These thoughts all dart behind my eyes, after the middle of the night, in front of the glow of villages burning, until I spill them onto paper.

I am a soldier. My words are my tears.

They don't wash away the fires.

CHAPTER 2

From the dark man in his darkness, my beloved, I turn; looking forward seven summers.

On the edge of mountains and plains, a bright clean palace gleams.

Within its halls, a woman walks; slowly, stiffly, smoothly, straight and tall.

Her long auburn hair is dancing with life; her face, however, can no longer show so much expression. Her royal gown of greens and browns, trails behind. Her servants pause to smile and bow.

They love the fragile smile she gives in return; they know she cannot give much more, and wonder about the tears they see on her cheeks. Some of them think they know why.

Some of them speculate wildly.

Some of them are correct.

She wants them to know—more than they know; more than they will be comfortable knowing.

One day, they will learn why they see those tears.

But, that time cannot come, until she takes a first step of hundreds.

Smoothly she glides, stepping out into her quiet garden, which she touches.

Slowly she glides, up the baked stone face of her tower, which she does not touch; although as always she checks it for wear.

She gently steps into her wide upper room, between its narrow encircling columns.

A servant waits, having ascended by stairs curving up through the floor. The servant has brought what she asked, and sets it on a tilted frame.

The woman nods to him, and with a gracious gesture she dismisses him.

He will do the same for her on each first day, each week, for years to come.

The woman carefully lowers her willowy body into a nearby tall-backed chair, billows of hair arranging in comfort around her.

She pulls the frame to her. Upon the frame: a shallow tray filled smooth with clay.

The woman casts her mind back through the years; back to the days when she leaped and crouched and stormed through life.

Then she reaches, and sinks a stylus-tip into the clay. Along with this she sinks her thoughts.

I am the Empress of Mikon.
I do not know how long I have, before the next great change.

My people have often represented my body and face; indeed, moreso than any woman's in history. Somewhere a sage is collecting a record of all my public utterances.

But, the paintings and sculptures and statues of me, are only of my body. Even my sayings do not reveal my soul, my mind, my history.

My people deserve to know, to remember, the truth about me.

I remember. I have failed in so many things, and most of my people do not know—or do not remember.

They *should* know. They must remember.

On a day to come, their disillusionment, though divisive, still will serve its place in the fate of the nations.

And, perhaps, this testimony shall also serve historians, helping them piece together events of the past few years. I held a central place in the history of our lands, of Mikon, after the most recent Culling.

I did not know what privilege I had been granted.

Oh, I surely asserted my "privileges"! I thought I snatched them by my will, from the anarchy of that time.

I was a fool.

Already I hear the ardent denials, from people who shout my name with such devotion. I treasure and bless those people in my heart, more than they can imagine. And those paintings and sculptures showing the ground beneath my feet becoming fertile, watered by my eye-closed tears—they are not wrong. No, they are far more right than they know. Yet none of them, nor the songs which call me "meek" and "stern" and "gracious" . . .

None of these tell *why.*

They don't even know from how deep a wound, to myself and others, those tears seep.

I dug my wound, bit by bit, filled with decay and ooze and bile. It swelled with infection.

It had to be lanced.

And even now, I pay the price.

but my price is small, compared to what others have paid . . .
for me.

Page by page she scratches her soul along with the clay.

Every week, a new blank tray. A day a week, a page a day; the fine, small letters she cuts in the clay, as if into powdered flour. It doesn't weary her, but emotionally. Emotionally, and in one other way.

She mustn't write more than one page a week.

She still has many things to do, many people for whom she must be strong, before she dies.

She will not kill her body through her writing.

Not yet.

❖ ❖ ❖

Whatever use it may be to scholars later, this is a testimony first—of the person that I was.

I am a maga; even though I haven't needed to use those skills in years.

But what I was, still echoes in what I am.

It would be misleading to say that I am no longer a maga. Every study affects the soul. My soul is still here; although my body has flowed away, as every mortal body flows—as the curving of a waterfall.

Scars and all, my soul is still here.

I am *not* against magi—not in principle.

But I was not a good one.

And that makes all the difference.

When I began what I considered to be my self-carved path to glory, I had not long passed my twentieth year; having spent some time already in preparation and training for the magical arts.

I'd always enjoyed my use of power—a habit that wouldn't soon change—and so had devised a clever scheme of revenge against . . . someone I had known as a girl.

I had been certain that I would escape detection.

I had been caught, of course.

This was when I learned true fear.

Had I been properly punished—and I *did* deserve death after some demeaning service—I might have learned wisdom through fear. But, my masters delayed my punishment.

I now suspect that they were debating, whether to risk the loss of my potential—to the world at large, or to particular schemes of their own, the Eye only knows.

Then the Culling began; thanks to fighting among the Cadrists.

I also know the Rogues had a hand in the Culling as well.

All the klerosa vanished; and the nations fell apart; and I was released when the Cadre disbanded. Why, I never found out; and had no wish to discover. I took myself away to survive in obscurity, not to become an expendable pawn: the fate of most apprentices.

That was a terrible year. Fool that I was, I tried to tell myself how exciting my life had become.

Then the fighting began to slacken as one by one the surviving Cadrists also disappeared. Bands of soldiers crossed the land, seeking any advantage, competing simply to live.

I also needed advantages—and resources.

So, I gathered squads; building them into companies. I thought of myself as daring, and innovative, and defiant—swimming against the currents of history!

Hardly. I threw myself headfirst downstream into the river, trying to swim more quickly than anyone else.

and . . . I who am thought an example of virtue today, was once . . . something else.

I was worse than any mere flirt. I enjoyed edging men in that direction, with or without my magic, achieving power for myself at their expense. And if it bothered them, so be it—what were they doing around me at all?!

Fortunately, I was distracted enough by my practical problems: I never gave my full attention to this addictive little hobby.

Yet, even now . . .

I feel such burning shame in my heart, I wonder if steel would quench it . . .

No.

This is only another temptation: to defy the price of what I have done, to pretend that I can make it go away.

What I have done is real—forever.

Further crippling myself will never help me. Adding to my crimes will only add to the burdens I carry beneath the unavoidable Eye.

I can be crushed beneath those burdens.

Or, I can let love to help me to stand—and to walk—and perhaps one day to run.

I do not believe that I shall be running again in this world.

I am grateful, even to walk . . .

Now my thoughts have turned that way, so I will follow the bend in the path I walked so poorly.

But, *not* that far. Not yet.

That cliff must be descended; but not yet.

CHAPTER 3

Along with this woman, I turn back my gaze, beloved; back to those fateful days: where I find the dark man—and his same dark struggle.

Seifas dips his pen into his ink, and debates of slaying one last man . . .

❖ ❖ ❖

The final apprentices now are rising from the shadows, trying to claim their masters' power.

My current commander, Portunista, is such a one. She makes it clear, that *she* is her only goal. To that degree, she is honest.

And, as long as her troops stay warm and fed, and have some time for leisure, I suppose they won't complain.

I would complain. I am a subcommander.

But to preserve that authority, I must stifle my conscience.

I hate it.

I can feel my soul eroding away.

I should just leave.

but I have nowhere to go.

. . . I should kill myself—rather than offer a silent assent to the dissolution around me.

What is my duty?

Should I risk my soul to chance that I might live, to see the return of justice?

What chance is that?

If I cannot decide—it might as well be *no* chance.

And if justice will not be fulfilled—then there is no hope.

And if the cries in my heart are hopeless . . .

. . . I might as well be dead.

I have a small knife. I bought it for this.

I see it where it lies, awaiting my choice . . .

I do not fear death, as other men do. I am one of the Guacu-ara.

If there is nothing, I shall not know it. If there is something, then I will fight or I will serve; and that is no different from now.

So, shall the cries within me be fulfilled?
The knife awaits my answer . . .

If the cries are only my wishes, they are not a reliable guide—my wishes are *not* the ground of All. I won't continue my pain for a self-delusion.

If the cries are only induced by the world around me, then they are unthinking urges. Only to fill such hungers would cast my mind into death—or else I am there already. I might as well complete it.

If the cries have only been trained into me by men, then where did *they* receive their notions of justice? From where I have said? Their *own* cries will only be hunger or lies!

I might as well kill myself.

A shameful act, you say? The act of a coward? Not the mark of a man or warrior?

But, if there is no justice, then why *should* I agree? From *my* own pride? To kill my life is the ultimate pride—the deadliest victory over mere instinct!

Should I agree, because of *your* pride? I might as well prefer my own—and then, to the knife!

Should I agree, for *you* perceive justice? How is *your* mirror then better than mine?? And if I cannot see justice, even the blurriest vision, *your* witness to me must *also* fail!

Even my reason can have no meaning: without true justice, my motives for thinking are only irrational.

So.
I am a cripple, deluded. I should completely free myself.
A knife to the artery stings but a bit.

A death in battle? What *can* a death *mean,* in a world without justice!?
I will seek elsewhere, for satisfaction—or else for oblivion!

. . . . . . yet, I choose to stay, still.

Why?
Not from lack of nerve or skill to do the deed.
Why??

Because, whatever else is real—so is my cry for justice.
It may not be what I think it is—but it is *something.*

What does this tell me?
To myself I ask: what do I hunger for? Why am I starving inside my mind and soul?!
I want to see the return of justice!
Ah—it is only my instinct, only my training, only . . .
Perhaps. Perhaps. . . . . .

Listen, knife. What rests beside you, there in the shadow? You I have known for a day. What is *this* I have known, for years?
This weapon, I say, is my aasagai.
No, you say; that is an axe.

Oh? And why should I listen to *you?*

Here is a rigid, finger-thin needle, as long as some men are tall, with sharpened pommel and infighting quillions—I hold it along the shaft of its length, and twirl it around myself for defense, until I punch past the guard of my foe . . . this is an *axe?!*

If you were to say "a spear" I might agree. It shares some traits with things called *spear.* It has no likeness to things called *axe.*

Yet, if I mistook, and held an axe instead, you *still* would be absurd to say "*not* an aasagai"—unless *you* had some accurate notion of what an aasagai *is;* and what it is *not.*

And I can tell this difference!
Mere desires of my heart, *are not* justice! Mere training is not of itself *justice!*
I *do* perceive the distinction, the disparity!
Somehow . . . despite any blurrings and flaws and mistakes . . .

. . . I must have some sight of true justice!

And, if justice exists . . . then *hope* must exist.
And you, knife, offer no hope at all.

Would Matron Cami be proud for me . . . ?
how I miss her

We of the Guacu-ara never were told of our parents. Our ranks were our brothers; our Matrons our mothers. But Cami *loved* us: the children she never would bear, whom she had forsworn for our sake.

I do not know where my birth-mother is; nor the only mother I ever have known.
But now I am sure that someday, somehow, my cry for justice *will* be answered.
And with that knowledge, I find I can sleep.
For tonight.

CHAPTER 4

The following day, Seifas assigned himself to scouting—again.

The sun threw shadows through forests, as he loped around close hills and quiet coves of lakes. The shadows and light lay patchy on him. Seifas embraced and used the shadows, sent by sun or stars; but even after the night before, the shadow of his life still lay on him.

He didn't embrace that shadow. He bore it in shame.

While on patrol, he wouldn't be fighting a losing battle against his commander's selfishness.

Yet, he also knew that by his absence the battle was lost.

Still, out all alone, he could forget the shadows in his life—

until he chanced on a forest glade, where a girl sat watching a flock of sheep.

Eighteen hours later, Seifas would record what happened—and so commit his journal to an empire not yet born:

> "The midsummer sun glares into the glade—reminding me, that what I do will be seen by the Eye. I can feel myself, there in those shadows once more, wondering what to do.
> "Should I tell the brigade?
> "Should I warn the girl and her family, to protect their precious flock?
> "Should I simply leave, saying nothing to anyone?
> "I . . . we . . . should be helping this girl!
> "But, we also need to eat.
> "Yet—if we take the sheep, then how do we differ from brigands??"

Weighed by his doubts, Seifas waited.

He wanted to pray to Macumza, the Agent who guarded the paths of the Hunting Cry. But only a Matron could have that communion—and now the Matrons were gone.

He would have even prayed to the Eye for guidance. But the Eye seemed far beyond every star in the sky.

Waiting was easier, and doing nothing.

So, he did.

The soldiers he soon was seeing, slipping through the trees, didn't wait.

They acted. Although, like many men, they couldn't even stalk a sheep.

The animals scattered; and in their distress, the shepherdess jumped from her rock in fright.

A woman and man, both in light armor, leaped from thickets, into the path of the girl.

"Gotcha now, my—aaaow!" yelped the man; the girl had smashed his head with her staff.

"Pike, really, you *are* impossible," muttered the woman, who reached and snagged the girl by her hair. The shepherdess shrieked and flailed with her crook; but the woman walked, steadily pulling the girl off balance. "Long hair; bad idea my dear," she mused. "Then again—keep it. You may find it useful in other ways . . ."

"Get a move-on!" snapped the sergeant to the others, who had paused in their chasing to watch and laugh. They returned to killing the scattering sheep.

Seifas was already moving.

The juacuar crept, outside the glade's wide edge, his belly low, his aasagai across his back. The girl might not be in danger, yet; surely the woman would remind them, Seifas thought, that they were men not beasts.

Still, the girl would be the key. If he attacked immediately, they might attempt to use her against him. If they didn't take her, he would follow them to find their camp.

If they *did* take the girl, then first he would kill her guards. Although he would spare the woman's life, if possible.

Seifas was a soldier—and he was of the Hunting Cry. He knew all plans were uncertain; and no one knew more than the Guacu-ara how an uncertainty could lead to death.

However well he planned his attack, he might be slain this afternoon—over a handful of sheep, and one poor girl.

Still; a better reason to die, than any he'd recently had—or could reasonably hope to ever have again . . .

"So, good friends!"

Seifas froze, balanced on fingers and toes.

He and the others stared with shared amazement as a fair-skinned, bearded man strode out of the trees.

The man was dressed in simple clothes—though something about them itched the back of Seifas' mind—and he carried a flutewood stalk.

This unexpected apparition calmly paced across the glade.

"I see, young miss, the market has come to your family," chuckled the stranger. "Did they offer you fair price?"

Even the girl had no idea, whether or how to answer! Not knowing what else to do himself, Seifas resumed his meticulous crawl around the clearing. Securing her freedom had now become more pressing—or, perhaps Macumza *had* sent help after all . . . ?

The sergeant tried some bluster: "Who're you?! And why're you here?!"

"I am merely someone seeking service, like yourself," bowed the smiling man, solidly settling near a slaughtered sheep. "I think that covers both your questions admirably! May I ask the price you promised to her?"

Seifas continued flicking glances back and forth between the glade and his chosen path, carefully picking obstacles out of his way.

"None of yer business," growled the leader.

Seifas could no longer see the stranger's face, but the man still sounded like he was smiling . . .

"That tells me these sheep, and this young lady, are none of *your* business. *If* that is the case, and if she requires, then I am prepared to *make* it my business." He chuckled again, and gave a slight bow to the girl.

Seifas would relive this moment, in his journal.

In some ways, he would relive it the rest of his life:

> "I feel my heart pound—with emotion? No, more! Something I've lacked, for so many seasons, threatens to blind and to suffocate me!
>
> "It is *hope.*
>
> "I am snarling now, blinking away the tears my heart is crying. I will *never* live without hope—never again!
>
> "I will find the hope to have, or seek my death in finding it!!
>
> "I can see the girl; she doesn't dare to hope; she *wants* to dare to hope . . . My heart is bleeding—its scabs fall away!
>
> "I promise her: I will share the hope I find, or seek my death in sharing it!!"

The soldiers didn't know of this doom, creeping toward them around the glade. They kept attending to the smiling stranger.

"An admirer, eh?" the sergeant snickered. "What, no ladies your own age to play with, out here in the hind end of nowhere?" The other soldiers chortled.

The woman whispered loudly to the frightened girl: "I'm sure you *can* do better than this peasant, my dear! In fact, I guarantee it: from these fellows here as well as their friends!"

Seifas felt his fingers digging furrows in the ground.

This woman, who would murder the hope of her common sister, would *not* escape him while he lived . . .

The stranger shrugged his shoulders. "I can listen all day long to your baseless slander. Eventually, her family will wonder where she is. In any case, I think you soon will be facing someone *far* more wrathful than I!"

"Well, then," retorted the sergeant, "we had better run away with our meal and our fun, if we want to live!"

You cannot *possibly* run away quickly enough, Seifas assured him silently . . .

"Come and stop us if you dare, you lone buffoon," the sergeant challenged. "Let us see that weed you carry parry steel! Clov, you get the sheep!" The youngest soldier began to move.

"You will be quite embarrassed, if I brought some reinforcement," smiled the stranger.

Seifas and Clov both jerked to a stop at this!—though Seifas instantly forced himself onward. Clov glanced around uncertainly.

"Look at the girl," continued the stranger, "then at me, then at yourselves. Who doesn't belong?"

Indeed, he looked as different from them as Seifas himself—although in an opposite fashion! Now, only one straight line through trees and brush divided the juacuar from his striking point . . .

"So, I am not from the area; therefore, cannot be here to see the young lady; who certainly is—my apologies, miss—a little too young to be courting."

Sweat ran down the sergeant's face. Was the stranger a scout for a squad? Or . . . was he perhaps a magus?

Seifas could feel the sergeant breaking beneath the strain; and knew his time had run too short. He wouldn't be able to strike the first blow . . .

"Clov!" the sergeant shouted. "Get the bloody sheep!"

The brigands tensed themselves as Clov edged forward, twitching his eyes from tree to bush to rock. He paused at the body nearest the stranger, trying to think what to do.

"I truly am sorry," the fair man said. "You *know* you shouldn't be taking that sheep."

Clov looked back at his fellows.

"Go on," the woman coldly ordered. "Let us see what happens."

Clov stooped, and reached a hand.

With a whistling crack, the flutewood *snapped* against his other wrist. The startled brigand reflexively dropped his sword.

"Tsk," the stranger chided; then, *whoop!* as Clov dove forward from a crouch, attempting to grapple. The fair man spun, without much grace—the flutewood cracked through the air again, flatting the brigand's neck between his helmet and studded jacket. The soldier fell, unmoving.

Seifas scurried, no longer worried about being heard.

"Oh, well," the stranger sighed, as the sergeant and the third of the brigands launched themselves into action.

The third man closed into striking range first. The stranger dodged his poorly-timed swipe by simply backstepping; then darted left and ahead, as the soldier swung a backstroke. But the stranger, inside the soldier's reach, blocked the stroke by raising the staff at a crossing angle.

After a pausing thought, the fair man punched the brigand.

A clever move for an amateur, Seifas thought: the stranger's hand had been held high to pull his staff on guard against the counterstrike—

—but the brigand's bulky helmet blocked the still-clutched flutewood, keeping knuckles from meeting the nose!

The fair man grunted; then flicked a finger into the eye of the brigand.

The third man *yelped* and threw his hands to his face—punching himself with his own guard!

The stranger's sudden dash a moment ago had put this man between himself and the sergeant. Now the two unwounded antagonists circled around the staggering third.

The stranger now kept quiet. Seifas watched, unmoving, filled with curiosity. The fair man shifted grips on the pole, his pale face pursed in thought.

Then with a grin, he glided in behind the central man, whirling his pole in a striking loop to harmlessly thump his enemy's chest.

"Char take ya!" cursed the still-blinking man, lunging a countermove—right into his leader!

"Fool! It's me!" the sergeant cried, and parried the strike. The stranger, rebounding the flutewood, pulled it around and thrust it over the middle brigand's shoulder. This creative gamble *paid*: the pole-tip pounded the sergeant, driving the nosebone deep in his skull.

"Sarge!" the man in the middle screamed, as his officer sank to his knees.

The stranger jumped back into a pre-lunge stance; and then, his hands neck-high, he thrust again—at the vulnerable gap between the vest and the helmet: *snap!*

The last man shouted and finally leapt to attack from where he was guarding the girl—but:

"Pike! Stop!" the woman barked. "Get back here!" The thin man yanked in his tracks; he backpedaled, twisting his face in rage. The stranger, who still was smiling, heartily twirled his weapon back to a hiking position, as he turned to face the guards.

"Enough of this," the woman muttered; she jerked a knife from its sheath and held it out to the throat of the girl. "Drop that stick and submit to the mercy of Pike, here—or else she dies."

Her tone was level and deadly.

The smile of the stranger finally faded.

"There will be little mercy," he said, "coming from *your* direction, I think."

Indeed.

A collapsed-carbon spike punched through the woman's knife-arm just above her wrist. Her hand popped open, dropping the knife, as the pick was yanked from her arm. Pike heard her gasp, and twitched his head in time to see a dark blur whirl in a three-quarter spin around the side of the woman. The blur became a blood-bespattered spectre—ebony-skinned, ivory-toothed, gripping a devilish tool, the sharpened pommel driven through bone, between her ear and eye.

The woman wasn't even looking at her fiendish slayer; yet she dropped from the pommel-spike with infinite horror in her eyes . . .

Pike tried to scream and turned to run.

He couldn't run fast enough.

"Afterward," Seifas would write, "we watched each other, black and white, at a cautious distance.

"The girl had long since run away to find her father and family—I am afraid I frightened her.

"But, I didn't frighten *him*.

"I do believe I impressed him, though: he didn't smile at me, at first.

"After a time, he spoke.

"'Well,' he said.

"'Well,' said I.

"'All manner of things shall be well,' he murmured. The ghost of a smile appeared on his face.

"'I am Seifas.' I did not add, 'of the Guacu-ara.' He wasn't blind.

"'I am . . .' and he hesitated.

"Then he said, 'Jian.' And smiled a little more.

"'Well met, Jian.' I did not know the name. 'You carry yourself with honor.'

"'I like to speak a little softly,' he said with a chuckle.

"'Your stick won't last very long,' I warned. 'Perhaps I can find some steel for you.'

"'Perhaps,' he agreed.

"And then:

"'Would *you* know someone willing to pay fair price for slaughtered sheep?'"

CHAPTER 5

A windy morning threatens rain, outside the upper room.

The woman doesn't mind. Any rain blown in, between the columns around the room, won't hurt the clay; nor hurt the ink with which she etches—nor anything else in the barely furnished room.

She *would* prefer a little rain today, she thinks. A little sun, to be sure; but rain would suit her better . . .

The imperial woman begins the wide new page . . .

And so, I let Seifas play the part of a menial scout, as often as he wished. I hadn't intended for him to actually *lead* his company anyway. I didn't want the competition.

Neither did I want to lead. I much preferred to command.

I tolerated the two real leaders among my subcommanders, because they weren't ambitious. And for other reasons.

I do not care to speculate on what I would have otherwise done to them.

I have no need to speculate.

I know what I *did* do . . .

. . . those memories sear me still.

But, these things had not yet come about, when Seifas returned to camp one day with a stranger.

"I need thirty krana," Seifas announced, ducking lean and tall into my command tent. "I have purchased some sheep."

In fact, he had already ordered a squad to retrieve the carcasses. A rather high price for the lives of mere sheep; worth a week's wage for two squads. And this money would not be returning through company vendors for recirculation.

Yet, we did need the sheep.

I almost ordered Seifas to just *take* the stupid sheep . . . !

. . . but—something distracted me.

He looked . . . different . . . from when I had seen him last.

I nodded to Hud, the frail young man from Keryth who kept my books. He answered my nod with his own, sparely, gravely; and went to the chests to retrieve some silver.

After all, I *could* always countermand the order later.

Seifas continued his report: how he had found the unexpected herd; how soldiers from an unknown brigade had tried to take the sheep for themselves; and how a strange, fair man had faced them down.

Seifas underplayed his own contributions to the fight. That was nothing new.

He also, however, was standing straight and tall, with a vigor in his eye and voice that he had never shown before.

Wonderful, I sourly mused—the juacuar had found a friend.

By himself, Seifas was only an irritant. He helped to keep unruly soldiers in line; but he couldn't sympathize with his troops. Which surely was fine with *me*—it meant he wouldn't build a following.

He probably would have been happier, as a permanent scout.

But I didn't want him happy.

He irked me.

I told myself that Seifas was a tool, thoroughly molded by his teachers in the Hunting Cry.

This is what I told myself—but still his presence pestered me; for he had something I lacked.

Seifas had a purpose greater than himself.

I wouldn't have minded, had his purpose been *me*. But, I knew I wasn't his highest authority.

Neither the Eye nor the Agents cared about us—this was clear enough in all that I could see. It even was clear in what I *couldn't* see: for the klerosa were gone, and new ones were not being raised! *Had* their masters ever cared about us?—then where were the servants?!

Gone, to the unseen—abandoning us to fight and die alone!

Gone, and good riddance. I never had liked them anyway. Justice had to begin and end with *me;* or else I became a tool in the hands of another.

But Seifas kept his sight on that unseen.

And I, in turn, had kept him near me, in my twisted fretful way. Resenting him, and scheming.

I would condition him to suit my self.

I could have ensorceled him to sleep with me—*that* would have been conditioning indeed!

Yet—I always found excuses not to do it.

I wouldn't admit my doubts to myself. Could I set my teeth into his soul? Or if I tried, would he draw *me* into that other world—where I refused to go?

I might be mastered instead—to a man I did not understand, who would not *ever* try to understand *me*.

Other men were willing to barter themselves to me.

He would not. I feared that gravity, and that anchor.

It is easy to say, the beast is not under the bed.

It is not so easy, to prove it by sleeping there.

How much more terrible is it: to deny and to test the things of light whose spears might slay one's self—even with joy.

I did not want to die. And his soul, which threatened to crush me if I prodded, I did *not* want to live.

So.

I had tried subtler things.

Some simple words, here and there; a mention of this atrocity or that. Look, on the horizon—another village burning! How long, would you say, from the color . . . ?

And I had fancied I was succeeding, etching his soul, little by little, day and night, inducing him to compromise, to look the other way.

To despair.

I hadn't known how successful I had been—until that afternoon, when he stood straight and tall in my tent, brokering foolish sums for stupid sheep.

Now my hateful game was blown away!

—and through my mind it flashed, how treacherous and how petty I had been . . .

I swatted that perception firmly.

Now the fool had a friend. I would have to nip this in the bud to start again.

Then, Seifas stepped forward.

I jerked in my seat, startled by my feeling, that he had heard my spite and meant to punish me—and frightened by my impression, that he would be right to do so . . .

But, he had only drawn a small, flat purse, from a pocket on his belt. Out of it, he tapped some silver krana onto the table, where Hud was entering sums into the ledger. The younger man's face didn't change; but, I saw the respect in his eyes when he nodded sparely again.

"Here!" I snapped. "Let us see this champion." And I stomped to the flap—although not quickly enough to keep from seeing Hud, adding a couple of krana of his own into the pile.

I snorted—and decided where this stranger would be put: gathering fuel from the pens. If he enjoyed the company of sheep so much, then let him try cattle as well! And let him discover, thereby, how fickle shepherdesses can be!

Yes; I taught him that lesson well enough.

But not yet.

That sharp cliff must be descended; but not yet . . .

CHAPTER 6

I charged from my tent, already hating a man I hadn't seen.

I cannot see him now.

But, I remember how I saw him, then.

As Seifas had said: a fair man.

He stands halfway downhill, surrounded by soldiers who seem to be wandering into position as they pass. They watch him, staring, unspeaking; he smiles to them in return, resting upon his flutewood staff, meeting them each with a nod.

Certainly he is fair of coloring. Curly, sandy-yellow hair; a short curly beard; a brief moustache. His skin is paler than any I've seen; compared to Seifas, simply snow. He wears a tunic of humble wool, very clean—which raises further suspicions in me: any mere peasant would *not* have clothes entirely unworn by rain and mud.

I stop at a distance to watch. A boy has pushed to the circle's edge, unlike the other nearby vendors' children.

The stranger turns precisely to the boy, squinting in thought a moment.

Then he squats to eye-level with the boy, and says:

"I see you have a sword-jumper!"

He sounds like Seifas, somewhat; though a higher baritone, befitting a smaller man.

"So, can you jump a sword with it yet?" he asks.

The boy is holding a ball, covered in elongrass netting winding into a line of strands.

I haven't the faintest notion what he means—jump a sword with *that?!*—and neither does the boy, who had begun to shrink away from the man's attention. But, his curiosity now has much increased!

I see some soldiers nodding; everyone seems to relax a little, yet grow more alert.

"*Did* you know your ball can jump a sword?" the stranger gently asks.

The boy is darting his eyes toward his elders.

A soldier mutters, "S'alright, lad. Speak up."

He gulps, then edges further in.

"What do you mean . . . sword-jumping?"

"Well! Sometimes a fighter must dodge a swipe by jumping something swung at him! Imagine! Here—" the stranger has leaped to the right, facing left in an on-guard stance. "Here is our hero, taunting his foe to a towering rage. 'Where shall I skewer my peacock again?!'"

The boy's eyes widen in wonder. Several soldiers are smiling now, but not in mockery.

"So, the villain," continues the stranger, leaping across to the opposite side, "snarls and savagely swings his axe or halberd, thus!" And with a looping whistle, he brings his pole around in an arc. "Striking here!" he points, and then steps back along his staff to put his legs within the arc. "But!—our hero *jumps*," and once again he leaps, inventively whirling the staff beneath him, "clearing the blow—or even pinning it down! Ha-HAAA!"

He flourishes, standing proud and straight upon the staff, flushed with exertion and grinning broadly.

"Well," he adds with a shrug, "any professional soldier could do it better. But, you have a lead on me," he points to the boy and his ball, "for *you* can begin to learn it early!"

The boy now shifts his excited attention, between his ball and the stranger.

"It *does* work a little bit differently, with a ball," the man allows. "I would be glad to show you."

And, he holds out his hand.

The boy is hesitating. "G'wan, lad. Let'im try," advises another soldier. I ruefully shake my head; to my surprise, I am smiling, too! The man must be a clown . . .

"I understand," the stranger nods, with a different smile. "You *do* have every reason to believe me. Yet to *act* on that belief, even once you have your reasons . . . it *can* be hard to step out onto a bridge, even when we have built the bridge ourselves."

I blink so sharply, my eyelids click.

This man is not a clown! He is—! What he is, is a . . . !

Don't listen to him! I want to shout, through my clenching throat. This is a *trick* of some sort! Can't they *see?!* Why are they *all* smiling now?!

I don't know whether the boy understands the man—but, he understands the surrounding smiles.

With only a tremor of hesitation, he gives the man the ball.

I force my muscles to twist into action: enough of this farce!

A hand falls gently on my shoulder.

I whirl, spitting, to face the threat . . .

. . . Seifas is standing calm and tall beside me.

"Watch," he murmurs.

He isn't looking at me. *He isn't looking at me!*

My fury floods my mind, as I turn back to the gathering crowd—

. . . the stranger is jumping the sword!

Having fastened the end of the twine to his ankle, he is swinging the ball on its leash through the air, near to the ground, jumping in a stuttering step to avoid the slinging cord.

"It works much better with a friend!" he shouts. "Then you can jump both feet! Come on and try!" And in a frolic, the boy and his friends all fling into the circle, leaping to clear the arcing ball.

I cannot move; the sight is incredible. Whenever the children stumble, they and the man all tumble down; and then they bounce right up to try again. The children shrill and giggle; the vendors can hardly wipe the tears from their eyes for laughing so hard;

the soldiers regale one another with yarns of war. Now the ring is clapping, and as the cord completes an arc, they raise a counting shout: "Ahoy! Bahoy! Chahoy! Dahoy! Eeoi!" Seifas, his long lean face the perfect picture of dignity, is laughing boisterous roars, his bright white teeth all shining . . .

I didn't laugh.
I seethed, and was seized with a burning itch to fly down the hill, to rend the joy of those people.

The force of that joy quelled me instead.
I didn't want to face it.
I was afraid to face it.

So I turned, and skulked to my tent.
As far as I know, no one even watched me.

I told myself I wasn't retreating. Let them have their fun. I was practical. I was pragmatic. Wasn't this partly what vendors were for?—to entertain the troops?
I didn't entirely succeed in ignoring the differences, of joy and fun and pleasure. But I managed not to think of it.
No . . . I managed to think *away* from it.
I strode into my tent, and poured a mug of mead, and sat and stewed. Even Hud had gone to join the escalating party. Fine. Whatever.

. . . and then to my mind, there sprang an image of me, dancing and singing.

How ridiculous! I had never once sung in my life . . . !
—but I remembered now, that I had *danced,* long ago.

I remembered: how I had danced the dances of little girls who wanted to dance the dances of women; how I enjoyed my play, how I had looked with a clean admiration—that which poisoned turns to envy—upon the girls who were finally ready to dance the very best dances.
I had wanted so badly to dance those dances . . .

I wept unblinking tears; refusing to admit that I was weeping, wanting to murder those memories.
I hated them.
I loved them.
I missed them.

But I refused to close my eyes and cry.

CHAPTER 7

The sun was gleaming like a beacon, my beloved; setting the air afire with glory through the western mists. Bands of men and women competed in chorus, rising in power every moment, until the sun departed to their gladful roars and answering cheers among the watching crowd.

Then lantern-poles were set; watch-fires lit. Vendors and soldiers together worked to bring out meat and mead and fruit.

Seifas had left a sullen muddle of mercenaries, in the morning; now a happy hamlet bustled, singing, dancing, kissing, jumping, playing, strumming, declaiming, feasting.

Seifas, while trying to find and assign some picketscouts, lost his sight of Jian. He expected to find the popular stranger at the festival's center—but, he couldn't decide where the "center" might be!

Eventually, an elderly potter, tottering to the meaders, gave the juacuar a solid clue.

Away from the main festivities, Seifas found an impressive knot of old campaigners, lounging near some short-flamed coals—a hot fire being unneeded in midsummer, but their bones appreciating the local warmth. Besides, even a minor fire would keep the punkie-gnats from swarming out of the ashes.

Jian leaned back against a log, mugs of water and cinnamon mead nearby, from which he drank in alternate sips. Also near was half a loaf of longbread, and some sticks of pounded quail.

He didn't speak, but only listened, quietly chuckling at the stories. No one seemed to notice him; each was enheartening every one with tales of high adventure.

Seifas saw that Jian could see him.

Jian saluted the juacuar with mead; then he placed that mug behind his reclining-log.

Smiling to himself, Seifas circled the gathering from a distance, approaching from behind, not to disturb the tellers. He swallowed some mead from the mug, then leaned across the log to hear the end of a knee-slapping tale involving mice and figs.

"I'm glad to see you again," said Jian, softly as another story started. "I had *thought* I would meet your commander, but—" Glancing over his shoulder he winked. "Seems I've arrived for a holiday!"

"We had no holiday planned," admitted Seifas. It took him a moment to understand how *odd* that admission sounded: yet Portunista hadn't made preparations to be celebrating Midsummer's Eve! Besides, he would have said the troops were not in the mood.

Nearby, women from the red-lamp tents were happily dancing, swirling in rings from one to another fire; they seemed in no particular rush to capitalize on compliments.

An altogether different mood, for everyone!

Almost everyone.

Seifas recalled his commander's face as she had returned to her tent; and tried to be diplomatic.

"Commander Portunista decided to spend some time alone, while she had a chance, in order to consider . . ." His invention failed. " . . . issues," he limped to an end.

"Is it time to meet her now?"

Seifas honestly wasn't sure. "I think she *should* meet you," he carefully answered, "and it might as well be now." Some time had passed. Perhaps she might be calmer.

Jian slid back, over the log, not standing into the firelight.

Seifas watched as Jian assumed the lead, beginning the way uphill; moving, not *exactly* from shadow to shadow, but from zone to zone of least attention. He did give a ready smile, to anyone who saw him, but: a slight of movement in the corner of the eye—*Was that the stranger?*—and he was gone, leaving behind a minimized ripple of speculation.

These odd impressions faded, as they neared the top of the hill; and Seifas began to worry: would Jian march into the tent headfirst?! Portunista's expression slashed through Seifas' memory: this needed delicate handling.

His fears came partly to nothing. Jian stepped briskly to a halt well-short of the tent, and rested on his flutewood pole, looking back across his journey in satisfaction.

The juacuar discreetly coughed. "Let me ensure that she can receive you."

Jian nodded once, and faced the tent. He seemed to be composing himself— and that struck Seifas a little strange, although he didn't know why.

The subcommander firmly rapped the wide tent-flap.

No answer.

He edged his head inside, incrementally.

Portunista sat in her chair, behind a table, studying documents and a map. Her eyes seemed reddish and squinty—as if she had been crying!

But Seifas firmly dismissed *this* fancy: studying maps in dim lamplight would easily make her eyes look bleary. On the other hand, he mused, that *did* bring up the question of why she hadn't properly trimmed her lamps, or even jotted wisps . . .

"*Well?!*"

Seifas restrained a wince; and then he stepped into the tent.

"At your request, Commander, I have brought the stranger to see you."

She hadn't really requested this; but Seifas hoped his respectful tone would calm her a little further.

Portunista stood, moving away from the map, and seemed to compose herself. Hadn't he seen something similar—?

An unexpected image flashed across his mind: himself, in matchmaking garb, arranging a noble couple's introduction—and with one of them stewing in a wretched temper!

Seifas rapidly spun to the flap, hiding a smile, just as Portunista ordered Jian to be brought in.

"*This* seems a good omen!" The no-longer-quite-a-stranger doubtless referred to the grin of the juacuar. Seifas coughed and regained his own composure.

"Commander Portunista now will see you," Seifas tried to announce—when Portunista herself strode out the flap!

Jian bowed low, with a respectful "Commander," as the juacuar moved to stand behind her.

"So," said Portunista frostily. "Thanks for helping my subcommander obtain some food for my brigade." Seifas couldn't clearly see her eyes from where he stood, but he suspected she flicked a glance toward the festival strewn about the hill below. So much for the sheep—indeed, so much for a sizable fraction of their supplies!

"The herding family thanks you, too, for such a generous compensation," Jian returned, and shortly bowed—the bag still hung on Seifas' belt, of course.

"Where are you from?" Portunista demanded to know.

Seifas' ears pricked up, and he focused intently on watching the man; who narrowed his eyes a little, and then so slightly pulled back his head, while shifting his grip on the flutewood staff.

"I come from a faraway land, as you can see—"

"Not necessarily," Portunista interrupted. "Seifas looks as different from most of us as you—and yet a few of his kind are born each year in every nation." Her triumphant smile was spread so wide, Seifas could see it from behind.

And then, in turn, he saw a startlement, even worry, on Jian's face. The pale man sighed and tried again.

"I apologize; but I am under an obligation, even the nature of which I mustn't reveal. I *am* a stranger to these parts, and I will need a . . . sponsor, of sorts."

"And you believe it should be us."

"I don't know why it shouldn't be."

"But you won't tell us where you are from."

"No."

"Nor who, if anyone, sent you."

"No."

"Nor why you are even here."

"Not at the moment, no."

"And if I handed you over to my interrogators?" Portunista asked with a sharpening edge to her flattening tone.

"It would hurt." The fair man matched her flatness, and her sharpness.

Seifas was disappointed at the hostility. But he couldn't fault his commander; she was only being prudent. Besides, after tonight, would *anyone* in the brigade agree to torture this man . . . ?

"I understand this looks suspicious," Jian continued. "If you wish, then I will leave."

"And what would you do if you stayed?!" retorted Portunista.

Jian bowed shortly once again. "I would commit myself to serving you, in every way that you deem proper—with the reminder that I have loyalties which may supersede your authority."

Portunista laughed unpleasantly. "Well!—*you* are an arrogant scamp! And if I told you to gather fuel from the pens? Would your loyalties supersede *that?*"

"As far as I know . . . no they would not." For a moment the man's face tightened; but then with a sigh of resignation, he grinned instead.

His confidence set her back on her heels.

"And you, Seifas!?" She turned and shot the juacuar a glance.

"*I* prefer to gather sheep and the heads of villains, rather than droppings," he gravely replied. "If *that* is what you are asking about. Otherwise," he continued, over her narrowing glare, "whatever you have him do, if you accept his offer of service, he *should* be required to help in defending our camp against attack."

Snorting at this, Portunista strode downhill and to the left, away from both the men. Sharing a glance and a shrug, they followed. This time Jian paced Seifas as a proper subordinate, two steps left and two behind.

Portunista breezed into an armorer's tent. A weaponbrace along one side held several swords.

"Here!" Portunista pulled a short and very plain sword from the brace, handing it to Jian. "We can spare you nothing better than a common battered weapon which has only failed a hundred faceless soldiers!"

The fair man carefully set aside his flutewood staff—not without some fondness, but with a definite air of finality.

Seifas swallowed a lump in his throat; and decided the boy with the sword-jumping ball would be given the staff for a keepsake.

Turning away from the staff, Jian accepted the sword.

Flexing his wrist, he tested the balance, twisting a few slow cuts through the air.

"No matter," he smiled to Portunista. "Any sword will do."

A moment of silence followed, while they watched each other.

Then he humbly asked,

"May I also be sheathed?"

Portunista blinked, then tossed him a worn but serviceable sheath, sewn from softened leather; and then not altogether meeting her officer's eye, she growled as she plunged from under the covering tent:

"Find him a place to sleep . . ."

Seifas could no longer hold in his mirth, but prudently softened his laughter.

Seven minutes later, a hundred and eighty-four men were dead.

CHAPTER 8

Portunista told herself she wasn't fleeing the forge; but she couldn't get rid of the feel of defeat. This "Jian" had met her stroke for stroke. She'd hoped to dislodge some useful information—or else to drive him away—but he seemed to have no pride to inflame or burst.

And so she stomped uphill, unsure of what she would do when she returned to her tent, other than pore once more over maps and rumors and figures. And drink, of course; the night was warm, the forge-tent had been hot—*that* was why she was flushing . . .

But she didn't want mead.

What she really wanted, was . . .

She altered her route, heading north across the top of the western slope and then downhill, into Gaekwar's side of camp. She had brought her only bottle of vania, whenever she last had visited him. He hadn't returned it, so probably kept it, while the brigade was on the move. He wouldn't be there now, but to the west downhill with most of her brigade, keeping a watch on his company-soldiers and muttering cutting remarks about cows.

She hadn't felt like visiting him for weeks, and didn't feel like seeing him now. She only wanted a drink; of something that wasn't mead. Something she *enjoyed*. *That* was what she wanted—that was *all* she wanted . . .

She ground her teeth in baffled frustration. What she *really* wanted—was to strike and smash and—!

And, she got her wish.

With a hooting roar, a monstrous form crashed out of the trees—not far in front of Portunista!

A line of hollering humans also poured into the clearing.

Portunista blinked in confusion, as the enemies charged the hill, swatting aside the empty tents—the creature's roars seemed to echo out of phase, downhill to her left, where the enemy line stretched out, charging upon her shocked brigade.

Then with a curse she remembered the squad, reported by Seifas. *That* had been to the north: *this* must be a retaliation. They would have *easily* found her camp, especially once the festival started.

The damned midsummer's celebration . . .

Portunista had wanted a target.

Here a target was.

The maga slashed her fingernails across her other palm, hissing from the back of her mouth with a rising pitch. The mystical pain increased the elemental Yrthen force she violently infused beneath her enemies.

The natural earth exploded—long rough parallel furrows, peeling back at the speed of sound, throwing men in the air, sharply slamming the monstrous mammal, leaving soldiers stunned and bleeding as the battle line behind them stumbled into the shallow trenches—their momentum broken.

Portunista smiled. Very satisfactory.

But she doubted that she would be able to use her personal variation of the Yrthrip skill again—unconsciously she flicked her hand, slinging blood upon the ground, as she squinted in the starlit night.

The creature was a shoulderbeast; ten wristlengths to foreleg top. Four men rode in wicker baskets: one each side, one upon the back, and one set in-between the topmost basket and the mahout who was guiding from a saddle on the neck.

The topmost basket held the commander. And the others . . .

. . . were jotting! She could hear them clacking away at some effect she couldn't recognize with all the noise.

Three magi. Only apprentices, or else she would have been dead already, but still—

The commander shouted a code, and pointed at her. His shortbowmen, near at hand behind the line, nocked their shafts.

Portunista craned her neck, as she trotted briskly to her left, wanting a better view of the fighting down the hill, while keeping an eye on her proximate threat: half a brigade and a magi-reinforced shoulderbeast. She still didn't know what those men were chattering, but most jottings required a line-of-sight—and now those bowmen were wending their way through the battle line!

Some cover, some cover, she told herself, her skin now prickling in panic . . . *any* cover!—well, *those* would have to do—

She slid feet first behind a stack of empty casks, as the shortbows sang, their missiles thunking oakwood slats, and otherwise whistling past her.

Good enough as shelter for the moment; but she'd easily be outflanked—besides, a waist-high pile would *not* be stopping a shoulderbeast! And *what* were those magi *doing* . . . ?

Portunista ground her teeth: she could not hold the line. She *must* escape downhill. If, she amended acidly, she could do it while flat on her back, before those men regained enough of their balance to . . .

. . . ah, wait; *that* might work . . .

She closed her eyes, and jotted an Yrthescrution.

Binding her scrution behind her lids, she 'saw' the nearby surface-pressures of the enemy line. Only a very few moments had passed—they were regrouping and picking their way across the scars.

Good.

Chuckling deviously, Portunista jotted an Yrthepool; letting the contours of her earlier ripping be her guide, for infusing just the right proportions of materia.

Guided by her will and skill, the Yrthe changed a prism of ground, five paces wide, knee-deep, and forty paces long, into a liquid consistent with water—but vitally reactive.

Even the shoulderbeast stumbled again, as its mahout drove it forward trying to reestablish the line. Its escape annoyed the maga; still she laughed while most of the upper line abruptly washed downhill in a tumbling roll of vitalized earth!

The enemy commander now was shouting for his mahout to be crushing her with the shoulderbeast.

Good. That fit *perfectly* into her plan.

She could feel the beast approaching, for she hadn't released her Yrthescrution yet. Portunista jotted again, pooling another forty-pace trough; but this time only inches deep—and wide as a shoulderbeast!

She set it several paces uphill of the creature, running it through her own position, pointing down the hill behind her soldiers' battle line.

Releasing the bind upon her scrution, Portunista rapidly blinked, rubbing her eyes and flushing away the microthin materia layer. The Yrthescrution's annoying aftereffects were more than compensated by the exhilarant rush downhill on a river of earth, much like a child on a slide: an escape while flat on her back!

The wave of vitalized earth didn't end with the trough. Portunista kept her concentration and her balance through her enjoyment, lying back and banking the rushing river with her will, tacking left and right, avoiding tents and such.

She fetched up moments later near the bottom of the hill; her soldiers steadily struggling in a battle-line to her right.

Releasing the earth around her, she staggered with relative grace to her feet, and hopefully looked back up the hill . . .

The creature had only suffered another stumble, hopping out of the earthen stream to better footing.

Portunista ineffectively wiped some mud from her face, spitting to clear her teeth, growling her disappointment.

But she had gained some time, to oversee her situation—although she hoped her opponent would urge an immediate chase, rather than charging her line or jotting down a strike upon them.

Here, at the bottom of the hill, she could see more clearly what was happening. Her troops had splendidly met the surprise attack, rushing against the invaders with high morale.

She couldn't see Seifas in the campfire-lit confusion; but she figured he wouldn't be among the front-line anyway. He would be somewhere uphill, striking out of the darkness like an ebony razorwyrm. She smiled possessive pride: these imprudent fools had called down on themselves the wrath of one of the Guacu-ara! She could safely leave the remains of the enemy's upper line to him and to his aasagai.

She *could* see *Othon* easily, though: Othon the Implacable indeed! He should have been mowing her enemies like a hailstorm scything grass. But the giantish subcommander hadn't been wearing his armor—now some soldiers from his company guarded his flanks, while he restrained his edged mace, lest he sweep his own men from the field. The fight was settling round him on both sides, like metal filings near a magnet; but with a balance as tenuous as a bubble.

Yet with half the enemy floundering to their feet, after tumbling down the hill, the chaos on the lower line was shifting decisively in her favor—and neither side was strong enough to prolong the battle's breaking point. Without klerosa, soldiers now were much less willing to risk themselves in battle.

The break would happen soon. As far as she could tell, by carefully checking the flows of the skirmish, she *would* have won already, if she hadn't needed to fight those magi and their shoulderbeast. Her soldiers' morale was *remarkably* high . . . probably thanks to . . .

Her mouth twisted.

. . . probably thanks to being inspired to celebrate Midsummer's Eve with so much gusto.

She doubted Jian was helping to hold the line, however—he didn't look the type. Probably he had run for cover the moment that he had heard the roar from . . .

Wait—hadn't she left the shoulderbeast *behind* her . . . ?

Her heart froze—she scampered leftward, trying to see more clearly. She had *thought* she'd only been hearing an echo off the nearby tentsides; but—

—there were *two* shoulderbeasts!

One of them was behind her line this minute!

She had lost after all—she wouldn't be able to stop it in time, before it tromped her defensive—!

Portunista's feet, and her thoughts, skidded to a stop. Now that she had a clearer view, she could see the truth.

Jian was playing with it.

> "I simply cannot describe what I was seeing any other way," she would write years later. "And, he and the beast both seemed to be enjoying their 'game' immensely!

"Later I learned that Jian had raced downhill, to help to gather the children away from the fight. Seeing my soldiers engaged along the line, the young and inexperienced beast had whooped and challenged them; while its mahout tried to goad it into position for charging up our line. And Jian had been the only man who was free to answer the threat.

"So he'd jumped and whooped in kind, waving his arms, calling the shoulderbeast's attention.

"Jian had drawn the beast—which remained oblivious of its mahout—into an open patch of ground behind the line; and he was speeding back and forth, jinking and janking, swatting the legs of the beast with the flat of his blade. The shoulderbeast plunged and spun, rearing and hooting, as in a primal dance, billowing clouds of summer dust in the flickering bonfirelight.

"And the purblind *fool* of a man, was laughing fit to burst!"

Then the situation changed.

Other adults had been gathering children into groups, but hadn't yet hustled them into the relative safety of the forest, lacking a definite order. Not being far away, the children were cheering Jian—and the shoulderbeast as well!

It didn't take the creature and its mahout long to recognize the sound.

The shoulderbeast jerked to a stop, facing the clusters of clapping children. The mahout, seeing a way to distract the defensive line, spurred his mount, shouting commands to which the beast was trained to respond.

Jian, no longer laughing, darted in front of it.

"No!!" he cried. "Not the children! Not the children!"

He stood his ground, waving his arms insistently.

The mahout pointed, and spurred his mount again, calling down a cursing taunt upon the fool in front of him.

The shoulderbeast, reacting to commands and goads, surged ahead, toward its 'playmate'—and toward the children beyond.

Jian continued to wave his arms, shouting: "No!!"

He wouldn't dodge again.

The children no longer were laughing and clapping.

The mahout, sensing victory, struck even harder with his goad—

The beast *plowed* to a halt, spraying Jian with dirt and grass.

One last time the mahout spurred his mount, shrilling commands to strike!

Snorting in annoyance, the creature rolled on its back.

"It was not," the maga will later write, "that the children in those days were barbarous. They simply hadn't expected to see this—yet, somehow they also had. So they responded like children.

"They could see the astonishment on the face of their persecutor—and thought it the funniest thing in the world!

"And when the shoulderbeast happily grunted, and wriggled on its back, as if scratching a spot that was hard to reach, the children literally rolled on the ground with glee—despite the sinister scrunching sounds!

"Even Jian stood frozen in bemusement.
"Then I saw him recover, shrug, and mouth the words, 'Oh, well . . .'"

The adolescent creature quickly rolled upright again, regaining its feet with a glorious sigh. It squinted in curiosity at the rejoicing children, whose guardians stood in confused relief.

Leaning on his sword, Jian flourished a courtly bow to the beast, inspiring another round of applause. Giving a grunt, the creature ambled away on a shallow tangent, settling to the ground between one group of children and the defensive line.

Portunista couldn't pull herself away from this fantastic sight. A few unruly children scampered to its flanks, shouting a combination of names, resolving into "Tumblecrumble." The creature practically preened beneath the praise—

A mother shrieked.

Jian whipped round to find the cause; even Tumblecrumble jerked his head in alarm.

One of the foes had broken through the line.

A heavyset lump had somehow survived the onslaught; he had decided not even to risk an attack on his enemies' backs, but instead was floundering full-speed toward the children!—seeing some helpless targets, and one distracted defender.

No one had noticed, before he had covered half the distance.

Portunista disentangled her thoughts and leapt into a run—*knowing* she would arrive too late.

The shoulderbeast heaved upright; but couldn't safely move with children underfoot—*he* would arrive too late.

Jian burst into a vicious acceleration, smiling no more . . .

he would arrive too late.

"I still can see the developing tragedy, in my memory," Portunista will write in her testimony . . .

❖ ❖ ❖

One boy jumps from the nearest pack, scampering up a nearby crate and thumbing his nose at the charging brigand; who alters his course accordingly. Jian is straining for speed . . . but now he will be even later, by more fractions of a moment.

The infantryman must pull to a halt to stab at the boy, spears not being the best for passing strikes, and the brigand not being a model of skill.

The boy is crouching on the crate, making himself as small as he can—but even this lout will be able to hit him. The boy sticks out his tongue, blowing in rude defiance.

As I race on, I give the highest epitaph I can:

I could have used a man, with the courage of this boy.

The brigand bugs his eyes and howls, combining with the rising roars of Jian and of the shoulderbeast, plunging the spear ahead and down to spit the boy, under the chin, between the knees, through the chest and out the back—

—except, instead, the boy leaps up, as the villain commits his thrust, heaving his legs and body above the spear, staggering slightly in midair—then *stomping* the shaft, pinning it to the crate!

"Ha-HAAH!!" the child is trumpeting, planting his hands upon his hips. The villain's expression is priceless.

"Ha-HAAAAHH!!!" echoes Jian, charging past behind the foe, slicing his sword entirely through the back of his neck.

"HAWWRRRR!!!!" Tumblecrumble roars, punting the remnants across the ground, and dancing on the pieces.

I stumble to a stop, laughing at the scene. Jian has slid to a halt himself, and spins once more to face me . . .

. . . but, his face then flashes from grin to grim; and he charges—straight at me!

What am I supposed to make of *this?!*

He hurtles toward me, his body lowering, fully striving—the earth itself is thundering, with encroaching mass as he approaches; and as he throws aside his sword I think:

. . . does he intend to *smother* me??

The past few moments have been too bizarre . . . I calmly watch my fate, trying to sort the meanings, to take the proper action.

But as he hurls himself, I've only managed to think:

Let him come—he shall find me no easy prey!

and . . . why is the ground still shaking?

Then he has wrapt me, indeed with force but gently, enfolding me and twisting, the thunder rising in crescendo, puffs of air buffeting us, and he grunts as I land on top, our momentum rolling us over until I come to rest beneath him . . .

How must my wounded pride have appeared!—eyes still wide; face still frozen in amazement; gulping air like a fish. Jian is finally face-to-face with me; his eyes are shining with mirth and success.

And then he kisses the tip of my nose!!

The effrontery! I cannot slap, or even sputter, before he spryly states: "You are *more* than welcome!" and with a spin he has rolled away, rising to stand with a shake of his head, perhaps to clear some dizziness.

Without much grace, I scramble backward to my feet, trying to reckon my situation . . .

❖ ❖ ❖

Portunista's brigade, meanwhile, had not been idle.

Seifas had now subdued—or otherwise removed—any remaining enemies scattered uphill. Othon and others had counterstruck their blows, driving hard against their enemies—who lacked expected shoulderbeast support and had to stumble through a pile of their own fellows.

The enemy commander *had* slain two of the northern pickets during his infiltration of troops into the area; but surviving picketscouts, having flanked the fight around the clearing, now were setting up positions just inside the northern treeline, cutting off retreat.

Consequently, as the attackers attempted a rout, whistlefletches flew in their faces. Yet their commander, the magus Gemalfan, remained unchecked.

Having failed to trample Portunista with his shoulderbeast—despite her being distracted by the battle's oddities—he now could read the writing of his fate upon the field.

So, Gemalfan madly urged his beast—onward toward the children!—the shortest line to safety for him lay across their mangled bodies . . . !

—one of his sub-apprentices hastily scrambled up the shoulderbeast, almost smeared across its side within his lacquered wicker-rider—

when an outraged Tumblecrumble intercepted Gemalfan's charge!

The impact staggered the older shoulderbeast, which bellowed and spun to counterattack.

An eardrum-rattling duel erupted: the mammals swiped and butted, trying to break the other's trunk-wide forelegs, pummeling chests and jaws and sides.

But Tumblecrumble lacked experience; also his elder's power and size—who, himself, was lacking resolve to defend the guarded helpless . . . unless perhaps he counted the screaming men upon his back!

On the other hand—one of those men was Gemalfan: a former Cadre apprentice.

Leaning forward, he jotted outward shot after shot of pentadarts.

The materia streaked in short sharp bursts to seek the heart of Tumblecrumble.

The mammal's leather hide, however, thick and tough and nonconductive, made for *some* defense.

They only hit with hammerforce—instead of blowing apart his innards.

Both onslaughts, mundane and magical, drove the younger shoulderbeast to his knees, his breath torn loose in gasps.

. . . and Portunista found that she was *not* prepared to let the creature die!

Each new burst of raw materia seemed to float quite leisurely from Gemalfan's fingertips, as Portunista watched with racing mind . . . sinking the enemy shoulderbeast to its knees in vitalized earth would hardly stop the pentadarts . . . time was slipping, *life* was slipping . . . !

Portunista felt her limitations settling chainlike down upon her—together with the implications of this single fight: her first real duel against a rival mage.

Over the year, she'd skirmished against some squads, even against a company once or twice; always letting her subcommanders lead the troops while she safely stood behind the lines, jotting a few effects.

Now she was fighting a *rival:* a magus with his own brigade.

And . . . she had done *well!* So well, she had forgotten she had never done the like before.

So well, she had forgotten that her rival might know more than her; might *be* more clever than she was . . .

might take something from her after all . . .

Every sickening thud of energy into the hide of the shoulderbeast, became a personal insult to the maga.

Tumblecrumble needed a shield.

Portunista gave him one—the only one that she could give.

Focusing her intent, the maga whistled as she inhaled, the cool air slipping between her lips and through her teeth—fusing Aire and raw materia needled in a ball-sized globe.

The wisplight drenched the beasts in bluish-white suffusion, mirroring the maga's chilling fury.

She bound the sphere into existence; with her will she *threw* it into the line of sight between the magus and his target.

Right in line with his—

—her head rocked back—*punched* above her eyes!—

The shock snapped Portunista's time-perception back to normal—but the wisplight hadn't failed.

It had been kicked aside.

She angled it back into the line, bracing for the impact—!
And again. And again. And *again* . . .

A corner of her mind protested: *how* long could she bear the backlash . . . *how* long 'til her willpower cracked . . . how *many* darts was she even *stopping* . . . ?!

But, she *did* stop *that* one. And *that* one.

And she *refused* to lose this duel!

If only she could hold on . . . maybe the infantry-line behind her could find a way to help . . . Feeling stronger even as her strength wore thin, she threw the wisplight in defiance at the face of the larger beast, driving the creature back through bluff, bouncing another dart.

Gemalfan, meanwhile, found this feat a rude surprise! He had never seen a pentadart defense—never had imagined one existed!

In his own near-panicked focus on the creature attacking him . . . he had forgotten the maga he had failed to trample.

The maga who had single-handedly ruined the charge of his upper line . . .

If *she* could do *this* . . . what *else* could she do . . . ?!

Gemalfan spat a command, ceasing to clatter his pentadarts; his sub-apprentices started jotting again.

Portunista felt her intention *snap!* apart like a strand of elongrass, winking out the wisp. She ground her teeth, in frustration, even with the strain relieved.

Now she knew what those servants had been doing: jotting dissipation spheres.

They couldn't intentively bind into place a sphere impervious to intention; but so long as they chattered, their master and his shoulderbeast would be immune to direct attack from magic.

Gemalfan *could* jott out, *if* his sub-apprentices heard his percussive effects and stopped their own in time. But his lackeys still were near to panic, unlikely to register subtleties; and he certainly *wouldn't* command them directly to cease, where his vicious and clever rival could hear!

But, Gemalfan believed he still could slay *one* enemy.

He told his mahout to gain the flustered attention of their shoulderbeast. It rose upon its hind legs once again—for the finishing blow on the fallen Tumblecrumble.

And Portunista was out of plans.

Reluctantly sighing, she gave up the shoulderbeast for lost.

She had failed.

But, she would devote the pain of this loss, to removing that man from the face of Mikon—!

And then—with a leap of her heart . . .

. . . she saw that others had *not* given up on Tumblecrumble!

There, around the side of the lumbering animals, darted Seifas!

Here, on the other side of the pair, stood Jian!

And the fair man was holding . . .

the sword-jumper ball!

While Portunista stared in blank amazement, the fair man tossed the elon-grass-netted ball up-over the pawing trunk-like legs of the older shoulderbeast, holding the other end, to which he'd tied an empty kettle of roughly equal size. Seifas caught the ball midair, and in a pre-planned move the two men ducked a crisscross run beneath the creature's stomach, pulling the fibers to fullest ten-sion—releasing the weighted ends with a flip, back under the shoulderbeast.

The spinning bands were humming, as the ball and kettle flew into a twin-ing knot between the animal's two front legs; not enough to trip, but hampering it, confusing it further, while it entangled itself, instinctively trying to guard its somewhat vulnerable underbelly.

And as it stumbled and thrashed—Portunista suddenly shouted in victory, recognizing a path to her vengeance!

She converted her cry to a boiling growl, focusing several wristlengths into the ground below the animal; then she struck her fist into her bleeding palm: the conventional Yrthrip technique.

The earth *did* ripple beneath the shoulderbeast!—globbing undulations, su-percharged by Portunista's emotion and will.

The dissipation spheres could only block intention of effect; they couldn't block mere physicality.

With a mewling hoot, the older shoulderbeast fell over.

The magi and the mahout had a moment and a half, to throw themselves to safety as the massive mammal keeled—

—whereupon they learned a lethal physics lesson . . .

CHAPTER 9

Tumblecrumble soon regained his balance, having been caught in only the edge of Portunista's concentrated earthen ripple. Quickly he crushed the elder animal's head—providing meat, in passing, for the feast the humans would surely enjoy on the morrow.

Gemalfan and his sub-apprentices *almost* leaped to safety from his mount: throwing themselves in the natural direction—

but not accounting for the momentum transferred by the falling shoulder-beast.

Any leap still landed them beneath the animal.

Seifas paced around the twitching mound of flesh as Tumblecrumble crunched the blocky, bony rectangular skull a few more times. Gemalfan had been a little more successful than his minions—the children were hurriedly being escorted away from the area, so that they wouldn't see him.

They could hear him, though.

He lay, screaming, from the pain of both his flattened legs.

Jian stood, arms folded, feet apart, between the children and the incoherent writhing magus. In the shifting bonfire glares, Seifas couldn't read that backlit face.

He knew his *own* heart's resolution, though.

His aasagai *pierced* Gemalfan's head, twice in rapid thrusts, through the eyes, into the brain, ending his cries and life.

"Hmmph," grunted Jian.

"Now he sees the All-Seeing," Seifas explained. "And his journey there was quick."

"Indeed," murmured Jian; and then, "How clearly they see, whom your sword instructs!" He began to laugh, a little shakily; Seifas didn't think the joke was worth the humor.

Portunista strode up then, demanding to know why Seifas had slain the magus without her permission.

"I didn't care to explain to her that I find torture distasteful," Seifas would write in his journal a few hours later . . .

46

"His droning became annoying!" I retorted; and saw her settle upon her heels.

Some might say my action meant nothing; that Portunista now held dozens of captives, and I couldn't save them all.

But I could spare Gemalfan—enemy though he was to me.

Besides, I doubt that we'll be wringing information from Gemalfan's men; all of whom have freely spoken of his dispositions.

And, if I read the signs aright, perhaps we might not ever be resorting to such cruelty again.

But quite a bit remains along that line, to be accomplished.

Altogether, circumstances favor us for now. We have assimilated a rival brigade, increasing our strength and seasoning our men. We have acquired a shoulderbeast, which—or who?—may be of help in later engagements. We should be able to easily find Gemalfan's vendors and supplies; and Portunista may discover information in the magus' texts. Morale runs high. Tomorrow I can pay a shepherd family for their loss, without a single worry.

yet . . . I wonder . . .

The Eye does seem to be smiling on us; but when my Matron Cami favored my brethren, she also was strengthening us for further service.

So—what are we being strengthened for? And why?

Or, is my perception of plan only illusionary?

If I believe He plans, then *this* may be a part of one.

But what if the Eye cares little for us, being so mighty and far away? What if we are beneath His notice, except for a casual whim of entertainment? The chaos of a Culling puts the teachings of our tutors in a new and frightening light . . .

No . . . I decided *before* today's peculiar events: the cries in my heart, are truly hope for justice.

Small as we are, we cannot be too small for the All-Seeing.

And our Matron taught us:

the Eye Above is the Lord of Justice.

So. I will wait, and watch events play out, before I cast my hope away.

No!—I have had a taste of justice at last!—and so I shall hold to my chosen course!

I will find the hope to have, or seek my death in finding it. I will share the hope I find, or seek my death in sharing it.

And now let us see what the future will bring.

SECTION TWO

DOWNSLOPE

CHAPTER 10

I look forward now, beloved; thirty years and more. The Empress sits no longer in her upper room, exposed to the sky, privately baring her soul to the world, pouring her heart into her tablets of clay.

There is no longer any Empress. There is no Emperor.

There, is the Arbiter.

He was not the first.

He would, however, be the last.

The clean-shaven elderly man who slowly walked the carpeted aisle, dressed in candlelight-yellow robes, knew about the Arbiter. Most of the people in every Nation, knew about the Arbiter.

This man, though, didn't know there never would be another Arbiter.

Neither did any scholars standing around him; nor the man who stood in front of him, wearing an eight-sided four-pointed star picked out in red upon his own yellow frock, above his heart.

The walking man stopped his walking, having reached his destination.

In front of him, a podium; upon the podium, a book.

The pages of the book were blank.

There would be others to be filled, everyone hoped; but this would be the first of the others.

The leader of the ceremony nodded to his peer.

The first man took the first step on his final path in life.

He reached; received a pen; and then in ink precisely drew these marks upon the page.

I, Khase Sage Exemplar, of Rosatta, port city of the independent state of Noi, hereby dedicate this chronicle: to the Eye, to the Orthogon, and to any people of Mikon who wish to learn something more about the coming of the Arbiter of our Era.

❖ ❖ ❖

He finished this sentence, beginning his final work. Only his death would end it. Khase had sealed himself to his task, as now he would demonstrate to his peers.

Khase raised his right hand.

His leader, the Sage Preeminar of the Rosatta Noi Orthogoni, held a thin metal wafer: a silver kran, unstamped by a nation. In one side had been jotted a sigil; out of the other, a unique arabesque had been carved with jotted precision.

The Preeminar said nothing; the Exemplar had already given all necessary words, on the page.

The Preeminar carefully reached, forward to Khase's hand; to the meaty portion opposite the thumb—he applied the silver wafer.

The sigil had been solely designed for this: as the elemental circuit closed, on contact with his living flesh, materia started reacting within the physical material.

Khase grimaced, holding steady against the branding burn of searing flesh and sinking silver.

The Preeminar quickly pulled away his fingers. He had not been burned; this effect had nothing to do with heat, despite its feel. But he didn't want to interfere with any operations of the seal.

The silver now was fused in Khase's hand.

Nearby waited an acolyte, a rust-red candle lit. She let some wax drip on the open page.

Khase held his right hand over the spot.

As he hoped—a drop of sizzling blood fell onto the wax.

Had there been no blood, the acolyte also had brought a stylus; with which the sage would have nicked his own hand.

But this was the better way. The wise respected even their superstitions: had blood not fallen first, that would have been a troubling omen.

Hot wax; vitalized blood: upon this mixture, Khase forced his hand— imprinting with the arabesque that now would be his sign forever.

This formality never would be required again, even for future volumes of his work. All Lifesearchers would aspire to seal their work, of course, with their final breath and blood; but circumstances didn't always favor that intention.

Khase Sage would gladly endure an occasional press of heated wax, however.

A tiny price to pay—to leave his mark in history.

This completed the ceremony. All the sages signed the book as witnesses; and then, along with the acolyte, returned to other duties.

Khase brought his book, to his chamber in the Orthogoni. He'd already laid his travel schedule; but like any author, he preferred to commit his ready words to paper.

Only a dusty prose, to many people.
For Khase Sage: the doorway to an adventure . . .

❖ ❖ ❖

Not many years have passed since the *Journal of Seifas* was delivered by the Arbiter Lestestauros, to the Promulgators, for publication to the people of all nations. At about the same time, copies of a single document were delivered by mysterious circumstance to every Sage Preeminar of Mikon: the *Testimony of Portunista*. The method of the deliveries, the existence of an apparent original, the peculiar features of the original and the copies, the combined testimony of the Preeminars: these, along with many textual evidences, provided robust arguments for the genuineness of the Testimony. The Preeminars, guided by the reception of the Journal among the people, authorized the publication of the Testimony as well, once Lestestauros had read and approved the document.

These widely available histories—penned by a man and a woman who each contributed centrally to the events postdating the Culling of the Era of the Anshu Pax—have been helpful in reconstructing and preserving the ideas and perceptions of many key figures of our recent history. Furthermore, they offer the most consistent records, to date, of the coming of Lestestauros. However, their limited scope sometimes omits details historians might consider important and useful.

I thus proposed to Hafis Sage Preeminar, of Rosatta Noi Orthogoni, that I should undertake a search into these events, while living memories still remain; and I was granted this privilege, as witnessed by my seal and the signatures of the Exemplars of Rosatta Noi Orthogoni.

This chronicle is my contribution to the collected history of Mikon.

❖ ❖ ❖

Sighing contentedly, Khase closed his book.
Now he was ready to truly begin.

CHAPTER 11

The late afternoon felt stifling still, despite the slope of summer's end, as Seifas walked back into camp, returning from patrol.

Mists were gathering over the forests. Seifas wished for a breeze, but wasn't expecting any during the Hazyslope side of summer.

Since midsummer the weeks had been largely peaceful, aside from the usual minor squabbles within a brigade—especially one that had recently conquered an enemy.

But the juacuar felt edgy.

It was time to move. Somewhere. Anywhere.

Preferably somewhere exciting. Somewhere with stocks for the winter, too.

Not that there was a hurry, yet, Seifas allowed, as he ascended the hillside assigned to his company. But—how could he put it? They had better hurry, *if* they wanted to keep from having to hurry, to keep from having to hurry . . . !

Seifas smiled at himself. What a difference fifty days could make, he thought. Ten weeks ago, the feeling from such an idea would have nettled him. Now he could laugh at the joke—while still of course taking it seriously.

"'Scuse me, sir!" piped a voice behind him.

Seifas had heard the person approaching; and had wondered who it would be.

"Yes, Dayva," he nodded in greeting. "A message for me?"

"Yes, *sir!*" saluted the girl, one of Gaekwar's yeomen. As usual, Seifas fought an urge to tell her to go *home;* brigades were no place for a teenaged girl.

But she probably didn't have a home anymore.

This was now her home, and she was doing her best to fit. Not too badly, either: Seifas thought she might one day become a decent officer.

If she lived long enough. And if her spirit wasn't crushed.

Normally she was a cheerful soldier, refreshing the world wherever she went—much as the first breeze of autumn would, cutting at last through muggy summer. Seifas felt vaguely sad, that whenever Dayva met him, the edges of her personality froze into a brittle uneasiness.

"Th' C—Commander wants to meet with you-all. Th' subcommanders, I mean," she stuttered. She still held her hand in salute; Seifas frowned at her lapse. His frown didn't help. "They'll be w-waitin' in th' usual place, f'r you t' get back from patrol. *Sir!*"

"Thank you, Dayva," Seifas nodded gravely. "Dismissed." The girl took three steps backward—finally lowering her hand—and sharply spun in place before she marched away in another direction. Well, sometimes the novices tried a little too hard. He doubted that she would rely on formalities very much longer. One day, not many seasons from now, she would be a sister-in-arms.

Seifas had never had a little sister.

Juacuara, for a reason no one seemed to know, *never* had sisters. Not of the Guacu-ara, at any rate.

He wondered whether his natural mother had carried any daughters . . . who she was . . . who his natural father was . . .

He wondered how many juacuara, when finally given some freedom, had found their natural families.

Seifas had never been given that chance, even to choose *not* to search. The Culling had come; almost the moment he'd finished his graduate classes, it seemed.

And then, he had run . . .

Seifas turned away from that thought, unable to face its pain.

Thinking of a family he would never be able to find, was a relief by comparison.

So: a sister. A little sister.

Well, if he *had* a little sister, he would want her to be like Dayva. He wondered what kind of woman she would become, with the advantages of a military training and discipline—

and then to his mind there flashed a face—a cold dead face; and cold dead eyes . . . eyes that had been dead *before* he struck . . .

the eyes of a woman who casually murdered the hope of a common sister, for her own amusement . . . not looking at *him,* but looking *ahead,* toward something too awful to bear . . .

Had *that* woman's spirit been crushed, long before?

Had *she* been once like Dayva, but then mangled?

Seifas pitied that woman.

If she'd only seen something before her, awaiting her as she died—then what hope did she have?

But . . . perhaps she had also seen something *within* her.

Then there might . . . just might . . . have been hope—even in that final moment.

If there was any justice.

And Seifas found himself smiling.

For the Eye was the Lord of Justice.

How astonishing! He had *hope* for her!—a woman he gladly had slain as a brigand, a *waste* of a person!

Yet, perhaps she hadn't deserved to become the person she had been. Perhaps she wouldn't have been that person, if someone had stood for her.

Seifas vowed: his little sister would *always* have someone to stand for her.

He shook his head—whole minutes had slipped by! His peers might be annoyed by his delay; but, the heat would only become more mild.

He loped around the western face of the hill, heading northward.

Chapter 12

Soldiers lounged around at rest, as Seifas passed through Gaekwar's side of camp.

Two of them were sparring using practice sticks. Their lanky commander lay nearby, apparently bored, oiling and cleaning his touted toy, a weapon he called a 'disker'.

Seifas stopped to watch the practice-duelists. This woman and man were the least of the soldiers of Gaekwar's company. Seifas knew the woman had been training hard, for nearly a year.

She still hadn't come very far.

Her sparring partner, previously part of Gemalfan's brigade, possessed more skill, somewhat—and much more confidence. Instead of training, *he* was merely performing.

The sweating woman, already bruised from previous passes, set herself on guard again, as her opponent swaggered into position.

"I promise," he drawled, "I'm going to make this *very* easy. All you have to do, is stop me from clipping you. Here I come . . . !"

With this facetious announcement, the man began advancing, steadily stabbing his longer practice-stick, in a looping overhand arc, right-to-left, high-to-low.

"Watch it . . . watch it . . . You couldn't stop it last time . . . Isn't it hard to parry a stab like this?"

The woman's eyes and guard locked onto that scorpion-gait.

"Can you count the timing right to parry it? Can you? Can you . . . ?"

The woman twisted her face in thought; she tried to gauge the attack, tried to figure the timing, tried to decide what parry would work—almost upon her . . . only another stroke or two . . .

His left hand looped around and tagged her head, striking with the shorter stick that doubled for his parrying-dagger.

The woman fell roughly.

"Too bad," the man guffawed, and stabbed her side with the longer stick. She didn't groan. "You really should learn how to watch two directions at once, you know!"

"That's a pretty good trick, Carl," drifted an even more languorous drawl from nearby. "Mind if you show it to *me?*"

Carl froze. A bead of sweat trickled down his face. "Errr . . . yeah, sure . . . Commander . . ."

Gaekwar stood, sleepily blinking away the afternoon sun. He left behind his short, blunt leafcutter-axe, and didn't even unstrap the disker from his forearm. Stifling a yawn, he sauntered to the woman.

"Stick," he said.

She handed it over; and crawled away to the side.

Gaekwar gave the stick a glance. "A little longer than what I'm used to, but it'll do for the moment, I reckon. That maneuver looks tough to parry, Carl. Mind if I give it a try?"

Carl swallowed. "Not a problem, Commander. But—no hard feelings, right?" A grin.

"Hmph . . ." Gaekwar tipped the stick some various parrying angles, deep in thought. "Right," he absently answered. "Go ahead when you're ready, don't mind me . . ." he faded off, squinting at the stick.

Carl nodded, grinned at the soldiers around them—none of whom grinned back—and then with only a brief hesitation, began his looping attacking advance.

Gaekwar looked away from his stick, to Carl's progressive attack, then back again. He pursed his lips, subtly turning the stick.

Seifas wondered whether Carl would have the nerve to blindside Gaekwar, too. He needn't have wondered.

A rapid-cycle *whishhing*—a faint explosive *puff*—
Carl pitched forward and to the right, gasping . . .
. . . then screaming in a muted whine between clenched lips.
Gaekwar had shot him with the disker.

He lowered the stick he had never used. His left arm, with the long contraption buckled between his wrist and elbow, still remained pointed at Carl. Gaekwar had smoothly brought it up to fire, not even trying to hide the movement, as normal as resting his hand on his belt, for no particular reason.

It had been casual.

The thin commander ambled over to his writhing soldier.

"Great move, Carl. But, y'know," he said, "you really should learn how to watch even *one* direction at once. Before you think of yourself as awesome, that is. Oh, wait." He knelt and pulled a metal disc the size of his palm, out from under the wounded knee, wiping it on the trousers of the other man. "I don't believe you'll *ever* be awesome. Mostly you'll be hobbling around for the rest of your natural life. You're dismissed from the company, Carl. Go and try to find a vendor to be impressed with you." He turned to walk away, sliding the disc through a slot in the spring-loaded cylinder, mounted on the shooting mechanism.

"Oh, and Carl . . ." Gaekwar stopped and looked back over his shoulder. "No hard feelings. Right?"

Carl didn't answer.

"Right?" the commander asked again. The disker pointed steadily at the wounded man—and not at his other knee.

"r . . . right . . ." Carl gritted out.

"Good," Gaekwar nodded. "There had better not be."

Carl resumed his moaning.

"Better move on along," Gaekwar advised as he ambled away. "Seifas over there just doesn't *like* to hear tedious droning." And he winked in the juacuar's direction.

"Decent practice, Meg," he added to the woman. "Thanks for the stick." He tossed it lightly in her direction; she caught it in midair, unsure if she should smile or not.

Gaekwar had already shifted direction: downhill toward the subcommanders' meeting place. "Get cleaned up, get some food, get some rest," he added over his shoulder as he left the area.

Carl shrank away from Seifas, as the juacuar resumed his march to the meeting place. The soldiers were quietly laughing, as they dispersed for dinner.

The longer stride of the juacuar easily caught and paralleled the angular subcommander. The slightly shorter man glanced up from under his free-floating shards of hair.

"Moooooo-ooo," Gaekwar said sardonically; with his fingers he mimed a scattering herd. Seifas knew his peer was fond of implying that people were cattle who wandered through life in response to whatever was prodding them.

"You left behind your leafcutter."

"Ohhhh," the 'cowherd' lazily mused, "I doubt anyone will want to take it. Don't you?"

And he smiled his lopsided smile again, while his fingers tapped a random beat upon the frame of the disker.

CHAPTER 13

Only Othon waited in the glade, at the bottom of the hill, when Seifas and Gaekwar arrived.

"Hey," Gaekwar called as he walked past. "Any sign of our glorious predecessor?"

"Gone fishing," the big man rumbled; the lanky subcommander laughed in reply. "For you-all," Othon clarified.

"Fine with me," Gaekwar announced, as he settled his scrawny frame into a cranny near the stream. "I guess I'm where he least expects!" He started cleaning his disker once again.

Othon, meanwhile, recommenced his careful pace around the small glade's arc. Seifas amused himself by trying to guess which tree the giantish man would choose today. He narrowed the probabilities down to three, before he heard the missing subcommander coming.

Dagon, in his official black-and-red garb, charged into the clearing at a walk.

"Finally!" the Krygian huffed. "I *do* have other things to do than lie around all day!"

"Drat!" Gaekwar grumbled good-naturedly, as he leveraged out of the crevice. "I guess this means I'll have to do some work around here after all."

"By all means," invited Dagon, "stay here instead, and play by yourself. More room in her tent that way."

Actually, Seifas mused, there had been plenty of "room" in her tent, since well before Midsummer's Eve . . .

"You can keep that fickle vixen to yourself . . . if you can," replied the 'cowherd', as he ambled back across the glade. "When she wants me, she can find me; and I'm not *overly* worried that *you* will be able to change that fact. How many nights have you 'played by yourself' in her tent, eh?"

Despite the thin man's casual saunter, Seifas could see his tendons tensing. Gaekwar didn't have his leafcutter handy, and Dagon did have his falchion. Furthermore, Seifas reluctantly had to admit, Dagon was *not* a completely incompetent fighter. Yet Gaekwar was gently lifting his disker into position.

But, in the small glade, a long lunge with the talon-shaped sword of the Krygian could negate any distance advantage offered by Gaekwar's unorthodox weapon.

It would happen, Seifas judged, in the next few moments, as Gaekwar passed by Dagon. Would he shoot first? Seifas didn't know—Gaekwar's idea of honor was somewhat different from that of the Guacu-ara.

Would one, or both, strike at the point of closest approach? Dagon's hand was twitching; but the Westerner could parry with his forearmed weapon, and for close emergencies he could extend a short triangular blade below its mouth. And at this range, a disc might sever a neck altogether.

Or, if Gaekwar made it past, then there was Dagon's favorite tactic to consider . . .

All eyes slid sideways, to the clearing's edge, as a tree was *stripped* from the soil with a rippling *crunch!*

Othon grunted, then lightly tossed the sapling to the side, for one of his squads to drag to their fires in the evening. His habit of expanding their small clearing, helped to keep his hulking body fit.

The habit served some other purposes, too.

"Weeds," he muttered, not looking at anyone, but with evident satisfaction. "*Some* weeds think they are oaks." He dusted his hands, clanking the gauntlets he'd donned for the 'gardening'.

Seifas managed not to smile, as the man from Manavilin Island lumbered out of his improvised lumberyard, holstering those menacing gloves in special loops on his belt.

Dagon swallowed sharply, and then stomped off at a tangent; so he wouldn't seem to be following Othon, Seifas figured. Gaekwar, on the other hand, cocked his eyebrow as he caught the eye of the juacuar, and chuckled—though very softly!

Seifas finally let himself smile.

But he also sighed. How many men around him hid their souls behind a screen?

. . . and, did *he?*

CHAPTER 14

As Seifas hiked uphill, to their commander's tent, he saw that Dagon would be passing near to Jian.

Children often would gather, after their chores were done, to play with Jian. This afternoon, a group of the older boys had brought some practice sticks, while younger children scampered on one of the earthen berms encircling round the hillside.

"You might *think*," the fair man said to them, "that parries should be wild and swooping. Instead you're more likely to flail around, if you *aren't* thinking!" This inspired a few laughs. "Really, the *best* kind of parries do the job with minimum effort, allowing you to conserve your strength for punching past the *other* fellow's defenses. *I* think the best commander to watch, in order to learn how to parry, is . . . Othon!" This earned a few more laughs, though incredulous ones. "Now, can anyone show me how Othon attacks?"

Jian and all the children laughed aloud, as the training boys—and even some younger children—mimed the massive subcommander, in exaggerated *swooshes*.

"True!" Jian agreed. "That is how he *attacks*. But—how does he *defend?*"

Some of the boys attempted to carry on clowning for laughter, but, *"No!"* Jian snapped, jolting them in surprise. "Watch," he smoothly continued past the reprimand, showing how Othon would inward-draw his arms for parrying, keeping the moves of the edged mace controlled and tight, " . . . until he's in a proper position . . . to *STRIKE!*" Jian launched an Othon-ish two-handed chop.

The children laughed again. Seifas chuckled, too—but, he also easily recognized the principles being used.

"That is what I want to practice today," Jian declared. "I'm going to work on keeping my parries tight. Now, would anyone like to help?"

"Me! Me!" Dagon mocked, a high-pitched squeal, causing the boys to jump again; some of the youngest squeaked in shock nearby.

As Dagon continued his condescension, Seifas saw the scowls on the faces of Jian and the boys were perfectly matched. "I'm a punkie loser and I can fight pathetically, too!" Dagon chirped. Abruptly switching tones, he growled, "But when I grow up, *I'm* gonna learn how to fight like a *winner!*" And drawing his falchion, he launched into a competent series of cuts and parries, slicing the air with his talon-shaped scimitar. "Come see *me* when your mothers decide to let you off their apron-strings," he sniffed, "and when you're worth a *real* soldier's time to teach."

"Yes," drawled Jian, turning back to the children, "you *also* can learn to fight a man by waiting until he's fighting someone else, then cutting him down from behind." To Dagon's shock—and the delight of the audience—Jian sprang into a clownish but accurate representation of Dagon's favorite tactic! "Punkie losers need not apply," he growled in a gravelly Dagon-voice, as he tiptoed from one imaginary fight to another. Seifas thought the children would belch out their lungs, from laughing so hard.

Snarling, Dagon threw a parallel slice that could have laid a kidney or backbone open, had he connected; but Jian spun away from the cut, and followed it with a parry.

"As you can see," continued Jian, while Dagon stood frozen in place, "Dagon prefers to cut low and behind from the side. It might have even worked, had I been fighting for real, rather than just pretending. Fortunately," he grinned, "a long thin pole is currently sticking in Dagon's ear, which gives me a chance to discuss his cut." He winked at Seifas; the children resumed their giggling.

As Jian stepped away, the juacuar removed his weapon gently out of the ear of the Krygian, wiping the wax on Dagon's jacket-shoulder.

"You should also notice my parry was tight and controlled, unlike the usual parries of *some* people I could name such as Dagon but won't . . ." Jian bowed to the clapping and cheering children.

"I can parry *anything* a clown like you could throw against me!" Dagon snarled. "That is," he regained a veneer of civility, "if you'll accept a friendly wager."

Jian weighed him from the corner of his eye, still smiling confidently. "Terms?" he tossed behind him, as he turned away from Dagon again.

"Since *you* don't even have a halfway decent sword for paying the bet, perhaps a service then. Clean my boots with your tongue!"

Jian rubbed his beard in thought and gazed downhill. "Then I wager *you* . . . a kiss!"

He turned once more to face his astounded taunter.

"Only Tumblecrumble," clarified Jian. "On the mouth." The children were giggling again. "Fair?"

"I accept!" bit Dagon through a ferocious grin. Sheathing his falchion, he held out his hand—but Jian walked right on past.

"If you think I'm fool enough to shake a backstabber's hand, you're going to be horribly disappointed later tonight," the fair man snorted. "Come along children! I'm sure that Commander Dagon has a meeting to attend, before we settle our bet."

The Krygian twisted his face in some different directions, trying to cobble together an angry reply . . . !

"You should probably wait to speak—until you're out of earshot," suggested the juacuar; whereupon Dagon swallowed, turned, and harrumphed up the hill.

CHAPTER 15

With her maps laid out in the middle, Portunista's tent was cramped. But this didn't bother the juacuar, who often crouched in corners while scouting or stalking. Fortunately, her quarters were cooling, with evening.

"Gentlemen," she began. "While decoding Gemalfan's disciplex, to learn what his plans had been, I discovered that he had deduced the location of—a Cadrist Tower!"

Seifas' spine twinged; he bated his breath, just in case.

"These towers weren't marked on official maps," continued Portunista. "But, by comparing *amateur* maps, appropriated from various traders who used to serve the Cadrists, the towers can be uncovered." She paused to smile triumphantly.

"Here!" Portunista stabbed her master map.

"The Tower of Qarfax!"

So.

Now there would be trouble.

Seifas bitterly sighed. All eyes turned toward him.

"*You* have something to say, Seifas?" Portunista asked with mild surprise.

"I garrisoned at that Tower, several seasonal slopings ago."

Anger started burning in the maga's eyes. She could easily work the math: he had joined her brigade bare weeks at most, after serving Qarfax.

"And why, please tell, did you withhold this information?"

"Because I didn't think you were ready to know it."

Dagon snorted at Seifas' answer. Gaekwar ducked his head, propping a grin behind a hand. Othon warily edged away from the line between the juacuar and their irate commander.

But Seifas focused on Portunista, daring her to explode. Her dusky skin grew pale with rage.

"And do . . ." she finally forced through slitted lips, "you think I'm ready now?"

"No. But I know you'll go there anyway."

He didn't blink or move, but easily breathed, regularly, in and out, trying to radiate a rational calmness.

But—later that night, requiring honesty from himself, he wrote down words of treason . . .

"She couldn't threaten to punish me with expulsion, or demotion; she knew I would gladly leave, taking along perhaps some soldiers with me. More important, her chances of success in any combat increased dramatically, as long as one of the Guacuara worked for her. She knew that, too.

"I waited; and I listened.

"Would she rant? Then I would leave: she wouldn't be worth protecting any longer, having become completely unobjective of herself.

"But—I also thought . . ."

Seifas' pen froze to the paper.

He remembered those moments; lifted his pen, past the ink he had trailed down the page, and tried again.

"But if her next sounds were percussive, a jotting . . ."

Did he dare to write it??

But he had devoted himself to trying *another* facet of justice—a justice upon *himself.*

He forced himself to relive those moments fully . . .

" . . . then—she would have discovered the length a juacuar can leap, from a tensioned crouch.

"I didn't need to lower my eyes to see her throat. In my imagination I could feel it crushing, in my hand, against her spine."

A bead of sweat fell onto the paper. Seifas lifted his pen to start another line, seeing again what he had imagined . . .

"We would land . . . there . . . further from the flap of the tent.

"Between myself and freedom, would be three enfuried men.

"At least three men would die.

" . . . and so would my soul."

There.

It was written.

Seifas read over and over again—what he was capable of.

"But," he continued, no longer bearing to see what he had written, "I would gladly sacrifice *myself,* to keep her from becoming a monster.

"Not her. As long as I live it won't be *her.*

"So I waited, to learn the extent of my failure."

CHAPTER 16

Portunista's throat choked.

She couldn't speak. She barely breathed.

Here she had been, blundering round in the back of nowhere—and at any moment Seifas could have given her what she'd been searching for!

She tasted blood; and forced away her irrational anger, swallowing and relaxing. This was *not* worth chewing her lips to a froth.

Her first impulse had been to peel back Seifas' skin—she had also learned a few new jottings from Gemalfan's disciplex, and wanted to test a theory of hers.

But killing the juacuar would serve her nothing. She needed the man—he was an edge that few of her peers could match.

Besides, she didn't really doubt that he would help her; though whether to win, or merely survive . . . ?

Portunista wanted to *win*.

She exhaled, as gently as she had inhaled, watching the deadly man who crouched on the other side of the maps . . . his eyes stayed locked with hers, his arms crossed lightly upon his knees. She watched him easily breathe . . . and knew that she would never intimidate him—not this way.

And from the corners of her eyes, she watched the other men, watching her watch him . . . waiting to see what she would do . . .

"Perhaps it is just as well," allowed Portunista. "I might indeed have failed, not knowing the things I know, if you had told me earlier. What matters now, is now I know."

Possibly not the most coherent statement she ever had uttered . . . ! But, she was pleased to see relief from Seifas, as he settled back onto his heels, with a nod. Perhaps he *had* been wondering how many quivering fragments she would blast him into.

Well, she thought . . . he should!

"Watching you two flare your nostrils, is *very* entertaining," Gaekwar drawled. "But if you won't be killing each other, I have things to do."

"I suppose," admitted Portunista thinly, "I had better hear what you may know, Seifas, before I finalize my plans. Please," she added, with an attempt at a smile.

So, Seifas told how he and nine other men had been recruited from Wye, a border fort between Lemalsamac and Noi.

"As far as I could tell," he said, "the magus picked the other nine without regard for who they were as long as they seemed healthy."

"Didn't much care who he got . . ." Gaekwar stroked his shaven chin. "Except for *you*. I don't buy it. Something isn't adding up . . ."

"Too few," Othon rumbled. Everyone turned to him. "Too *few*," he insisted confidently.

Seifas shrugged. "His tower wasn't the size of a keep. And he barracked us on the bottom floor. Then again," he pondered Othon's implications, "the dell in which the Tower stands, provides at least two klips of clear diameter field. We set a couple of outside-roving pickets—I was one myself—but certainly not enough to properly cover the treeline."

"Too few," Othon repeated, nodding once in satisfaction.

"What was your squad expected to do?" Portunista settled into place, her anger now forgotten. "Why exactly were you there?"

"As a garrison. 'For mundane threats,' as Qarfax said."

"Hmph!" Dagon interjected. "What 'mundane' kind of threats would bother a Cadrist?!"

"Brigades and their scouts," Portunista mused. "Or maybe bandits. As you can see on the map," she briefly flung her hand, "the area *is* remote. Demimen hordes? Giants?"

"Exactly," Dagon nodded. "Even a 'juacuar'," he slightly sneered, "isn't good enough to kill a brigade—or a horde, or anything else like that—and for bloody sure, a squad of faceless mercs would *not* be tipping the scales! And does anyone *else* remember what was going on, that Qarfax might have been specially worried about?"

"Plenty!" Portunista snorted. "Cadrists had been launching wars against each other for nearly a year and—"

"Dying," Othon darkly finished. He slid his eyes to her; she yanked her line of thought to a halt.

"Disappearing, yes," she nodded. "Aside from killing each other, too."

"Like the do-gooding mouthpieces." Dagon didn't look at Seifas, but the man of the Guacu-ara knew at whom that barb was aimed.

"No!" retorted the juacuar, although he quickly reined his irritation. "All the klerosa vanished *at once*; the Cadrists began to disappear later, in a *progression*. Yes?"

Portunista nodded. "That seems right."

"Someone who kept his ears clean, would have heard enough to know the difference," Seifas added as an aside. Gaekwar blinked and Portunista tilted her head; but Dagon jerked and reflexively rubbed an ear. Seifas smiled.

"So, did Qarfax disappear on you?" Gaekwar asked.

"In a way . . ." Seifas shuddered.

He told how they had found the magus, on that final night.

Dagon whistled lowly through his teeth. "So, we could end up burned to ash, hm? I hear the coast is lovely in the autumn . . ."

"Clothes." Othon squinted as he thought the matter through.

"Right!" Gaekwar snapped his fingers. "You found his clothes and things piled on the floor, you said? Around the ash?" Seifas nodded. "So he hadn't moved," the 'cowherd' mused, his drawl receding as it often did when deep in thought. "Scorching? Damage from smoke? No," Gaekwar murmured, as Seifas shook his head. "So he didn't *burn* to death—not in any conventional sense. Talk to us, Portunista."

"Well . . . there are several methods . . ." But she trailed to silence, unable to give a fitting suggestion.

"So—let's take a tally," Gaekwar resumed his ironic drawl. "We're talking about a powerful Cadrist . . . right?"

He flicked a glance at Portunista, who nodded: "Like many Cadre members, he was a researcher. Into principles of superspace, as I remember the rumors. Very strong in Yrthe and Watyr: he wrote a textbook we were taught from."

"Superspace," Dagon muttered, "hm . . ."

"Rogues."

Othon let the deadly word slip into the chilling air.

Outside, the sun was setting. Seifas could smell the autumn, in the back of his mind. Earlier on that afternoon, he had been praying for its arrival.

Now he felt decay, and death.

"Did you see *any* sign of Roguents, Seifas?" Portunista asked; with perhaps a tremor to her voice . . .

The juacuar shrugged once more. "No. But how would I know? We didn't find a signature nailed in his entrails on the ceiling. Yet, Qarfax certainly died," he emphasized in understatement.

"Oh, *this* gets better and better . . ." Dagon sighed, with equal irony.

"So . . ." Gaekwar cleared his throat. "We have a powerful Cadrist," he started again, "who can probably mulch a horde of demimen, if he puts his mind to it; and who also feels reasonably safe in mucking around with the fabric of space. He hires one *very* good fighter, and a passel of mediocre ones, as some protection above and beyond whatever geegaws he's woven around the area. Nevertheless, whatever he was afraid of *still* apparently whomped him, not even bothering Seifas and the others. Yet Portunista thinks we oughta traipse on out there anyway—which not only means we're risking our arms being handed to us by maybe a ticked-off Rogue; but *also* we have to worry about being zorched by anything trip-wired into the place!" And he inhaled dramatically. "Did I miss anything?"

"It might not have been a Rogue!" protested Portunista. "The Cadrists were fighting one another, remember?"

"Then why should we go?" asked Dagon, not unreasonably. "They'll have looted his place already!"

"Clothes," grunted Othon again.

"Exactly," nodded Portunista. "Whatever killed the magus didn't kill *you*, Seifas, or your squad. You *did* find everything still in place, untouched, yes?" He nodded grudgingly. "Something, or someone, strong enough to kill Qarfax so easily, hardly would run and hide at hearing you and your squad coming up the stairs. Therefore, either it only wanted to kill him, or else to kill him and then get one or two particular things: because it left the other things behind. *I* say odds are good, that *we'll* still find them there. And if the Tower *has* been looted already, then someone will have probably set off any traps, and we shall be quite safe."

"On the other hand," Dagon wryly remarked, "this would seem to mean that Cadrists didn't kill him—*they* would want his raw materials and equipment for themselves, wouldn't they? At least the 'geegaws' from his body, right? So . . ." he finished, "do we feel better, or worse?"

"Worse," muttered Othon, shaking his head.

But Seifas sighed, for he could see the light in Portunista's eyes. She was looking beyond these problems, to the obvious reward.

She might one day be like Qarfax!

Of course, thought Seifas, *that* had not helped Qarfax . . .

CHAPTER 17

Portunista's attention wandered, with her imagination; she could practically *taste* the power awaiting at her destination! But soon enough she *did* recall the meeting still in session; and found her subcommanders lost in useless speculation.

"Gentlemen!" she clapped her hands. "I think we have some hope!"

Despite their dubious looks, she forged ahead.

"Qarfax clearly could have only expected Seifas to beat an opposing force of no appreciable size—the others just as clearly were hired to protect his back, and maybe provide more targets for enemy fire. Yet Qarfax hired them *anyway!* They must have made *some* contribution to the tower defenses, whatever they are—so *now* those defenses must have a *hole.* Which *I* intend to exploit!"

"Of course," she added, seeing some skeptical looks remained, "greater power provides for greater authority . . . to share with my faithful subordinates!"

Dagon widely grinned at this. Othon rolled his eyes, but patiently sighed. Gaekwar snorted; yet he also settled back to consider a marching route.

Seifas only looked at her again.

She didn't like him looking at her like that.

"Get some dinner," she told them, "and be back within an hour. A week and a half, or two, to march," she muttered thoughtfully, as the men unwound and stretched, and exited.

Seifas was the last to move.

"Step carefully," murmured the juacuar to her as he left. "The distance between life and death is less than you think."

That sounded disturbingly cryptic. Did his fair-skinned friend have anything to do with that . . . ?

Her thoughts returned to Jian, as they had often done since Midsummer's Eve. She paced distractedly through her tent, chewing her lip. Who was he, really? Why was he here? He never did anything notable—helping the vendors, sparring a little with Seifas. Keeping away from her, mostly. She wondered what he might have contributed to her meeting, imagining how he would have looked, trying to guess what he might have said . . .

Bah! She kicked a cushion. It flew across her tent with a solid thump.

Very satisfactory. So she kicked another one.

Feeling much better, she trod out the flap to find some dinner—maybe some longbread and quail . . . He would probably be near the quailcotes. She could order some pounded quail on sticks, maybe talk to him, figure out something useful . . .

Mulling this over, Portunista wended downhill in the deepening gloom of twilight. She hadn't gone far when she heard that voice—

"You're ready for kissing now, I see!"

Her feet tangled—with her throat it felt like! Spluttering, she whirled around . . . ! She only saw some nearby backs of people.

She spun some more directions, just in case.

Meanwhile, Dagon answered from within the crowd: "I'm ready for *you* to kiss my boots, if *that* is what you mean!"

"Well said!" was the hearty reply; the crowd lightly laughed.

Now Portunista knew where to look, and leapt atop an earthen berm, following as it encircled the hillside, clearing the edge of the crowd.

"Commander Dagon and I have a bet to resolve," said Jian to the gathering. "From myself: *one thrust!*" He quickly lunged, though not toward Dagon. "And from him: *one parry!*" He threw out a hand to the glowering man.

Silence.

"Ahem," coughed Jian theatrically. "Your cue, good sir."

"Get on with it," Dagon nervously growled. "I'm getting hungry; maybe I'll visit the stockpen, before you clean my boots."

"And *that* is Dagon's condition for my loss!" said Jian, resuming his rhythm. "*If* his parry succeeds, then *I* must clean his boots with my tongue—and he didn't exactly specify a time or place, so who can tell what foulness he may stoop to—or stoop *in*, eh?" Again the crowd laughed; not a few clapped. Portunista only shook her head. Why must he be so headslappingly . . . fair?!

"And in return, should his parry fail—I never said I would *hit* you on *target*, sir . . ." Jian grinned, as Dagon's breath caught short. "Though I shall certainly *try*," he added, and Portunista snorted. A fine idea, to throw away *that* advantage . . . "If he cannot parry my legitimate thrust to his chest," and she tapped her foot in exasperation at *this* naive slip as well, "then he must give a kiss to Tumblecrumble . . . on the mouth!" Jian flourished to the crowd's delight.

"Are you ready *now??*" Dagon fretted, looking around at the failing light.

Jian settled into a comfortable stance, within clean striking distance. "Ready and on-guard, good sir! Prepare yourself accordingly!"

Dagon whipped his falchion into a ready stance, dead center of his mass, where he could easily parry in either direction. "You didn't say that *I* had to use a stick, dear *boy*," he smirked.

"Quite true," Jian smiled in return . . .

. . . sounding no less amused, and yet . . .

Portunista blinked. Was she imagining—?

"Quite true. I didn't. I take it you're ready now."

"Anytime!" the Krygian snapped.

"Anytime . . ." echoed the juacuar nearby. Dagon jerked his head and eyes—
—*Go now!* thought Portunista, *he's distracted*—!

But Jian turned round and saluted his friend, slowly so Dagon would *not* mistake it for the thrust. "It's good to know Howclear is here," he said to Dagon, "lest your blade should slip a bit. I wouldn't want my supper ruined." Then he returned on stance. "Ready as well!"

Fine, thought Portunista, let him lose . . . he deserves it after his blunders . . .

With a *snap* Jian stabbed from where he stood, then followed smoothly with a lunge. Dagon barked a laugh and whistled his blade—!

But there was no clang.

Even in the dimming light, everyone could see the stick, touching Dagon almost in the center.

"Pucker up, dear sir."

Jian recovered to attention, with a salute, as the crowd erupted. Dagon stood frozen in shock; but Portunista smiled in surprised appreciation.

Then, Dagon raised his hands. "Silence! I have something to say!" The noise abated somewhat.

"Congratulations, *sir*," he gritted through his teeth. "Clever timing: in this purply haze, I could hardly see a competent disengage. *However*," he continued, "would you be willing to give me a chance to recoup? Double or nothing?"

"Don't do it!" "He'd not've given *you* th' chance!" These and other calls came out of the gathering; ones that Portunista heartily agreed with!

But . . . "Before I consent, I must hear the terms you are offering, sir."

"Torches," stated Dagon. "Plenty of 'em. Also, I think you did *not* quite *fairly* play with me . . . *sir* . . . for if you disengaged my blade, it *wasn't* any straight thrust!"

"That's debatable, Dagon!" Seifas warned.

"True!" returned the Krygian smartly—angering Seifas *must* have seemed better than kissing Tumblecrumble—"But debatable either way. Correct?" He turned toward his opponent. "Shall we *see* for certain whether you played by what you said?"

Jian considered this a moment. Then, "Done!" he granted. "Torches!" Dagon cried, and people ran to fetch them. Portunista found that she was growling beneath her breath . . . but at least he couldn't *really* lose . . .

"And just to keep things interesting," added Jian, "I voluntarily reinstate my *own* end of your terms!"

Portunista's jaw popped as it fell open. Even Dagon's eyes went wide. "As you say!" he crowed. "The crowd is a witness!" The maga *stamped* her foot in frustration—

"Commander Portunista!" Jian turned round to her. She hadn't known that *he* had known that she was near!—caught off balance, she nearly tumbled off the earthen berm.

This did not improve her temper any.

"Would you kindly wisp the area for us, please? I wouldn't want for Dagon to be cheated by the flickering of the torches."

"Done!" she barked, and whistled up some floating globes.

"Same shot!" Jian announced; then he came on guard.

Dagon grunted, face and body tensing tight as steel, as he brought his falchion into line. "And no feints!"

"Certainly not. One straight shot. If you're ready."

"Ready!" gritted Dagon, his eyes boresighted on the wooden stick, as if by force of will he could destroy it . . .

With a proper stab, Jian set up the shot—and then lunged home.

"GRAAAHHH!" Dagon roared, falchion flashing in the brilliant sea of orangish-white—!

He roared. But didn't clang.

The blunt wide tip was resting just about dead center of the Krygian's chest.

"I didn't disengage you last time either," Jian smiled up at him.

"Now—!" the fair man spread his arms to quiet the crowd as the cheering began again. "You have a problem, Dagon. You bet me double or nothing, but frankly there isn't any point in kissing Tumblecrumble twice. So, to *me*, your second terms seem rather open."

Dagon started to dispute, but the juacuar stepped forward and overtly stared into his ear. The Krygian leaped away in panic: "Get *back* from me, you freak!"

"Only checking," Seifas warned.

"So I was thinking," Jian continued, with relentless cheerfulness, "I'll choose something you consider yours, to kiss. And as I've had that kiss already, I'm glad to report your account is almost clear. Fair?"

Dagon looked dissatisfied with this; the logic seemed suspicious. But, what else could he do?

"Agreed," he mumbled.

Jian saluted Dagon and the crowd, and then he strode away; downhill through the cheers. Portunista huffed a sigh: a *perfect* opportunity for him to extort his enemy—altogether wasted!

But, as the crowd and Seifas started hedging Dagon toward the edge of camp that Tumblecrumble favored, Portunista turned to follow Jian.

Dropping nimbly off the berm, she trailed him from a distance.

He walked in unobtrusiveness, often changing direction, finding the path of least attention.

When he reached the quailcotes, he asked a vendor for sticks of pounded meat—just as she'd expected.

When his sticks were ready, he turned to leave—

and found the maga waiting, holding cups of mead and bracing up a loaf of longbread with her arm.

"Do you mind?" she asked. "I could use some company, while I eat tonight." Good start, she thought and pleasantly smiled; very smooth. In fact, he looked a little thrown off-balance . . .

"Send some extra sticks of quail to me," she told the vendor, and then turned to suggest her tent for solitude . . . but Jian had already moved away.

"Thanks! That sounds fine!" he told her over his shoulder. He walked to find a nearby fire, and there he settled back against a log. No one else was at the firepit, but it wasn't private. Seven paces distant, some of Othon's company were heartily shoveling down their evening meal, as a sapling crackled in their fire.

Jian began to nibble neatly on his skewered strips of quail, pausing for a sip of mead. Portunista pulled the bread in halves, and tossed him one.

"So," she started, and she munched her bread. "Very impressive. You don't even care if he kisses the beast?"

Jian shrugged. "I'm not worried. If he doesn't, he will undermine his own authority, showing himself to be a man who breaks his oaths—though granted, of a minor sort."

Portunista nodded. Very clever—devious even. "And if he fills your terms, he looks a clown." She took another bite of bread. "But, you might have lost."

"So?" he asked, and looked at her directly . . .

. . . she saw that he was utterly insane . . .

She tromped down on that burst of fear, and drew the clear conclusion.

"You rigged it."

He chuckled and sipped some mead.

"No. And yes. Sort of. I didn't fix it so I couldn't lose." He smiled a most unnerving smile.

"But . . . if you *had* lost—!" Maybe he *was* insane . . . ! Had she just spit out a chunk of the bread . . . ?!

"Nothing a jug of water couldn't fix. I didn't say that I would *swallow* anything, nor that I'd lick his boots all totally clean at once." Not an especially comforting explanation, the maga thought! "I'm sure it would've tasted vile," he added.

"But—you would've looked—!" The implications dawned on her.

"A fool?" he finished for her—with a grin she normally would have described as diabolic. "As you can see"—he paused to take a grateful-looking sip of mead—"I didn't have much to lose; and plenty to gain, no matter what. I played it fair and in good temper; had I lost, I would have paid the same. People probably would have bought me supper for a week," he chuckled.

Portunista's quail arrived. The boy who carried it scurried away when Portunista scowled at him—his grin and Jian's seemed *much* too close for comfort.

She shuffled some things around in her mind, while they ate together in silence. She absently hoped that Jian hadn't seen that bit of bread fly out of her mouth . . .

On the other hand—she had to swallow a grin herself, when she caught him perusing her, over his meal. She had slipped into a few old habits, calling attention to herself . . . and away from that bit of bread, she hoped . . .

Jian had *seemed* to constantly give *away* his advantages—but now she thought he must have been *securing* them while doing so.

"Are you *really* that good with a sword?" she asked, hiding her interest under a tease.

"No," he chuckled. "And, yes; in a way. I *did* win the bet, after all."

"How?" she asked, more forcefully than she'd intended.

"Surely you don't believe I'm going to *tell* you all my secrets just like *that!*" he laughed. "Dagon led *himself* into it, through his overcare and pride. Seifas probably knows the trick—or any of several regular veterans. It wouldn't hurt for you to talk to them a little anyway, you know."

But, she decided she would *not* ask Seifas, or anyone else. *Now* it was a challenge; a minor one perhaps, but if successful, maybe with interesting rewards . . .

Wait . . . He was finishing up, and . . . Was he preparing to *leave* her at the fire? *This* was hardly something she was accustomed to!

"And what about that gibberish at the end, about the terms already being fulfilled? What did that mean?" she rattled out, off the top of her head. He *was* about to leave her there . . . !

"You mean you have no clue?" he winked.

And then he strode away into the dark—probably to return his cup and sticks to the vendor and quailer! she slunk, thinking to herself—

and then she nearly choked on her bread.

She was absently rubbing the tip of her nose.

CHAPTER 18

I now look forward a week and a half, or maybe two, beloved—only twelve days at most.

The dark man lies in darkness, guarding as the others sleep. The nearby firepit-glow does not even reach the ceiling overhead.

On occasion, Seifas looks up from his open journal, inches from his face. When—or *if* his turn to sleep does come, he shall pillow his head upon his book, not even rolling over.

He has no wish to press the scabbing cuts upon his back.

"Being in Qarfax Tower again, is making my flesh to creep," he writes.

A question nags his mind:

What had Qarfax felt, before he died?

Better to contemplate the recent past than worry about the future, he decides. So he puts his pen to paper once again.

"This afternoon—was it only this afternoon?—we met to plan our squad's approach, to the Tower in the dell. Portunista wouldn't hear of bringing more than just a squad, betting all our lives on her impression of a hole I somehow left in the Tower defenses . . ."

Seifas' pen trails off, as he looks around and listens.

Did he hear something? Was it wind . . . or a lost soul's moan?

. . . Wind. Even the lightest touch of a breeze upon a draft-hole under the eaves, might have made a noise as Seifas has heard. Or imagined he heard.

Where was he at . . . ? He scans what he wrote, to reestablish his thoughts . . .

❖ ❖ ❖

She also insisted on bringing each subcommander. Maybe this only shows how much she doesn't trust us in her absence; but we four *do* maximize force with minimum complement.

Dagon suggested we take some expendable troops for "testing" trap situations. Before that villainous line of thought could be accepted, I neatly turned the tables by proposing we bring Jian—leaving the impression that *he* would fill this role.

Dagon leapt at the proposition.

Othon and Gaekwar didn't seem to mind.

But Portunista's response I watched most closely.

Increasingly, she has been seeking his company. Sometimes this can be clearly explained. Some of the vendors and soldiers, serving as porters, broke into a rousing syncopated chant, early on the second marching day. Natural curiosity led myself and Portunista both to investigate.

Jian had taught them, and was leading the chant.

We also found him going from man to woman to man, carrying part or all of their loads, a few minutes each.

When Portunista saw this, she rode away again, looking somewhat uncomfortable.

But she never stayed away. I watched her as she rode or ate nearby at times when he was not behaving oddly at all.

She didn't always speak to him; and when she did, it was only a minor question or politeness. Still, anyone could easily see she wasn't treating other troops this way.

So—when Dagon recommended that we bring an expendable man along to help us "clear out rooms," I saw an opportunity and said: "Perhaps take Jian. He might serve us well."

"Perhaps," admitted Portunista. "He has proven he can quickly think; and if we lost him, it would hardly matter."

But, her eyes were not so nonchalant . . .

❖ ❖ ❖

And Seifas ceases writing; hearing again the quiet sighing touching on some distant flue.

Does it herald a change in the weather, he wonders?

Why does it seem like a warning of tragedy . . . ?

CHAPTER 19

Now I turn back several hours, my beloved; to watch the squad arriving.

Seifas, having scouted ahead, met them at the treeline. He waited, watching the woods around them, while they got their view of the dell.

"That," Dagon muttered, "is just about the shortest, squattest 'Tower' I've ever seen . . ."

"It's bigger than it looks from here; we're still a long way off," Seifas reminded him.

"Right," Gaekwar mumbled. "Compared to that little bitty tent down there, it's huge."

Seifas gave a nod. "I've flanked a little left and right of our advance, and also when I first arrived. But, I haven't seen another sign of anyone."

The Krygian snorted softly. "Huzzah for the *Hunting* Cry, eh?"

"It isn't as though we're magical," Seifas growled in bitter nervousness. "If I am *not* given time to work, then I cannot scout *anywhere* thoroughly!"

That was aimed at Portunista, who thinned her lips. She *had* insisted on coming here, as soon as her brigade could settle camp, after arriving late that morning and choosing a spot a little way past the valley's pass.

"We're here," she said. "So let's do something *about* it."

"I suggest we wait to get a feel of what is out here."

"Fine. Don't wait too long."

The juacuar withheld a sigh. Kilopaces away from camp, at the end of afternoon—of *course* they couldn't wait too long! Thanks to her.

Seifas knew that *he* was the only one in the squad who could feasibly keep on a mission after sunset, isolated in the woods.

So, unless they were settled in the Tower within the next two hours or so, they would have to camp somewhere nearby. Where the owner of the tent—or anyone in the Tower—might try stalking them.

And he would be their only real defense.

"Is this a natural dell?" asked Jian.

Twelve weeks after meeting him, Seifas still had no idea how much Jian knew about this sort of mission; but at least he'd asked a pertinent question.

"No, I think it isn't," answered Portunista, with a final glare toward the juacuar. Then she closed her eyes and chuffed a brief semantic sequence, while the others watched and waited.

Short, thick yellowed grass carpeted the smooth wide bowl; no trees, no brush, no hedges. Four swift brooks rushed down the slopes, diving below the center of every wall through low, wide openings. Next to the sluice of the southern wall: one door, offset and narrow. The tent had been set nearby the southern stream, within a hundred paces from the door.

After a minute, Portunista shook her head, opened her eyes, and blinked away thin flecks of Yrthen materia. "I can't exactly tell," she grudgingly sighed. "The valley *has* been artificially shaped in small respects, but . . . more like sandings, or even polishings here and there, I think. Smoothings. Also," she deepened her voice in worry, "something in the dell itself—*under* the dell—is interfering with my scrution."

"So . . ." Gaekwar drawled, "do we go in *now,* wait until the sun goes down, or wander around and try to find whoever owns the tent?"

"Let's just wait a bit and think," said Portunista—then winced at Seifas' smile.

So they settled into place.

Seifas took a moment to appreciate his favorite time of year: autumn's upslope had arrived. He eased his mind by contemplating colors: the quiet slow explosions of the trees, measuring weeks instead of an instant.

Jian had settled beneath a honey tree; its leaves were well on their way to matching his rust-colored shirt. Its sap would make him sticky on the back, however! The absentminded man might take some ribbing, Seifas figured; but would probably think it funny, too. Especially since he had only bought the shirt that morning, after hearing Seifas tell the reason Dagon wanted to bring him along!

He certainly wore the shirt quite well: Portunista had given Jian an appreciative look, before the hike.

So things were progressing steadily on *that* front; yet, Seifas vaguely felt disturbed whenever he thought about it now . . .

"Hsst!" This came from Portunista, too brief to be a jotting. Moments ago, Seifas had heard her chuffing again, trying another Yrthescrution. She knelt upon one knee, head on hand in thought—but with the other hand thrown out behind.

Pointing along the line, *between* them and the brigade.

"Someone's coming; from that way," she whispered. The men crept closer to her. "I was checking to see if there was something unusual under the forest, like in the dell—there isn't—and *footsteps* just appeared back there."

"Coming into your sensing range?" Jian asked.

"No!" the maga shook her head. "Several paces within. They just *appeared*, between one moment and the next! Human weight, not too large, two-legged. Boots I think, but soft ones. Soon we'll see; he's coming directly for us." She brushed her watering eyes until they cleared.

The squad lined up across the path of advance; while Seifas concealed himself, preparing for trouble.

Then the humming began.

CHAPTER 20

Portunista certainly hadn't expected a casual humming!

Moments later, a short man rounded the path. His broad face exhibited plenty of smile marks, especially near his deeply twinkling eyes. Short black hair receded smoothly from his forehead, going well with dark gray trousers and field-jacket.

He tromped to a stop, loudly threshing leaves in his way.

"Oh me! Oh my!" He popped his hands theatrically.

"Onto *what* have I stumbled here?"—by his jerky pacing and pitch, he was-n't surprised in the least. Then his speech smoothed out, while keeping its tenored edge: "Four shady-lookin' gentl'men, a lady whose squint could kill—ease up, doll, or those lines'll be permanent, trust me on this—an' . . . lessee . . ." Not even moving his eyes, he kicked a pebble into the brush—eliciting a grunt. "Oh, yeah, a jaaa-guar!" Seifas rose from the brush like a spectre. "Haven't seen one o' *yous* in a while; good t' see ya now. Don't go gettin' cat-a-stro-phic on me, 'kay? I jus' wanna see the people I'm talkin' to. 'Sides, *that* shrub couldn't'a'been comft'ble." The short man grinned and rubbed his hands, as if deciding what order they all should be eaten in.

"This wouldn't be Qarfax by any chance," Gaekwar muttered to Seifas; who snorted: "Not even close."

"Qarfax . . . Qaaar-faax . . ." The man darted his eyes above their heads, as if searching his memory. "Can't say I ever heard th' name." He perked, standing an inch or two straighter—not that this came to much—and tipped his head to the side. "Does he have somethin' to do with th' buildin' down there in th' lake?"

Portunista wasn't sure that she could spot a fellow apprentice, set loose by the chaos of the Culling; but she didn't think this man possessed the underlying aura of a Cadrist's power.

"He looks more like a thug." She eyed him head to foot with some distaste.

His eyebrows twitched with his faltering smile, before he resumed that un-settling grin.

"Nice voice! Betcha sing pretty good when y're in th' mood. At least, I betcha *keep time* pretty good, eh?" He grinned even wider and winked.

"WHAT!" she bellowed—was that an innuendo . . . ?!

But, "Tickety-tockety-lickety-split," he chattered while snapping his fingers; then "BAM!" he pointed at a tree. "Or, th' like," he shrugged. "'Sides, y're th' only one here 'thout an obvious weapon, an' no off'nse, y'ain't got many places t' hide one."

The maga blushed with fury: her shirt and breeches weren't *that* tight!

"Don't zap me, doll; that was a com-pli-ment, case y'hadn't noticed. Okay, so, who's in charge?"

"The doll," Othon rumbled.

"Ah." The stranger nodded; then bowed to Portunista. "It's really quite . . . um . . . fetching. Really. I'm sure it's entirely practical; it *looks* practical! Just . . . um . . . well-cut, yeah . . . help me *out* here, guys, I'm dyin' . . ."

Portunista didn't expect—or want!—for someone to help the little weasel . . . ! She was thinking of "fetching" the remains of his hair to test a jotting theory of hers—but . . .

"You mentioned something about a lake, I think," Jian offered.

"Yeah! A lake! Right! Like I was sayin' . . ." The slightly stocky man hustled over to the treeline's edge. "Thanks, pal," he muttered, before he continued: "As y'c'n see, *what* we have here is a lake . . . 'xcept," he shook his head amused in wonder, "there ain't no lake."

And he changed the shake of his head to a satisfied nod.

Again, silence.

He looked around, guarding his expression.

"I take it from sap-boy's snappy save, that yous didn't know this was *s'posed* t' be a lake, hm? Now, *either* yous wand'red out here in th' middle o' Eyeforsaken nowh—" He cut himself short with a "sorry," and a harrumph. It occurred to Portunista that he was trying to "spare her," as the "lady" of the group, from his profanity.

Now she thought that steam might be emitting out her ears . . . !

"—wander'd out here in th' middle of nowhere, 'thout a map," he continued, "*or,* yous know a bit o' somethin' 'bout this place I don't. So . . ." he shrugged elaborately, and walked a few steps back into the woods along the path, turning to face them again. "So what's th' scoop here? Hm?"

"We *don't* know you, and you're not in any position to ask us anything," Portunista declared. He didn't wilt beneath her glare, but did hold up his hands.

"Okay! No need t' get hos-tile. I'll go first."

He cleared his throat. "My name . . ." He paused, and looked around at everyone in turn. " . . . is Pooralay."

Dagon snickered. "Well; that's inoffensive enough!"

"Yeah, well, I'm an inoff'nsive kinda guy. So kiss off, doll-boy."

Dagon choked and Portunista watched him turn a lovely shade of reddish purple! But before the Krygian could act . . .

"Hi! I'm Jian." The fair man walked to meet the stranger with a smile and outstretched hand.

"Uh . . . yeah . . . call me Poo, I guess . . ." He shook Jian's hand. "Yeesh, guys, where'd y'find this clown? Is he simple, or what?"

"Expendable," muttered Dagon.

"Actually," chuckled Gaekwar, "he found us."

"Ah." Pooralay carefully watched as Jian, who shrugged, resumed his place in the line. Then he squinted his beady eyes, and tilted his head. "Do I know you?"

Portunista's temper doused in shock; her hearing felt as sharp as knives . . . *Know* Jian??

The fair man thought on this a moment. "I am certain," he replied—very carefully—"that we have never met, and that I don't know *you.*"

This didn't seem to satisfy the little man, but with a muttered "Yeah . . . okay . . . my mistake, I guess," he turned back to the others in the group. "Um . . . okay; wristboy, how 'bout you?"

"Uh-uh," Gaekwar corrected. "Now you tell us why you're here." He emphasized this with his disker-laden arm.

"Okay . . . I c'n unnerstand y'bein' nervous 'n all . . . but howsabout pointin' that thing somewhere po-lite b'fore I get annoyed."

Gaekwar didn't move; but Pooralay did. With a fatalistic shrug, he sauntered over to the 'cowherd', putting his torso inches from the disker.

"Now y're sure t' hit me. Feel any better?"

—a blurring hand—

—the disker's springy whine—!

Gaekwar gasped and caught himself from leaping backward.

Pooralay had stuck a short thin knife between the disker's channeled metal slots, blocking the shuttling mechanism.

Instantly plenty of weapons were leveled . . . but Jian only watched while stroking his beard.

"Kinda jumpy, aincha?" Pooralay grinned. "Don't move, or y'might get stuck. I ain't nicked y'r arm—yet. Like I said," the short man flicked his eyes around at them, "I jus' don't like t' be annoyed, is all." Pushing the disker gently to the side, with a "Watchit," Pooralay pulled the knife from the works. The disc spat weakly out. "Prob'ly gonna need to check those springs," the stranger suggested—Gaekwar looked as though he had swallowed his tonsils. "So big guy, how 'bout you?"

Pooralay turned to face the spiky end of an edged mace. "You gotta name, or are y'-gonna be imp'lite to someone who's ver-ti-cal-ly challeng'd?"

The "big guy" squinted, and then replaced his mace inside the wooden frame upon his back. "Othon."

"Fair 'nuff; you 'n th' kid with th' sap on his back're all okay in my book. You too," he nodded to Seifas. "I'm okay with jaguars on gen'r'l prin-ci-ple." He stepped five paces back, to regard them all again. "Okay, so y'wanna know why I'm here."

He paused, and then inhaled.

"I'm lookin' . . . f'r the Well at th' End of th' Wood."

CHAPTER 21

Pooralay led them down into the dell, chattering amiably; though Seifas noticed he stepped on Dagon's foot in passing, probably for laughing at him again.

"Actsh'ly," the stranger said, "now that I'm here, I'm even *more* sure that I'm at th' prop'r place. Well," he added, after a moment's thought, "not *complet'ly* sure, but ev'rythin' seems t' be tallyin' up that way."

They watched in all directions as he led them down the slope. Being in the open, made the juacuar feel nervous. The kilopace of clearance round the Tower gave an ample firing field.

"So, okay," the little man continued, "what's th' *end* of a woods? It's like y're askin' where the end'f a blob 'r circle is: *nowhere*. Sure you c'd have an arm o' th' woods thrown off like here or there—hell, most woods got a hunnert 'r thous'nds of 'em—but what makes that 'the end'?" he crooked his fingers. "Nothin'. It c'd be th' b'ginnin' just as eas'ly. So, I figur'd that once you get t' th' *middle* of a woods, basic'ly you've establish'd an *ob-jec-tive-ly dis-tinc-tive* part o' th' woods. Right? Y'can't go any furth'r *into* th' woods, once y'reach th' *middle*— 'cause *at* that point y're goin' *out* again. And *that*," he ended, "is an *end!*"

He turned with hands spread wide in triumph, walking backwards, waiting for applause.

"That seems logical," nodded Jian, deep in thought. He seemed to be the only person taking Pooralay seriously yet.

"But why," he asked, "would you be looking for this Well?"

The short man blinked and stumbled, and the others stopped in amazement. "Y'mean y'never *heard* of it?!"

"Um . . ." Jian shrugged, looking around, " . . . maybe I've led a sheltered life so far?"

"Yeah . . ." Pooralay mused. "Yeah, okay, *that* I c'n buy . . ." He shook his head. "So, anyone want t' 'xplain it?"

Dagon rolled his eyes. "It's a kiddie tale."

"A *legend*," Portunista corrected—coming to Jian's defense, as Seifas saw . . .

"A *treasure*." Gaekwar pointedly stared at Pooralay.

"A *risk*," asserted Othon, folding his arms.

"A *prophecy,*" Seifas emphasized.

"Well . . . that's helpful!" Jian smiled—perhaps at his pun.

Pooralay grunted. "Yeah, it's all o' that, I guess." Then he recited:

"The Well at the End of the Wood
delivers both evil and good.
Make your choice and leap into strife.
Learn the price of death and of life."

Seifas and Portunista studiously recited the poem with him. Gaekwar sounded embarrassed, but still he chanted it. Dagon only rolled his eyes again, and turned away; perhaps to keep on watch for trouble. Othon didn't join the chant, exactly; but he clearly rumbled "life."

"'Kay. So y're *not* all ign'ramuses. I was b'ginnin' t' worry." Pooralay scowled at Jian, before resuming his downslope pace.

"So . . . basically . . . nobody *knows* what the Well may be."

"Well, no . . . heh-heh-heh," Pooralay chuckled, at his own pun. "But it's obvi'sly somethin' worth findin'."

Dagon snorted. "Yeah, sometimes second sons of merchants or nobles, with nothing better to do, get all decked out to gallivant around the countryside, looking for the thing. It's an excuse to look good for the ladies, get into fights . . . They call themselves 'errants', like *that's* supposed to be impressive."

"Confidence tricksters also harp on the Well," Gaekwar added, staring at Pooralay.

"True errants *do* exist," insisted Seifas. "But they're very *rare.*"

"We weren't taught about the Well by our instructors," Portunista said—not as far as *she* got, Seifas silently amended!—"Maybe the history teachers knew something about it . . . or . . ."

"Researchers," Othon finished.

"Superspace researchers maybe?" Gaekwar gestured at the Tower.

"Who knows?" shrugged Portunista. "But we're working at it backward. We would have to know *about* the Well, before we could begin to guess who knows—or knew—whatever . . ." She trailed off, thinking. By her thirsty look, Seifas supposed that she was dreaming about more power than she had imagined.

The juacuar decided, that whatever it took, he *would* prevent her from finding the Well—for her own good.

And a darkness settled on him, for he knew what he was willing to do—to keep her from becoming a monster . . .

They finished their hike downslope, each of them in silence—even Pooralay.

Then as they reached the tent: "This is yours, I guess." Gaekwar jerked a thumb.

"Yeah . . ." The little man absently waved, striding past without a glance. Then he sat and stared by turns, first at the cubic Tower now looming over them, then at the grassy valley all around.

Meanwhile, Seifas eyed the tent, then scanned the far encircling treeline. "But," he said to everyone, "he hasn't been *staying* here."

It took a moment for Pooralay to register this. Then he grinned and cocked an eyebrow. "Yeah . . . oh, hey, you're good!" He assessed the area once again himself. "Yeah, I got here 'bout three days ago. Set th' tent up kinda as a decoy. Guess I shoulda come down here an' scuffl'd it some at night, t' make it look more lived-in."

"So, you've seen activity in the Tower?" Portunista asked.

"Not a peep," he shook his head. "But that don't mean a thing. Been sittin' aroun', scoutin' th' area, tryin' to get th' lay o' th' land." He chuckled again, sardonically. "Tryin' t' get up gumption enough t' tackle th' door or a sluice, or work m' way up to the roof and look around."

Seifas motioned for the squad to settle in; they kneeled or squatted comfortably, beneath the azure deepness of the sky. The sunbeams slanted down with friendly fierceness, yet with definite lack of heat. Winter would be coming soon; and Seifas paused a moment to enjoy the feel and smell and sights, inhaling them, forcibly banishing darkness away from his thoughts.

Then he padded over to the little man, and sank to sit beside him.

"Let us play a game." He smiled with equal menace and goodwill.

"D'pends on th' game, don't it?" "Poo" smiled back in much a similar manner.

"Your accent comes from Tafel, probably Tafeltop itself."

"Sharp ear!" Pooralay chuckled—it hardly took a genius to figure *that* . . .

"You're good enough with knives that you aren't carrying any weapon larger than the two long daggers holstered on each belt, at hand."

"Bloody good eye. Remind me never t' fight a jaguar . . ."

"However, the knife you used for blocking 'wristboy's' disc from launching—"

"Gaekwar!" "Wristboy" interjected. Pooralay arched an eyebrow at the juacuar—but Seifas knew the information wouldn't be much gain: he doubted any farming mother named her son an ancient word for "cowherd" . . .

"*That* knife," continued Seifas, "was a balanced throwing dagger."

"So?"

"You haven't been camping in the tent; where would you 'come down from' at *night* to make it look more slept-in? Only the trees around the rim."

The little man had stopped his grinning, though his eyes still twinkled.

"When we detected your approach, your feet just seemed to suddenly plop on the ground from nowhere." Seifas didn't tell of how they knew this. "You clearly weren't surprised to see us; yet you purposely scuffled leaves as you got closer. Why? To make us think you *always* move so loudly, perhaps. Either your eyes are sharp enough to spot me in that brush, or else you already knew that I was near, and made a solid guess of where I'd be most likely hiding. Jian was standing with the rest of us when you arrived, and never turned his back to you— and yet you knew the sap was on his back. You watched him lean against the honey tree." Seifas smiled, matching evaluating stares with Pooralay.

"You were in the branches of the trees—close enough to see us; maybe to hear us, too. And then you quickly moved a little further off, quietly and unseen, dropping down to meet us on the path. You surely possess the necessary hand-speed and precision."

Seifas stopped a moment. His "sparring" partner didn't bat an eyelid.

"Portunista over there was right." Let him know her name as well, Seifas thought; if he's heard of her, he might also know she commands a group of companies, and that might help forestall some future problems. "You're a thug."

Pooralay conceded with a sigh.

"I am Seifas." The juacuar gave him a greeting hand. No reason not to be polite, he thought. Besides, a thief might soon be useful . . .

A hesitation—then Pooralay accepted Seifas' hand. His shake seemed genuine. "I'm not confessin' t' nothin', y'unnerstand . . . but rottin' good for you.

"Okay! That leaves doll-boy ov'r there, whose name I couldn't care less about—"

"Dagon!" "Doll-boy" growled.

"Whatever . . . Okay, *my* turn now." He clapped his hands together, and resumed his shadowy grin.

"There's an encamp'd br'gade 'bout sev'nty-seven hunnerd paces south o' here, 'r so."

No one expressed any shock; this didn't seem to disappoint him. "I take it this ain't news t' anyone. I'd make some c'nclusions from *that*, 'xcept there ain't no point, 'cause I follow'd you here from y'r camp! Yeah, I *thought* that might get more reaction!

"Shadowed you at an angle, 'bout a hunnerd paces t' y'r left, followin' down th' stream t' mask my noise. Y'didn't swing wide enough," he winked toward the juacuar.

On seeing Seifas' self-chastising scowl, the little stranger not-unkindly laughed: "Don't knock y'rself too hard upside th' head; you were obvi'sly inna hurry t' get here—or maybe someone else was inna hurry. Y'didn't strike me as th' sort to rush a job like that. Th' lady here runs the gig; Othon said so, but she obvi'sly *ain't* th' squaddie leader. So she's got a higher rank. Justa guess, o' course."

"Good guess," Portunista admitted grudgingly. Not a bad idea, however, to let him confirm the scope of her authority . . .

"Meanin' *she's* th' one t' blame for hurryin' out here late in th' day." Seifas had to forcibly smother a kindred grin; Portunista wasn't amused.

"Sap-boy didn't know that this was s'posed to be a lake. He seems a little wet b'hind th' ears, but no one told 'im diff'rent, so I'm guessin' you weren't comin' here for, let us say, th' u-nique ge-o-gra-phi-cal features of th' region. Y're here for the Tower. You were 'xpectin' a Qarfax fella; and y'figure he's in the-o-ret-ic re-search. That makes this a Cadr'st Tower—even though it don't much look like one," he wryly observed. "Lady's prob'ly a maga; word is, mosta th' Cadre's va-porized themselves. Two an' two t'gether, y're here on a gadget-lootin' run, give y'r brigade some punch." He shrugged. "Maybe I c'n help. Eyecansee, *I* c'd use some help," he sighed. "I hate t' mess with magi." Turning, he regarded the Tower. "Guess that's gonna change, huh?" And he sighed again. "Place gives me th' heebiejeebs. I kinda gotta feelin' 'bout it. I *trust* my feelin's!" he declared, and spun back around to the group.

"Well, it isn't like you *have* to 'mess with magi,'" Dagon said. "You could just hike on out of here; go find a lonely merchant-lady to fleece."

"Whassa-matter? Y'think y'r odds are bad with me aroun'? Sure I thoughta tailin' out," admitted the little man, "but I *didn't* come here f'r th' loot . . . Well, y'know, maybe a little, just f'r my 'xpenses . . . Hey!—why'm I 'pologizin' to *you* guys?! Y're just like me, only taller, 'n' rookies! I ain't here f'r treasure! *I'm* here 'cause—!"

Smothering what he was going to say, Pooralay sulked instead. "Y're just here t' get y'r brigade some firepower. Whoop-de-floggin'-do. Good luck, and have at it. J'st stay outta my way."

"And power over life and death and good and evil doesn't count as 'firepower' . . ." Gaekwar said acidically.

"Who knows j'st *what* it counts as?" shot back Pooralay. "Who said it's 'power'? Sounds more like knowl'dge t' me. But then, *I* don't have *your* obvious *decades* of 'xperience, decipherin' multi-millennia cosmic *hooey!!*" And he spat in Gaekwar's direction.

"Could be both," Othon murmured, looking at the sun descending in the west. Seifas knew that Portunista also would consider knowledge power . . .

"So, why here, do you think?" asked Jian politely. Pooralay huffed for a moment, eyeing Gaekwar—who recalled his crippled disker! The lanky man edged off, looking nonchalant, and crouched as if on watch behind them near the tent—while he surreptitiously started repairing the workings.

"Yeah . . . okay . . ." Poo threw threatening glances at the rest of the squad, but did appear to be calming down. "Why here. Good question. Betcha made a wunnerful kid in school. Well, once I d'cided t' find 'The Well,' I went t' Tafeltown's Orthogoni. Kinda scorched fr'm all th' fightin', but still in pretty good shape. Busiest scribblers I ever saw. Them'n th' Promulgat'rs, goin' in and out, alla th' time. Makin' copies t' help replace th' books that were lost in th' fightin', I guess. Overheard that most o' th' other Orthogonies also were hit, some o' them directly. No total losses, but . . . anyway," he moved along, seeing impatient scowls nearby. "I kinda wander'd in while they were busy. Figur'd they wouldn't be int'rested helpin' a . . ." He sighed again. " . . . a thug, like th' lady said—helpin' me, findin' somethin' like th' Well. Always kinda liked researchin' maps 'n such. I coulda . . . borrowed . . . books I guess, but it just . . . didn't seem right . . . Whaddayou smilin' at, sap-boy? So, okay, I go in, mess around, avoid some people, find th' maps—best maps in th' world at an Orthogoni."

He shook his head, staring at the ground, focused on his memories. "Never knew there were so many forests in Mikon. Th' rottin' cont'nent's thick with 'em! A million square klips at least, up in the Middlelands, and mosta th' maps o' there're older'n dirt. But first I concentrated on th' local stuff; y'know, Casio an' Lemalsamac, some of Krygy, not too far inland. Kinda pokin' around, eyes're gettin' bleary . . . then . . . bam!" he jumped. "Just like a target, right there on th' *page!!*" Pooralay looked at them. "I mean, I never knew it would *happen* just like . . . !" He faded off, controlling his exuberance.

"Four rivers," he began again, more calmly, bending down to scribble on the ground. "Well, brooks, actsh'lly. They're bigger on th' maps than here, an' I can see why, now: more water here 'rigin'ly, w'd make th' brooks more swoll'n backin' pressure." After looking around at them, he then continued. "Comin' from th' four points on th' compass, down from these here mount'ns to th' north, an' from those ridges there," he pointed. "You guys came in through the pass back there, th' southeast corner; most sensible way t' bring a big group into th' area, and it's close t' where y're camped."

"And *I* bet *you* camped on the *northern* side of the dell," inferred the juacuar. "You wouldn't need to watch your back as much."

"Yeah, good guess," agreed the little man. "I'm sure you guys got maps— didn't y'see the lake right smack b'tween th' rivers?!"

Everyone but Jian looked pointedly at Portunista, who folded her arms and tapped a booted toe.

"Qarfax *could* have bribed—excuse me, *requested*—the mapping guild to keep his privacy; and *obviously* the trader maps were drawn by people who had *been* here. What does it *matter* anyway?! Let's *go,* before we're camping in that puppydog-tent tonight!!"

"Testy minx," Pooralay muttered. "So, I'm thinkin', hey, a map-sized lake, outta th' way," he hurried along as Portunista spiked a glare in his direction; Seifas could hear the 'cowherd' chuckling—very quietly!—behind them. "Buncha natural signs're pointin' at it, so t' speak; it's in the middle of a *wood,* right? And best of all, get this—there ain't no rivers leadin' *out-a* th' valley! Betcha didn't notice *that,* eh??" He proudly grinned, as their expressions changed to something more like awe than skepticism.

"Where's the wa-ter *go*-in?" he gleefully observed. "Has t' be down a *hole;* and lookit, what d'y'see?" He pointed behind himself, not needing to look.

The brooks were diving into sluices, one in every Tower side—with nothing coming out.

"Rotten blood!" Gaekwar snapped his disker back together, and rejoined the group.

Pooralay was almost dancing in excitement. "See? *See?!* It's a *well . . .* in th' *middle . . .* of a *wood!* An' th' *middle* of a woods is gonna be th' closest you c'n get t' bein' at its *end!*" He clapped his hands together with a smack, whirling toward the center of the dell, delighted as a child who's found the treasure stashed for Stilleve Day. "And lookit, lookit, surprise, surprise! It's a WHOLE . . . EYE-BLINKIN' . . . *TOWER!!!*"

And throwing back his head, he cackled and hopped and shook his fists for joy!

"SO!" he spun again to them, with another popping *clap!* Their faces—even Dagon's—had become slack-jawed and wonderstruck.

Everyone's face, that is, except for Jian's. He was standing with his hands on his hips, and grinning.

"Who wants t' go in with me?!"

SECTION THREE

FIRST NIGHT

CHAPTER 22

It looked like any other tower door.

But Seifas knew it wasn't.

"Be careful," said the juacuar, as Pooralay knelt beside it.

"Ah-duhhh!!!" the short man slapped his head. "C'n you c'ntribute somethin' a little more *specif'c?!*"

"Qarfax changed this door somehow."

"Y'mean it's gonna turn me inside-out?"

"No . . . maybe . . ." Seifas tried to puzzle what he had seen.

"Then *git,* y'gangly shadow-throwin'—!" Pooralay broke off in mumbles, reining in his temper. "All o' yous, back! Left, right, anywhere, not in m' light!"

Ignoring the glowers at his back—but they moved, including Dagon—the thief returned attention to the door. He pulled a thin metallic stick from one of many jacket pockets. Crouching close to a side, he probed the doorjamb with the strangely-ended implement.

Seifas thought to tell him that when last he'd left the Tower, no one was alive within it. But he caught himself before he spoke: he didn't know if anything had happened during the slopings since. And he heard the rumblings . . .

"Nothin' I c'n find," the thug reported, not too happily. "An' there's no lock t' pick—"

"—ah-DUHHH!" retorted Dagon at this obvious announcement.

"Okay, doll-boy, *you* c'n be th' one t' push th' door wide open, then! G'wan, it *seems* t' be complet'ly *safe!* Can't y'hear th' noise inside!?"

"This is why we brought the red-shirt 'sap-boy'," Dagon smugly answered.

"True enough," the fair man said. "You all stay back, and let me test it—"

Seifas reached with his aasagai and poked the handle-latch, pushing the door slightly open.

"GAH!" Pooralay cried. "Dammit, lemme get back from th'—!"

"It didn't hurt me when I left it last time," Seifas said. "And *you* decided it had not been trapped."

Pooralay sighed. "Y'wanna fill some details in f'r some of us?"

Seifas briefly told him of his garrison.

"A pile-a ash. Great." The little man stared sullenly into the narrow darkened gap. "So, who goes first?"

"Jian!" Dagon said.

"No, I will," corrected Seifas. Dagon tried to protest, but—"Silence!" said the juacuar. "I was last to leave this place, and I shall go in first!"

Dagon aborted his complaint; perhaps because the juacuar had pointed around with the aasagai. The needled tip was floating like a wasp a fingerwidth from Dagon's face.

"Be my guest," he gestured to the door—while staring at the tip. "May be better anyway . . ." he muttered.

Pooralay warily stepped away, as Seifas pushed the door more open with the aasagai, letting sunlight stream into the room.

"It's the basement," he announced, half to himself, as the noise increased.

"Hmph. Funny place, *above* the ground," Gaekwar drawled.

Seifas nodded. "Very true. What you see," he told them as he crossed the threshold of the large stone room, "is what we called the 'basement.'"

"Kind of stupid, weren't you?" Dagon said. The group was gathering round the door, while Jian was next to step inside.

The juacuar looked back to them. "This *was* the basement, at the time. The doorway you're all pressed against, opened to the floor *above*."

They froze, except for Jian, already wandering curiously.

"Be my guest," Othon grumbled—then shoved Dagon in.

"Careful," Seifas warned them, as he barred the stumbling Krygian with the aasagai. "In the middle of the room, there is an open hole."

"*I* don't see a hole," said Portunista as she squinted.

"Maybe that's b'cause th' door ain't wide enough f'r you an' sunlight both, doll." After a poisonous glance—which the short man disregarded as he checked the doorway's inner frame—the maga whistled through her teeth. Floating wisp-lights lit the wide round room.

"Thanks," absently nodded Poo, as Portunista walked inside, then "Oomph!"—she kneed his ribs in passing.

"So, what we *have* here," Gaekwar mused as he and Othon followed after, "is an empty level of the Tower . . ."

"Half a level." Othon bounced his forehead off the oaken beams above.

"Three quarters of a level," Seifas said. "An intervening space above us holds some gearworks."

"They run *that*, I guess." Portunista gestured at a plank which hung from thickly woven rope. The rope led to a metal ring from which two smaller ropes descended into eyebolts in the sturdy plank. The main rope dangled through a hole above, itself the size of the hole below the plank.

"Exactly," Seifas said. "Although I think there *are* more gears than needed for this simple lift."

"You've been up there?" Gaekwar asked.

Seifas nodded, edging to the hole and peering up into the crawlspace depths. "I was curious one day while I was off my watch. The mechanism operates by pulling these." Two other finely woven cords descended from the hole above, connecting to some levers set on each side of the plank.

"Wait, wait—back up," Dagon waved. "What about the *door?* Where does *that* door lead?"

"Out," Seifas smiled. "See?" He pointed to the dell outside. The floor was gleaming oranger as the sun descended to the final hour. "Going *in,* it used to open on the next floor up, where our garrison was stationed."

"Yeah? And where did *that* door lead?" Dagon asked.

"Also out. Right there, outside that door."

"So . . ." pondered Gaekwar. "What if guys went out *both* doors at once?"

Seifas grunted wryly. "We were told to *never* use the basement door, except in an emergency. When Qarfax died, the door upstairs led *nowhere* any longer."

"Pooralay!" called Portunista.

The little man anticipated her. "No sigils on th' frame, or near th' door," he answered. "Nothin' near th' door at all, 'xcept f'r this here lever." He tapped a wooden brace, next to the door, into which ran another rope, knotted thickly at the bottom. "Wonder what it—?"

"We *also* were told to *never* touch that lever!" Seifas warned.

"Yeesh, okay, no probl'm!" Pooralay backed away.

"What's the pail for?" Jian inquired. From simpler rope, a large tin bucket hung beneath the plank.

"Drawing water," Seifas answered. When he yanked a thin cord down, it pulled its opposite number up, thus racheting up the opposite lever by a notch. The deep and steady rumbling underneath them now was joined by different clanks and rattles overhead. The plank and pail descended slowly. Seifas pulled the other cord, making the plank to stop. "It goes up similarly," he added.

"Why a plank?" the maga wondered. "Why not just a pail?"

"To get to the works above, of course!" Dagon snorted.

"You mean, if they break down?" retorted Portunista.

"Right!"—then Dagon winced.

"Probably to reach the gears below," corrected Seifas.

"You mean, if *they* break down?! " the Krygian answered witheringly. Now it was Seifas' turn to wince.

"Interesting," Jian observed. "How *does* a person reach those gears, should something happen? Not by the plank!" he quickly added.

"Doors?" suggested Othon.

"No," said Seifas. "None I ever found."

Portunista sniffed. "Qarfax studied superspace. He could jott and bind a tesser—he must have bound one on that door," she pointed. "Getting into places wouldn't *be* a problem for him, nor for anyone helping him."

"Which brings us," Jian concluded, "back to why he has a plank."

They all considered this, for a minute.

"Well!" said Dagon finally. "Let's send Jian into the hole!"

"Ready!" Jian hopped onto the plank. Dagon blinked, then smiled in anticipation . . .

"Wait!" protested Portunista. "*I* am going down the hole!" Incredulous looks surrounded her. "We're *in* the tower of a Cadrist; *I'm* the one most qualified to figure out what he's done down there—"

"—if anything . . ." interrupted Poo.

" . . . *and* it's *my* brigade!"

"I think you shouldn't go alone," warned the juacuar.

"Fine," she snapped. "Hold still!"

She leaped on Jian, pulling her legs around his waist until they dangled behind the plank.

"Don't even *think* . . . " she growled beneath her breath, "of trying *anything* . . . "

The startled man blinked once or twice . . .

And then he said: "Let's go!"

CHAPTER 23

"That *don't* seem overly safe . . ." Pooralay muttered.

"Qarfax was heavy and tall." Seifas sounded as if he was stifling a chuckle, while watching the couple descend into the pit. "I think the plank will hold them both."

Pooralay angled an eye at Seifas. "I didn't mean th' *plank* . . ."

Jian and Portunista sank beneath the level of the wooden floor. Around them rattled machinery. Jian pulled one of the lever-cords, jolting the plank to a halt.

"Well?" he loudly asked.

"Well, *what?*"

"Will you whistle up some lights? I didn't bring a torch . . ."

She expelled a sigh, and cursed herself. What in all nine hells had she been *thinking?* Her imagination promptly gave her answers to that question . . . but she firmly clamped her imagination.

As a consequence, she clenched her jaw so tightly she could barely focus her intent or even whistle.

It took several tries to get some wisps.

"Any problems?" Blue suffusion softly lit his pale and curly hair, she noticed . . .

"Focus, dammit!" Portunista growled.

"Ooookay," Jian recoiled, then shrugged and started examining their surroundings. Portunista did as well—being careful *not* to look in his direction.

The lights showed millhouse wheels, set along the walls in frameworks. Streams poured down and over them, vanishing below. Although the cords had disengaged the gears, up in the headworks space, these wheels continued turning under force of falling water, working other shafts and gears nearby within the pit.

"Seems a lot of effort for a water well!" Jian was speaking loud enough to hear, but not intrusively. Portunista wryly smirked at his consideration.

And remembered *not* to look at him . . .

All the distractions were giving her trouble in keeping the wisps in existence. So, she unbound them all but one.

"Are you okay?" Seifas boomed from above.

"Just fine!" she yelled. "And trying to think!" The men above could light the sconces she had seen upon the 'basement' wall.

She guided her one remaining wisp over to a wheel—the southern one, she thought.

"Neat!" she heard Jian say. "I had forgotten you could *do* that!"

Ruefully she shook her head and smiled. Here she was, sitting on a full-grown man who still said "neat"! Well, maybe it fit; they *were* on a sort of swing . . .

She put the wisplight through a series of acrobatics, darting it over, around and behind the machinery, dancing among the shadows, scampering through a millwheel's massive spokes.

She tried to pretend she was only exploring meticulously.

But Jian was laughing.

She could *feel* him laughing, in her, under the rumbling machinery. She was showing off, and *enjoying* showing off, not for her own sake . . .

. . . but because she was making him happy.

She had to look.

She put the wisp through a complex series of curving loops, for keeping his attention . . . and turned and looked at him.

Was he laughing as a ploy—the way *she* laughed sometimes?

No. She could see his face.

He truly was enjoying *her,* her skill and ingenuity, for those were *her* in action, her enaction.

So she spent another minute, cleanly feeling and enjoying Jian enjoying *her.*

The wisplight floated to a hover, her attention drawn away. And so he surprised her when he turned to see her watching him.

They blinked together.

"You should smile like that more often." This she heard or felt him say. Was she smiling? Was her smile like his?

A corner of her mind concluded that his eyes must be the wisplight color, for his irises shone white. His pupils, though, shone deeply black; blacker than the shadows farther than her light could reach. She wanted to *reach* into those shadows, and discover what was there. She wanted to curl up in those shadows, safe and warm beyond the world . . . where there was only healing and nothing that would ever hurt her . . .

"Ahem . . ." She heard a cough, from in the shadows. She was there right now . . . Wasn't she? Was she? She looked around, in her security, and saw the restful nothing, which meant there was nothing to be fearful of . . .

"AHEM!" Now the cough was more insistent. "Portunista!"—that was her *name.* Someone was saying her name, who didn't fear her, didn't hate her, didn't want to use her. Maybe he would say her name again . . .

"It's hard to learn without a light to see by, Portunista!"

And with a physical shock, machinery noise asserted itself. She could hear, but couldn't see; she could hear him, but she couldn't see him. *Why* could she not see him?! She could hear and feel him; she could even taste his smell, the-smell-that-was-*him* and no one else. Why couldn't she see him? She wanted to see him!

"Why can't I see you?!" Portunista shouted, her security evaporating. Something was wrong. Everything was right, but something still was *wrong!*

"I think the wisp burned out. Can you make another?"

Her attention fully returned, to her self.

With a snarling sigh, she whistled up another light, nearby. Jian looked curious more than worried, although he *did* blink several times, his pupils having dilated in the darkness.

"Was there a problem?" he asked. "Did something happen? Was something wrong?"

Her anger at herself spilled over. "No, nothing happened! Everything was right—*Nothing's* wrong! Just be *quiet* for a moment!!"

He recoiled; and her heart was wrenched—because his smile was gone, and there was hurt within his face. *She* had put it there; for no good reason.

But she was angry—she wanted to be angry at *him*—so she didn't apologize. What could she say?—that she had plunged them both into darkness, because she had let her attention slip while searching in his eyes?! She might as well tell him that she was a scatterbrained fool!!

"What are you *waiting* for?" she demanded. He had already shrugged her harsh words off—she thought she had seen him mutter "Oh, well . . ."—"We need to go farther down!"

"As you wish!" he cheerfully answered; then he crinkled his face in concentration, as he considered the racheting cords—pulling one would raise the other on its notching lever. As he worked to operate it right, she watched his nose—*not* his eyes!—his nose was twitching at the tip; not a lot, just a little . . .

The plank *jerked* into movement, and she bit a curse in two. Had she *actually* been thinking of nipping the tip of his nose?!

She sent the wisplight off again, as straight as if on rails—*No dancing!* she determinedly told herself—and kept it steady during their descent. As they passed the bottom of the wheels, she ordered another halt.

The wide stone well showed polishing down to this point—by jotting, she suspected—but below the wheels the sides were rougher. She whistled up another wisp successfully, and sent it farther down. By its light, she saw the well wasn't only more natural here, but also narrowed from a width that was almost the same as the room above, into a throat a little wider than the plank. This rocky throat drank down the streams into a rushing water which seemed to be racing—she oriented with the Tower in her memory—yes, south. A river underground.

Something sparkled in the light, around the river's throat. What was that—?

"Say," Jian interrupted her thoughts. "Isn't that a ledge?"

"What?" she answered absently, while trying to decipher what was being revealed beneath them—

"A ledge of stone," Jian clarified. "I think it's solid all the way around the well down here."

She looked up to where he pointed—and she saw he was correct.

She sent the upper wisp to slowly pass along the ledge. It seemed built sturdy enough . . . or maybe . . .

Closing her eyes, she chuffed in syncopated tones, focusing her intention and attention. Flecks of elemental Yrthe coalesced beneath her eyelids as she concentrated. Binding her jott, she scruted the ledge, and also the walls around them.

Ah; they *had* been jotted into their current shape!

And . . .

Her eyes popped open in surprise; ferociously she blinked to flush evaporating Yrthe.

"That *must* be uncomfortable," Jian said sympathetically.

"It could be worse," she wryly snorted, drying the tears from her cheeks. "It could be Phyre." She ignored his wincing "Ouch!", and looked around again with natural eyes.

"We need to reach that ledge," she told him.

"I don't believe that you can safely leap there," Jian replied in doubt.

"Look!" she exclaimed. He turned toward her. "No, not at me!" she waved. "I mean look over *there!*" He dutifully followed to where the wisplight trailed; a shaft was spinning one small wheel in barest contact with the wall, at the ledge's level.

The wall there glowed with sigils—very faint but deeply purple in the wisplight.

Jian whistled in appreciative understanding, almost leaning from his seat to get a better view.

"Hold *still!*" Portunista warned. "And look . . ." They locked their eyes together on the wisp, following as she traced around the ledge, revealing what her scrution had detected. The sigils encircled completely to a height above the ledge about two wrisths. On every cardinal compass point, a small wheel spun in contact with the tracing.

"Wouldn't they grind away the . . . um . . . sigils?"

"I don't know," admitted Portunista. "It depends on how they were made, I guess."

"So why would anyone want to scrape them?"

Portunista sighed. "I don't *know*—which is why I'm wanting *over there!*"

"Oh. I see. Well . . ." Jian considered the plank-lift they were sitting on.

"I think . . ." the maga murmured, squinting in the soft blue light. "I think those contact-wheels have sigils on them, too. It's hard to tell, they're spinning so fast . . ."

"I have an idea! We'll swing back and forth, until we get you close enough to jump!"

Portunista flatly turned her gaze to him; he was nodding his head, quite pleased with his idea.

"Even *if* I did that," she retorted, "how am I supposed to get back *on?!*"

This shaved his satisfaction somewhat. "Ummm . . . I swing over again and you jump?" His suggestion faltered under her increasing glare. "Well," he offered, "if you have another plan, I'm certainly willing to try. How did Qarfax get there, do you think?"

"He probably tessered over, and then back again."

"Couldn't he do that from above?" Jian looked up to where the subcommanders waited.

"I don't know. I guess so, but . . . then *what* was this plank-thing *for?!*" And Portunista sighed again in irritation. "Okay," she relented, "fine! *I* can't think of another way, so let's try yours."

"Since the ledge goes all the way around, we'll simply shoot for that part right in front of us . . . erm . . . I mean behind you and in front of me."

"I'm going to leap *backwards?!*"

"You can't leap over my head," Jian shrugged, "and you might snap my neck if I leaned to let you jump. Just turn around on my lap. When we swing close, pretend that you're a girl again. You've launched yourself from swings before—right?"

Frankly, Portunista couldn't remember. She *was* entirely certain, though, that this was a freakishly stupid idea!—but she *did* want to see those sigils up close.

Studiously not looking at Jian, she folded her legs and rotated round, until she was facing the same way as he. "Whoop!" he wobbled, as their weight shifted, bobbing the plank, throwing her backward onto him. Her heart was pounding like a mule-driven rock-breaker, as they struggled to gain their balance . . .

"Hold *still,* blind your eyes!" Sweat trickled into her collar.

"Um, that reminds me, Commander . . . I can't see *through* you, so I *won't* be able to help you decide when to jump."

"Better and better," she groused. A prudent corner of her mind provided some visions of her leaping *back* to a swinging Jian, from a damp stone ledge, over a pit, leading to an Eyeforsaken underground river . . . !—she pounded that thought away. One thing at a time.

"Okay, here we go!" Jian said.

They started pumping back and forth.

The swing gyrated in the air.

Portunista was about to lash out with a reprimand, but he soothingly answered her first: "Wait, we've got to do this together, Commander. *You* lead, and I'll do my best to follow." Fine. She'd lead. That suited her, she simmered.

She tried to put aside the unsettling aspects of the situation, and pretend that she was a girl again. She bent her legs—Jian bent his beneath and with her—and then they smoothly straightened.

Nothing much happened. But they didn't wobble.

She throttled her frustration, and continued the rhythmic motions, shifting her body's gravity along her legs.

Her impatience soon abated: now they were moving! Steadily she breathed in rhythm with their movements—she knew she must prepare her nerve to jump, but put aside that worry while she concentrated on the immediate task. Back—forth . . . back—forth . . . a little farther every time . . .

The breeze across her face invited a vivid vision—light no longer bluish black but yellow-bright as summer day, her tresses long again and flying in the air's caresses . . .

"Doing well, Commander!" Jian sang out, distantly in her ear. Yes, but she must gauge the arc for maximum effect. Too low, and she would not be carried far enough. Too high, and forward motion would be transferred to momentum rising, and again she wouldn't carry far enough. Green grass beneath her tree lay warm with falling sunlight speckling shadows through the leaves around her as she traced along the ground expected consummations, playing, working, with a serious joy . . .

Except . . .

Something still was wrong . . .

Hitched breath, nearly breaking rhythm—she came to herself again. No, it wasn't going to work. They were at the point where balance lay; more force would only push her higher in her leap, not farther—it *should* have been enough! Why not—?!

"The hole!" she shouted.

"Yeah, the rope is bouncing off the edge above us! I can feel it! You aren't going to reach it, are you?" He truly had wanted *this* for her . . . but Portunista pushed away the warmth this thought evoked—especially in their present circumstance! She jerked again, against their rhythm, imagining what the men above might *also* be imagining . . . !

"Lower down—I need more rope!" she gritted out between her teeth, her temper rising. By the fires below, if she must *be* in this ridiculous situation, she was going to make it work . . . !

"I don't know . . ." pondered Jian, loudly in the racket that disoriented as the sounds kept shifting through their swinging.

"It'll *work!*" she told him. "Just . . . pull that lever—"

"No, wait . . . the cord is really what controls it, the lever just gives—"

"I don't care, just pull the lever!" Now the time to jump was near; she was becoming vastly nervous, and therefore *much* more resolute—

"Portunista, wait! This isn't going to work!" Now Jian was shouting, too; though still he seemed to hold back out of worry for her ears.

He might as well have been throwing oil on fire.

"Just pull the lever!!"

"If we go much lower, you'll need to swing much higher to get back to level with the ledge, and that'll mess your—!"

"We'll be closer, too, so do what I say and PULL THE EYEBLINDED LEVER!!"

Above them, their companions crouched around the hole, intently staring into pitchy deeps where bluish glowing only emphasized what they could not perceive. Long moments earlier, the rope had started heaving back and forth with escalating vigorousness; and now it was shaking as well as pitching.

"I don't even *want* to know what's happening down there," Gaekwar drawled.

"Probably clawin' large holes in his throat . . ." muttered Poo.

"Can you *see* them?" Dagon asked with bored annoyance, as he leaned against the wall back near the open door.

"I don't dare to lower a torch down there, as long as the rope is swinging like this," explained the dark man testily.

"Well I can *hear* them over *here!*" the Krygian snorted. "What are they saying??"

Portunista's shriek, especially clear in its intensity, drifted to them through all the machinery noise.

"Pull the lever," Othon reported.

Dagon sighed, shrugged . . .

. . . and pulled the nearby lever.

"Actually," he corrected them with a grunt, "it *pushes,* instead of pulls . . ."

The knotted end of the rope shot up from out of the lever-brace, toward its ceiling-hole, although the knot itself caught there, unable to farther rise.

Jian and Portunista, struggling over control of the plank, felt the tensions all give way on the cords.

"Oh, spew . . ." the maga whispered in horror.

Then they plunged into the pit.

CHAPTER 24

A hideous sliding grinding sang above the four men round the well.

"Uh . . ." Dagon blinked, near the open door. "Did *I* do that?"

Between the ticking moments, Seifas tried to figure whether he could drive his aasagai into the rope, so that the indestructible shaft might bear the weight of his falling friends . . . was Portunista a friend—?

But someone thought more quickly than even a juacuar.

With a grunted snarl, Othon seized the diving rope, bracing himself at the edge of the hole. Shards of thread spit from his hands: the rope *smoked* to a halt! Seifas winced reflexively—but then saw Othon wore his battle gauntlets.

"Wrong lever." The giantish man was eyeing Dagon balefully.

"Sorry," the Krygian shrugged again. Then his eyes rolled upward toward the ceiling, as an ominous rumbling drifted down from overhead. The thin pull-cord, having been wrapped around a special gear or wheel, serenely sailed past Othon's staring eyes, into the void.

"That," Pooralay mused, "does *not* bode well . . ."

Seifas dashed across the room in leaps; Dagon dove aside as Seifas lunged to stab the knot which was caught in the hole above. Even *its* sharp tip did not go far into the sturdy knot, but Seifas pulled down anyway, leveraging the rope.

"Pull!" he ordered Dagon; who regained his feet as Gaekwar slid into place. Once they had gotten their grips on the knot, the juacuar yanked out the aasagai and added his own hands. The three men *heaved* their bodies down, against increasing pressure from above.

"Something's trying to come apart!" The 'cowherd' Gaekwar shook his face to fling the sweat away. "We've got to pull the tension tight again!"

The toil became more difficult; but as they worked the rope into its first position, feeding it into the wooden brace, the troubling sounds receded in intensity above.

"'Bout anoth'r han'width . . ." Pooralay told them, standing watch on the brace. Then he pulled the lever down in place, its opposite end impressing the rope above the knot—the knot pressed up in return, increasing the lateral pressure of the lever.

A few more burps and bumps—and then the series of events above them stopped, although the rumbles from below continued on as usual.

"We were told, *NOT* to touch that lever!" Seifas reminded the panting Dagon.

"Sorry!" Dagon repeated. "Why does he even *have* this lever?"

"Who knows," the 'cowherd' said, wiping away the stringy hair now plastered to his brow.

"Who *cares?!*" Othon added in his strain. He still was holding his rope in place, and tendons stood out redly on his neck.

Now recalling their dangling companions, three men rushed to Othon's aid. But Dagon took his time, ambling over. "C'mon," he said, "it's only Jian and Portunista and a plank and rope. It *must* be easier than pulling trees!"

"Bad angle," grumbled the proud Manavilon.

"Sorry, guys, my arms ain't long 'nough t' really help," the thug apologized; the other two each grabbed a section under Othon's hands. "Hm," he added. "I s'pose this rope ain't *that* rope. Oth'rwise," he pondered while the others raised the plank, "this woulda gone back up when that went down. B'sides, th' knot-hole stopped that rope, but this'n kept on goin'. Somethin' up there mus' be addin' friction, too; oth'rwise th' rest o' th' rope woulda fallen with th' cord . . ." He looked into the pit. "Guess they mus' be on there still."

"Why d'y'say?" gritted Dagon, who had, under glares, joined in the hauling.

"I doubt y'd be sweatin' *that* much, pullin' up an empty plank with three more men t' help, doll-boy! O' course," allowed Poo grudgingly, "they might be dead weight, too." He knelt and shouted into the hole: "Ever'one all right down there?!"

"We're just fine, thanks!" came a glad shout in reply.

"Nothin' fazes that boy . . ." Pooralay grinned.

Soon they pulled the couple from the well. Othon, with assistance from the others, lifted the plank until the sitters' feet were clear, then twisted around to gently set them down.

"Thanks, Othon!" Jian reached up from where he sat to clasp a massive forearm. Othon knelt to sit and rest. Portunista, on the other hand, had leapt—or rather stumbled—from the plank, as soon as her feet were over the floor.

"Fazed," the 'cowherd' mumbled beneath his breath to Pooralay, who nodded "mm-hm" in agreement. The maga's short dark hair had lengthened a little during previous weeks, and normally flared, up and out, in careful wavy swoops. Now, bits and pieces straggled everywhere; and she seemed unable to blink while gulping air.

"What!" she snarled, seeing their look. She tried to squint her eyes in a glare, which didn't quite work.

"Nothin'," Poo and Gaekwar said in unison. Gaekwar wandered quickly to the door; the sun now touched the treetops edging the dell. The thug meandered over to Jian—who lay on his stomach, looking back in the hole.

"So," said Pooralay, casually, "what were y' *doin'* down there?"

Jian opened his mouth, but—

"*I* will tell you what we *saw*," announced the maga, glaring more successfully at Jian.

Portunista gave the squad a brief account of their discoveries in the pit—no need for too much detail over certain points, she thought.

When she reached their fall, Seifas told her what had happened. Portunista turned her glare on Dagon; although curiosity now was blunting her anger.

"Why," she muttered to herself, "*does* he even have that lever?"

"Well," continued Jian, seeing Portunista deep in thought, "we fell a ways before you caught us. Right for the throat of the hole . . . *wsshh!!* Except," he shrugged, "we couldn't see the hole anymore, because the wisps had doused again. But," he hurried on, with a cautious glance toward Portunista, "once you caught us, Othon, and the . . . mm . . . excitement had lessened, Portunista whistled up another light. Now, here's the interesting part—"

"The throat of the well was encircled with sigils," the maga absently interrupted.

"Down to the water's edge," Jian nodded. "I mean *right* to the edge. Where the river rushed beneath it, the throat was smooth as if it had been razor-cut . . . ow," he coughed, "bad analogy. Still, it *was* completely strange."

"So, were the sigils doing anything?" Gaekwar asked.

"They were indeed," Jian nodded. "Portunista can explain it better, though."

"Hm? Oh." The maga turned to face them; then sat down on the floor. Her knees felt wobbly, she decided . . ."I tried an Yrthescrution once I got my bearings. Sometimes it can help me understand a sigil when I'm in proximity. But I've never seen these kinds before."

"So, you *don't* know what they did," pronounced the Krygian.

"Oh, I think I do," she snap-returned. "A scrution always has at least a little overflowing of perception. Like when you're focused on a blade, you still see other things. But I didn't realize what I was seeing, till Jian said something about the bucket being in the water."

"The plank was used for a waterwell, I guess?" Jian shrugged.

"But I wasn't sensing where the water *should* have been," continued Portunista. "The scrution told me that the throat continued *past* the sigils—*not* into a rushing river!"

"How *far* past?" Gaekwar asked.

"Another hundred paces, easily. *Then* I found the water. I could feel its flow, against the throat of the well . . . but *not* remotely as quickly!"

Jian dipped his hand into the pail, placed behind the plank; splashed around; and then drew out his hand with a flourishing spray.

"That river was there! *And* it was flowing fast."

"Superspace," Othon murmured.

Chapter 25

With the sun's descent into the forest top around the grassy bowl, the air was turning chill and damp, filling full with shadows. The juacuar insisted they explore the floor above, before the full night fell.

"This is where we quartered," he explained, while leading up the narrow stairs which curved along the inside of the Tower. Here the sturdy lumber ceiling rested rather higher. Past this landing, stairs continued winding.

Where the narrow crossing hallways met, a rock-lined firepit showed no signs of recent use. In every wall of every hallway section stood two doors, totaling sixteen. The sky's light filtered indirectly in through deep and open windows, at three of the hallway ends, including on the stairway landing. Sconces lined the walls between the doors; but Portunista whistled wisps, until the torches could be checked and lit.

Directly across from the entry landing, at the southern hallway's end, stood no window—but a door. After careful scrutiny by Pooralay, Jian—at Dagon's order—opened it.

Only a blank stone wall.

"J'st like Seifas said. Int'restin'," Pooralay murmured.

"*More* interesting," added Portunista, "this one *also* has no sigils."

"You mean, Qarfax bound a tesser here *permanently* into place?" Dagon blinked, and thought this over. "Could he *do* that? I mean, he had to sleep eventually, right?"

"Cadrists don't—or didn't—see the world the way we do," explained the maga, with a touch of wistfulness. Being in the Tower, seeing only these few things . . . she could *taste* that power, that distinction, that position in her world . . .

"They remained awake, to enjoy the duty of sleep," said Jian, softly. Then he blinked. "Sorry . . . you were saying?"

"I don't know what you're talking about," she irritably replied . . . *what* sort of drivel was *that* . . . ?! "But a Cadrist could attend to dozens, maybe hundreds, of his bindings at a time; and he could keep them all in place, or many, even while his mind and body slept." She didn't have a clue how this was done, or what the feeling would be like; but *someday* she would find it out . . .

"So, people could go in and out this door," the lanky 'cowherd' brought the topic back on track, "as if it was the door downstairs. Why would Qarfax do that?"

"He never told us," Seifas shrugged. "He never told us *anything* about this door. He only told us, *never* use the basement door, except in an emergency. As you can see, the windows for the garrison floor are slim and few. We never noticed different heights," he ruefully admitted.

"I've got an even better question," Dagon said. "If Qarfax could create a tesser with those sigils in the well, why not put them on the doors? Why bother with a bind at all?"

The maga shrugged. "I haven't a clue. Maybe he was going to, and never got to do it? Maybe scribing a tesser-sigil as large as this door, was something he hadn't discovered, yet."

"But why would he do it at *all?*" Gaekwar exclaimed. "It doesn't make sense! No more than him rigging a seat to go down in the well, when he could just jott himself there when he wanted!"

"I don't *know!*" Portunista was becoming *very* tired of saying this; it wasn't improving her mood. "I simply don't know how tessers work, so I don't know what their limitations are. *If* we ever reach his private rooms or laboratories, *maybe* I can figure something out from his notes. *That* is why we *came* here," she reminded them impatiently, "*not* to stand in this *hall!!*"

"Why *y're* all here, not me," the thug corrected idly. "*I* came here f'r the Well."

"And?" Othon asked.

Pooralay shrugged. "I dunno. It's a well, an' I guess it's at th' end of a woods. But it don't seem t' mean or t' *do* anything—not anythin' worth discoverin', I mean. Like 'ista says, maybe there's some notes upstairs."

"First we check *these* rooms," insisted Seifas. The longer Portunista took to reach those notes—*any* notes—the better. And discipline dictated they ensure the barrack rooms were clear.

"Fine," Dagon said. "Send Jian in."

Pooralay snorted. "Y're gettin' t' sound like a brain-flogged macaw. 'Send Jian in, send Jian in, bwa-CAAAWW!'"

"Just get *on* with it," Gaekwar demanded. "I want supper!"

So they settled in. The thug began to examine a door, by wisplight and the torches being lit by Othon on the wall.

"These were only barracks, right?" Gaekwar asked, fiddling with the disker.

"That is what they *were*," the juacuar confirmed. "But who knows what has happened here, in the slopings since?"

"I thought a good burglar could wipe through a check in a moment or two," Dagon sulked. "Or maybe you failed basic thievery?"

"Oh, I c'd do it that fast, if I wanted to. But the fancy stuff is f'r 'mergencies, or for showin' off. Speed kills."

"'Oh, I *could* do that, if I *wanted* to,'" Dagon mocked. "*That's* sure easy enough to say."

Pooralay looked back at him. Then he turned around completely, pulling out an ohre from his pocket. "Okay, doll-boy, check this out." Setting the coin upon his left hand's thumb, he flipped it into the air.

It didn't come down.

"Pretty smooth, hm?"

"Cute street trick," the arrogant Krygian said with contempt, as Pooralay walked to him. "It's in your fist. Probably never left your thumb."

"Guess y'r eyes ain't even as good as I was 'xpectin'," Poo replied. "Nor y'r ears. Any of th' rest'a yous, see and hear th' coin go up?"

Jian raised his hand. "I did."

"Okay, I did, too," Gaekwar admitted, interested in spite of himself.

"You snatched it out of the air that fast?" Dagon dubiously stared at the fist.

"Nah." Pooralay opened the fist, under Dagon's nose.

It was empty.

Portunista had wandered over, to look more closely for herself. Not taking his eyes from Dagon, Pooralay reached and stuck his *right* hand into Portunista's thick dark hair.

"Hey!" she exclaimed as she batted his hand away . . . then choked.

He held the ohre on edge between his thumb and index finger.

"*Very* nifty!" nodded Jian.

"Hey, 'ista," Gaekwar grinned. "How come that never happened whenever *I* did that?" This earned him the expected spiky glare, but he continued grinning all the same.

"I snatched it *that* fast, doll-boy. That's how some of *us* do magic, sister," Pooralay winked to the maga. "So, unless y'wanna kick th' door in y'rself an' check fer traps *that* way, stay outta *my* hair!" he added over his shoulder to Dagon—who edged even farther down the hall.

The thug went back to work, but not for long.

"What," Portunista mused, "would a mage be like, who could move that fast?"

"Lethal," rumbled Othon.

Portunista pondered this. True, in terms of teeth and tongue and throat, a mage could only jott so fast. But still . . .

With a smile, she sauntered over to the little man, and knelt beside him.

"Would you perhaps consider giving some private lessons?"

Seifas sighed in disappointment for his commander . . .

Poo's hands froze.

He slowly turned his head in her direction.

"Doll," he said, very deliberately—faltering her smile. "If y're talkin' 'bout payin' me gold, don't bother. I c'n pick up all y'r gold, whenev'r I want. If y're talkin' 'bout payin' *anoth'r* way . . ." and he narrowed his eyes even further, "y'r tent looks too crammed-full already. I de-cline." He returned to work.

Seifas suppressed a laugh: *that* didn't happen often . . . !

Portunista was much less amused.

"Considering who I am," she slid her voice like steel through her lips, "and what I can do, you might want to treat me with more respect than you've shown so far."

Again, the thug's hands froze.

Again, he slowly turned his head toward her.

"True 'nough," he allowed. "But then, y'might wanna watch what kinda threats y'make, considerin' how closely we're sharin' this hallway . . ."

—yelping indignantly, Portunista leaped, crashing backward into the wall behind her at an angle—

" . . . *and* considerin' some of us's hands're quicker than th' Eye." The thug returned to work, grinning in satisfaction; Jian softly chuckled.

The maga pushed herself off the floor, bracing against the wall, her eyes nearly popping out of her head in fury. How dare he—he—!

Then her fury melted into growing horror. Staring at the thug, who whistled a bawdy dancing tune, Portunista edged her hand to her practical—well-cut!—shirt, undid the second button, and reached inside.

She drew the ohre-piece out.

"Hope it was good f'r you too, doll."

Gaekwar whistled.

"Hey, 'ista," Dagon began. "How come *that* never happened when—"

"Shut up!" she barked.

Pooralay leaned away from the door. "Done!" he announced.

"Okay!" Jian walked over—very carefully looking *not* at Portunista; but smiling and winking at the little man once his face was out of her line of sight. He composed himself, squarely faced the door—and with a loud "Ha-HAAA!!" he threw it open and leaped into the darkness beyond.

A moment's silence.

"All clear!" rang out his cheerful baritone. "Um. I think. Anyone have a light?"

"One down, fifteen t' go." Pooralay stepped to the next door over.

"This is going to take *forever*," Gaekwar groused.

It only took an hour, though. There were fewer interruptions.

CHAPTER 26

"I am ready for supper, *now!*" Gaekwar's drawl was absent.

Seifas shook his head. "We were fortunate we found nothing on this level—"

"'Fortunate'?!" interrupted Portunista.

"But," continued Seifas firmly, "we should scout one level more, before we camp tonight."

"Why?" insisted Dagon.

"Safety," nodded Othon.

"It's not like we'll be sleeping up *there!*" persisted Gaekwar.

"No," Pooralay sighed, "y're sleepin' down *here*. Where somethin' might still come t' getcha."

Gaekwar froze in mid-retort; then also sighed. "Never mind. Let's just do it . . ."

The stairway wound along the Tower wall, up through another median. Instead of any open room this time, it passed a single door, set in the inner wall which paralleled the outer curve.

The sun had set; and through the narrow open window opposite the door, the stars were shining in their nightly blaze. The stairs wound onward into a gloom above.

"Seifas—how many more floors?" Portunista asked.

"Only one. The top—where Qarfax died. He slept and took his meals up there. We figured this was where he worked; he often used this door, but warned us—"

"—never to touch it," several voices chorused.

"Well, 'ista, go on!" said Dagon. "This is where you wanted to be!"

She flatly glared at him.

"Pooralay, check the door," she ordered, not even looking toward it. She noticed he worked more quickly than before; maybe he was hungry, too . . .

"Sigils all over th' frame," reported the little man, continuing his sweep.

"Of course there are," she sneered at Dagon. "He would *guard* his laboratory."

"An' th' handle's false," the thug concluded, leaning back to rest.

"What?!" Portunista turned and stared.

"Handle's just for looks. Hey, jaguar! Y'ever ac'shl'y *see* th' mage go in?"

"Once," Seifas answered. "Others did as well. He used the handle—but, I saw he *also* put his palm upon this plate." He indicated near the door, a finely arabesqued rectangular slate.

Portunista was already chuffing softly, in contemplation.

"Flog it," she muttered a minute later, and wiped the Yrthe from her eyes. "I don't know *what* the sigils do. I mean, they act as a lock, awaiting a key—that's obvious—but what the key is or how it works, I haven't any clue."

"Anything *else* you saw or heard?" the Krygian asked the juacuar, who only shook his head. "So," Dagon mused, "I suppose that means the magus wasn't jotting to make it work."

"That helps us, doesn't it?"

Dagon blinked at Jian's sincere remark; and so did Portunista. But the Easterner's inference did make sense . . .

"No jotting," she perused. "Gloves, Seifas? Maybe a ring?"

"He *did* wear rings," the juacuar confirmed. "No gloves."

"So maybe only the hand," she said. "I think if such a lock required a ring, the plate would have an appropriate shape."

"Too bad," Othon sighed. They looked at him. "No hand."

"Yeah," Pooralay winced, "that's right. A pile-a dust upstairs."

A minute passed.

"Well, that's it!" Gaekwar gave a single clap and turned around. "I'm off to start the fire—!"

"Hold!" commanded Portunista. "We aren't out of options yet! *If* the sigils have been inscribed to read his handprints, *those* might still be found in his room."

"You're kidding," Dagon said; but Pooralay was nodding.

"Yeah," he agreed, "it's poss'ble. Some tape and powd'r might do th' trick; which o'course I happen t' have. Betcha got some powd'r, too, hm?" Portunista ignored his tease; as a matter of fact, she *did* have some talcum powder. She would use his, however.

"Or," she moved along, a little sourly, "*if* these sigils need a ring, it might be somewhere up the stairs."

"In his pile of ash!" suggested Jian.

"*Or,*" the maga forcefully concluded, drowning that unnerving image, "*if* they need his living flesh, we *still* may be in luck."

"Y'think he kep' a spare *hand* inna jar, up in his room?!"

"Woman's secret," she smiled mysteriously. Blank looks confirmed that only *she* knew where to find his living flesh.

"*I'll* be lighting the fire downstairs." The 'cowherd' hastily turned again—

"I will need you *all* to help me search!—so come along!" Portunista marched upstairs, sending the wisplight on in front.

"We're gonna end up in *all* these rooms before the night is over," muttered Gaekwar; but he followed along obediently.

After one more half-turn around the Tower, Portunista reached the final door, also set in the inner wall.

There it was.

Here *she* was!

This was it—the *real* beginning—everything she had been hoping and dreaming about!

Dagon, though, provided some perspective.

"It doesn't bother you at all a Cadrist *died* in there?!" he nervously snapped from several steps below.

Her neck popped icy water beads. She had, in fact, forgotten that completely in her eagerness; despite Jian's casual comment only a minute ago. Had he been reminding her, politely . . . ? No matter. She firmed her voice before she answered:

"Not in the least!"

"Crazy minx . . ." floated up from down around the curve, but Portunista couldn't tell who said it. Part of her mind decided it wasn't Jian, however, and . . . What did she *care* what *anyone* thought?! Jian included!

"Step aside, and let me get t' work. No plate up here," Pooralay added for the men below who couldn't see the door. "I guess that's how the jaguar got inside."

"Go ahead," she said, more calmly than she felt.

What might she find inside—waiting for them?

Waiting for *her.*

She forcibly recalled her logic about their chances . . .

"Complet'ly clean," the thug announced, disgustedly. "Wasn't even locked." He cursed himself in mutters, for not attempting the Tower earlier . . .

"*That* means Qarfax wasn't keeping *important* things up here . . ." Dagon was probably right, Portunista had to admit . . . But flay his bones!—he *didn't* have to sound so smug about it!

"Not in here, perhaps," she said defiantly, "but he *didn't* place that sigilplate downstairs for nothing!"

"So, go on in!" the Krygian said.

"All right! . . . I will!"

. . . but she didn't.

a *Cadrist* had been brutally slain inside this room . . .

. . . and she . . .

was only an apprentice . . .

A minute crawled across her.

Then Dagon said that Jian should be let past so *he* could go in first . . .

"Okey-doke!" agreed the irrepressible man.

"What if a Roguent's in there?" That was Gaekwar.

"Oh . . . um . . . I'll tell it there are people *more* worth eating somewhere else than Qarfax's room!"

Portunista sighed. Could Jian take *nothing* seriously—?!

. . . she didn't want to see his helpful cheerfulness scraped rawly away in bloody screams, along with his face and his chest and—

"I will go," she said.

And she did.

CHAPTER 27

Portunista arced the wisp into the room, as she thumbed the latch and pushed the door part-open, bracing it while kneeling, hoping any attacks would be directed where she wasn't.

Not that this would likely fool a Rogue . . .

She shot more whistled lights to every quarter of the room, as well as near the center. Then she rolled, half upright, through the door.

She had to force herself to see . . . because she didn't *want* to see . . . would she be driven mad before the torment . . . ?

She only saw a large, well-furnished bedroom.

"Nice roll, doll . . ."

Portunista couldn't tell if Pooralay was making fun; and decided she didn't care.

The bedroom of a Cadrist . . .

She would have a room like this, one day, she promised herself, slowly standing, quieting down her nerves, marveling in the opulence.

In fact, she could have one tonight! No one else would want to sleep up here, inside a dead man's room.

Besides—*she* was leader. She could requisition any room she wanted.

Most importantly, she would do this to defy her fear . . .

"Are you dead yet?" Dagon's inquiry floated up the stairs and through the door.

"Still alive, thanks for asking! You can come in now! Be careful, though," she added as the door swept open. "There's a dead man on the floor."

"Yeah," the thug observed, respectfully. "Sort of."

Several paces away from the door, deposited as if at random, lay the pile of ash. And some clothes and rings, and other things.

"Eerie," Gaekwar murmured as he entered, darting his attention and the disker three directions all at once, and fingering his axe's shaft. Othon entered last—and even then, the room did not feel smaller. Pooralay was lighting lamps.

"*Nice* bed," Dagon nodded. "Big enough to hold us all . . ."

"Tonight just me," said Portunista.

"What?! You *can't* be serious!"

She sighed, while poking through pillows: "I have a headache . . ." She might have to find a comb or brush . . .

"That *isn't* what I . . . never mind," Dagon sulked. "Whenever that thing comes back tonight, don't yell too loudly or else you'll wake us up downstairs . . . What *are* you doing??"

She smiled triumphantly. "Living flesh from Qarfax!" she announced . . .

. . . and held up a hair.

"*That* counts as *living* flesh?" Gaekwar asked.

"The root of it does." Portunista brought it over to show him and the other subcommanders. By the lamplight, they could see the tiny bottom glob. "If you don't yank the root, the hair keeps coming back. We won't need *any* powder!" she told Pooralay. "Come on, I want to try it on the plate right now!" She pushed past everyone.

"Closer to the firepit, closer to the food, I guess . . ." Gaekwar sighed and followed after.

But Pooralay and Jian were crouching near the remains; Seifas paused to watch and listen.

"Either almost instantly," Jian was speaking in a hushed evaluation, "or, he was *held* somehow. Right?"

"Yeah . . ." the thug agreed. "Pretty good, kid."

Jian acknowledged his compliment with a small and sober smile, as he stood. "Only a pile, not a trail," he said to Seifas as they left, with Pooralay not far behind. "The fabrics are *in* the dust-pile, too. He wasn't moving."

Portunista waited for everyone to join her at the locked-door landing. She was certain this would work—her smile was swelling just about to bursting! Now they all would see her victory, and so she turned to touch the follicle to—

"Hey, Portunista!" It was Jian.

"What?" she snapped, annoyed at the interruption.

"So, what *is* your powder for?"

She blinked for several moments . . . "*What?!*"

"Well, Pooralay has some powder for lifting fingerprints, although it doesn't seem we'll need it. I just wondered what you used yours for," he pleasantly inquired.

She glared at him a moment. "Chafing," she flatly said.

"Oh. Just curious. I thought it might be makeup, since, y'know, you *are* a woman . . ."

"Jian!" she grated. What moronic conversation *was* this?! Granted, she *did* always bring some things of that sort in her belt-pockets, just in case she needed touching up before a meeting—she *was* brigade commander, after all—but . . . Scourge him! This was supposed to be her moment of triumph! It was *not* supposed to be a lecture on a woman's uses for talcum powder . . . !

"Chafing," Othon agreed.

Portunista felt invisible strings, dragging her head around in his direction. Pulling off a gauntlet, the gargantuan man unbuttoned a pouch on *his* own belt. With his hairy-fingered ham of a hand, he pulled a tiny vial from which, uncorked, he gently tapped into the gauntlet's leather lining.

"Helps the skin stay drier. Makes the cloth and leather less abrasive. Keeps the smell down, too."

"That makes sense!" Jian was intensely interested. "I sure wish *I* had some of that."

"Here. I have plenty."

"Thanks!" Jian pocketed two of the flat tiny vials. "Which reminds me, I really should put on my gloves . . ."

If someone had told Portunista that the longest string of words from Othon's mouth she'd ever hear would be about some talcum powder . . .

She shook her head. The *next* time she had even the faintest notion of wanting to nip Jian's nose in the dark, she'd order Gaekwar to shoot a *disc* through her brain . . . !

And so, having altogether forgotten about her pride in her victory, she pressed the follicle to the sigilplate.

CHAPTER 28

In the bluish wisplight glow, the sigils seemed to float, first above, then below the surface of the plate.

Portunista knew what happened next was not exactly such a trick of eyes and light.

As the follicle touched on the arabesque, a violet pierced the blue, spreading in an instant over the plate.

Portunista heard the doorframe "click"; she pushed the handle . . .

. . . opening the door.

Gaekwar tried to speak; failed; and then in quiet awe began again.

"Seifas . . . Did you ever actually look *inside* the door?"

The dark man slowly shook his head. "No. None of us were ever close enough."

"Sooo . . . this *might* be normal," Dagon judged. "Or might not."

Beyond the door, were branches—several hundred paces in the air.

Purple misty twilight pooled within and under leaves. But up above . . .

Pooralay regarded this, then looked behind him out the southern window. "C'rrect me if I'm wrong . . . but ain't it darker here, than there?"

"A couple hundred kilops west of here . . ." Portunista drank the sight, feeling insignificant. Could a magus really jott a tesser *that* far distant? No, it had to be the sigils.

Othon sniffed. "And spring," he added—then he sneezed.

"So, it's several *thousand* kilopaces north-northwest," Jian concluded, sounding quite impressed. Portunista blinked. Of course: just as they were on the autumn upslope, spring would also be beginning north of the equator. Not *too* far north, however—this was more like never-ending summer.

"What did we do wrong?" Gaekwar asked.

"Nothing." Portunista shook her head. "This is it. The hair worked fine. This is his security. This is not his laboratory. This is how we *go* there."

"*Anywhere* out there," said Dagon ruefully.

"No, wait—think about it," she answered. "Qarfax needed sigils on the door to go this far. The next door must be relatively close, even if he tessered to it."

"Yeah, but why'd he bother doin' this at all? He c'd just brick up th' door, an' . . . I dunno . . . 'beam' h'mself right t' th' lab fr'm in his room," observed the thug. "Y're sayin' th' lab is really b'hind this wall, an' when we find th' next door it'll lead t' where this'd norm'lly go. Right?"

"Because he was a researcher?" Portunista shrugged. That sounded less than confident. "Depending on what he was doing in his lab, then 'beaming' to it might be dangerous. And this," she waved, "might be an experiment, too."

"A mighty large number of 'mights'," Dagon snorted.

"Okay, fine," retorted Portunista. "There's a few more minutes here . . . I mean out there . . . before the sun will set completely—so we'll just fan out and *look*."

"In the treetops," Gaekwar dryly said.

"It isn't all that hard!" the maga exclaimed in exasperation. "Look, the trees are woven close together; branches *large*, plenty of *handholds* . . . See?!"

She demonstrated this by stepping through the door.

It shot away, in an arc, to the right, behind her.

She turned in time to see the portal close and vanish.

Anger turned to ice.

"Spewing blinding bile . . ."

She was alone. In a forest. Deep in the Middlelands. Thousands of thousands of paces away from her brigade. And night was falling.

In an Eyeforsaken *tree!*

. . . in the distance, an inhuman shriek erupted.

Answered by another, distinctly closer . . .

"Okay . . . okay . . ."

She spent a minute muttering this at various speeds.

Nothing was okay. But she needed time to seize her fear.

First things first.

Slowly, carefully, Portunista reached to balance on a limb.

Slowly and even more carefully—her hand was jittering so, it took a quarter-minute—she put the follicle into the smallest pocket on her belt.

"Think it out," she told herself.

She was doomed if this was just a trap. Dead . . . ? Not necessarily; but she might need a year or more to walk to southern lands.

She was young and strong. She could make it. Probably.

Assuming it was *not* a trap, the *real* door to the laboratory should be somewhere near. Probably on the ground: it would need a framework which would be more difficult to have constructed up in the trees. She could jott some wisps to help her search—although those might attract whatever had screeched in the distance. Maybe morning would be a better idea . . . She even could spend some days to quarter the area; fruits that might be edible hung from the trees.

On the other hand, her friends—her *officers,* she corrected herself—would not go back to her brigade and leave her here. Well, Dagon might . . . but she was certain the others wouldn't. Because . . .

. . . well, because they *were* her friends.

They certainly didn't have much other reason to be loyal to her. But she'd bet that right this moment, they were searching for another hair.

Jian would certainly be; and she realized, she *would* bet her final drop of blood on that.

Although he'd probably do the same for Dagon, too.

That thought only irritated her. But the combination of annoyance and of . . . hope . . . helped to further clear her head.

So. Where could she expect the portal to appear?

Behind her? No, she couldn't hope for that. Qarfax would have wanted the next invader attempting the door to be befuddled.

And yet, the next one through the door, on any *normal* occasion, *would* be Qarfax—who would *not* appreciate disorientation every time that *he* stepped through. So, the door would probably reappear along some limited positions . . . such as on a circle!

Yes, she thought as she peered through the dying daylight; the door must always vanish moving right: branches with older cuts had grown above the fresher cuts.

And in an arcing path!

So. She felt much better now.

Now she had more hope.

Several minutes had passed already; her friends should open the door at any moment. Somewhere on that radial arc; probably forty-five to sixty degrees on either side of straight across from where she stood—because if it was seen when it returned, it *wouldn't* be so fuddling as a trap!

Qarfax was a clever man; but she was clever, too. She was also willing to bet that she could find the *other* door, if she was wrong about this door returning—or about her . . . friends.

And she bet the follicle would unlock it. *And,* Qarfax wouldn't likely run the same trap going *out;* she could probably open the door, once she was *inside,* and step out onto the stairwell landing like the door was normal.

And *then* she would *demand* to know why no one had come to help her . . . ! Where *were* they?

As if on cue . . . "Portunista!"

She couldn't exactly discern the direction among the baffling branches, but it wasn't far away.

And it was Jian.

Of course. He *would* insist on going first.

"I'm over here!" she yelled, cupping her hands around her mouth, trying to give him a better direction—she found that she was smiling wider than her cupping hands! She forced herself to gain composure—mustn't let him . . . mustn't let *them* . . . see how glad she was to—

—*thrashing leaves above her*—!!

her body hurtled forward and down, instinctively diving away from the sound . . .

. . . off her branch . . . !

Too shocked to curse, she threw her arms in all directions, scrambling for a handhold in the tumbling world around her, eardrums shuddering under the hideous scream above.

Her body struck another branch, and seized it . . . tasted blood—she must have hit her mouth . . .

More shrieks near but not so near; the nearest creature held its cry. She looked—she thought it must be 'up'—toward a shredding thrashing, vision spinning dizzily, a stormy blackness, pounding with a strength and speed like lightning, at the branches in its way.

She licked her teeth and swallowed blood, and whistled.

Blue light burst above her—glinting from a razored beak.

An enormous hunting bird *screeched* in surprise—in other circumstances its expression might have been amusing!—flinching from the intervening ball of eldritch power. It seemed no monster, other than its size . . . although its proportions didn't seem quite right . . .

The wisp, however, could only bluff not block the creature; despite its seeming composition of a thousand radiant needles, it held neither heat nor mass. A hungry kitten could, in perfect safety, bat it easily.

The giant killer bird looked *very* hungry.

And it saw her in the light.

She broke the bind and doused the light; without a pause she whistled up another wisp as far away as she could jott.

The bird's head snapped in that direction. Portunista stilled herself, in fear and dizziness. *Take the bait!* she silently pleaded, adding spice by drifting the wisplight idly off along a tangent.

Other avians now descended on the light; but her particular persecutor only pondered skeptically.

How intelligent *were* these things . . . ? She had to *hurry;* her body was cramping from clinging to the branch, unable to gesture for a different jott. She angled the wisp behind the bird, bringing it marginally closer. It turned to watch, but not completely around.

"Go away!" she desperately commanded, under her breath. She had to *hurry,* because—!

"Portunista!" Scourge the man . . . ! Couldn't he tell he shouldn't be coming closer?!

No, she realized—because he wasn't afraid of anything . . .

More shouts distantly rose, shouts for her—but her stomach wasn't curdling for *those* shouts.

By now she could determine Jian's direction.

The raptor could, as well.

It swiveled its head, locking with lethal precision.

Her mouth was twisting along with her stomach . . .

—she heaved herself into a scrabbling run along the branches, whistling lights in all directions. But not toward him. She heard the creature behind her shriek and dive in chase. But not toward him. She pulled herself through vines and branches, trying to climb and arc around to where the door might be.

But not toward him.

"Jian!" she shouted toward the damn-fool man. "Go *back!* Back to the door! Keep low! Birds will attack you through the trees!" That sounded inane, but she didn't care. "I'll meet you there—just *run!*" He'd better run . . . she'd flay him alive if he made her wait for him at the door . . . !

She could hear the others, shouting for her and shouting for Jian—

Wait . . . no, she *couldn't* wait!—the rotblooded bird was gaining on her . . . ! but—

The shouts were coming from the wrong direction!—not from where she thought that Jian had come!

Snarling, she veered to the right—four talons plowed the wood behind her.

"Jian! The door has moved—after you went through! Don't listen for me—listen for *them!* They're where the door is *now!* Run *that* way!"

The creature shrieked again behind her, this time with a different pitch. What—?

Talons crashed in front of her! She darted left and down, wriggling past more branches in the deepening darkness, tasting wood-chips in her teeth. She must have been detected by another bird, which the first had tried to drive away.

She ripped a fingernail pulling herself across a branch. *Two* birds . . . she had to get around them—

No! This was a cul-de-sac! Too many branches, too many trunks! Had they *driven* her here? She had to go back—!

An avian head *smashed* through the thinner branches above, striking where she would have jumped. The black eye glared—in triumph? hissing—freezing her blood, freezing her muscles, her instincts overriding her will, crushing her down, yet knowing, *knowing,* a murderous claw was pulling back to strike—

"MOVE!!!" she screamed to herself—but there was nowhere left to go—

—the avian eye blinked twice in wide surprise.

"bw-SCREE?!" Almost a question . . . And now a grunted exhalation, from it and from—

"Hi there, 'ista! Whoa!" Jian leaped cheerfully onto the feathery back, dislodging the balance of the bird, which looked at least as shocked as Portunista, flapping and scratching and slipping its wings and talons every which way, before—

"Whoa . . . ?" Jian's eyes were popping, too!—he scrambled gripping on the bird's rotating body like a barrel, rolling over, rolling off . . .

Rolling off the branch!

outraged shrieks . . .

One was from the avian; plummeting down with Jian through branches to the ground, far below.

Portunista thought the other was hers . . .

Or was it from behind her? She turned to see an even larger avian, poised to strike, trying to freeze her once again.

She couldn't tell, exactly, for her sight was full of rippling blurs. Once she blinked, everything was clear.

"Scream for this," she told the creature, teeth exposed behind her lips, inhaling through her teeth and tongue and crooking her first finger thrusted—peeling off a line of feathers, leaving bleeding skin behind.

That elicited a scream. Very satisfactory. The creature jumped and flapped away. Not altogether satisfactory, then. But the night was young.

A corner of her mind reported, calmly and insanely, that her theory was correct: the veckinesis jotting from Gemalfan's disciplex could be applied on parts, not only on the whole. Or, rather, that depended on what the jotter thought as "one whole object." Gemalfan's fight against her might have had a very different ending, otherwise. Jian might now be dead.

Oh.

He *was* dead now.

So, it didn't matter. Nothing mattered.

"Portunista!" Close by and from far away she heard the cry. But it didn't matter. It was only Seifas, tugging at her arm. "Commander, we must hurry!"

"There is no hurry," she calmly explained, as if to a child, "because it doesn't matter."

"Wh—? Commander? More aasvogels are arriving! This way to the door! Have you seen Jian?"

"There he is." She pointed without looking, eyes locked only straight ahead; she carefully picked through branches, moving steadily away from where she pointed . . . "He is down there. Birds are eating him. On the ground," she added. Yes, the ground was crucial, far away, down there behind her. Where Qarfax's laboratory door must be. The laboratory she had come to find. Jian had wanted that for her, for *she* had wanted that, and so he now was down there where it was, because . . . he . . . she . . .

Seifas swore. How amusing. Seifas never swore. She would have to make him swear more often.

She wondered if these birds could swear.

The upper door was standing open, straight ahead, not moving now. Her men were standing near the door, not moving either, trying not to draw the birds' attention, she supposed. Didn't they know it didn't matter?

She smiled.

Shock was on their faces. Seifas was telling them something. She didn't want to hear what he was telling them. So she didn't listen. She looked around, instead; in the sky, and over treetops. Many birds were flocking to the area. Good.

But, they weren't looking where they should.

"So, he's bird juice now, eh?" That was Dagon. Someone else was talking to him, softly, and she couldn't hear.

She would kill him later. First, she would do other things.

She pulled her wisplights into the sky, all of them still lit. How interesting— her focus must be growing stronger . . .

She whirled them high, up where the birds could see.

Then she pulled the lights all down to her.

Now the birds were looking where they should.

She set the wisps to rest among the branches. But if some went out, it wouldn't matter.

Nothing mattered.

Someone shook her shoulder, yelling in her ear. It wasn't Dagon, so she didn't kill him.

"The birds must all come here," she said; very rational, very clever. That was why she now was here. That was why . . . Jian now was . . .

"If they don't come here, I cannot kill them," she continued; and she sighed contentedly, for she could see the birds were coming now. "You should go back through the door. If you decide to close it, I won't mind. It doesn't matter." Dagon, on the other hand, could stay. She thought it should be fun to throw him with the veckinesis to the birds.

Whole clouds of monstrous birds . . . Or fifty. Or twenty. So large, they seemed like clouds . . . One was floating in, hurting her head with its shriek, watering her eyes.

"Be quiet," she said. Or maybe she shrieked . . . so that the bird would understand . . . She revolved her hands and arms, jotting an Airebelle onto its head. Look at the silly thing, shrieking now! Look at it flop in convulsions! Look at its head exploding slowly! Look at it dropping down through trees! Down onto the ground, where . . .

Another bird, the one that she had peeled some feathers from before. How funny, that she had to blink her eyes again to see it clearly. Just like earlier. She didn't silence it; could an aasvogel curse? Why, yes it could, quite fluently, when its eyes were yanked from its skull! The way that Jian's blue eyes were now being yanked from his skull . . . Its curses made her head hurt more; so she dropped the bind on her first belle, jotting one for this bird now.

She now understood, however, that Airebelles weren't killing these fast birds fast enough—not when there were so many. So she spread her fingers wide, and clacked her tongue in sharp percussive rhythms. From those fingers shot raw bursts of materia, pentadarts—from the fingers of each of her hands they shot. The air was filled with blood and feathers.

But there wasn't blood enough, because she hadn't drowned.

She had watched the older girls so long ago; they had danced in hope of bringing life into the world. She was killing hope of life and hoped to kill. The men were killing with their dances, too: lanky, angular Gaekwar slicing with his rounded axe and rounded discs; Pooralay in bloody patterns drawing in the air with knives; Othon crushing skulls and feet and wings with edged mace; Seifas stabbing fore and back and to the side, the aasagai, the stick of death, teaching aasvogels, the birds of death, what was death. Even Dagon with his falchion . . . wasn't that amusing?

No.

Nothing was amusing anymore. Nothing mattered.

A temporary lull; the storm of birds grew darker overhead. Quickly precisely jotting, she pulled and pushed each man back through the door. They weren't expecting that! Seifas even cursed again! There they were, back in the Tower, looking at her.

"Do whatever you like with my brigade," she said. "Because it doesn't matter anymore." There; that would stop them killing all the birds. She hadn't yet killed Dagon, but since nothing mattered, she decided to spare his life. Jian would have spared his life. Though Jian might have tricked him into kissing a shoulderbeast.

She wouldn't scratch her nose, although it itched.

She turned her back on them. Plenty of birds were left—and much, much larger ones were on the way! She could kill as many as she wanted . . . !

But . . . what did it matter? There was no point in killing any more—nothing mattered.

Death descended again.

She could feel them descending, tons of feathers, skin and razored bone, crushing her already, in anticipation.

And now at last she had to face the truth . . .

. . . she didn't want to die.

Because if nothing mattered, then her death or life could never matter; only nothing could await her, if her life could never matter. Only, her life mattered to her: only her life, paper-thin and terrible, between complete incalculable *nothing* . . .

The fact of the matter, now she learned, was that she wasn't strong enough to die.

So she lashed—not in strength of vengeance: if only *her* life mattered to her, what could vengeance matter? Not in strength of any purpose; *she* was her only purpose, and no single point could be strong by itself. She lashed out only in fear, her fear increasing with approaching death, her failure growing with her fear, failure bringing certainty of death. The weight of deadly failure crushed her down, crouching her into a ball, muttering, "I matter; I matter; I *do* matter . . ."

Then into the smothering wall above she screamed—

"Someone tell me that I matter!!"

The only answer she received was creatures screaming in her face, her face upturned defiantly to hopeless death . . .

. . . that—and, faint beyond the muffling feathers . . .

"Ha-HAAAA!"

Insulted screeches rent the air—a feathered body plowed into the living cloud above her.

Jian had charged them—riding the back of an aasvogel!

From the seething cloud of bone and feathers, he *stretched* out in leaping free, reaching for the branching cluster where she crouched, tumbling down beside her with a grunt; covered in sweat, and dirty feathers, bark and sap and shallow scratches here and there.

And laughing so completely he could hardly stop to breathe.

"Where shall I skewer my peacocks *again!?*" He raised his fist in triumph to the raging birdfight boiling round and overhead, as the hunting avians, driven to the edge by deadly prey, frenzied in destroying one another.

Not a shout of hatred, but of victory; by daring ingenuity he had fairly played and won.

He wasn't being spiteful.

He was saluting them . . .

"Ahhhh . . ." he sighed exhausted in his mirth. "Hi, Commander! We'd better move along, before they see we're here!" He looked around to get his bearings, then began to drag himself into a run to reach the door.

She couldn't move. She couldn't blink. She wasn't sure she even breathed.

He stopped before he ran, and turned to check on her.

"Oh, by the way, Commander, thanks for lighting the area up!" He offered her a hand. "I hadn't any clue where I should nudge my ride! I doubt I could have held on any longer, either. Wow . . ." he added, looking at the corpses and destruction. "*You* guys sure were busy. Ouch. Remind me not to fight you!" He laughed again. "Commander . . . ?" he asked—offering still his outstretched hand.

She didn't take it.

Pulling herself up, by herself, refusing to look at him, she staggered toward the portal.

"Sorry, Commander," she heard; and then she felt him push her. Just a little; but she stumbled through the doorway, falling on the landing's floor. The others all had drawn away so she would have more room to come through quickly.

An aasvogel's talons crunched the branch behind her, piercing with a cry of failure.

"Heard enough o' *that*," Pooralay said; while Portunista panted on all fours, she looked up under a bracing arm, and saw the thug was peeling something from the sigil-plate. Behind her, blurring scenery shifted, as the portal 'moved', clearing the door of obstacles, closing with a thump.

Leaving her in the dark again, hearing her breath—and the breath of the squad around her.

Especially Jian, in the dark, beside her.

CHAPTER 29

"*Now* I am going down to eat!" Gaekwar laughed exhaustedly.

"Too bad we can't have fresh meat waiting for us after that!" Even Dagon seemed to be enjoying the camaraderie.

"Ha! My friend, we'll have meat aplenty!" Portunista's memory reported that she'd never heard the 'cowherd' calling Dagon a *friend* even *once* before . . . "There should be a severed bird already down the stairs. Chopped its head, and kicked the body through the door!"

"Foul roast!" Othon snorted—Portunista could practically hear his smiling strength, however.

"I'm afraid so," Seifas sighed. "Aasvogel meat *is* tough and stringy. Then again, we were only taught about the full-grown birds; these chicks may be more tender."

"Chicks!" chimed in two or three together.

"Yes; adults are not as small as those. Qarfax must have set his tessers near a nesting ground."

"Just how large do those things grow?!" Dagon demanded.

"Large enough to hunt a shoulderbeast, or even wyrms," Seifas somberly answered. "No one knows the limit. Giants roam the Middlelands."

"How can something so large fly?" marveled Jian.

Before the juacuar could answer—"How'd you get up on th' back o' one-a those turkeys?!" Pooralay roared.

"Wasn't easy!" chuckled Jian. "Good thing I put on my gloves," he added, with a touch of wonder in his voice. "Just like riding a barrel made of feathers!" he laughed again. "For a while we bumped around the lower branches of the trees; she was trying to shake me off, or knock me off, or anyway get back up through the canopy into the open sky. It was *very* dark down there . . . But sometimes, we were gliding beneath those trees . . . as if floating through enormous castle halls. She eventually got used to me, I think, and decided I wasn't going to hurt her; so she calmed and got her bearings, and then she swam through the air until she found a channel back up through the branches. I *could* hear this other racket going on—but, it seemed like she and I were alone in another world . . . and then we shot up through that clearing of living leaves and branches, and we plunged into a lake of stars! She spread her wings and cried for joy, and . . ." he sighed. "And I kissed her neck, as I clung to her feathers. I thanked her for the things we shared. I hope I dream about them . . ."

"You kissed . . . the back . . . of a killer . . . bird . . ." Dagon flatly said.

"Hmph!" chuckled Jian. "Do you have no poetry in your soul?? Even if she was my enemy, how could *she* not love the life she lives, even more than I? And if she couldn't, then I would love it for her, for her sake; such an experience, as she *is,* ought to be loved. But, I think she must also love what she does. And if we are loving something together, I would be a traitor *not* to love her, even if she was my enemy; for we share that love. If we must fight, then we will fight; but I would love her anyway. And if she cannot love me . . . then I will love her still, though I die—for she is my sister, even if she cannot know me for her brother."

"You should try to love cows sometime . . ." Gaekwar muttered cynically.

"You," said Seifas softly, "should have been among the Guacu-ara."

"Pooralay!" Jian exclaimed. "What happened with the door?"

"Blindwitted idjit!" Poo retorted. "Didn't y'see what happen'd when 'ista went through th' door th' *first* time? What didja 'xpect w'd happen when *you* jump'd through?!"

"Well," he answered—Portunista heard him shrugging in his voice, "I figured the door would close again, of course. But we had to find her. And I'm expendable." No rancor or regret, only a fact. Her heart and stomach twisted together . . . "I meant, that I was surprised the door stayed open when the *rest* of you came through. How did you manage that?"

"Th' way I woulda managed it th' *first* time, if y'd'a waited, y'punkie-brained fool! Got a strip o' paper rolled on a spindle in m' pocket. It's been treat'd with an ex-tract, made fr'm honey trees 'n other stuff. Peel it back, cut offa slice, an' then it c'n hold things together. Handy, in *my* line of work." The maga heard his thoroughly devious grin. "So I scotched that hair we found, onto th' plate. Good f'r in-ter-ro-ga-tions, too. Put it on some hair'n . . . rrrrrrip!"

Everyone was laughing, even Seifas.

Everyone . . . but her.
Why wasn't she laughing?

Because.
Everything now was right. And everything was wrong.
Everything mattered, now. And that was worse than *nothing* mattering.

If he had never come into her life, she might have *always* been content with nothing mattering but herself.

When he was gone, she knew the truth. When he was there, she knew the truth.

The truth, was that she wasn't the most important thing in all the world. The truth, was that it was better for her, *not* to be the most important thing, the only thing, that mattered to her.

It *hurt*. It hurt in different ways. She *hated* that pain . . . why wouldn't he leave her *alone* . . . ?! He was laughing, laughing in her pain . . . she *hated* that pain . . . she hated . . . she hated *him* for doing this to her! She *hated* him for bringing her a truth she did not care for! She would show him . . . she would show . . .

"I will show him . . ." Portunista muttered. "I *will* show him . . . he *can't* do this to me . . ." She whistled up a wisplight, and refused to hear how shaky she was sounding. One erratic wisp appeared . . . was it dimmer?

"Um . . . Portunista?" Jian was looking at her, with those innocent eyes. Why did *he* not ever seem to hurt?! He was *laughing* at *her*, laughing from the grave he didn't have . . .

"He won't get away with this . . ." she promised him. But—she couldn't face those eyes, those eyes that didn't hurt, that never seemed to thirst, those eyes she couldn't set her teeth into, invulnerable to her, only giving, always ready to give, and never seeming to *need*. She sobbed and fell against the inner wall, throttling down her sob with rising fury.

"He *won't* do this to me! He *won't* hurt me like this and get away with it!" She pounded her fist upon the wall.

"Not to sound nervous, or anything . . ." Gaekwar nervously drawled. "But I think I missed a part. Who are you talking about, again?"

She ground her teeth and groaned. She *would* strike out, strike out and not be hurt, *strike* at the man who hurt her, strike at . . . at . . .

"Qarfax!" she exclaimed. "He's *laughing* at me! He thinks he's smart, and that I cannot get to him! But I will! I know where he's weak!"

"He's dead," Othon pointed out.

"He thinks he's won," she grated, "but he hasn't! He thinks I cannot get to him! But I can! He hurt me when I tried to find his laboratory . . . but I won't give up . . . I *will* get in, and I will do it *tonight!*"

Gaekwar stood, and very carefully walked to her. Portunista was sure that he meant well; she could see his eyes.

She understood those eyes. He wasn't understanding her.

And that was fine. She was comfortable with that.

But Gaekwar wasn't the one she wanted to understand, and wanted to be a mystery to . . .

"Commander," he said, looking her in the eye with the eyes she understood. "I'm not being funny anymore. It's time to go downstairs, and get cleaned up, and eat, and get some sleep. Tomorrow, if you want to go through that door and look around," he sighed, "I guess we'll go. We'll back you up. But you need to rest—"

"To hell with the door! I *will* defeat the magus tonight!" Portunista declared. Gaekwar's eyes showed anger and frustration now. *That* was what she wanted to see!—that look that told her *she* was in command, that *she* was the most important . . . !

She looked down and to her left. Jian was shaking his head, his own eyes narrowed, though not in fear or anger.

"Gaekwar's right, Commander . . ." Every time he called her that, she felt a blade-tip pierce her heart. He was *mocking* her . . . ! "Tomorrow morning you'll feel better, and then we'll beat the magus' traps for sure; and then—"

"Tonight!" insisted Portunista. *Jian* couldn't order her around! She was the commander! He *said* so, but she *knew* he didn't mean it . . . ! "Right now! *You* don't have to do a thing! Just watch . . . just watch . . ."

She turned to step away from the wall . . . she nearly stumbled over Jian, who still was sitting . . . why would he not move?! All he had to do was *move* . . . She would show him . . .

Portunista ignored the way the landing tilted wildly in the flickering light, as she focused her intent. Gurgling, bubbling, she infused into the wall, left of the door, the right proportions of the elemental Yrthe.

It took her longer than she had expected . . . she was so *intensely* tired . . . but she wouldn't stop. She would show him . . .

"Look," she rasped. "I'll show you. Do you see?"

"Yes." Jian sighed. "I see." *That* was what she wanted to hear in his voice. Resignation. To the inevitability, of *her.* She smiled.

He wasn't smiling.

She bound her jotting into place, barely, softening a swath of stones: an Yrthepool, in the wall.

She exhaled through the curvature of her tongue behind her teeth, sharp as a small explosion. With a finger flick, her veckinesis pushed the mud; and *further* she exhaled, a tear pressed seeping out of an eye, spots gyrating blackly in her vision. But she would not stop, even to inhale . . . *she would go through* . . .

The wall fell, wetly.

There it was.
The laboratory.

She sent the wisp into it, where it shivered, dully, luminating secrets now exposed for her to take. She breathed the painful air, and blinked, and forced the vitalized stone to puddle inside on the floor.

Finally. It was finished.

She had won.

Except—she still must enter the secret room, consummate her victory, justify her actions with success.

One step forward.

Twice.

. . . a rising whine, inaudible almost—sounding familiar—

"Portunista, get back!" Jian was pushing, pushing her away, from her victory, *from her prize—!*

Was that a fear she finally saw in his eyes . . . ? Fear of her?

fear . . . for . . .

The silence and darkness crashed open with bright strobing bolts of materia, lancing from every quarter and also the center point, striking down from on high . . .

—striking down on Jian—

She heard him grunt with every hit. But he didn't scream.

He fell—before a bolt smashed into his face, she saw his eyes on her . . . no longer afraid . . . because she was safe . . . But he didn't scream.

She saw him crawl in lurches across the floor, dozens of bolts, hundreds of bolts, hammering down onto him. Away from her. But he didn't scream.

She saw him roll in a fetal ball behind a chair, seeking any cover from the relentless energy-storm that shattered the chair into kindling, lancing past it into him. But he didn't scream.

She saw him twitch and then lay still. The pentadarts continued pounding for another tick of time; then stopped.

A single thread of smoke arose in a wavery line, from behind the wreck of the chair, breaking into curling shards.

But Jian did not scream.

She wanted to scream, for him. No, she didn't want to scream. Her throat was sore. Her soul was sore. Hadn't she just wished for this? Wasn't it funny?

She tried to laugh. She heard the whine, mixed with her broken laugh, and stepped to embrace and welcome—

—the ragged hole jerked left, and she felt something, someone, wrapping her, cushioning her . . .

. . . indeed with force but gently, enfolding her and twisting, the thunder rising in crescendo, puffs of air buffeting them, and then he grunted as she landed on him . . .

"Jian . . . ?" she heard her voice, as wavery as the smoke that had been rising from behind the chair . . .

"No, 'ista,"—a whisper she knew, had known before in moments of quiet happiness, but for which she no longer felt that feeling . . . "I'm Gaekwar. Quiet, 'ista, shhhh . . ." Why was he saying that? She wasn't crying. Was she?

He turned her over slowly, as they lay upon the upward stairs, placing him between her and the landing.

"Listen to me . . . Commander," Gaekwar whispered. "Please be very quiet. If it chews the floor to pieces, we'll have a harder time escaping."

She couldn't make sense of anything he was saying. Maybe he could see it on her face, because . . .

"Listen to me, Commander . . . are you listening? Whisper to me softly . . ."

Too many things went through her mind at once, and she started giggling . . . a giggle like the distant scream of a ghost.

"Okay," he said, holding her close . . .

And Portunista pounded the floor, with her right hand, over and over; with her left she clutched the back of Gaekwar's fighting jacket.

He held her close, so no one else would hear.

CHAPTER 30

She sobbed into his shirt, not thinking, only racking with her sobs. But she was very quiet—so the others wouldn't hear.

Somehow . . . it helped. She didn't feel as though her brain was made of broken glass.

To blow one's nose upon a former lover's shirt, she decided, must somehow make *everything* seem more real, afterward . . .

"Alla yous okay up there?" came a shout across the landing.

Raw materia instantly thrashed the floor and wall.

She stifled a yelp, pulling her left hand under Gaekwar after being struck with molten chips. Muffling a curse he swatted his hair—wasn't it good, the hair on the back of his head was so short? she thought within her quieting grief. Otherwise, a spark might have worked its way to where he couldn't get it out . . .

Despite this idle thought, she found she now could focus better. The bind upon the latest wisp had been long lost; she whistled up another one, now much brighter, steadily floating above where she and Gaekwar lay. He turned to look across the landing; together they could see remaining members of her squad, looking up around the corner of the narrow curving stair.

"Sorry," mouthed the thug. Gaekwar motioned for them to go downstairs. They did.

"Now, Commander," Gaekwar tried again—with his smile and drawl that once had attracted her so much . . . "I need you talking to me, *very* softly." Portunista nodded. "Tell me what is shooting at us over there. I think I recognize it, but I want you to confirm it."

"Pentadarts," she said.

"Five were shooting? I mean five sources."

"Yes, that's right."

"Can you tell me when they fire?"

"When they hear sufficient sound," she said, smiling very faintly; Pooralay had demonstrated *that* . . .

"I agree. What else sets them off?"

137

Her eyes unfocused, as she sent her memory back into the minutes earlier—her breath began to catch again.

"Mo . . . mo . . . movement . . . when people move . . ." A stray thought crossed her mind—if Gaekwar said one word about a cow, she'd scalp him to his skull . . . ! But he didn't.

"I agree. *Any* movement?"

Any movement? What did he mean . . . ? She tried to think . . .

and in her memory, she saw Jian—being hammered mercilessly; trying to escape and failing, trying to protect her and succeeding . . .

protecting her from being blasted into smoking pieces . . .

"Jian is still in there," she said.

But before she could continue, Gaekwar spoke.

"Tell me of pentadarts, Commander." She didn't answer; she was still untangling all her feelings.

"Tell me of pentadarts, Commander." Not annoyed, just persistent. Blast his eyes . . .

"Pentadarts," recited Portunista, "are high-kinetic bursts of raw materia, not directly elemental in their composition. They transfer kinetic force, with little burning, through conductive material. Metal especially is susceptible to a pentadart attack; while thickened leather armor, such as could be made from plates of shoulderbeasts, can insulate the victim from the deadlier effects."

"What are those effects, Commander?"

She swallowed. "A pentadart, when striking the torso of a living creature, transfers . . . a kinetic shock into internal organs. The vic . . . victim's body . . ." She crushed an urge to cry again, and made herself continue, " . . . will often not be damaged on the surface. But, internal organs such as lungs, the stomach, or the heart, will rupture. Other organs often flatten from the transfer of kinetic force."

"How many pentadarts hit Jian, Commander?"

She breathed two times. And then again. And then she looked at Gaekwar, in the eyes—the eyes she understood.

"Too many," Portunista said.

He nodded.

She sniffled once, to clear her nose. "Sorry. I'm okay."

"I can tell. I'm glad," he smiled, "because if I try to jump that gap, I'm worried those things will toast my buns."

She giggled very briefly; and felt better.

"Gaekwar," Portunista said, looking up at him. "Thanks."

"You're welcome. I liked him, too. He . . . mm . . . well, he wasn't a cow. Y'know." He shrugged, and turned around, rotating off her to the right, reclining on the stairs against the inner wall.

Portunista carefully leaned forward, cautiously preserving the scraps of rationality she had gathered, studying the landing. Gaekwar watched her, as she thought the situation through; and he smiled.

"Hey, Commander . . ." Portunista slid her eyes suspiciously, hearing his whispered drawl. "*You're* not one either."

She snickered, "You are *so* full of cow-juice," and batted his ridiculous bangs of hair.

Then she sighed, and firmly wiped her nose again.

"Okay," she said. "Now I've got a plan."

CHAPTER 31

Having found the strength to think about the past few minutes, Portunista now recalled a fact that gave her hope.

"Watch," she murmured to her subcommander; the wisplight floated over to the gap.

Both of them tensed for the fusillade. But nothing happened.

She smiled as, almost playfully, she bobbed the wisplight in and out of the gap. No rising whine; no crashing devastation.

She looked at Gaekwar; his own smile mirrored hers. "*Any* movement?" he asked her once again.

Now as she danced the wisplight in defiance of the generators, Portunista finalized her plan.

"Hsst! *Hsst!*" she called, trying to avoid the sensors. Seifas' head appeared around the corner, further down the stairwell. "Poo!" she mouthed, and gestured to the juacuar. Moments later, Pooralay edged into view.

"Tape!" she mouthed, while miming a pull and a strip. The thug held up the roll.

"Throw it!" she instructed him with mouth and mime. He sighed and glanced quite pointedly toward the wall-gap; but he did as she asked.

The tape traversed the distance without trouble.

Pooralay's eyebrows perked; but Portunista gestured for him to retreat to safety.

Sliding over, Portunista quickly gave a kiss to Gaekwar's cheek; he rolled his eyes at this.

Then she whispered once again: "Now, watch."

She had been studying some new jottings, from Gemalfan's disciplex, practicing in secret during Hazyslope—she didn't like for others to see her failures when she practiced.

Now, into the gap, she jotted one wide plane of Silveraire.

Gaekwar nodded as she moved the mirrored surface. As expected, no attacks.

"Great, Commander! Let's get moving!" That is what he began to say and do; but she stopped him.

"They still will respond to sound," she murmured. "And I can also deal with *that*," she added, watching his confusion. "But—I won't be going past. I am going *in*."

140

Sighing in exasperation, Gaekwar tried to argue; but she looked him firmly in the eye and told him: "Hush!"

He blinked, and closed his mouth. She continued:

"I *am* the brigade commander; this *is* my expedition; and *this* is my responsibility. I came here for this laboratory, and I *will* possess it. I wish . . ." She felt her lower lip starting to tremble, so she bit it. "I wish that I had taken your advice. But I didn't—so, here we are. I know now how to defeat it; and I am going to do it. I won't go off my head—but neither will I let his body lay in *that* room overnight! So." She paused to smother several types of anger . . . "I will take care of both those problems now. I hope," she added.

"If you're so set on going in, then let *me* do it. You're the co—" But he silenced, at her look.

"That's right," she said. "I am the commander. And, I am the maga. *I* can do this; *you* cannot. I am the one who put you all in danger; and I will be the one who will take care of what I've done. So, when I go to do that, if I gesture to you, you run on past behind me, go downstairs, and put our supper on the fire," she wryly smiled. She knew what his expression meant, and so she continued: "If my plan goes wrong, *you run anyway!* I will fall into the room, and draw the generator fire, and so you should get safely past. Then you can do what you want," she finished. "For I will be dead, and so no longer Commander," she did not explain—but it wasn't necessary. Gaekwar got the message.

She thought that maybe he would argue . . . then she saw him, in his eyes, reevaluating her.

"As you command," he finally complied.

She didn't peck him on the cheek again. That had been appropriate, before: one last thanks for helping her, by being who he was. Now that time was past. She was the commander, he was the subordinate; and both of them, to their surprise, were comfortable with that. She grasped his forearm, receiving and giving strength.

Then she stood and moved away from him, over to the stairway's outer wall. It wasn't far; but she wanted him to understand that she would do this by herself. She waved for him to go back up the stairs, away from her.

She didn't want his lungs to crumple.

One deep breath, to steady herself. And then she realized, she didn't *need* much steadying—which, a corner of her mind ironically reported, was a pleasant change of pace . . . !

Then she jotted an Airebelle around herself.

A deadly silence fell.

The echoes from the stone, the bare caress of moving air, even sounds from Gaekwar that would normally be imperceptible . . . *all* were gone.

Only sounds within the belle remained: the beat of her heart, the saliva she was swallowing, her shallow rapid breaths.

The silence of a living grave.

The belle redirected *all* the air it contacted, to the Puria. *No* sound could enter—and so no sound of hers would reach the laboratory.

But the redirection worked both ways: if she moved the belle, then its inner curve would inescapably scoop a vacuum.

The way that she had burst the heads of aasvogels.

Beads of sweat were trickling down her skin.

Gemalfan's disciplex had not revealed the answer to this problem. But it *must* be something simple, for she knew this *was* a common Cadrist jotting. Air must enter, to replace the air departing. But the silence mustn't be defeated . . .

Shutting her eyes, she felt the shape of her intention. She had made the sphere complete, but—there was something strange . . .

Opening her eyes, she looked and saw the stone wall of the Tower to her left. Interesting . . . There was real though ephemeral elemental Aire, mixed with raw materia, intersecting and extruded through that wall to form her sphere. What would happen if she took a tiny step away . . . ?

She had bound her jotting on the second button of her shirt. She risked the tiny step, the belle moving in conjunction.

With a softly smacking pop, the left side of the belle failed, rupturing the minor vacuum already accumulating.

She deeply breathed, in relief; the fresh air tasted good.

She continued edging rightward, discovering she could still maintain her bind despite the leftward rended hole. What would happen when the belle's surface touched the inner wall . . . ?

It flattened to fit the shape.

Well! Inspired, she felt around more closely. The rending when she'd moved had been extensive; more than she had first detected: behind, below, and to the left—wherever the belle had been jotted through the Tower stones.

Very interesting. She could now be sure she wouldn't smother or explode—the aasvogels' necks must not have moved enough to overcome the seals around their moving heads.

However, all these gaps would be about as silencing as the columns holding up an outdoor temple!

She knew she shouldn't have to jott the belle again at every step. What was the solution . . . ?

The belle's flattened shape, along with its persistence where unrent, provided her the clues. A few moments more of experimenting, and she found that she could use the bind to fix the gaps by re-extending her intended shape.

She stepped ahead, altogether off the stairs, and then repaired the shape behind her. Good. Now there would not be another new gap; unless she leaped into the air! Crouching—she tested—only pooled the belle, around her in an arc; and standing up again allowed the belle to resume . . . its . . .

—her skin pulled all directions!—her eyes evaporated!—her eardrums stretched to bleeding! her breath yanked from her lungs! which seemed to help a little bit, though now she couldn't breathe . . . !

She cursed herself: her crouch had scooped her atmosphere across the inner surface of the belle; standing had decreased the pressure drastically!

Don't drop the belle! she commanded herself. There *had* to be a way around this—but she never would find it if she didn't face the pain. If she collapsed unconscious, the sphere would vanish; so her pride and body would be bruised, but nothing worse.

Probably.

The belle could be ripped by accident, without destroying its existence overall. So . . .

Reaching to the left with her intent, she . . . erased . . . a minor hole.

The recompression nearly brought her to her knees; she gulped the air until she could gain her control.

But, *now* she was prepared.

She stepped, with just the slightest quavering in her chest—behind the screen of Silveraire.

Then she turned to face it.

It mirrored her reflection.

She looked nervous.

She expected that she wouldn't hear a warning whine of charging energy; but she thought the plane of Silveraire, although as thin as atoms, would reflect the first few bolts—and not be kicked aside the way a wisplight would.

Then a surge of fear: she should have checked to see her shield would hold *before* she stood behind it—!

she thought of Jian, lying dead—because of her.

She stood in place.

A quarter minute ticked away.

She was still alive.

She started to breathe, finding she had held her breath while waiting. Despite a subsequent dizziness, she held her concentration. Firming her expression—she reflected grim determination now, she gladly saw!—Portunista beckoned Gaekwar.

She watched him on her jotted mirror, as he trotted past behind her, feeling him deform the belle like a bubble.

She saw worry in his eyes.

She could understand that.

Now, next: turn and jott a second plate of Silveraire, to her right, her throat vibrating strongly to produce a tinkling glassy sound, as she smoothed the mirrored surface with her palms—

—she gasped! pain!!

—head rocking, pounding blows!—heart leaping into her teeth!

She ground her teeth, biting on her fear. The shocks were not yet physically harmful. And they quickly ceased. The Silveraire in the gap had warped and bulged, twisting with the pounding of her mind. But it had held.

This time. For the bursts of one brief moment.

Her sweat hit stone in spatters. The sensors must have heard her after all! Or, maybe they'd heard Gaekwar running past, and then hair-triggered afterward when she started percussive jotting . . . ? She'd hoped the hole she had put behind her for a vent, would not emit enough—

Damnation! The *hole!*

She had placed it on her left, *because* she had been facing *down* the hallway at the time. It must be turning as she turned—yes, she felt it, to her left but pointing down the stairway as she faced the Silveraire—closer to the gap! And so, of course, when she had turned to jott the silver on her *right,* the hole had pointed *toward* the silvered gap—in line with every generator!

Blind her eyes . . . she was such a *cretin!*

. . . did she even have the faintest *clue* what she was doing . . . ?!

She could leave, she thought as she sealed the sphere, erasing a new hole behind her. She could think it over, get some food, get some sleep, maybe even pass the deadly opening once again to sleep upstairs . . . up in the room and bed of Qarfax—who *was* more clever than *she* was after all . . .

. . . leaving Jian to lie alone, where she had killed him with her pride . . .

In the Silveraire, her nose now wrinkled, in determination. . . . had he ever seen that, too . . . ? what would he have thought of it . . . ?

Now she saw a snarl.

Qarfax would not win.

The maga took a step, closer to the furious destruction that would burst her innards to pieces . . .

Portunista smiled, however. What could the pentadarts do to her that was worse than the pain she *already* felt inside?

There. She felt the belle making contact with the edges of the gap in front of her. She pushed, expanding her intent, until the sphere had sealed the gap.

Now let's see if they can hear me! Portunista wryly thought . . .

Firming her resolve, she jotted to her left: another pane of Silveraire.

No vicious shocks.

And now for one last panel, overhead.

The effort nearly swamped her . . . her vision wavered . . . her binds would vanish—leaving her staked naked to the sight and sound—

She bore down hard upon her bindings.

They steadied.

Four large planes of Silveraire; one large Airebelle; a wisplight, too . . . at least she was long familiar with *that* . . . !

Three jotting types, six binds to hold, between one slip of concentration and her life.

She held it all, counting slow to sixty, steeling her intentions and resolve. She could do it. She was ready.

Portunista closed her eyes . . .

. . . and slowly stepped again.

A corner of her mind observed that she had thrown her arms out wide, in automatic reflex, mirroring the balance she maintained. The Airebelle would follow without a problem, bound upon that second button of her shirt.

But, she still had five more bindings that she had to move . . . at the proper angles . . . at the proper distances . . . not the smallest gap allowed to let a sensor find her body . . . stay the proper shapes—keep them in existence—

she was losing balance—! straw of towers wobbling—!

—she threw away her wisplight bind, and seized the shields—!

They held.

Barely.

Sweat was falling from her hands. But she didn't care. She paused to swallow, breaths and other beatings in her body filling all her hearing . . .

She stepped across the threshold of the gap within the wall.
Now the sensors *all* would have their firing arcs upon her.

She told herself the situation hadn't *really* changed. Two or three, or even one, would doom her to a frightful death; so what did all five matter?!
More precisely—something mattered to her *more.*

She stood some moments, still; regripping on her fear and concentration, feeling as if sensors were caressing her, watching for her to uncover, waiting to embrace her . . .
She very nearly laughed. She very nearly killed herself by laughing.
She truly was besotted, wasn't she? Her weakness was so pathetic, it amused her. Jian was *dead*—only honor and revenge remained for her to take, however far she could.
And she *would!*

Her binding grip was sure as frozen diamond, as she stood upon the solid puddle she had melted when she pushed the wall into the laboratory. She now rotated, half a turn; sealing then re-rending her belle, until she faced the wall-gap once again.
Whistling up another wisp, she snapped her head around to send it soaring toward the door on her left. The dazzling Silveraire reflections didn't break her concentration; still, almost instinctively, she altered the wisp's intensity, remembering how that had felt when it had dulled before by accident.
Very satisfactory . . . One more jotting *might* be more than she could manage—but she didn't need another.
She would defeat the Cadrist *now!*

Planting her wisp in place, she walked with her ungainly binds, following the wall inside the laboratory. Only two or three more steps—and now she stood beside the door!—a little disappointed not to see a matching plate, but that was fine—her plan allowed this possibility. She was certain it would work . . .

her mind exploded.

—*hundreds* crashing, ricocheting reflective surfaces, still transferring fractions of kinetic force onto the fragile mirrors—
She shrieked inside her soundproofed bubble, first in pain and fear, and then in anger—*Why . . . ?!* What had she done *wrong?!* She was going to be plastered onto this stupid door—!

She bit down on her scream, converting it into a growl, as storms of pain and force threw water droplets flying off her face, her hair, her hands. Intuitively, she dropped the wisp and Airebelle, to redirect her focus on the floating sheets of almost-nothing set between the onslaught and her death.

Darkness and the sound now crushed against her mind and body both.

Four bound jottings, and she dared not drop a one—nor could even try to jott another—muscles cramping and spasming, arms refusing at first to obey, then drawing inward from their splayed positions, feeling for the handle, praying to *whatever* might be listening that it wouldn't be false like the hall-side of the door—!

The handle worked.

She wasted pushing at the door in crumbling panic, feeling her mind *ripping* with the shields—no, she had to pull it *toward* her . . . ! Had she reasoned this correctly—?!

She *had!*

The landing and the narrow tower hallway; not a jungle.

She needed light, but dared not jott.

"LIGHT!" she roared. "I need a torch!—blast your bleeding eyes!" She cursed and shouted, concentration strained and failing . . .

She might run now . . . through the door . . . run away, and escape and live . . .

—no —she *refused* —Jian was still in this room, where she had killed him with her pride

—and she—was going—to *win*—!

Portunista stood in place, bearing the pain that he had borne, defying the room's defenses to kill her, crying out for light . . .

A torch curled blazing around the corner, bouncing off a wall, skittering down the floor.

Good enough.

Nearly vomiting from the effort—slowly and precisely Portunista tore a sticky paper strip, dropped the spindle afterward—stuck the tape onto a breeches-leg, fingers wet would drench it—

Slowly and precisely she unbuttoned one belt-pocket, bending down her head to see, straining in the mix of strobing flickers orangish bluish white—sodden clinging hair now stranding, funneling the sweating salt into the burning corners of her eyes—synaptic shocks eroding her control, foretasting the final agony, her body being smashed from deep within would be *relief* compared to this—!

Slowly and precisely, she carefully dragged her dripping fingers up across the inside of this smallest of her pockets . . .
. . . lifting out the follicle of Qarfax.

She placed the hair between her shaking lips—wiped her trembling hands upon her shirt, her breeches, on the door, *anything* to dry them . . .

the pain was irresistible—
—against her will, she stumbled forward, through the door, sobbing with the single fleeting moment of *relief*—unconsciously, she tried to drag her shields—
—which couldn't follow through the doorframe—

—*three silvers slipped and vanished*—
a single warning—she collapsed, the right—a bolt, nicking her head in passing, spinning her around . . . *everything* was spinning . . . her brain throbbed nauseating . . . *hold* the final silver, but it shattered her intention, raking shards across her mind . . . *all* striking round her, blasting searing chips of stone . . . they couldn't get to her, she was in the doorframe lee . . . but they ate away the stone, had torn the door apart already . . . she was screaming through her teeth and couldn't stop, they heard her screams, relentlessly they sought her blood and body—

. . . but she . . . was going . . . to *win* . . . !!

The hair hung from her lower lip . . . she seized and pressed it to the sigilpanel . . .

The sigils worked.
She had told the generators, that *she* was their master.

Her keening faded with the echoes of the blasts, leaving only gasping with relief.
She wiped her left hand one last time upon her breeches, pulled the tape from where she'd placed it, twisted round to face the panel—
—and taped the hair, onto the sigils.

It had worked. She had won.
. . . no, it wasn't over yet.

She scrambled to her feet, and charged into the laboratory, whistling wisplights everywhere. There, along the quarters and the center of the round room's ceiling, hung the generators, pestles resting on internal gimbals that allowed rotation.

Her throat was hoarse; but she didn't need her voice to do this jotting—only her aching jaws and raspy tongue.

She hammered every generator to pieces—with her *own* pentadarts.

Now, it was over.

She forced herself to deeply breathe, regularly, in and out.

"It's safe!" she shouted—or tried to shout. "Come on up!"

"Hmph." Pooralay snorted from the gap behind her. "D'pends on whatcha callin' *safe* . . . "

"Better leave the hair . . ." she told him.

"ah-duhhh," he mumbled, pressing sticky strips already. The other men were entering the room.

She had to sit. The scarred and pitted wall, between the gap and door, felt good to lean against.

"Not to be a next-day general, 'ista," Gaekwar said, "but why not tape the stupid hair onto the panel *first?*"

She shook her head . . . needed a drink *so* badly . . . water would do . . . mead would be better . . . aasvogel blood was almost worth considering at this point . . .

"It only would have opened onto the nesting grounds again," explained the maga. "The hallway and the laboratory needed to be linked, before the panel could affect the generators." She wondered in her calm exhaustion what the other door looked like, so many kilopaces distant. It probably simply opened onto normal space, and thus was still intact—unlike this door! The tesser would be on the entry-side, of its special doorframe. The other portal-side would end up here, inside the laboratory's doorframe edge, an inch or so away from—

She closed her eyes. Trying to puzzle this out any further, only made her head hurt worse. A thought drifted across her mind, however, and she opened her eyes again, looking to the floor.

The floor in front of the frame, inside the room, was stone—and covered with sigils.

She allowed her eyes to drift as well, showing her what they would . . . a thin stone parquet covered the laboratory in plating, and every plate was sigilscribed. Except where she was sitting. When she had smoothed the vitalized blocks of stone, having pushed them into the room, she had covered up the sigils under the gap in the wall—mostly forward, but left and right a little, too. And then she had stepped from *that* new layer, onto the uncovered floor, when she had moved in front of the door.

Of course. *That* was why the pentadarts had fired. Qarfax had anticipated a mage might hide from sight and sound.

She weakly cursed her deep stupidity. She only had needed to step through the door, into the hallway—not too far, to avoid detection by the generators through the gap instead—and then they would have ceased their firing.

Assuming, she reminded herself, that she had thought enough ahead to leave her shields behind. Her shriek of rage and fear had not been helpful, either. She was too exhausted even to laugh; still it was bitterly funny: she would have been much safer, if she could have shut her mouth a few more moments . . . !

Well, a win was a win.

She closed her eyes again, unable to stop the gently welling tears. Behind her eyes, she saw Jian moving, still alive, stumbling, rolling, crawling on the sigiled floor, drawing death down *onto* him with every move he made. He hadn't had a chance.

And, it would have been *her* . . .

She wept again, softly, too depleted to prevent imagination from providing detailed picture-feelings: *this* is what Jian must have felt—as he had struggled, carrying death away from her, so that she wouldn't have to share it . . .

how had he *done* it . . . ? how, without *screaming* . . . ?

"About bloody time," she heard the Krygian's muttered satisfaction. She didn't have to open her eyes and turn her head to know that he was standing near the blasted chair behind which Jian had tried to find a final hopeless chance.

"I *seriously* suggest you shut up now," Gaekwar softly warned him.

Let Seifas stab the fool, she decided. She didn't have the energy to kill him yet herself . . . and, she *had* decided not to kill him, anyway, earlier, minutes ago, hours ago . . . hadn't she? Yes, before Jian had smashed through hopelessness, answering her cry, saving her from death, after *he* should have died . . .

He wouldn't be jumping out of the darkness, on the razored edge of victory, this time.

She needed a drink; she deeply needed water. *Maybe* she wouldn't cry again, even later sleeping in a dead man's bed.

No. She *wouldn't* cry again. Never again.

She raised her hand to wipe her eyes.

"ow," she heard.

A corner of her mind observed that she had recently exhaled, and that if she didn't soon inhale she *would* be passing out.

Another corner thought that passing out would be just fine.

Another corner firmly vetoed *any* notion of passing out! But neither had she yet inhaled.

Another corner calmly noted: her tears had now been sucked back into her eyes, perhaps because her lids had opened wider than they should. The trails of moisture felt to be freezing solid. Bracing; but uncomfortable. On the other hand, now she wouldn't have to wipe her tears away . . .

Another corner told her where the mumbled "ow" had come from.

Another corner tallied all this up, and so concluded: her wits had finally cracked. The voices must be beginning now. Her troops would dress her in a long-sleeve shirt, tie the sleeves behind her back, and haul her in a wagon looking for any honorable way to be rid of her—feeding her until then with a long and cautious spoon.

"—eyes of the watcher by *night . . .* " Seifas murmured in reverent terror. This did *not* make Portunista feel any better. She tried to bat away the hope that gripped her throat insanely.

"It . . . it isn't possible . . ." Dagon sounded throttled, too. She followed his voice and his scuffling feet, as he backpedaled into the wall with a thump.

She scraped her head around to her right—not to her left, not to where she couldn't bear to look, but to her right. The stones of the wall passed under her faintly itching nose; then the wall planed off into a gentle distant curve.

There was Dagon. She could bear to look at him. She wanted to see his face. She wondered if *her* face looked that distraught.

She had to breathe. She had to know.
She chose to look.

Continued right, around to what had been her left. She passed her eyes across the other men. She didn't care to see them; she could see them any time she wished. What they thought, wasn't important.

Except they also saw what she was seeing; demonstrating she was not insane.

Jian was standing to his feet, behind the sharded chair.
His face had not been harmed.
His arms and chest had not been harmed.
His curly sandy-colored hair, which caught the wisplights' glow so well, had not been harmed.
His shirt . . . *that* was harmed. It hung in tatters off his chest.
He shook his head as if he'd just been dunked in icy water; but unlike herself, no sweat was oozing from his body.

Another corner of her mind was noticing that his chest had plenty of much the same hair as his beard . . .

Jian removed his shirt, the red of which seemed black as blood within the bluish light; and started laughing quietly.

"So much for that, I guess," he said, and gently laid the shirt upon the shattered chair. "I hope I won't be needing *that* again, anytime soon . . . !"

She inhaled, rawly.

He turned toward her sound.

"Hey there, Portunista! I am *so* glad you're okay!! I was worried, for a minute. Aww . . ." he looked around, in regret. "The lab's a wreck." He sighed apologetically. "I'm *awfully* sorry. Almost looks like all those aasvogel thingies packed themselves in here with Tumblecrumble for a fight! I know you were hoping that you would find *something* useful in here . . . But," he added, in good cheer, "who knows! I bet you *still* can find a *lot* in here worth keeping! But, let's start tomorrow morning—'kay? I'm hungry." He walked to the mouth of the wall-gap.

She followed him with her eyes.

"I'll go start the fire, okay?" Jian suggested helpfully.

And then the man who should have been a dead man left the room.

CHAPTER 32

The dark man lies in darkness, guarding as the others sleep; the nearby firepit-glow does not even reach the ceiling overhead.

Seifas has recounted many happenings this day, as much as he remembers. He knows that soon his watch will end; but unlike the others he will not be sleeping in the garrison chambers. Instead he will sleep on guard, near the fire.

He hears the breeze moan faintly once again, and smiles, for now it almost seems a pleasant friend.

If only he could shake the feeling that it heralds tragedy to come . . .

"Well," he writes, "we have already faced tragedy several times today—and hope remains.

"Although this latest incident unnerves me, when I think about it . . ."

All of us wandered down the stairs, as if caught into a dream—all, except for Jian. He bounded down ahead of us, full of life.

Gaekwar's fire—which he had lit while Portunista fought against Qarfax's defenses, saying that he did *not* intend to starve while she was killing herself—gave us plenty of warmth inside the chilling Tower stones. Jian suggested we each take turns in washing ourselves with water from the well below.

I seemed to awaken, as I washed away the blood and grime with cold fresh water, cleansing cuts across my back from one of the aasvogels, drinking the water in with my skin as well as with my mouth.

Jian refused to wash himself until we all had been refreshed, saying that preparing Gaekwar's kill would be a messy job. When we returned, one by one, we found some aasvogel portions roasting on the firepit. We watched the food that he had prepared for us; he put the carcass out the door for any scavengers to eat. Then he bathed himself; and with the bucket from the plank, he spilled clean water down the stairs and hall to help remove the blood.

Then we ate as we had washed, watched and waited—in silence.

I wondered who would be the first to speak.

I thought it might be Pooralay.

I hoped it would be Portunista.

It was Dagon.

"How did you do it?"

Jian blinked, once or twice, as if he didn't know whom Dagon addressed; and swallowed the meat he was chewing.

"Excuse me?" he asked politely.

"How did you do it?" Dagon repeated, flatly, like a man whom dice have turned against, now facing debt's reality. "How did you escape the pentadarts?"

"I . . . . . . didn't," answered Jian, cautiously.

"So why are you alive?"

Jian considered this a moment; then looked up at Dagon again. "They malfunctioned?" he brightly asked, like a boy with an answer in school that he hopes is right but isn't altogether sure.

Jian returned attention to his meal as if a minor puzzle had been adequately solved. Dagon mumbled to himself—"Malfunctioned . . . yeah . . . that's it . . . a malfunction . . . of course . . ." And since he drifted into silence shortly afterward, maybe he did convince himself of this.

No one else said anything, until the meal was over.

Then after finishing, Jian stood up, stretched, yawned, and said, "Well!—we've had a busy day! Since I don't have a shirt anymore, I think I'll go curl up beneath a blanket, on one of those grassy beds . . . what did you call them?"

"Quitches," I answered.

He yawned again. "Quitches," he repeated. "See you all tomorrow!" He walked down the stairway landing hall. "I guess I'll try *this* one . . ." He chose the room next to the upward stairs. "Oh . . . has anyone claimed this room already?" He turned toward us deferentially, blinking sleepily as we watched him.

"Aren't you worried a Roguent might attack you if you're by yourself?" Gaekwar asked, quietly.

Jian smiled. "I haven't seen Rogue Agents here, or even any evidence that they've been here. Have you?"

"*I* would've thought a pile of Qarfax-dust would count as evidence!" Dagon sneered.

"Really?" Jian inquired. "So, what part of that suggests a Rogue to you?"

Dagon began to retort—then stopped.

"Mmm-hmm," nodded Jian. "Here we are, in the tower of a Cadrist who experimented and researched, installing confusing and lethal mechanisms, *and* who had expected an attack, while his peers were certainly fighting one another. I repeat: do we have *any* positive evidence that a *Rogue Agent* killed Qarfax? Any *positive* evidence that a Rogue has *ever* been to this Tower?"

This would have helped me feel better about our chances of surviving overnight.

Except for how the conversation ended.

"Are you saying you don't *believe* in Roguents?" Dagon tried regaining some of his sneer.

Jian stopped smiling.

One old sconce-torch smothered on itself, near the hallway end, flickering shadows over Jian.

Watching us. Watching us, watching him.

"Do I believe that Agents of the Eye rebel against Him?" Jian answered softly. "Yes. I do."

I tried to swallow; my throat was dry. I wonder: do we, even we of the Guacu-ara such as I who ought to know better, slur the descriptions of such creatures so that we will not have to face the implications—that even lords of Heaven might rebel . . . ?

"Do I believe in Rogue Agents?" And Jian slowly shook his head: "No. I do not."

He turned away from us, to his chosen room; and put his hand upon the latch . . . and paused.

Looking down, at an angle, as if into a distance, he added,

"At least . . . not anymore."

He went into his chosen room, closing the door behind him.

The silence settled around us thickly—silence within the crackling of the fire.

The silence of an eternal burning.

Sometimes, mundane realities save us from a morbid introspection. My bladder needed relief.

Saying nothing, I walked the stairway hall; into the flickering shadow.

I do not remember what I thought, when I passed Jian's room.

Turning to the right, I walked downstairs into the 'basement'.

Normally, it would be foolish to relieve myself into a well from which I would later be drawing drinking water; but now I know why Qarfax had told us we could: the rushing river at the bottom carries all our waste away, quickly and efficiently, constantly refreshing.

Then I realized, I was relieving myself into a tesser.

The strangeness and disparity *was* worth a chuckle; and that dispersed the darkness, somewhat.

I finished; and then I said, "You may come downstairs." Had I heard the boots, despite the rumbles and cascades below? Or had I sensed the presence in some other way—as one of the Guacu-ara?

I don't know. I know I suspected and hoped that I knew, who would come down the stairs.

I was right.

Portunista carefully climbed, down the stairs of extruded stone, steadying with her back to the outer wall. She sat on a lower stair; her soft boots dangled over the floor.

"Yes?" I asked, knowing what she would discuss, but wondering how she would choose her path. I walked across the room to her, kneeling two stairs lower; I wasn't looming over her nor was I sitting much beneath her.

I could look into her face . . .

She didn't speak. I waited.

Then she said:

"Seifas . . . what are errants?"

I watched her face so carefully . . .

"Errants are men or women, commissioned by the Eye Himself, typically through a dream."

" . . . why?"

"Usually, to find something. No . . ." I cast my memory back to certain classes given in the Hunting Cry. "To *search for* something. The errant is given no guarantee to find it; but the search itself would serve for other purposes."

"Are they always . . . sent . . . to search for something?"

"Perhaps they aren't. I don't know," I honestly answered. "I suppose it could be a task of any sort."

I watched her as she thought her next question through.

"What are the signs that a man . . . a person . . . is an errant?"

I heard her lapse, but managed not to smile.

"Errants are men and women only, such as you or I," I said. "Not even a mage or warrior neccessarily. A baker or a tavern-keeper might be called to serve."

This surprised her, I could see—hadn't she heard the stories?

But then she added, "Even clowns, I suppose."

I hardly dared to breathe. "Yes," I said. "I suppose."

"There are no signs by which they may be recognized?"

"They are always difficult to kill," I told her softly. "*Very* difficult—whether battlemage, or baker."

"Why?" she asked, like a child, listening to the stories of the sky.

"The Eye Himself has chosen them, and so protects them. It would hardly do to set a person to a special task, and then that person prematurely die!"

"They cannot die or be killed or be defeated?"

"They can fail—if they choose to fail. Or they may be defeated, as the Eye allows some plans of His to be defeated, in order to protect His goals in other ways.

"Even so—if I fought against an errant, I would expect to badly lose.

"Even if he was only a clown."

"Do they die?" she asked.

I looked her in the eyes, and said: "In all reliable stories I know, the errant *always* dies—accomplishing the purpose for which he, or she, is called."

I saw this hit her like a slap.

"They live so that they may die. They expect to die at any time. Not a bad way to live, once one becomes accustomed to it . . . to die for a purpose . . ." I drifted into musings of my own.

We sat in silence another minute; then she stood to leave. "Is there anything else?" she asked, already turning to walk upstairs.

"Magical force will usually fail, when applied directly to an errant."

She froze on the stair; I heard her breathing stop.

"I don't know why," I added.

She didn't look back to me; although she moved her head.

"Seifas . . . you *know* those generators weren't malfunctioning."

I nodded. "The bolts could shred a chair and shirt, but not the man behind them."

She walked upstairs again; so she didn't see my smile.

I wondered—I wonder: for her sake, I hope she accepts the hope that has been given to us.

And yet . . .

What if I am wrong?

. . . what does it mean—to believe, and not to believe?

CHAPTER 33

Dark clouds billow over Dichosa, my beloved; although some gleams of gold shoot through to touch the city on occasion.

In her upper room, the Empress thinks back seven years and more—back, to her first night in Qarfax Tower.

Yesterday she glided through the glassless window of her fana . . . and then stared, blankly, for an hour at the clay.

She had done the same the day before.

Two days now, without a single new word engraved in the clay.

Nevertheless: she remains determined to compose her testimony. So she reaches out once more—to write of a betrayal.

❖ ❖ ❖

On that night, I paced a dead man's room, thinking on a man who wasn't dead but lay asleep instead, below me on a bed of quitch.

How should it be, that he could sleep in satisfaction on some dirt that any vagrant might acquire—for I was sure his sleep was sound and full—while I, who claimed a bed of kings, could only circle restlessly?!

Bah—I would *plunge* into my *own* bed I had won with sovereign effort, and be comfort to *myself* . . . !

But, although I paused to do just that, the bed lay cold and empty still. The sheets and downy pillows and the firm supporting mattress—weren't *alive*.

I saw and felt instead, the mossy living grass.

I'd slept on quitch before, resenting it as being beneath ambition.

And yet, I'd always slept upon it well.

The simple grass had given comfort, despite how I despised it. Yes . . . comfort and enjoyment in its gift of sleep, two living things together in a harmony . . .

Instead I'd gained my dead ambition: I would be the only thing that mattered in my bed.

And with that thought, another thorn was sticking in my mind. I had discovered, earlier that evening: if I mattered only to myself, then nothing mattered, even my own self. The fear of life and death provided by that revelation still was curdling on my tongue. Now I sought to overcome this fear.

When had I become aware of that despairing knowledge?

The first time I had thought that Jian was dead.

Why had *that* affected me in such a way?!

Because . . . to Jian, I mattered.

He gladly risked his life for me—with no regrets, with no coercion, no compulsion, nothing to gain for himself by doing so . . .

not even expecting thanks.

I had never *mattered* to a man like that, before.

To overcome my fear of life and death, I had been driven to convince myself *I mattered:* that my wishes were sufficient to establish such a truth.

But, I had failed. If I hadn't mattered to someone else, then I would have lost, and would have *been* lost, whether I had lived or died.

Jian had shown that I, I myself, truly mattered.

and . . . Jian mattered to me.

This was *deeply* bitter.

I preferred to be a fortress to myself. To be, instead, invested in *another's* value, left me open to attack!

And yet I still could taste the fear I'd felt: when I had seen a point, itself, has no true strength. A single point can't even claim existence!—except by postulation, by the *grace*, of something other than that point.

So: it was weakness, or else . . . what? *More* weakness, in dependence . . . ?

No! I was *strong!* I *had* defeated Qarfax's traps, through my strength of mind and body! That was something to be *proud* of, something to set against my prior despair . . . !

But then, why *hadn't* I been strong, earlier, in those forests? Yes, I had succeeded in slaying some avians. But my attitude, and the meaning of my accomplishments, had been completely different—for my victories against them would have been completely worthless, even if I had defeated them all.

Yet my victory over the generators *mattered;* and *would* have mattered even in my death. So, where was the difference?

Jian had shown I mattered, but in *both* the cases—so *that* was not the crucial factor.

But now I remembered: after Jian's apparent second death, I *had* admitted to myself, however vaguely:

Jian mattered to *me.*

So. There was strength in this, after all.

I wasn't satisfied. Strength there might be, but also terrible danger to myself. I would be vulnerable.

Most of all, to Jian himself.

What if he betrayed me?

How could I ensure that Jian would love me?

And here was the nub, at last! I *wanted* to be *loved*—worse, I had discovered that I *needed* to be loved.

As a pretense of something to do, rather than think about that, I stripped from out of my unclean clothes—sodden still with blood and sweat as well as water—and flung a wardrobe open.

A royal robe commended itself. I tried it on. Very satisfactory: its quilted fabric and fur would soon be warmed; and in the nearby mirror I could see a queen—a furious queen!

A queen within a dead man's robe, too many sizes large for her, like playing dress-up . . .

Never mind. It was mine. I didn't need a mirror.

I wrapped the robe around myself, and cinched it up, and then resumed my march around the empty bed, dragging the tail of the robe behind me like an outraged bride.

How could I ensure that Jian would love the way I wanted to be loved? *That* way lay more safety; a measure more of control. I would minimize my vulnerability.

The simplest answer was: make him addicted to me. Then I would be indispensable. I knew how to do that.

And after all, wasn't this what I had wanted down in my heart for weeks?

Good! I thought. *Everything* has led to this. *Now* I could satisfy my wishes in such a way that wouldn't make me seem a fool, and which would serve me properly!

But, I was still a fool.

CHAPTER 34

Now I had made my decision; and I would act.

I plotted my assignation, as if an assassination.

Part of me recognized that I was about to attempt a treacherous thing. Furthermore, Jian himself would probably try to reason me out of it. After all, he wasn't Dagon.

Who raised another consideration: I wanted to get this done with minimal interference from anyone who might be feeling possessive, resenting the new competition.

And I didn't want to wait any longer.

Sneak in tonight, accomplish the deed without detection—except by Jian, of course—and then . . .

Well, I wasn't thinking of that far ahead. I wanted it done. I wanted what I thought was safety, only on my terms.

And, I wanted the satisfaction.

I jotted an Airebelle onto myself, leaving the usual puncture behind me; then I left the room of Qarfax, ghosting silently down the narrow stairs, excitement bringing alive each nerve, matching my wits against my men.

I passed the next landing down; the laboratory's two gaping maws held no more attractions for me that night.

Here was the garrison landing. I stopped, several steps above it. *He* lay just beyond the inner wall. If only I could tesser . . . ! But I couldn't, yet. I would have to improvise.

And I could do that very well.

My only real concern was if a man came up the basement stairs, while I was making preparations. That would wreck my plan—until another night—but otherwise would not be problematic. I would simply drop my Airebelle, in case they somehow sensed a special silence, and then inform whoever came upstairs, or round the corner, I meant to use the well-room for a privy. The robe would be embarrassing, but it *could* be easily justified for what it was: a substitute for filthy clothing.

Doing what I wanted without the others knowing I had gone down to *him,* would be harder.

I jotted a sliver of Silveraire, silently within my belle, edging it round the corner, angling it like a mirror.

Dagon stared, ready to kill.

I jumped, too shocked to even defend—!

. . . then I realized: he wasn't moving. Except for his eyes.

A moment later, I figured it out: in my nervousness, I had smeared the normal alignment of Aire and basic materia, so that now it magnified what I was seeing. The mirror was showing me Dagon, as he sat beyond the firepit, keeping our first watch.

I tested my discovery, over long minutes. I had little else to do—with Dagon so alert, I couldn't slide into the garrison room where Jian was sleeping, or even try another tactic to disguise my entrance.

So I watched, at first impatient—and then with curiosity.

Dagon only moved his eyes, from one target to another: dark, murderous eyes. All his face seethed with hate; aimed at every door behind which other men were sleeping.

He also looked across the pit sometimes, where Seifas lay asleep; his back was set to the fire, resting his head on something not a pillow.

Did Dagon look at *me* like that, when *I* could not see him . . . ?

I shivered; and resolved to never fall asleep again with Dagon in a room . . .

Surely Seifas couldn't know about this concentrated hate, and also sleep so soundly. Or, did Seifas even care? I myself would not be fool enough to stab a sleeping juacuar; but what stayed Dagon's hand? Fear of being discovered?

Probably fear of Seifas, I decided. Such a murder would be, paradoxically, easier to get away with while in camp.

But, Dagon sent his gaze most often, and most harshly, toward the door of Jian. Not surprising, given their relationship since Jian's arrival; also only likely to increase with Jian's infatuation with me—which is how I saw the matter, and how I wanted to have it seen. When that happened, I expected to need to murder Dagon, or arrange to have it done, lest he should cause me problems. The other men I could trust to keep their place.

However, this begged a question: why had Dagon *not* decisively struck already against the man whom he *already* had hated the most?! The fair man posed a *far* less physical threat than one of the Guacu-ara!

. . . was Dagon simply scared of *everyone?*

I pondered this; and waited for his watch to end.

I came to no conclusions on that night—or none that I admitted to myself.

But now I can see; and now I admit, what I *could* have seen, but didn't want to see:

when one's *self* has become an inflammation, then every *other* self can only be feared—and hated as an enemy.

how well I know this, from experience . . .

CHAPTER 35

Time passed, slowly. But it passed.

I saw Seifas wake. Dagon reacquired his normal nonchalance; although I now could see the signs beneath.

Dagon chose a room, and closed its door, leaving Seifas to keep his watch alone.

Seifas stretched, near the firepit, on the floor, having pulled out a tiny vial from a belt-pouch. Opening his 'pillow' . . . Ah! An answer to a mystery!—a leather-covered book! He must have kept it in a trouser pocket. From within the book he picked a writing bone, dipping it into the vial.

Seifas kept a journal.

He lay on his stomach, leaving the healing scars upon his back to open air, his nose almost on the page, his hand precise and quick despite dim light—too dim for any normal man to read and write, but not for juacuaran eyes.

Why so dim, I wondered . . . ? Because, only one torch remained alight; and as I watched, it also sputtered and then extinguished. Older torches needed some attendance—but Dagon had been too intent on his hateful thoughts; and now the great and cautious juacuar was too intent on writing his book!

Still, a meager firepit glow would be enough to show me, if I walked onto the landing. Seifas quickly settled into a habit: write one page, look around, and then begin another. Plenty of time.

Gemalfan, in his disciplex, had written of an incidental property of Silveraire—one that now would serve me well.

I waited, until Seifas gave the area a piercing gaze.

Then I quickly jotted a plane of Silveraire, halfway down the hall, toward the firepit, filling it in from floor to ceiling and wide from wall to wall. With my smaller mirror still in place, I now could see the dim reflection of my section of the hall. I specially bound the jotting, securing the image of my hallway half, and then revolved my plate around its axis, like a cattle gate.

When Seifas next looked up, he still would see my hallway section—just as he had seen it before!

True, he *would* be seeing it reversed, as with a normal mirror; but in a symmetric hallway such a difference wouldn't be instantly notable. A close inspection might have shown the stairways leading up and down had now reversed positions; but in chancy light this seemed unlikely. Besides, it only had to last for half a minute.

I walked around the corner, to Jian's door.

What did I feel?
Too many things.

I placed my left hand near the handle of his door, and bound on it another, larger Airebelle—for of course my current sphere was pooling on its surface, not surrounding it. With my other hand I pushed the latch, opening the door within its silent belle.

Dark inside—too dark for me to see. Now I had to take a risk. I whistled up a wisp, but fashioned it in the new alteration I had discovered that evening.

It burst into its existence, but not brightly; glowing as faint as starlit mist instead. Showing Jian asleep upon the quitch.

No furniture to speak of; only wooden framing in the far left corner, holding the grass and patch of dirt upon which Jian was sleeping. The frame was long, but wasn't wide enough for two.

Not under normal circumstances, anyway.

I stepped with care into the room, then shut the door; and as it neared my un-moved wrist, I dropped its belle and yanked my hand inside, gambling that the small remaining "snick" would not be heard by Seifas—nor by Jian.

Now that I was in, I dropped the Silveraire plate outside: at worst the juacuar would only see the firelight stretch a little further down the hall.

I was in. I deeply breathed.

My conscience twinged; I tromped it underfoot.

I had come too far, I told myself.
I owed this to myself, I told myself.
Jian owed this to *me,* I told myself.

Then why not let him choose to give it?
Because I want it *now,* I told myself.

I am so ashamed, for what I did that night.

CHAPTER 36

Short pegs hung above the bed along the wall. I jotted a larger Airebelle upon a peg, filling most of his room, and the next one over, leaving one small cleft for us to breathe fresh air.

Still he slept.

I released the bind upon my smaller belle. He would hear me now, and might awake too soon unless I acted carefully.

Still he slept.

One more jotting . . . and this I wanted Jian to hear.

I started thrumming, deep in my throat.

Yes, this sound was more than any human might emit in certain situations—just as stories say of magi. When combined with jotting, it can . . . interfere . . . with the intents of other people.

I would render Jian susceptible to my suggestions . . .

But, then I stopped myself.

Not for shame of what I wished to do, I am ashamed to say. Something else occurred to me.

Errants, Seifas had said, resisted magic. And Jian had been immune to pentadarts. No matter; I knew other ways to reach my goal.

No matter.

With those two words, I threw away what I had learned that night about reality—because the implications didn't comfort me.

I wanted to matter to Jian. It mattered to me that I matter to Jian.

I refused to think of what Jian might think, about the matter.

I lay myself, covering us within a dead man's robe, to betray the fairest man I ever knew.

I began.

Jian turned and stretched beneath me. That was fine.

Jian opened his eyes as he awakened to me. That was fine.

I raised myself above him; showing him my *self* in my pride.

Jian's eyes focused onto me. That was fine.

And then he spoke.

As he opened his mouth, fear sliced into me.

What I wanted, was for him to worship me.

What I feared, was that he would repudiate me.

What he said, was:
"So.
"This is how it is to be."

That was not exactly fine. But it would do.

And then he pulled me down to him.
And he was glorious.

Soon I had lost my grip on everything—but on him.
I didn't care.
I curled up in the darkness, safe and warm away from the world,
where there was only healing and nothing that ever would hurt me.

CHAPTER 37

I slowly awoke; feeding my soul on comfort and safety.
I *mattered*.

Then my eyelids popped in shock.
Under the door, light was seeping.
Daylight.

Jian's breathing changed beneath me as he awoke as well.
Daylight. This would be embarrassing.
To put a bold face on it would be better, I decided.
But, not just yet.
I kissed him on his nose.
"You should smile like that more often—" but I put my finger on his lips to hush him, holding him close before I faced the world again . . . drinking our contentment.
Then I faintly whispered, "Quiet, Jian. I need to think." Wasn't there some other way to save my dignity, without parading brazenly—?

Jian replied, in equal whisper,
"As you wish, my wife."

I heard my throat clearly click.
"What?!" That was what I tried to say. A dehydrated throat, belated prudence, and a dozen wild emotions, all conspired instead to make a quiet croak!
Jian began to chuckle. "I'd best get up before you change back into a frog, I guess!"
He disentangled from our couch, from his thin blanket, and from my thicker borrowed robe . . . a minute earlier, he would have found it far more difficult extricating himself from *me!*
I dared not speak: my brain was reeling, trying to sort out too many things—be furious, or laugh at his naivete?!—and I would *not* announce my presence here, if possible.
Jian quickly dressed, and buckled on his shortsword. It *did* look good on him . . . but I was *not* about to sanction this idea of being *married*, of all things!
Still, he had me at a disadvantage: I couldn't upbraid the impossible man without alerting all the others that I had gone to *him* last night!
Yet he somehow understood my wish for some discretion. Edging to the door, he put his ear against it, nodded, and then tiptoed back to me again, smiling with his blasted cheerfulness!

He didn't touch me—I suppose my glare had *some* effect!—but he whispered: "They're eating breakfast around the fire. Be prepared; I've got a plan."

With a wink, he listened at the door again—probably to ascertain that someone wasn't passing by—and then he quickly, smoothly left the room with minimal movement of the door.

I stood and cinched my robe around me—*my* robe now, most certainly, and *not* Qarfax's! I eased to the door.

"Good morning! We made it through the night together after all!" Coming from another man, *this* boisterousness *might* have seemed suspicious—

"Look!" shouted Jian. "A Rogue Agent!"

I nearly bit my tongue: he sounded so sincere, I almost thought he meant it! Then I cursed his foolishness: now their attentions would be surely redirected, but only for half a moment—nowhere near enough for me—

"Ha-HAAAH!" Jian's cry receded down the hall; over frantic scuffles and a muffled comment on his mother—"FIEND!" he thundered. "YOU MUST DIE!!"

I threw his door as quietly as I could, and with the briefest right-hand glance, I heeled myself around the corner to my left and up the stairs.

My glance was enough to see that Jian had drawn his sword and leapt the firepit, scattering men behind his charge downhall.

I surged up stairs, two at a time. Below I heard Jian laughing.

"I'm sorry for the joke," he gasped. "You ought to see your faces!" And now I could hear him *folding* up in laughter, bouncing joy up stony stairs, echoing in my heart: I couldn't help but laugh a little, too.

I reached my room—*my* room now; it hadn't felt that way the night before. Perhaps because the clear light shone through sashes of the window slits.

Or, because Qarfax's ashes now were smeared across the floor . . .
my breathing froze against my dash upstairs—

—then I laughed in horrified amusement: from the streak's direction, and my memories of my leaving, I had dragged the robe across his ashes in my haste!

I almost disrobed instantly; but too late now for squeamishness: I had been quite intimate in and with this robe already!

What I really wanted, I decided, was a bath. Some breakfast, too, but first a bath. Last night I had observed, although I hadn't cared to notice, a bathing basin made of brass, sitting on a rug of fur.

I wasn't keen on lugging water buckets up those stairs; but then I realized, that such a clever magus who enjoyed his comforts, might have made provision for this already.

Putting some trust in him—a trust established on his lethal ingenuity!—I searched the bathing tub more closely. Soon I found small sigils traced above a pair of holes, near the top-edge of an end. They matched with two brass pipings down the outside of the tub and through the rug, into the floor.

Excellent! I'd heard of tubs like this, although I hadn't yet enjoyed one! A minute of experimenting; and then a stream of steamy water poured into the bath. A nearby dresser carried bathing implements, and even towels.

I set aside my robe, and climbed into the basin, leaning back to let the rising water slowly cover me. I broke some soapbark chips to swirl for froth, luxuriating in the smell and feelings, sighing in contented closing eyes . . .

Someone walked into the room.

Before I could yelp—

"Good morning, Portunista!" Jian announced; his voice shone like the morning sun outside. "Oh, that's a good idea! Congratulations!" I suppose he meant my bath.

"What are you *doing* here?!" I sputtered—but then I saw the answer.

"I brought breakfast!" he smiled, just like a child who had fixed up food for parents on a holiday.

I couldn't find sufficient phrases for a proper cursing. Partly, it was difficult to do so in the face of his affection for me. Also, I *did* want to eat some breakfast.

And our love's euphoria had not *entirely* vanished; the water was reminding me, with rising splendid power!

On the other hand: I suspected why, from his perspective, he had brought the food. And he might as well have given proclamation we had spent the night together!

My imagination melded these disturbing thoughts.

"Jian," I said, attempting calmness. "Did you tell anyone downstairs that you were bringing breakfast to your wife?" He was placing barely balanced meats and travel-bread upon a tray he'd found across my room.

"Ah, um . . ." He looked up somewhat vaguely as he thought about it. "I don't believe I told them I was bringing food to *you*. Although, why *would* I take two breakfast servings up those stairs?" he grinned at me. "And since I didn't mention you, the answer to the second question also is a 'no.'"

I sighed. The sizzling breakfast meat, the aromatic soapbark, and the water's rising kisses—all were eroding steadily any ability to think. The fact that Jian was in the room—my room—*our* room?—wasn't helping, either.

"Jian, please; I have a favor." There wasn't any use in shouting at the impossible man. "*Don't* tell anyone that we are . . . wife and husband . . ." I managed not to lose my temper. "Not until I give permission."

And he shrewdly looked at me.

And I knew my ploy had been transparent.

But I didn't care—so long as he would do what I requested.

"Okay," he answered quietly. "I will not tell anyone, until you give me your permission."

Again I sighed, and leaned back in the bath. Clearly, he would be firm about our being married, even if only in private.

Then my mouth began to water for the stronger smell of food, as he walked to set the tray upon the bathing cabinet.

"You know . . ." I heard him judiciously say, "that basin looks as though it could *very* comfortably hold *two* people."

And, as usual, he was correct.

Afterward . . . I reclined upon him in my bed, looking at the sunlight playing on the ceiling overhead . . . not focusing on anything, just looking. *My* bed now—not a dead man's bed. The bed itself no longer seemed a cold dead thing; two living things now shared it in their mutual contentment. Had our spirit passed into it . . . ? I lazily perused. And what about the quitch? I once had heard that quitchgrass had a spirit of its own, to share with those who slept upon it. Was that supposed to be good or bad? Probably good. It certainly seemed to *feel* very good. Better than this bed? Or only different? *Something* about that grass was bothering me. I couldn't hold the thought; I let it drift away, and didn't worry. The thought had come already more than once.

The light's reflection from the polished floor, diffused, had crossed the ceiling with the passing sun. *Now* the men would have conclusive evidence: taking extra food upstairs was one thing; staying there for hours was another.

I vaguely cursed beneath my breath; but this annoyance couldn't breach contented joy. Let them know. At least their confirmation now would come from Jian's own coming up to *me*. So, it didn't matter.

No, better: *everything* mattered now. Now it was *fine* for everything to matter.

This trace of a thought reminded me of husbandry, somehow. My satisfied inertia dampened even that annoyance. I am brigade commander—and soon I shall be a *queen,* I dreamily thought. I could have a consort. That pleasantly settled *that* ridiculous notion.

I breathed, enjoying breathing; and I shifted once or twice, enjoying movement. Everything was very satisfactory. I was *glad* that I had gone, to do what I had done— I ignored the base intentions for my going—I was *glad* I hadn't tried to sleep alone in this dead bed, and joined with Jian instead upon his bed of living grass.

And now my bed was also full of life.

And Jian had come to *me*.

The grass would do much better in this room, I thought. I'd order Jian to bring the frame and sod. Or cut new sod, if necessary, since the grass must now be dead from want of light and water after spending seasons in that room. Here it would surely grow, lush and green—with water from the basin, even!

The grass . . . *Something* about that grass was bothering me. I couldn't hold the thought; I let it drift away, and didn't worry. The thought would come again; for it had come again already more than—

"Jian!" I shouted—or I gulped, as panic cut through bliss. I bolted upright on the bed, and looked down at the startled man.

"Someone has *been* here!" I exclaimed. " . . . and planning to return!"

SECTION FOUR

COMPLICATIONS

CHAPTER 38

I look forward thirty years and more, beloved.

Beneath a summer sky, a caravan carefully wends its way, curving gently around green hills, northward.

Every night its leader, Khase Sage, consulted maps; some as old as he, others far more ancient, a couple drawn more recently by scouts or curious locals hewing their livelihood here along the edge of the dangerous Middlelands. He also wrote, comparing notes from earlier travels, grading and compiling sources. When a work had satisfied him, he would pen it in his Chronicle. Along with Khase acolytes traveled: quick riding, lightly armed, these young men and women made their copies of his work and carried finished entries back along the trail, to any near Orthogoni; returning once again, to serve their master.

Eventually, the caravan arrived: entering in between tall ridges of a certain tree-filled valley. Khase, standing in this southern gap, looked north: higher ridges clasped the valley east and west; snowcapped mountains crowned it to the north.

The sage could barely sleep that night. Another bit of data, for the sake of his completeness, lay within a walking reach.

A beaten trail led through the southern pass . . . and here, a site of some brigade's encampment: rusted metal fragments and some charcoaled pits attested this.

The aging man strode northward through the trees. Yes, he saw, honey trees grew thickly in this area, and showed the scars of tapping long ago for syrupy sap. A wide stream flowed, down and north nearby.

It ended in a lake.

The caravan commander walked up next to Khase Sage, and whistled in commiseration.

"Sorry, Exemplar. We came out all this way, 'n' everything *looked* all right. But, I suppose it's a bust."

"Not true, Commander!" Khase's voice rang piercing bright, very fitted for a lecture hall. He stood with fists upon his hips, and smiled in satisfaction. "I expected this *precisely!*"

"But . . . this here's a *lake!*"

"Yes; and the maps all told us we would find a lake, did they not?"

"Well . . . yeah, I guess they did. It's just . . . I thought . . . It's not a lake in th' stories!"

"Yet the Journal and the Testimony clearly indicate that it *had been* a lake!—one that Qarfax probably renovated for himself."

"Oh. I s'ppose they *do* say that, now that I think about it . . . But, why would it be a lake *again?*"

"Send your men to bring our skiff from its wagon, good Commander, and together we may find the answer."

"Hm." He gave the order to a yeoman. "I *thought* you might be usin' that to, I dunno, go down a river or somethin'. Guess I didn't put th' pieces t'gether." The senior officer paced back up the nearby river edge while waiting. Khase joined him.

"What do you see?" asked the sage, teasing with an edge of expectation.

The soldier snapped his fingers. "Th' lake is backin' up the river, from th' water pressure. There's *dead* grass under th' water here!"

"Very good eye, Commander Trent! And so this also tells us—what?"

"Th' stream was once a lot less wide—b'cause it used to drain out fast! It wasn't bein' backed up by th' lake."

"Exactly."

"Although," Trent mused, "I woulda thought th' grass'd be long gone by now."

"As usual, Commander, your good eye has found a detail of importance," Khase sincerely said; though also with amusement in his *own* eyes at his joke. "Yet the grass *is* dead. So, when did the lake fill up?"

"Over years. It reached its current level years ago, backin' up th' river *then,* but not b'fore."

"Which means, there have been changes in the water level, fitting with a significant incline beginning here along the present water's edge."

Trent whistled once again. "But . . . the books *do* say the lake was here originally, 'fore Qarfax came . . . assumin' this here *is* th' spot."

"Good man!" Khase laughed. "Best to *not* assume ahead of verifying. That is why we brought the skiff! Go on," he urged his friend.

"So, why's there grass here now? I mean, back then? Qarfax woulda found th' river here when he arrived to build his tower, right?"

"Very, very good," agreed the sage. "Observe these rocks and ledges: they smoothly fit the river's shape, and so they *must* have been eroded by it—which takes time. Yet the river only *recently* became this wide, as shown by this dead grass beneath the water, as you found. When Qarfax made his changes to the lake, he *would* have left a muddy swath behind: you're quite correct. But!—grass grows faster on rich mud, than it decays within a fishless river!"

Trent scratched his head. "'s gone by me, Exemplar . . . Though yer right about the fish. There ain't no minnows, even."

"You did quite well, Commander. I myself had not considered how important dead grass underwater here would be for validation."

The soldier nodded at this compliment. Minutes later, other troops arrived and quickly got the small boat ready for deployment.

"Come along, Commander!" Khase hopped into the skiff. "Let us find the answer to your mystery!" Trent gauged by eye the sage's fitness—the other man was twenty years his senior—but after all, the skiff could only hold two men. Trent decided he could row, if the sage became exhausted; and besides, he wondered what the sage was hinting they would find.

"I am glad the water is so clear," said Khase as they smoothly skimmed across the surface.

"Even so, I sure can't say that *I'm* seeing much, Exemplar."

"Not surprising," grunted Khase as he rowed. "The Emerald Army probably left some traces of their camp, but I doubt that we could see those traces from this height above the dell—sloping deeper down below us, if we *have* located Qarfax Valley."

"Then what're we doin' here, Exem . . . ?" Trent's voice trailed away.

"Eh?" Khase shipped his oar. The officer had also ceased to row, and now was peering down into the lake with his good eye. "Tell me what you see, Commander," Khase grinned.

"A floggin' massive pile o' rocks . . ." the soldier's voice was hushed in awe. He looked around to ascertain where it was lying underneath them. "I . . . I hadn't thought it out, I guess . . ."

"It *can* be somewhat difficult, to keep in mind the *implications* of the story: how the pieces fit together. Even sages have that problem; which is why we go to look." Khase mopped his brow while carefully leaning above his own skiff-side. "There *should* be, not a tower, but the *ruins* of a tower, under the middle of a lake, which until recently was *not* a lake, yet once had been a lake before! And, here we are."

While Khase studied all the shapes below, Commander Trent looked up from deep-drowned stones, to all directions round: the lake, the distant wooded ridges, the northern mountaintops—he saw the mouths of two more rivers pouring through the trees.

And he knew—he simply *knew*—that even though he couldn't see it, there *would be* an eastern river. He could reason out exactly where to look, and didn't doubt that he would find it.

But, he *would* go look; to consummate his reasoning. And he knew how he would feel when he had found it:

Like a sage.

Like a child.

"It's like . . . like bein' in a *legend*," whispered Trent. "Like I could touch it. Like it's touchin' *me*."

"Legends are our history, Commander. Legends touch us every waking hour, and within our dreams as well. That is why we should respect them—and *remember* them," Khase added, with a gentle criticism.

"Rotten blood . . ." Trent felt a tear rolling down his face.

For several minutes they stared into the water, with an oar-push on occasion to ensure a better view.

"It's kinda like we're flyin' over history . . . or somethin'. Here we are; perched up in th' sky—'cause back in *that* day this'd've *been* the sky—lookin' down on where those people fought an' died, an' where those monsters almost killed 'em all. And Jian's down there, just a speck beside those things . . . but he's laughin' at 'em anyway, not carin' they were gonna bury him—'cause he was busy doin' what he *always* did, for *her* . . ."

"Thank you, Commander."

Trent looked up, suspecting mockery: but—Khase Sage Exemplar bowed to him most seriously. "*That* is how I should have been considering the remnants we are floating far above. Instead—I am ashamed: for I was only feeling bitter that I cannot go myself to see." He sighed, and looked again. And then he smiled. "I believe I almost see Commander Seifas down there, too . . ."

"When yer ready, Exemplar, let's pull on over to th' eastern lakeside."

"A capital idea! I wish to seek for something there, for validation!"

"Th' river mouth, perhaps?"

"I hadn't thought of that; but, you are right, that *also* would be worth the trip. No, Commander Trent; I was thinking: if we *have* located Qarfax Valley, we *also* should discover some significant remains of fallen timber in the southeast quarter. And the final river mouth should be just north of that direction, too! Shall we look?"

"At once, Exemplar!"

Off they struck, across the lake again.

"You should be a Sage, Commander Trent! I see you have an eye for it!"

The one-eyed soldier laughed, at the joke and at the expectation of another link with history, of being touched by legends.

"Too old to start that now; but, I b'lieve I'll tag along with you awhile!"

CHAPTER 39

"Now, explain again why you would think that someone's coming back?"

Portunista tried to sigh between her gulps of air. But she couldn't fault her 'cowherd' subcommander's gentle sarcasm: after flinging on her still-moist clothes and hurtling down the stairs, she had careened into their midst as they were sitting round the firepit looking bored . . . and *then* had only had the breath to say that someone else had been here and was planning to return.

"The grass," she panted. Jolting from an idle joy into the shock of revelation, plus a dash downstairs—all of this was making her feel ninny-headed. Moreover, she had left them all down here with hardly anything to do, while *she* had been—

"The grass . . . ?" said Othon, prompting her.

"The grass . . ." she said between her breaths, "is *green* . . . "

"The quitchgrass?" This was Jian, arriving more sedately on the landing down the hall behind her. Portunista nodded.

"Well," Gaekwar drawled, "they *say* the grass is always greener on the other side . . . " She snapped a glare around at Gaekwar's smirk; he arched his eyebrows, darting glances clearly aimed at her and Jian.

"You didn't seem to care about the grass last night when we were clearing out these rooms, *Commander*." Dagon scowled like thunderclouds above a cliff. "I guess you've had a closer look since then!"

Exhaling in exasperation, Portunista slammed a nearby door, and plunged into its room.

Jian ambled up the hall; then he casually leaned against a wall with folded arms, and smiled lopsidedly:

"Punkie losers need not apply."

Dagon ground his teeth, and clutched the pommel of his sword. "You little scratworm-colored—"

"One thrust. One parry. No clang," Othon rumbled. "Twice."

Dagon froze.

The fair man seemed relaxed—but *his* hand also rested on his pommel . . .

screeching—!
—everyone jumped—

Except for Jian.

"I wouldn't make her angry," Jian advised. The screeching stopped, then started over, mixed with muttered curses.

Portunista scrabbled backward from the room, bent over low . . .

. . . to drag a frame of quitchgrass, in a scrape along the floor.

She flung a hand triumphantly:
"The grass . . . is *GREEN!*"

"Yes, I must agree with you, Commander," Gaekwar soberly nodded. "The grass *is* green. So?"

"Hmm . . ." Pooralay contemplated this and stroked his chin . . .

—then his eyelids snapped in shock. "Oh, spew . . . !"

Seeing this on someone else's face was worth her efforts, Portunista thought.

The understanding dawned in Seifas, too: "They *all* look green and healthy."

"Every one," she nodded. "Anyone who *had* been paying attention last night would remember it *now* at least," she added, glaring at the Krygian.

He wasn't impressed. "So what?!"

"How long for quitch to wither without water in the dark?" asked Portunista pointedly.

"Uh. . . ." Gaekwar blinked.

"A week." Othon now was catching on.

"Or seven days at most," agreed the juacuar.

"The quitchgrass should be dead, *slopings* ago; but it isn't," Portunista said. "How long ago was it replaced?"

"Only five to seven days," Seifas nodded.

"How many days have *you* been here?" Portunista turned to Pooralay.

"Three. Then yest'rday, and then this mornin' makes a week—more 'r less. Just b'fore I got here. *Blind* m' eyes . . . !" Then, "Wait a minute . . ." he muttered, and tapped his finger on his knee while he considered other implications.

"No one else is here," continued Portunista. "Why would they replace the quitch in sixteen rooms and then depart—unless they were expecting to *return?!* So, *when* can we expect them back?"

"Within a day or two!" Jian was sounding quite impressed. "Perhaps today!"

"Exactly," Portunista said. "No point to cut new sod at *all,* unless you plan to use it—probably sooner than later, hm?"

"We *are* inside a Cadrist Tower, though," Dagon said. "What if Qarfax jotted something on the grass, or scribed some sigils in the frame, or something?"

Portunista started to reply . . . but then she closed her mouth again.

Berating herself, she shut her eyes, and chuffed an Yrthescrution.

She slowly shook her head a minute later. "No, there's nothing there that I can find," she told them, and then she shook her head more quickly as she flushed away materia from beneath her eyelids. "I admit, a jotting *may* still be there—but, should we risk that someone *didn't* cut the sod?"

"It *was* a good idea, however," Jian sincerely said to Dagon; who looked surly at the compliment.

"So!—we can anticipate these people back at any time," the maga moved along. "What *else* can we infer from all of this?"

"There's sixteen beds of 'em, at least; maybe more if there's some couples." Gaekwar couldn't help but smile.

Portunista wasn't amused. "Maybe more if they're a *brigade*. They make their preparations, then they leave, and yet they *don't* go check the *unlocked room* upstairs. Or if they did, they didn't touch a thing. Did any of you notice any looting?"

"I sure didn't!" answered Jian, helpfully.

The maga winced; still she added, "Me neither," a little forcefully, "and I had *lots* of time to look around this morning and last night." That wasn't true, exactly, but it made her point. "They didn't even take Qarfax's rings from his remains."

"The pile looked just the way I left it, after slopings," Seifas verified.

"And yet they're coming back. Back with *who?*" Portunista asked, knowing they would know.

"A mage," Othon said; the maga nodded.

"Or with magi," added Jian.

Portunista blinked—she hadn't thought of that . . . "At any rate, with someone else to further search the Tower—someone who could benefit from taking certain risks, or who would want to see the situation fresh and undisturbed. And *that's* a mage—or magi."

"And at least as many troops again," said Dagon sourly. "I doubt they left their mage-or-magi all alone, out in the wild, while they prepared some beds. No—there must be *several* times as many yet again, or else they might as well have *all* come here at once! And, after all the fighting in the Cadre—well, like Portunista's saying: if we're up against a mage, then we'll be facing a brigade." This earned some nods from everyone; except from Pooralay, who added:

"An' they're comin' from th' west, across th' ridge." The others stared at this announcement. "Hey," he shrugged, "I *know* I wouldn't miss a buncha chunks cut outta sod, out in th' woods. There ain't no grass—or chunks—like that, out in th' *dell* where we can see; an' *I* checked round th' treeline first when I arriv'd."

"I didn't even have the time to do a treeline search." Seifas said this with a pointedness at Portunista.

"Well, there wasn't any ev-i-dence along th' line," the thug continued. "An' I wasn't in a hurry to go pokin' in th' Tower, *specially* not without some signs of what was goin' on inside. So I was quarterin' up th' valley ev'ry day: first th' north, 'cause that was where I meant t' sleep . . . I mean instead of down in th' tent. Nothin'. Checked th' eastern side th' next day; nothin'. I was checkin' south when yous showed up, although I'd made a faster run-through when I got here. An' I know yous drew a blank as well, c'rrect?"

"Only where I wandered east and west across our path into the valley—and that wasn't far," the juacuar reminded him.

"That don't matter," Poo insisted. "Now we're talkin' about a comp'ny at th' least an' maybe a brigade, on th' *march,* an' not too far away already, 'cause their scouts intended to get *back* t' them and then t' *lead* th' whole group *to* th' Tower in a week, week-an'-a-half. Travel time, y'see: back 'n *forth.* Not five-t'-seven days *away.* Th' scouts were gonna meet 'em *three* days out! Y' only got here yest'rday y'rselves; an' I *know* y're smarter than to only have a jaguar scoutin' for y'r whole brigade along y'r march. Did *any* of y'r scouts see *anything?* Nah," he said, "or this all wouldn't be a hairin'-out surprise. They *gotta* be comin' from th' west."

"Tough." Othon stood among his blinking peers, and walked to lift the quitch-frame in the air. It took some effort.

It took *Othon* some real effort!

"Tough," he said again, and thumped it down.

"You mean that they were strong enough to carry *those* things all the way from where they cut them, back into the Tower," Jian inferred. "Hm?" he noticed quizzical looks. "There isn't any dirt in here, upon the floor," he told the others absently. "Those quitch beds have some solid slats beneath them, so they wouldn't dribble dirt as much as fresh-cut sod."

"Point," the thug agreed. "An' no such trail o' crumblies in th' dell. They couldn't altogether hide th' cuts . . . I'm expectin' that we find 'em west . . . but they sure ain't dumb completely."

"*I* would call 'em dumb!" the 'cowherd' said. "Or else they're frightened of their boss. That, or they're fanatics. It'd be a chilly day in hell before I lugged a bunch of sod in wooden boxes through a forest, 'cross a dell, and up those stairs! Just in case you're thinkin' along those lines, Commander," Gaekwar grinned.

She rolled her eyes. "Okay," she said. "One of you must go and bring the troops: after everything I've gone through here, I mean to *keep* this place!" she growled.

"Wait a moment," Seifas cautioned. "Our brigade controls the southern pass; and even though it would be hard for them to hold against a force attacking from inside the valley, *this* would be a *much* worse place for them to make a stand."

"Unless you're in the Tower," Dagon said. "And then you've got a serious advantage."

"Sure—if you're a Cadrist in the Tower!" Gaekwar snorted. "But we can't begin to fit the whole *brigade* in here! And 'ista isn't Qarfax."

"Still," said Portunista—with a glare; she didn't appreciate being reminded that she wasn't so experienced . . . besides, she *had* defeated all those traps . . . !— "we seem to be in much the same position. If the enemy attacks us, thinking they can take the Tower from a handful of defenders, then our companies could hit them from the sides, along with higher-ground advantage."

"Assuming," sniffed the Krygian, "that they're dumb enough to never send a scouting screen."

"Whatever," Portunista sighed. "*Let* them notice our brigade! They'll be less encouraged to attack us with their fullest strength, and we can hold this place with fewer troops! In *any* case, we need to put our soldiers on alert."

"I'll go," the 'cowherd' volunteered, and stood to stretch. "I need a new supply of discs, and even if I thought that blasted door would work again, I'm *not* about to pull them from a bunch of killer birds."

"Hey!" Jian took out a silver kran from a pocket on his belt. "Buy me a shirt?"

Gaekwar winked: "You won't be getting cold at night, I think!"

Jian shrugged and grinned lopsidedly: "I *do* have other things to do. A green shirt, please," he added. "I expect I'm through with red for a while."

"And green won't show up grass-stains easily!" added the lanky subcommander.

"Gaekwar!" Portunista snapped; he jumped a little at her tone and saw her pointing at him. "*You* don't leave until I sort the laboratory. You'll be taking what I pack you with, in case we lose the Tower." *That* evaporated all his smugness . . . !— she was tired of them discussing her in roundabouts.

"Now wait a minute! After fooling around all morning—*not* inside the lab," he added, "*now* you're saying we might be under attack at any moment! We need—!"

"Nope," she firmly cut him off. "You *will* stay *here* one hour, and I'll have you gone by lunch. You," she pointed next to Seifas, neatly squelching Gaekwar's further protests. "You go scout the west; bring Othon, Dagon and the thug."

"They'll see us coming, if they're close already," grumbled Dagon.

"Fine—then kill them! Then they'll know that someone's here who means to fight, so maybe they'll slow down and think it over, giving *us* more time to get our act together. Why are you still here?! Get moving!" she demanded.

"As you wish, Commander," said the juacuar. The others didn't like it, but they went. Good.

"Jian!" she turned.

"Yes, milady?"

Portunista momentarily lost her voice in irritation: he had promised *not* to call her "wife" in public, but "milady" wasn't much improvement.

"Jian!" she said again. "Go do . . . whatever . . . something . . . useful!" What *could* she order him to do . . . ?

"At once, Commander!" Briskly saluting, he spun upon his heel and promptly headed down the stairway hall. At least he seemed respectful; she suspected, though, that he was making fun . . .

"Gaekwar!" barked the maga, stomping past the 'cowherd'—

"Coming, Midama."

She stopped. And turned.

'Dama' was the title of a leader of an army of brigades.

But she could see that Gaekwar wasn't mocking her, although he smiled beneath those long stray locks of hair.

"Be patient," he quietly said, as he passed her with a shoulder-pat. "Whoever may be coming back, he doesn't have our Dama. I bet on us."

He walked upstairs—leaving her remembering his loyalty the night before . . .

. . . and wondering if she would *ever* understand a man at all.

CHAPTER 40

Sixteen eyes watched Seifas and the others leaving Qarfax Tower, my beloved.

Four eyes watched from in the western forest edge. The mismatched studded leather armor of the hidden men reflected minds and bodies worn down densely, like old roots: scraggly, dirty . . . desperate.

"Flamin' bile. We got squatters," mumbled one.

"They ain't all outta that there tent, I'm bettin'," said the other. "Must be more nearby."

"Just venturin' perhaps?"

"Then why ain't they all camped out on th' dell? B'sides, I don't intend t' stick around an' ask that jaguar!"

A spit. "A jaguar's just a man, like anyone else; 'n' they c'n die, like anyone else."

An eyebrow raised. "Them jaguars might be men, but they sure *ain't* like anyone else! I don't care *what* y'tell th' others. I was there when all you did was loot a jaguar's body for that axe; an' I was there when he was killed, which you were *not*. That jaguar company ate up two brigades, like *that!*" A finger snap. "A floggin' Cadrist had t' kill'em, an' *still* they kep' him busy enough t' let *another* Cadrist sneak up close for whackin' *him*. Biggest bloody mess I ever saw . . . You wanna fight th' jaguar, you go on. I'm headin' back."

A snort. "Th' Mad One won't be happy hearin' squatters now're at th' Tower. Person'ly, I'd rather face th' jaguar than th' Mad One."

"*I'd* rather face th' Mad One than th' jaguar!" A pause. "We're so complet'ly thumbscrewed . . . Let's go left. I figure these're scouts for some brigade, an' they'll be campin' south, down near th' pass, more likely'n not. We'll go north around, an' cross th' eastern ridge . . . get outta th' district altogether."

"We could go down an' offer to join."

"An' fight th' Mad One?!"

"Yeah, good point. Okay, let's go, b'fore they figure out we're here."

The two men faded deeper back into the forest, angling northward.

Six eyes also watched from underneath the eastern treeline.

Four of them belonged to soldiers, better armed and armored than the western scouts. Their cloaks were draped around their well-kept darkly painted armament; their steel was dulled by smoke of fires for damping down the sheen.

But every edge was buffed, sharp and razor-smooth.

These two men were watching the dell in confident alertness, ready to strike, ready to wait.

Yet when they eyed the man between them, wariness replaced their confidence.

Artabanus never looked wary.

His scouts perched, ready to dive into battle; but the gaze of Artabanus struck the land already, conquering it. He carried no weapon, wore no armor. Nor did he need them.

"One of the Guacu-ara . . ."

The scout on his left *now* wouldn't wager an ohre on the black-skinned man surviving another week.

"Clearly, he must die," declared Artabanus.

"A juacuar might be of use," suggested the man on his right. "By all accounts, not many have survived."

"He is a threat, for he does not serve me," Artabanus replied. "And should he cease to be a threat by his own choice, then he will have betrayed his former masters. I do *not* keep traitors by my side, especially killers of his caliber." Artabanus flicked his unblinking gaze to the man on his right—who swallowed.

"Clearly," the scout agreed, "he must die. Shall I slay him myself, Midomo?"

"If I have commanded, strike him down, though fifty other men may crush your bones beneath their blades. However," he allowed, returning his attention to the dell, "*this* juacuar survived the deaths of all his corps—and so is not within your capability, I think. *I* shall slay him, as I choose."

"But, if you have commanded, I myself shall strike him down," affirmed the scout.

"The other men you see may die or live to serve me. Any magi with them shall be slain at once. There *shall not* be another Cadre War: I shall reign alone." He didn't have to order them to bring him any disciplex or other mage material. They knew.

"*All* power shall be mine."

"All power to Artabanus," they reverently echoed.

"Now, I will return to camp," the magus told them. "If these we see are from a brigade, they likely shall be camping yonder." And he sparely gestured to his left. "I shall commission other scouts to check. You two stay. One shall report to me if necessary. If you find lone scouts, subdue and bring them to me. We shall discover what is in their hearts and minds, by splitting them open."

"As you command," they murmured in response.

He pulled away from their position—a fluid movement, drawing after a breeze that chilled their faces.

Minutes passed before one man would dare to ask the other:

"Shall we be seeing a better future? Or a worse?"

The other man dared not reply the words within his heart. Instead he answered, "I shall live to see the future."

He answered without hope.

Another pair of eyes, across the valley in the northwest corner, locked upon the form of Seifas, disregarding any others.

These two eyes had shadowed the progress of the western brigade; creeping close to hear the talk of scouts, when they had thought that no one else could hear—speech of fear and atrocity.

The Mad One might be such an opportunity as these eyes were seeking. Then again, the hands below those eyes must still survive to pluck away the rotted fruit: evidently now a spider lived within that shell, attracting souls grown drunk on heady fumes exuding from the ruin of the tree—and poisoning what it hadn't yet devoured.

A stronger leader might provide a different opportunity, and difficulty, toward the same result. Behind the eyes, a voice had whispered that another leader might arrive from eastward soon.

Did that leader now wait south, from where the wind was bringing traces of "brigade encamping" to the nose below the eyes?

A leader with a juacuar.

Another different opportunity; but, all combined together in the plan now set in motion by the Way of Things.

Into the wind between the winds, the mind behind the eyes did whisper: brother . . .

Affirmations came at once; eager to complete the number.

By addition? Or elimination?

Any possibility would play into the blue-steel taloned hands.

A Culling of a sort would be enacted here, uncovering the path into the future.

Many screams would echo on that path.

But—there would only be one cry.

Along the northern treeline, four more eyes watched Seifas, in the distance, as he trotted up the dell.

A finger pointed, tipped with stubby bone: "One of the olden killers!"

"An auspicious moment: murderers gather to feast on yonder corpse of stone."

"From the east and west and south, the clay-hearted come."

"The Lord of Slaughter shall be pleased, I think."

"Shall we be pleased to join the feasting? Has he brought us here for this?"

"One monster shall arise to take possession of the power of the corpse of stone."

"And shall be stronger after slaying every rival."

"Yet, as weak at first as having given birth."

"Then we will strike, and trample down the corpse of stone beneath our hooves, so that *no* monster shall possess it; and then we may leave these lands of murderers."

"You see our path correctly, Kambyses. Now, let us tell our tayasi, so they shall know to strike with all our power, pleasing Orgetorix Lord of Slaughter!"

Barest pause. "I most earnestly pray the Great Lord shall be pleased." A knotted forearm slid across one sharpened tusk, to show this deep sincerity.

And back into the northern mountain forests drifted both the Ungulata.

Seifas never saw these things; nor did Portunista; nor did Khase Sage discover them.

But *I* have searched them out, beloved—with my power that destroyed them.

Eighteen eyes watched Seifas and his squad, if *my* eyes also count. How many other eyes, from high above or deep below, were watching history converging on this valley?

One other at the least, that I know.

CHAPTER 41

"Vellum is *heavy*," grumbled Gaekwar.

"So? Walk faster, the sooner to put it down," retorted Portunista.

Noon had been a difficult hour for the maga. Trying to decide what she should keep at hand or send away, while quickly sorting through the wreck upstairs, had gnawed her temper raw.

Thankfully, a pentadart did not transfer much heat when striking; consequently books and scrolls deformed beneath the force of impact, rarely being torn unless their pages caught a shallow-angled strike. Ideally, what *had* been lost could be restored by following the records.

If she kept the Tower.

But, she couldn't count on that. She had to save the most she could—and yet she had to keep at hand whatever might be useful in a fight!

In the end, she packed up any reference to a jott she didn't know and wouldn't likely have the time to study soon—except for what she found that might involve defenses for the Tower. Those she kept aside, to study.

Everyone had brought supplies in sacks, including Seifas; small enough to set aside for fights or moving fast, with nothing sorely missed except for traveling food thereby.

All those sacks had now been packed with books and scrolls.

"You should've gotten Othon," mumbled Gaekwar as he tottered down the narrow stairs: one of the sacks had been the larger man's!—and now held codices which wouldn't fit inside the others.

"You volunteered."

"To go to camp—*not* to be a packing-ass!"

Portunista followed him across the 'basement'. Jian was lying on his stomach, his arms stuck down the well and moving in a minor rhythm. She'd find out what *that* meant in a minute . . .

"Gaekwar!" Portunista cut his next complaining short. "The troops should stay in place, until we've got a better notion of what's happening. Make sure they post patrols and guards, double-thick; and have the sergeants keep their squads together, on alert. At any sign of fighting in the dell, the sergeants should advance their squads, attempt to contact one of us, and otherwise engage the flanks of enemies—for harrying *only*, unless they hear from one of us. If our soldiers march, the vendors must withdraw, back through the pass, and wait for a signal: so make *sure* that they'll stay ready to move. That should keep them out of trouble for a while; they'll also be able to freely flee in case a battle goes too badly. Squads should be assigned to act as scouts for them." She rubbed between her eyes. "I guess that's it. You're free to make whatever other plans seem best within that framework."

"As you say." He sounded somewhat dubious.

"I'm trusting you with this. *You're* the subcommander who can talk with them the best; and they'll do what you command them to."

He rolled his eyes. "Mooooo . . ."

"All right," she smirked. "Go ready the herd, and then return. I need my best men here. And bring my other change of clothes!" Last night's basement dousing couldn't thoroughly clean her shirt and breeches from her sweat and aasvogel blood; and she flatly refused to wear those robes all day.

"Midama." He shortly bowed, and turned to leave.

"Bye, Gaekwar," Jian called out, his arms still in the hole. "Remember: green shirt!"

"Don't get too many grass stains while I'm gone!"

"Jian!" Portunista called, hands on her hips, turning away from her subcommander as he left the Tower.

"ah-hm?" he absently answered, still fixated on the well.

"I told you to do something *useful*, not . . . what *are* you doing?!"

"Checking something. Care to look? I think you'll find this interesting."

Curiosity drew her closer.

Jian, she noticed now, was lying upon the rope, so that it wouldn't slip into the hole. The rope ran back beneath him, coiling briefly on the floor before it rose again back through the hole above.

Most of the rope must already be below, she inferred; the seating plank as well. She carefully knelt and edged to peer into the pit, confirming her conclusions.

Beneath the plank a lit torch hung, tightly tied at midpoint balance to the stapled short cord for the water pail. Jian was swinging the plank, and so the torch, back and forth.

"It's awfully dark down there: *this* way I can see the different parts . . . for about a moment at a time," he sighed.

Portunista whistled up some wisps.

"Oh! Hey, thanks!" Jian smiled. "Of course, we've seen those spindles down there grinding on that band of sigils . . . more precisely, grinding away at four *discreet* locations on that *continuous* band of sigils. Do *you* have any further notion of what that's all about?"

"No, not really. It isn't like I've had much time to think about it recently."

"Well, I have; but I don't know what I'm thinking *of.*" The maga chuckled softly at this somewhat absentminded statement. "Why a continuous band? Why not plates, like on the door upstairs? I'll bet it's making some effect in all directions—like that smaller band down there which generates the tesser. Yet it doesn't seem to be affecting anything within its curve—not the torch and plank; nor us when *we* were down there. But the spindles *are* in constant movement. So, perhaps it's generating something *outwards.* Careful, watch your face." Portunista jumped a little—she had been attending so completely, she had never really noticed he was drawing up the plank while talking to her.

"But," added Jian, as he doused the torch inside the nearby pail, and started switching out the two below the plank, "the band is way down there below the level of the ground. Whatever those things do, it must be generated down there, too: below the Tower, out in all directions."

Something tickled Portunista's memory . . . "Yes, that's right! When I was Yrthescruting yesterday, I sensed an interference—at about that depth."

Jian arched his eyebrows; Portunista nodded, and began another scrution—but . . .

"It isn't any good," she sighed, a minute later. "I can tell that something's there, beneath the dell and centered on the Tower . . . but I *can't* make heads or tails of anything *else* about it!" She flushed out bits of elemental Yrthe from beneath her eyelids.

"Thanks for trying anyway." Jian shrugged; then brightly added, "I'm betting you can figure it out eventually!" Despite her irritation, Portunista had to smile at Jian's undauntable optimism.

"Setting that riddle aside . . ." Jian leaned over the pit again; she followed after. "Look at how those other sets of gears are linking to spindles, leading up through the floor."

She nodded. "Up behind the walls."

"Right. Now, come hear *this.*" He swung himself around to stand, dusted off his knees—Portunista smiled again, at his vague and futile swipes to dislodge bits of wood-dust from his curly chest hair, too—and walked to one point on the curving wall. Following, Portunista saw a brass device, shaped like a forking branch, lying on the floor nearby. He picked this up and handed it to her.

"If you'll put those in your ears, and place the other end on the wall, you'll confirm what we just saw."

She felt her eyebrows climbing up her forehead, as she heard a whirring clearly through the tube.

"Where did you get *this??*"

"From Pooralay, before he left. I asked him his opinion about the shape of the Tower, so he let me borrow this to test for confirmation. Here, there, there and there," he pointed to different places on the wall, while he approached the door. "I marked the spots with talcum powder. Helps with chafing, too," he winked.

"So, there are channels in the walls." She ignored his teasing; although she also flushed, to her annoyance. "I mean the . . . wall? No, the *walls.*"

"Square outside, round inside," Jian agreed, and knelt at the open door to draw the shape into some dusty ground outside. "Leaving channels in the corners, for machinery, sending force to gears above us in the ceiling space."

"So?" He had spent an hour doing *this?!*

"So—wouldn't you say it's overkill? Four complex, and rather large, machinery columns—for a chairlift! Even with a bucket on the bottom of the plank, it doesn't make much sense. But, come upstairs!" He bounded up the narrow stone extrusions; Portunista followed more sedately. Halfway up, she figured out what he was going to show her . . .

"*Two* long hallways." Jian stood on the landing, pointing as he made the counts. "*Four* short halls, because they cross each other. *Four* small rooms per hallway fraction: sixteen rooms altogether. The rooms are all rectangular." Well, true; but *that* was hardly what she figured he was going to show her!

"Now, come in here." And into his room he went. Portunista hesitated, trying to make this match what she had thought that he would say.

"This had better *not* be some elaborate ploy to get me alone in your room again," she dryly told him, hiding her confusion. "We've already wasted time enough this morning."

"As I recall," he lightly replied, "you came down to me."

Portunista gave a gasp. Before she could decide if she should be angry at him—for reminding her? for using this as a retort against her . . . ?!

—he turned to her, and told her:

"You will *never* convince me that we wasted our time this morning."

now she needed to gasp, but couldn't . . .
she opened her mouth to . . . what? say something? kiss him?
she waited in expectation to discover what her mouth would do . . .
"My wife," he added.

And she shut her mouth.

She felt as though he had tricked her somehow. Ignorant, calf-love-struck, naive . . . !!

He turned away, leaving her emotions a tangled mess, leaving her mentally cursing . . . him? Her? Both of them?

"Behind this wall, you can hear the machinery again . . ." Did she detect some disappointment in his voice? He'd better get used to that . . . !

He paused, and sighed, and looked back toward her; in the dimness, she saw only patient expectation.

If she hadn't been wearing the sound-tube, hanging from a string around her neck, she would have walked away, leaving him there. She had lost all interest.

"Although in truth," she would admit years later, "my interest hadn't been *lost*. "I had *crushed* my interest, to avoid the implications of whatever he might say . . ."

But, she still had the tube; and a shred of social propriety urged her to fill the implicit request. So, she set it in her ears again, and walked to put the sensor on the wall.

"Yes, it's the machinery," she sighed.

"Loud or soft?"

"Soft," she answered; then . . . "No." Her brow furrowed; her nose-tip twisted a little, as she contemplated what she heard.

She didn't see that Jian was smiling softly on that quirk of hers, like someone watching a sunrise or a waterfall . . .

"I think . . . I think it's just as loud as behind the wall below. And yet it sounds . . ."

She glanced at him; but by this time he had hidden his smile. "Finer," he suggested. "That's what it sounds like to me. The machinery is smaller, closer together, doing more things."

"Doing what?"

"Don't know," he admitted. "You're the maga, however, so I figured it might help you later. All four corners sound the same," he added as he walked into the hall. "And we aren't just talking about the built-in channels of a circle in a square. Draw it out, and you'll discover these partition walls are closing off significant portions of this floor, at those corners. It can't be more of the same machinery as behind the wall downstairs: *that* would sound fainter *but* just as blocky, so to speak."

"Instead it only sounds . . . finer. More sophisticated," said Portunista. Jian nodded. "I wonder, why didn't I hear them last night?" she muttered.

"It'd have to be really quiet to pick them up without the hearing-tube. And later, when it *was* really quiet—well, you *did* have other matters on your mind . . ." Jian reminded her with a grin. Blast his eyes, he was doing it to her again! Every time she seemed to have a grip on herself, he flustered her somehow, leaving her off-balance.

"I didn't try to explore the laboratory, because I didn't want to distract you," he said in apology, as she followed him up the stairs. Why not? she fumed to herself, you distract me enough already . . .

"It does appear, however," he continued, "that the radius of the laboratory is less than can be accounted for by the landing here." And he wistfully sighed, like a boy looking into an armory that he couldn't explore at the moment. "Last!" he clapped his hands together, "but not the least . . . !" and bounded up the stairs.

When Portunista reached the upper room—*her* room—she muffled any thought of it being *their* room—she found him standing in the middle looking upward with a satisfied smile, hands on his hips.

Now what? she wondered in irritation. The tour so far, though moderately interesting, had *not* been exactly helpful.

Portunista looked up.

Her jaw sagged down.
Above them, engraved into every bit of the circular ceiling—
—was a map.

"That's . . . that's . . . That's a *map!*"

"Yes . . ." Jian answered cautiously. He looked back down to see her staring up incredulously. "It's a map," he slowly agreed, as if perhaps expecting a joke. "Isn't this what you were studying, this morning? Right before you sat up in bed and shouted, 'Someone has been here'?"

She snapped her head back down to glare at him, commanding herself to close her jaw. "Of course! It's a map! So?" She attempted to say this casually, as if she'd known all along—but she could tell from Jian's expression that now he wasn't buying it. Still, she certainly wouldn't admit that she had spent *the-Eye-knew-how-long* staring blissfully up at the ceiling without a clue, or a care, of what she was seeing . . . !

"Now, as you can see," he continued, trying to keep his amusement down, "the map shows us the valley around the Tower in minute detail, all the way out to the ridges and mountains." The contours suddenly shifted into perspective for Portunista—the engraving was only a slightly different shade than that of the stone of the ceiling, itself abnormally smooth. Jian was walking to where he had pulled a taller chest of drawers over next to one low table. At least, she didn't remember those drawers being in place there earlier.

Then again, she upbraided herself, who *knew* what else she had overlooked in this room since arriving last night?!

"The most interesting thing, however, can only be seen by getting up close to the map," Jian said, carefully checking his furniture placement. "And, may I add by the way, this ceiling is *far* too low to match the height of the Tower outside? *And* the machinery in the walls continues up to ceiling level, too." He paused, nodded, then turned back to her with a gesture of invitation.

Portunista, still cursing herself for being so unperceptive, stomped to the table and pulled herself up onto it.

"I had to balance myself with a hand on the wall," the fair man warned. "One of the legs of the chest of drawers—"

"I have *excellent* balance!" She kept her hand away from the wall, and mounted the chest of drawers.

It *did* begin to wobble, as she rose into an ungainly half-crouch; but she threw out her arms without touching the wall, and inched her face to the ceiling. She wished that Jian would just *tell* her things straight out, instead of making her find out for herself . . .

She missed it for the first few moments, concentrating on the extremely fine detailing instead. This engraving must have cost a fortune—

Then she realized: she wasn't looking at an engraving.

The surface was flush, as well as smooth.

She looked even closer.

Every last detail was part of one, massive . . .

"sigil . . . !" she breathed; or maybe squeaked. She turned and tilted her head to look across the ceiling's surface. "This is a sigiltracing!"

The awe of trying to fathom such a complexity, blended together along with her inconvenient posture and unusual viewing perspective—

The chest of drawers wobbled with her increasing disorientation.

Her balance shifted violently back and forth, her body instinctively seeking to reestablish its center of gravity.

She waved her arms in all sorts of directions!—she was pitching over—!

She tried to curse, but all that escaped was an angry "Eep!"

Jian caught her.

It wasn't a graceful catch, partly because Portunista was a little taller than Jian, and partly because she had already twisted further over, like a cat, trying to land on her hands and knees.

Consequently, she bounced off his waiting arms—both of them grunted with the impact—and found herself standing next to him, still braced in mind and body for an impact with the floor.

"Uh!" she exhaled; then wobbled once again as her muscles unclenched and her center of balance steadied.

Instinctively, she thrust out her hand, and braced herself on the table—completing her humiliation.

"Don't even *dare* to say 'I told you so,'" she growled.

"Now, not being a magus, I haven't a single good idea why Qarfax would do this. So," Jian asked, "what do you think?"

Portunista's disorientation, which she'd begun fighting down, now rose again; and she cursed herself for not being able to let go of the table, yet . . .

Then she laughed at herself, silently and bitterly.

She had expected Jian to say "I told you so" anyway.

"I don't know," she muttered.

Jian didn't say anything. He only looked at her with expectant hope.

"What else do you want me to say?!! " she exploded. "I DON'T KNOW! I don't *know* why Qarfax did this or that, I don't *know* what's under the dell, or how tessers work, or how *any* of his sigils work, and I haven't been able to get a scrution to be worth more than *dung* the whole time I've been here, and my eyes are getting sore, and I nearly broke my neck just now, and—so just—stop *looking* at me like I know what I'm *doing!!*"

She slumped, back against the table, and glared at the floor, and imagined ripping out his throat if he tried to comfort her.

She did hear him walking across the floor . . . but not to her.

Instead, he clambered onto the bed.

—did he expect her to just jump up on the bed with him, like he was some sort of medicine for her misery?!

She raised her glare, ready to curse him.

He wasn't looking at her.

He was lying with his head at the foot of the bed, closer to the center of the room, looking up at the map—squinting his eyes, pondering what it could mean.

She took a few slow breaths. Jian was clever in some things; but he wasn't a magus. He had about as much chance of figuring out the functions of a sigiltracing, as *she* did of reading whatever was written behind the stars.

But, he had done what she had wanted for him to do, although she hadn't said it aloud.

He had left her alone.

Yet he hadn't given up. He still was trying his best.

Portunista chewed her bottom lip, and sighed. She really *was* an idiot . . . if *she* didn't try, who *else* was going to figure it out?!

Bowing her head again, she closed her eyes, focusing her intent; and began to jott an Yrthescrution. The elemental materia coalesced beneath her eyelids, her eyes seeping tears as they tried to flush the Yrthe. She put the discomfort aside, and sent her intent to the stone of the ceiling above.

There it was—and there was the tracing, across and within its surface; in-fused with plenty of Yrthe, as well as other materia. Linked to a whole other room of machinery in the ceiling above them.

And vastly more complex than she had even begun to imagine.

Where to begin?
She didn't have the faintest clue.

So, she tried to get a simple feel, for its shape in total.

She tilted her head, deep in thought. How peculiar—now she seemed to be looking down on the valley from high above. The trees and streams and contours all were there; there were the ridges and mountains, too; there was the Tower. But, it wasn't like looking at any map, or even seeing it like a bird.

It was . . . like *feeling* every tree and shape, in detail, all at once. She didn't have to move her focus here or there. *All* the map, *all* the sigil, twenty-four paces across or more, seemed to be one point—a point with the strength of a unity.

Was *this* . . . how the Eye beheld the whole world . . . ?

Something was happening, as if in the corner of her viewing, yet right in the center, too. She couldn't determine what it was—she unconsciously tilted her head in other directions, understanding intuitively she wasn't properly *seeing* it yet.

. . . was the sigil triggering?

Yes . . . the scrution itself was activating it, blending with it somehow, com-pleting parts of its circuitry where she hadn't even guessed there were gaps. Whenever she focused too closely on the details, she lost all perception of what the whole was doing.

So, perhaps she should start with *what* was happening, rather than trying to start with *how*.

On impulse, she sent her scrution in other directions around the room, reaching up from the floor, as the sigil itself was *teaching* her to reach—seeing the room without seeing it, accepting the whole before trying to figure the de-tails. She wouldn't have had any hope, before, of understanding what she was seeing—because, she knew and would now admit, she lacked some skills and knowledge that must be gathered first in other ways. Experience itself might help, perhaps . . . ?

She turned her head, her body not guiding but echoing her intentions; not restricting, but responding to what her intentions could achieve.

She didn't know that she was smiling; immersed within, and radiating, the joy of discovery.

She wasn't thinking about her self, at all.

She compared what she was feeling through her scrution, with her memories of sight—letting each inform and complement the other, inferring and learning the meaning of what must *be* . . . There was the basin; the tables, wardrobes, dressers, chairs. There was the bed. She could feel where Jian was, on the bed, and even 'see' that he was looking up at the map . . .

 . . . trying his best to figure it out.
Trying his best, to serve her.

She walked to him, and knelt, and kissed him lightly on the forehead.
"I'm sorry," she told him. "Thank you for being so patient with me, when I'm in a mood."
"I suppose," he thoughtfully answered, "that this means the threat will now be ramping up considerably . . ."

She would have blinked, except that would have interrupted her scrution.
"What?" was all she could think of to say. Had she heard him correctly . . . ?!
"Well," he said, pointing upward—she inferred it from clues in the scrution—"*those* little glowing dots are clumped together exactly where we left the brigade; so, I figure those *other* dots, over there, and there and there, must be—"
"Wait . . . hold on . . . WHAT??" Her 'view' tilted as she lost control of the scrution, her eyes popping open, blinking away the materia. At the last moment, she reached reflexively with her intent, and did something she would have said was impossible.
She bound the scrution into place, as she opened her eyes.
The wonder of the previous moments dampened her normal annoyance at having to flush out the Yrthe with her tears; the wonder, and the confusion. Could Jian jott after all . . . ?!
He slightly moved his eyes, to look up at her instead of up at the map; smiling, and raising his eyebrows—which looked very strange and comical from her vantage. And he continued to point.
"See?" he said. "*You're* doing that, right?"
Portunista looked up.
The map stood out in even greater contrast and detail.
And very fine points of orangish red, covered the edges of three of the compass-quarters.
"I expect . . ." Jian yawned and stretched, " . . . *those* four points, running across the dell toward our front door, are Seifas and the others. Although we *could* be under attack already from scouts," he allowed. He rotated round and off the foot of the bed. "I'd better go check. Be back in a minute!"

And off he trotted.

Portunista, however, was watching the masses, gathering from the east, the west and the north.

Each mass was somewhat larger than the blob of dots at the south, near the mouth of the pass.

And each was slowly moving, over the ridges, over the mountains, through the forests, toward the middle.

"Oh, *scrat*," she breathed . . .

CHAPTER 42

With his long legs, going downhill, Seifas easily outran the others as they returned to the Tower. He paused at the door, watching behind them, waiting for them to catch up.

The door popped opened behind him: "Hi!"

Seifas twitched in startlement; then he decided that Jian must have seen them approaching from one of the windows—or maybe he'd heard the feet of the others. Othon's armor was certainly clanking loudly enough at least . . . !

"A large brigade is approaching from the west," Seifas said; Jian had to jump aside as the squad rushed past him into the Tower.

"Ah!—good! It's larger than ours, and there are two more marching in from the north and the east!"

Seifas followed him up three stairs before this thoroughly penetrated.

"Hold, wait," muttered the juacuar. "What?!"

"*More* brigades?" Dagon's bushy eyebrows climbed to his hairline.

"*Good?*" Othon blurted.

"Oh, no I don't mean that it's good there are more brigades," clarified Jian, sort of. "I mean that it's good that we've got some verification for Portunista! Wait till she hears!" And he dashed upstairs, like a boy on Stilleve morning.

A minute later, they reached the uppermost room.

"Whew!" Pooralay squinted at the ceiling. "So *this's* what y'were doin' in here all mornin'. My 'pologies; thought y'were messin' aroun' with somethin' else . . ." he grinned.

Jian opened his mouth, but Portunista trod on his foot. Just in case.

"*Now* I know what I had been sensing beneath the Tower," she announced, overriding whatever Jian had been going to say instead—an "Ow!" escaped amusedly from his mouth. "That was a web-like feeling, and I didn't know what it did. But obviously, it detects and positions intruders wherever they are in the valley."

Jian furrowed his face in thought as he gingerly rubbed his foot on his calf. "Did you say that the feeling extended out *past* the dell?"

Portunista turned to reply . . . but nothing came out of her mouth.

"The reason I'm asking," he mused, "is because I sort of remember you telling us something about it *not* extending past the dell; which the map's detection certainly does . . ."

The maga sighed.

"You *did* discover how to work the map," Jian hurriedly offered. "That was nifty! Um . . . Seifas," he continued, ignoring Portunista's sullen look, "I'm a little confused about how *you* could verify the western brigade. It's just now crossing the ridgeline, and that's . . . mmm . . . about ten klips?"

The juacuar considered the question irrelevant at first; but, he happened to see Jian's eyes flick back in Portunista's direction. Then he understood.

The fair man had only meant to *help* their commander, not undermine her; now he was trying to cover her embarrassment.

Seifas could sympathize. Besides, on further thought, it *was* a pertinent question. The distance and time didn't seem to add up; and a prudent commander would want to know why.

"We found where the sod had been cut, about a thousand paces into the forest: just as our commander had reasoned." Portunista perked at hearing this; and Jian gave Seifas a tiny grateful nod. "I ordered the squad to wait in ambush, while I ran ahead. I reached the ridge, and saw the leading elements coming uphill through a sizable meadow. Far too many for us to fight directly."

"An' some'v'us ain't really so good at gettin' ready to ambush anyway," muttered Poo. Othon traded shrugs with Dagon.

Seifas pointed to the northern group: "These are very likely demimen. Only the Middlelands lie in that direction, and there is even less advantage to entering over those mountains than from the west or east."

"Unless y'spend so much'f y'r time in marchin' up an' down mountains, that one or two more don't make any diff'rence," Pooralay agreed.

"*This* gets better and better," Dagon mumbled. "I'd rather fight off those *other* two brigades than mess with a horde that size."

"Allies?" Othon asked.

Portunista shrugged. "Would demimen make alliance with a *human* brigade? Besides, the western brigade must know that Qarfax is missing: so why would forces cooperating with *them* even bother to *try* sneaking into the area from an unexpected direction?"

"To secure their perimeter, outside in?" Dagon speculated. "Still'd be faster than marching them all to the southern pass, then *back* to perimeter camps. Anyway, it's hardly likely they're coming to trap and dispose of *us*," he wryly added.

"I guess we'll see." Seifas flicked his glance to Jian, who was carefully contemplating the layout. What sort of tone had he heard . . . ?

"The scouts over there on the eastern rim, bother me most, I guess," continued Jian. Two orange dots rested in the treeline. "I wonder how long they've been *there*. Still, it might be a reasonable way to initiate contact with the eastern force," the fair man suggested, as he lay down on the floor, setting a pillow beneath his head. "Send someone out as if he's going back to camp, like Gaekwar, then loop him around behind those guys, and start a conversation." He nodded to himself, then noticed the others were staring at him. "Um . . . well, my neck was starting to get a crick, so I thought that this would help," he shrugged. At least he hadn't jumped back on the bed itself, Portunista groused . . . "Hey, I'll go if you want!" Jian offered. "I'm not all that sure I can sneak around behind them, though . . . besides, that hardly would tell them we're friendly. *Would* they shoot, do you think, if I walked up to them directly instead? They'll already know that we know that they know that we're here, and so that we know that they're there—right?"

Portunista decided that sending *Jian* as an emissary would be the *very* last thing she'd consider—though Dagon was saying, "Good idea!" with a falsely cheerful demeanor . . .

"Let them stay," she said. "At *this* point, scouts are hardly worth bothering with."

"Unless they interfere with reinforcements," Dagon retorted. "Commander," the arrogant man infused the word with sarcasm, "*I'm* gonna go, to bring back an archery squad, for garrisoning the Tower windows. I'd better be leaving right now, in fact . . . with your permission," he added, in a tone that dared her to disagree.

"Fine," she tensely replied. "I think that's a *fine* idea. Have them bring a cart of supplies, in case we're holed up here for several days. And bring a reinforced infantry squad as well." Portunista flicked her hand in his direction, dismissing him.

After he left there was silence, as they returned to the map.

Three larger brigades didn't allow many options to talk about.

"Well!" Jian hopped up and stood. "Does anyone have any plan of how to survive a fight in here?"

"Run," Othon said.

Jian digested this recommendation, absently nodding; then: "That's a good plan!" he brightly agreed. "I'd better go make us some lunch, I guess!"

And, he did.

CHAPTER 43

"Where are my scouts?" the thin man mildly asked.

"Most certainly scouting," one of the eight hulking men who followed nearby respectfully answered, "as you have wisely decreed."

"Are they to scout and not return?"

The nervous lieutenant scratched one of his numerous scars, not daring at first to reply to this mildly rhetorical question. "Shall I slay them when they return, for being late?" he offered.

"Perhaps," interjected a second brute, "they are already slain."

"Have *all* my scouts been slain?" the thin man asked.

The second soldier, Rester, shrugged; it wasn't his concern. The officer known as Harvester twitched, however. *All* the scouts? He'd sent only two, ahead of the march, to ensure their readied quitchgrass still was fresh. He hadn't thought to send more than two; not the eight he had sent before, to make the Tower ready for the coming of his lord. Why would there need to be more?

"Perhaps opponents surround us, Misire," suggested the third lieutenant. He wasn't worried. He put much faith in his sword.

And more: he knew the thin man's secret. All eight hanikim did; and so they addressed the leader of one brigade by the title reserved for kings—and those above kings.

But this was just the beginning.

"Perhaps," agreed the mildish man, and stopped in place, gently turning a beatific gaze upon his advancing people. Whoever was nearby, whatever they were doing, paused every minute or so to genuflect to him.

They knew what cost would be extracted from them, if ever they failed to do so.

"Ender." The mild man raised a hand. "Stop the Devouring Army here. Harvester, we shall send more scouts in all directions." He paused, and breathed in satisfaction, while Ender roared the new commands.

Harvester, meanwhile, twitched again. *More* scouts in *all* directions . . . should he have done that already?

"Misire, I beg the blessing of your attention, please." He knelt on the forest floor, his head chest-high to the scrawny velveted figure.

"Speak." A calm and distant smile.

"Misire, I've learned in the last few minutes, the soldiers I earlier ordered to scout for our flanks have been lazy and craven. Please, allow me to slay them for you, and find new scouts whom you can trust."

"It is well, my loyal servant. Slay the treacherous failures, and raise new scouts to take their place. For the all teeming multitudes are *mine*—surely my army's increase never shall end."

That, Harvester thought, was true enough: the brigade had absorbed every village that it had encountered so far.

As criers relayed Ender's roars, the brigade now trudged to a halt. "I beg to leave, Misire," Harvester said. The robed man flicked his hand, dismissing his lieutenant, who hurried away.

"Enemies all around," the magus mused. "Is this the first of blows from above? Or has a rival found his way before me?

"If I turn in that direction," he continued, "I see BLOOD AND DEATH AND CLAWS AND DEFEAT AND *VICTORY!!*" he screeched; his eyelids sank into his skull. Harvester winced again—and ducked behind a wagon as soon as possible, just to be sure he wouldn't be summoned back.

"Someone is there," the magus panted—his seven other hanikim, hearing The Voice, knelt behind him. "Someone is taking what I want, and there are enemies all around—too soon, too soon, I am not ready, blood must boil . . . !" One surviving baby began to cry nearby. His mother hastily smothered him.

Better to smother, than to be heard by the Mad One.

"He Who Fills The Cavicorn approaches; and the minions of the Lord of Slaughter; and . . . and . . ."

The subcommander known as Biter, dared to look upon his lord.

Biter considered himself a servant and master of terror.

What he saw now, however, filled even *his* heart with fear.

He saw terror, on the face of Praxiteles.

"The Doom of Bricks . . . !" the magus frothed. "Ahg! Can't see, I don't want to look! It isn't possible—it isn't fair! He can't *be* here! Loss, loss . . ." the magus mumbled. Then, "NO! The War continues! We shall conquer, we have foreseen it! All shall be ours! We are strong and eat the Truth, and having expelled it, we make new truths! We can win . . . we can win . . . every Culling proves it . . . it is only a matter of time . . . Do I want to go there?" the magus asked, in his first voice. "We *don't* want to go," the second voice insisted. "But yes, WE DO! The secrets are there, that guarantee victory; *we* are the first, so we shall have them first, they spit on us, but we are the *first!*"

The magus danced a jig, pumping his fists in the air. No one laughed. They waited as sheep in pens.

"We are the first . . . but we are *not* the first, someone is before us . . . some-one . . . we forget who . . . but Gamin is first . . ." the magus rasped a reptilian hiss. "He knows, I know. Gamin was braver. Gamin was first! Now *we* have the advantage, *and we shall NOT let go!*" His long and ragged fingernails dug his palm; blood dripped. "The Lord of Slaughter isn't first," he mocked; "for he fears! I do not fear him. I do not fear his minions. Yes, *I* am the worst, for I am the first, and so I do not fear!" He laughed. No one else laughed. "I, I, *I am* the worst . . . ! The first and the worst . . . I wasn't the first, but now I am . . . I AM THE WORST, DO YOU HEAR? DO YOU FEAR??" he shrieked toward the unseen Tower.

Silence followed.

"I do not fear . . ."

Biter thought that Praxiteles—or, rather, Gamin—wasn't convincing him-self of this very well. But, he kept his opinion to himself. Biter needed no con-vincing, to be afraid of Gamin.

"It isn't worth my time or effort, no . . . this is a . . . an *opportunity.* Yes! Op-portunity waits at the Tower of Qarfax. Not worth my time or effort to fight, but worth someone else's . . . He Who Fills The Cavicorn shall fight, sweeping away what isn't worth my time . . . I want to see *her!*" the voice of Praxiteles clearly an-nounced. "Nfff . . ." he shook his head, like a dog with a flea in his skull. "No, I am *not* going there . . . I am going . . . going . . ."

The eyelids of the magus relaxed, half-closing sedately again.

Gone, Biter thought, carefully bowing his head.

"Biter, you shall remain, overseeing our encampment," Praxiteles pro-nounced, with the air of a man standing bored in an art exhibit. "Swelter, you shall stay as well. Flooder, Stinger, Thunder," he addressed the three most phys-ically daunting men, "follow me. I am going *around* the Tower."

Better you than me, Biter thought to his peers.

Rester stood and sweated, as the others moved away. *He* had not been men-tioned! Was he supposed to stay? Or leave?

Choices were dangerous things to make, in the Devouring Army.

CHAPTER 44

"Excuse me . . . um . . . Commander?"

"Hi! Jian'll be fine!" The fair man waved at the puzzled soldier who stood at the door of the upper room. "Glad to see you! I guess this means that Dagon and Gaekwar *also* are back . . . oh, but I knew that already," he murmured half to himself, looking to the papers he held, as he lay on the bed. "Please come in," he absently added. "You'll be the first relief-watcher. There's the map," Jian pointed up, ignoring the awestruck stare of the soldier. "*Those* dots, we think are demimen, but we aren't sure yet. No word either about the other two sets. The southern dots are us, of course—I mean the brigade. It doesn't show dots in the Tower. Probably isn't important. *Your* job," he continued, "will be to keep a record of movements." He flapped the sheets on the writing slate. "So far it's been fairly quiet this afternoon: a couple of dots—scouts I mean—from the western brigade, tried to circle round north to the eastern side, but then were intercepted. I *think* that one survived to be taken prisoner. This other scout," he pointed, "was following *them,* until they got caught. Apparently he's a lot better, though, even in daylight—he's managed to get pretty close to each of the eastern pickets without them ever seeing him."

"What about those other four?"

"Definitely from the western brigade as well. They've been acting awfully weird." He furrowed his brow in thought. "They meandered around the northern quarter all afternoon, just south of the northern group; generally heading east, but sometimes reversing their course." He squinted. "It *looks* like they're on their way to the eastern brigade for sure, this time. Whoever they are, they easily handled a couple of interceptions from the northern group. So keep your eye on them. I mean if you can: I expect you'll be seeing a lot of activity once the sun goes down, and it may get kind of confusing . . ." *Even more than this?!* the soldier thought. "Whatever else you do, keep track of Seifas and Pooralay when they go scouting later tonight. And let us know if any significant group makes some kind of move from their camp, especially toward our brigade or the Tower. You won't have to tell us what enemy scouts are doing, like the ones relieving their pickets now along the northern and eastern rims of the dell. Just be sure to keep good notes. Oh, and speaking of which, *you'll* be relieved around midnight I guess."

Jian spun round on the bed to sit, and then stood up. "The bed is *great* for watching, without your neck being cricked! Though writing's a little hard like that," he allowed as he left the room.

Lying on the bed of Commander Portunista, wasn't entirely unattractive to the soldier; but he also considered it tantamount to suicide. The pale-skinned man had never seemed to be an idiot; decidedly odd, but more of a wit than a fool . . . Did Jian perhaps have *permission* to lie on her bed??

The soldier added this to the word of how often Portunista had been observed near Jian while on the march to the Tower; and then he reevaluated some of the speculation he had been recently hearing . . .

Outside, night was falling. Inside, soldiers bustled, settling themselves into places and routines, under freshly refurbished sconces. As he trotted downstairs to the garrison-floor, the fair man greeted the troops; they mostly returned the greeting with equal cheer.

"How're things goin', Jian?" One grizzled veteran stood on cooking duty, over a bubbling stew.

"Quiet, so far. Everyone else has had some, right?" He ladled out two dishes. "One is for the Commander," Jian explained.

"Don't forget th' most important thing," the captain grinned, saluting Jian with the stirring spoon.

"Ah! Ouch! That stew is *hot!* Um, good job!" He gingerly set the bowls to the side, before tapping a keg to fill two mugs with mead. The veteran had a good laugh.

"Here, use this." The older man rigged a contraption around the bowls of stew.

"Oh! I had been wondering what those pegs in the top of the bowls were for!" Jian held up a stick of wood; from each end dropped a knotted string to cinch around an angled peg. "Now it's like a balancing scale!" the curly-bearded man decided; and smiled a secret smile.

"Yep. Y'learn a few things, portin' food for more'n one person. Carry the mugs in the crook of your arm."

"Thanks, gaffer!" Jian stepped carefully back through the lounging soldiers. "Hot stew comin' through—gangway!"

The soldiers shook their heads, smiling for the clownish man, as they oiled and sharpened steel.

"I'm sayin' that he'll be back in under a minute," the gaffer winked, as Jian climbed up the stairs again. "Any takers?" Some betting commenced—for less than a minute.

Jian came down again: minus the mugs and bowls of stew, but wearing a lop-sided smile. Laughter followed him down the hall.

He paused at the firepit, and opened his mouth; but, "Spoons!" the gaffer said.

"'The most important thing,'" repeated Jian, and joined in the swelling laughter. He bowed to the cook, saluting the older man with the spoons he received. "It's been a long day," Jian sheepishly shrugged, and smiled as he walked back up the hall again. "Pay up, m'boys, pay up," the gaffer announced behind him.

The only good cheer in the lab, however, arrived with Jian.

"Hello, Portunista!" he called across the room. "I brought your dinner!"

"Mm, thanks," she vacantly answered; she was studying some of Qarfax's notes, after hours of sorting and cleaning the room. Jian put the bowls on a nearby table, safely away from any writings, but brought her a mug.

"Mm, thanks." She took a sip, without looking up, and set the mug aside.

Jian looked around at the tidied laboratory, now well-lit by lamps and sigiled wisps.

"Don't forget to eat the stew before it gels that gummy stuff on top."

"Mm."

Jian walked over to one far end of the room; then paced across it, in deliberation.

"Things'll be awfully crowded downstairs for a while, looks like," he said.

"Mm." She turned a page, and scribbled a note on a nearby pad.

Next, he walked to the blast-pitted stone between the original door and the gap in the wall. "I wonder, where will they put their supplies?" he murmured, carefully pacing across the floor again. "I guess it'll be in the basement."

"Mm."

Jian surveyed the lab once more.

"I wonder," he mused, "where *Qarfax* put his supplies . . ."

"Mm." Portunista drank another sip of mead.

Jian reflectively scratched his beard, then walked to a side of the room. "No lights over here," he mumbled; and spent a minute tracing the curve of the wall. Then he nodded in satisfaction.

"Hm!" he announced.

"Mm," she replied, and turned another page. He smiled a smile of progress being made, and eyed some nearby equipment.

Jian's attention eventually landed on a square table. Sigils were etched into parts of its surface-frame. The stone within that frame, however, was glassy smooth. Jian walked over to it and reached a finger—but then he paused before he touched the surface.

"Hey, 'ista! What does this table-thing over here do?"

She sighed, looked up from her work, and took a longer drink of mead. "It's another map. The straight-line sigil turns it on; the circle turns it off. I have no clue what makes it work, or what he used it for," she added vexedly, returning to her studies.

Jian shrugged and pressed the activation button. With a nearly inaudible hum, minuscule fractions of polished surface raised to varying heights, contouring the land around the Tower.

"Keen!" Jian said. Portunista kept to her books. She had been impressed already, hours ago.

Jian now spied a globe, small but finely sigiled, resting in a niche within the table-frame. He spun it. Nothing seemed to happen.

Next he pondered two small sigil-wedges; one pointed left, the other right. He pressed the left.

The map shuffled, and when it resolved, the scope had widened to show more land.

"Very keen," murmured Jian in satisfaction. Pressing that sigil over and over, brought the map to a span of thousands of kilopaces.

Two blue knobs now jutted up, widely separated on the map. Jian tapped these with his finger. Nothing happened. He wiggled them gently. Nothing happened.

On further examination of the frame, he found four other sigils, shaped like arrows instead of wedges. These redrew the map, in the direction pressed; thus 'moving' the map around.

Jian played with these; as the final daylight faded out of the two narrow windows, leaving the laboratory lit by magic and natural light. Occasionally, he would roll the sigilball in its niche; but still this seemed to do nothing. Two more wedges pointed up and down; however, they did not have any sigiltracings. Jian attempted to use them anyway. Nothing happened.

Portunista, meanwhile, had more practical problems.

Her brigade most certainly lacked the power to defeat even two larger forces, much less three. So how could she possibly keep the Tower?

Qarfax could have defended himself, of course; and yet, he *had* believed that he should hire some guards, as Seifas had said, against mere natural threats.

And yet, *not* against large numbers of natural threats, she reminded herself: no juacuar, not even Seifas, not even backed by nine other soldiers, *could* defend the Tower against a brigade—and any one of the warring Cadrists at the time would likely have brought an *army* of brigades.

Qarfax could have protected himself against a Cadrist, *or* against a Cadrist's army; but probably *not* against them *both*. One would have overrun him while the other took his attention.

And yet, Qarfax had *only* hired nine normal guards, and one juacuar.

So: Qarfax had likely made *other* provisions for Tower defense—plans which did *not* include Seifas, nor Qarfax himself.

Seifas, and Portunista's other subcommanders, together with a couple of squads, *might* be enough to repel a sally from any brigade the size of hers; but surely they couldn't defeat a brigade outright, thus nixing the risk of a siege.

And she faced *three* brigades, larger than her own—from which she would soon be cut off.

And she was not a Cadrist herself.

She absolutely needed that extra defense.

Therefore, she had spent the past two hours perusing scrolls and books for hints about such a defense. She was fairly certain her current stack contained the answers she needed.

Unfortunately, Qarfax had written them mostly in code.

Gemalfan's disciplex had not been all that difficult to decode, because the magus had still considered such information to be potentially useful in a trade. His coding had only kept casual viewers from learning too much.

This was different.

She rested her head on her hand, and thought.

A single word, as she was thinking, caught her eye:

four-faces.

It caught at her memory, too. Where had she heard of this, in reference to Qarfax? Not in the past few days . . . further back than that . . . Yes, that night near the end of Hazyslope, when she had announced her plans to her subcommanders. During Seifas' story about what had happened at the tower, he had mentioned something . . . about . . .

yes!—Qarfax had claimed *four faces* guarded him, so that he would *never* be caught by surprise.

That sounded like something to do with the ceiling map. But *its* divisions were only natural, formed by the streams . . .

. . . the *four* streams . . .

diving below the four Tower *faces* . . . down to millwheels, constantly running machinery . . . including *four* spindles, engaging their sigils continuously . . . no: continuously engaging only *one* radial sigil, at four distinctly different points . . . !

She rose to her feet, and carefully walked to the gap in the wall—the wrecked door being less than redundant now—trying to balance the weave of her reasoning.

"Hey, 'ista!" Jian called out. "Mind if I stay here and work with this table some more?"

"Fine, whatever . . ." she absently waved her hand in his direction.

She quietly paced, down the stairs, passing Gaekwar at the garrison landing.

"Ready for my report?" he asked.

"Later," she said, not looking at him. She didn't see his lopsided smile.

"I brought your other change of clothes," he added. "And also a shirt for Jian. Where should I put 'em?"

"Up in the lab," she vaguely replied; and having passed him, forgot him completely, leaving him staring in curiosity.

The subcommanders had claimed the 'basement' for themselves; but only for convenience, not for privacy. Soldiers were bringing in crates from a wagon outside, placing them so as to ease a defense of the open room. She stepped to one side, out of the way.

She still could feel her intentive bind maintaining the Yrthescrution within Qarfax's ceiling map. She would need to release that now, she supposed—even *if* two Yrthescrutions *could* be bound into place at once, they'd only provide conflicting information. She flagged an infantryman, and told him to run upstairs to alert the watchguard not to panic if he lost his dots for several minutes.

She gave the soldier an eighty-count to deliver the message. Then she began.

First she released the bind on the scrution three floors overhead. She hadn't realized, before she released it, how *relieved* that part of her mind would be. But, she didn't remain at rest. She knelt, and placed one palm on the floor, where she could focus with least distraction; and jotted a new Yrthescrution.

She sent her intent down into the well, searching its shape; finding the four turning spindles, and also the sigilband. Outside that band, within the rocky depths, the web that she had perceived the day before still lay, defying her understanding.

So, she tried to simply perceive the shape of the field as a whole; pulling her focus back, keeping as much of the field in her view as possible.

A smile crept onto her face; for now she could see:

four fields, each one slightly overlapping the other.

She sent her thoughts out further . . . whatever they did, the fields did end before reaching the edge of the dell—as Jian, she ironically grimaced, had helped to remind her. And yet, the detection radius of the ceiling map *did* stretch to the ridges around the valley.

So. Four distinct 'faces', surrounding Qarfax Tower. And documents hinting otherwise at a special Tower defense, made use of that term sometimes: "four-faces."

Clearly, unlike the map above her, merely scruting the jointed field did *not* activate it. Probably just as well, she decided: she didn't know how to control it. What did it even *do?*

Control . . . the disparate fields *were* linked in a way, by that common band from which they sprang. Would the control be a similar single-source?

Simplicity, she told herself. If this was a *defense,* what could she expect about it?—if *she* had designed it, what would have been her priorities?

To hold large forces at bay, or even to neutralize them, until she defeated any rival magi. And fighting against such rivals would likely require an intense concentration, at least as much as Seifas would need when dueling master swordsmen.

Too much concentration to guide the defense. She should be looking for something, then, with pre-scribed behavior instructions, like the pentadart generators.

She narrowed her focus somewhat, and began to scan, forth and back in a slow rotation of radius; allowing her intention to wash across the 'surface' of the subterranean fields. The forest for the trees, she reminded herself . . . She couldn't understand the details yet; so, she should look for a larger pattern— and she *did* detect a uniform repetition of insane complexity—and then, for some discrepancy . . .

—like *that!* There, centered in one of the fields: a solid object, about two handwidths across; covered with sigils—sigils she couldn't understand and hardly dared to probe.

This must be the control device.

The maga sighed, partly in satisfaction at her reasoning's consummation, and partly in frustration. Qarfax would have known exactly where he placed his artifact, and would have been able to reach it intentively almost instantly, as he wished.

But *he* would have known what to do with it, too . . .

"Portunista!"

She jerked, her concentration broken, the Yrthe falling from under her eye-lids. She raised her head; Gaekwar was kneeling in front of her.

"Finally," Gaekwar smiled his ironic smile. A corner of Portunista's mind was now reporting that he had been trying to get her attention for more than a minute.

"Yes?" she replied in an icy tone—no reason to let him know that she'd been oblivious of his presence . . .

"I think you should come upstairs. You won't believe this, unless you see it yourself."

"Just tell me straight out. I've had a long day."

He shrugged. "Okay: Jian is feeding the bird."

"And . . . what does that mean?"

"I told you you wouldn't believe it."

"No," she corrected, with straining patience. "I don't *understand* it. There's a difference. What do you mean, he's feeding the bird? *What* bird?"

"The bird that tried to kill you. He's feeding it."

Now she began to wonder if maybe she'd fallen to sleep on the floor of the basement. This conversation seemed unreal . . .

"The bird . . . from the forest, last night?" she prompted.

"Yehhhhhp," he drawled, grinning fit to burst. "He's feeding it haunches of pork."

She opened her mouth to ask, what in the *hells* of the lords of perdition that bird was doing *here* . . . !—but closed it again. "Okay," she relented. "I'll come see."

She picked herself off the floor, and stomped to the narrow stairway, wondering what she would have to deal with now.

CHAPTER 45

Portunista stepped into a scene from the fabric of dreams.

Here was the laboratory, with tables and books and shelves and equipment, testament to the will and the labor of Man. Here there was light, bound by artifice magical and mundane.

There, within one arcing span of wall, was life abundant, the verdant trees and the flowering fruits of a tropical forest half a world away—a forest she recognized. Its light shone living and beautiful: starry gleaming and crimson-violet clouds.

The laboratory hummed of the settled and antiseptic. Through the breach came all the noise of a living world, poised on the edge between sleeping and waking.

Jian stood, bridging the gap, feeding a meat to the bird.

The fair man turned his head to them, and put his finger to his lips.

"She's a little skitterish," Jian explained, softly with an even tone. "But don't be whispering, either; it sounds like hissing to her." Even the sibilants in *that* sentence were making the avian edgy. Jian turned back to the animal, twice his size though still quite young, trilling lowly to her. A stack of meat was lying at his feet.

"Where . . . how . . . ?" Portunista had too many questions.

"The meat was in a supply room. I'll show you in a minute."

One snip . . . A corner of Portunista's mind kept on replaying this creature's blindingly quick attacks, while her feet were taking her slowly into the room at an angle. The thing would only need one snip. Those haunches couldn't *possibly* be as fresh as Jian himself . . .

"With your permission, Midama, I think I'll stay right here." Gaekwar took a position near the gap; he would help keep anyone else from disrupting the hazardous balance that Jian had somehow attained.

The aasvogel could easily dart into the laboratory at any moment—and Portunista couldn't possibly make it to the outer landing, if the avian now attacked. Nor was there anywhere for her to feasibly hide in the room.

She *might* be able to kill it—but not soon enough to save Jian, if it chose *him* as its first target. The blind-minded man was standing right *next* to the thing . . . !

"Jian," she carefully said—and the avian's black inhuman eyes locked onto her instantly, instinctively gauging vectors . . . "Jian, you *must* step away from the bird. That animal *isn't* a pet."

Jian clucked softly, drawing the creature's attention back to himself. "Of course she isn't a pet," he murmured. "I would be insulting her, to treat her like that! She is more like . . . a lover, I think. I am learning from her; she is learning from me; and so we are communicating." He was silent a moment. "I want the love we share to grow."

"Jian!" Portunista grated. "She . . . *IT* . . . is a killer . . . *bird!* It doesn't love *anyone!*"

The impossible man looked back at her a moment, with that quiet smile. "*Surely* you aren't jealous of a killer bird, milady."

Portunista briefly considered blowing the innards out of the animal, or screeching some denial that would probably make it react into spearing her "husband" like a quail on a stick!—but, either of those responses might be interpreted as her being jealous of a killer bird.

So, she forced herself to calm.

"No," she replied, reasonably and calmly. "I am not jealous of the bird."

"That's because, unlike the bird, Portunista doesn't give a hoot!" The maga whipped her head around to impale the 'cowherd' with a glare; but the lanky man continued to grin, as he lazily leaned against the edge of the wall-gap—carefully aiming his disker at the aasvogel.

"Good," said Jian. "Because, to be honest, I think she may be jealous of *you*." He softly laughed. The avian shifted on its branch, edging closer to Jian; but its eyes were locked back onto Portunista.

The maga decided this conversation was only allowing the men to enjoy the situation at her expense. If the fool *insisted* on putting himself into this position, then he *deserved* to die. She would just have to . . .

. . . trust him.

Years later, contemplating her thoughts of that night, she would write:

"Behind me lay a path, which I could follow with my mind, clearly enough; but it led beneath me up to a veil. Did it stop behind the veil? Or did it continue on?

"It *had* continued on before. But, did *that* guarantee that it *still* would continue?

"Perhaps Jian *was* insane. Perhaps he was making a sentimental mistake. The path behind me told me that *neither* of these was likely true; but, there *were* many parts of that path I still didn't understand.

"Yet Jian wasn't merely a thing to be analyzed. Jian was a *person*. Perhaps he could see beyond the veil, and wasn't merely imagining that he saw.

"Trusting what I could see was very important; and one of the things I *could* see, was that he *usually* knew what he was doing. But . . .

"Trusting my analysis, could carry me to the veil, and it could give me some idea of what *should* lie beyond it.

"But trusting *Jian,* personally . . . did I dare do that?

"I wish I could say I chose to step through the veil.
"I decided instead, that I was too tired to care.

"I *told* myself I didn't care, and wouldn't care if he died.
"I lied to myself—to avoid the risk of a personal trust."

"Fine, Jian, whatever," Portunista sighed. "She can be as jealous of *me* as she wants, so long as she stays over *there.*"

And so she turned away from Jian.

It didn't help her to feel any better. Instead of exhausting herself with worry . . . she only felt exhausted.

She began to examine the room more directly—how *had* Jian done this at all?

The tablemap quickly caught her attention.

"Jian," she asked, "*why* is that little ball on the table?"

"It activates the tesser-generator built into this wall," he answered. "I thought it was meant to move the map around, by rolling the ball in its niche. Except, of course, there were other sigils for doing that. Then, after you left, I noticed the niche was beveled down to halfway below the middle of the ball. There didn't seem to be any point to that, except to allow some fingers room for taking out the ball. So, I took it out."

Portunista couldn't resist looking up, to see how things were going over at the portal. Jian was holding out an especially heavy haunch; the avian nicked its flesh and bone—the length of a forearm or so from Jian's own flesh.

The maga's stomach clenched; she looked away.

"So, when you removed the ball . . ." she prompted.

"The sound of the table changed. You probably noticed already." Actually, she hadn't, but neither could she remember what kind of semi-audible hum it had made before. "*That* hinted that maybe the ball would be useful somewhere else than in its niche. There weren't any other obvious holes; so I touched it to the map. Poom," he softly exclaimed. "The wall disappeared, and rain began to blow in the room—from a shower out at sea. You saw the water on the floor, right?"

"The giant killer bird eating out of your hand had first attention, I'm afraid."

"Awwwww," Gaekwar drawled. "She *does* give a hoot . . ."

Portunista pointed this time, along with her glare. Her subcommander didn't stop grinning, but at least he *did* stop talking.

"The map immediately scrolled to put the ball at the center. Using the arrows, not the brackets, moves the portal laterally; the ball stays in the center. Pick up the ball to close the portal. Nice design."

Portunista wondered whether closing the portal right that moment would slice the bird in half. But, then it would also slice *him* . . .

"Jian," she tried to achieve a tone of pleasant casualness, "step into the room for a moment, hm?"

And she flashed what she hoped was an innocent smile.

Jian looked only suspicious and amused.

Then he bent for the largest remaining ham. "Here, Milady," he murmured to the animal. "Watch the ham . . . watch it . . ." He waved it back and forth between them; the aasvogel tracked the meat, tensing itself to strike. Portunista felt her nose *twist* with a burst of . . . jealousy?! *Was* she jealous of the bird? So *what* if Jian was calling it by her name . . . ?—*her* name?! She didn't want that name from him! Blast its eyes, the bird was a *something,* not a *someone* anyway!

Jian threw the ham far into the trees; the adolescent aasvogel leapt in chase, twisting through the branches, nabbing it before the haunch had bounced three times. "Well done, Milady!" Jian called out. The avian scree'ed in their direction twice, shortly. At being complimented? In farewell?

Probably telling its siblings and cousins about free food nearby, thought Portunista sourly . . .

Jian had already stepped back over the threshold, so she plucked the ball off the map. The portal snapped from existence, leaving the curved stone wall.

Jian sighed and nodded, toward the vanished portal. Then he walked to the map.

"I don't suppose that anyone has a towel, or something?" he asked, keeping his hands away from anything. "I'd rather *not* have my new green shirt to be smelling like 'dead pig'. Just in case I see Milady again." He winked at Gaekwar; the lanky subcommander shook his head, and chuckled.

"No, I do *not* have a towel," said Portunista.

"Not a problem," he shrugged. "I think I saw some goods like that, in Qarfax's storeroom."

"Which would be, *where* . . . ?"

"See the short blue spike on the map?" Despite her temper, Portunista found herself looking for it with a rising sense of discovery. There it was, dead center; the colored spike had risen up from the table after she'd lifted the ball away. "Now, *that* spike represents a location Qarfax taught this table to learn—specifically, the aasvogel nesting grounds. Now try pulling out the map-table's focus." He waited patiently, prudently keeping his hands away from anything.

With another sigh, though partly from her growing pleasure at finding out something useful and important, she set the sigilball in its niche—the hum *did* shift, just as Jian had said—and did as he had suggested.

Hours ago, not long after noon, she had discovered most of the map controls; the excitement she had felt at that time was now returning, increased with the expectation of accomplishment.

When she had pulled the focus out, farther than she had tested before, a second blue spike appeared, amidst a mountain range, hundreds of kilopaces north and west of the Tower. She easily focused the map on that.

Restraining, with some difficulty, a shiver and a smile, Portunista carefully pulled the sigilball from its resting niche. With only a look at Jian to reassure herself that she was doing correctly—a look she found she barely resented right that moment—she touched the spike with the ball.

It sank beneath the ball; she felt but didn't hear it finely grinding. As the ball touched down upon the nominal surface of the map, it twisted and jolted within her fingers—she yanked her hand away with a curse, although she wasn't hurt.

"Oh, sorry. I think it only does that with the *blue* spikes."

She started to shoot an indignant glare at Jian . . . but the scene behind him caught her attention.

Where the wall of stone had arced, now gaped a shallow cave.

Ignoring her irritation in the glow of her amazement, Portunista stepped around the table's edge, toward the cave.

The lights of the laboratory illumined stacks of crates and barrels. Who *knew* what Qarfax had buried beneath this mountain?!

One object stood especially out in the careful piles.

A mirror, tall and wide, framed in gilded leaf.

"I've poked around a little in there already," Jian was saying behind her. "Mostly I only found some normal tower storeroom things. Although," he added, "my search was not very thorough. I lugged a stack of salted haunches back into the lab, for us to roast. Then I tried the *other* blue spike—and who did I find, but my flying partner, moping around alone! The other aasvogels must be shunning her right now, after she accidentally started that birdfight."

Portunista didn't give a single burning feather for the bird, *or* its troubles . . . She stopped her approach with a jerk—she was standing so close to the portal, she could see a faint transparent film in front of her eyes. Her nose was almost brushing it.

"Even though I searched around," continued Jian, "I didn't touch the mirror. I figured *you* would want to be the first of us to look it over. And after all, you *are* the maga." Silence for some moments; then, "Well? What do you think?"

But she couldn't bring herself to cross the threshold.

"Where . . ." She swallowed and started again. "Where does the cavern lead?"

"Nowhere," came the answer from behind. "As far as I can tell, it's simply a natural fissure deep in the heart of a mountain. It isn't large at all." He paused again. "I didn't see anything in there—dangerous I mean." Another pause; she didn't move. "Portunista?" Now he sounded worried. "Is something wrong? Are *you* seeing something?"

"No," she answered, faintly.

She was lying.

What she saw, in her mind, was an image from the night before.

She saw herself, stepping through a portal much like this one.

And she saw that other portal, closing behind her, trapping her on the other side.

And she imagined Jian: lifting the ball from the table, after she entered *this* portal—

—she would die, smothering, *long* before she could possibly melt through klips of stone.

Or, perhaps he would lift the ball as she stepped across the portal's membrane—bloodily bisecting her.

how would that feel? how long would she live? would she go mad before she died?

Burning hot into her mind, the memory came, of what she had wanted to do, to the aasvogel . . .

She laughed, once, a chuff of air. They'd probably think she was jotting. Didn't she trust Jian?

If she wanted that mirror, she would have to personally trust him—as a person himself—not to kill her in her vulnerability.

The possibility also remained: that Jian would abuse her trust.

True, she knew of several facts that gave her grounds for believing she could trust him with her life. Including a promised commitment to her, that she didn't want to accept.

Yet without an active personal trust, given freely by her choice, the facts were merely facts, shedding their light but only as far as she could understand them— or as far as she *chose* to see them.

And the facts might as well be dead. They couldn't make the decision for her.

Would you even want them to? asked a quieter voice within. Is that the sort of person you are, to let your decisions be made by something other than you yourself?
No.
Then choose. Will you, you yourself, trust Jian, he himself? Or not?

And then another voice, a spiteful ironic voice, asked:
Won't you put your faith in Jian?

She could feel her brain constricting, her teeth baring . . .
"Jian," she said. "Would you step away from the table, please?"

A moment passed. Then two. "The table?" He sounded truly perplexed. Of course he does, one of those voices told her, a voice she didn't want to hear—after all, he trusted *you* to not be hurting *him* . . .
Well, he didn't trust me not to hurt that bird! she retorted.
The voices were silent. The quieter voice had no need to speak, when it could flash up the memory of her feelings and thoughts when she had asked Jian to step back into the room, away from the aasvogel. The other voice kept silent, betting that this would make no difference.
That's right! she said to the quieter voice. You see? I *couldn't* be trusted!
The voice replied no further.
She told herself this was a victory.

"Jian," she said; a feeling like grime was washing down her hair, down her skin . . . but she wouldn't stop . . . "Step away from the table now." She made it an order, not a request.
What would she say, if he asked her why? So I can be sure you won't kill me, Jian? Because after all I've seen, and all you've done, I still don't *want* to trust you, Jian? Just shut up and do what I tell you, Jian?

"Oh."
And that was all he said. But it was enough. She knew that he knew what she meant.

Once, long ago, in an idle moment during her apprenticeship, she had wondered how it would feel to be turned into stone.

Her heart was doing that now.
  the most horrible thing she had felt in her life

She opened her mouth to tell him to never mind . . .
  . . . she shut it again. It was too late. It was already done. She would only look a fool.

She listened to him walk, slowly, across the floor. "Okay," he said; but there was no cheer, no joy in his voice. "I'm over here near Gaekwar, Commander." Not Portunista . . . not 'ista . . . not even milady . . .
She stepped through the portal.

She stood in the heart of a mountain; a heart where no light had shown for ages of ages—aside from one occasional light provided by someone from far beyond.
She looked up, around. The cavern did not continue very far behind the portal—a fissure less than a third the size of the laboratory.
One constricted hole of a heart within a mountain of stone . . .

"So, where is the wall?" Gaekwar was asking Jian—but his jocular drawl sounded strained.
"What . . . ? Oh . . . it's still there, I think, behind the portal. The tesser is terribly thin, you know. It's being generated by a slight extension running around the wall, lined with sigils even smaller and more complex than the ones on the door—maybe Qarfax scribed them after further refining his skill. The ridge is pretty hard to spot, unless you suspect already that something is there." Jian seemed to be making apology. For what? thought Portunista bitterly. *He* had found the thing . . . !
Not her. After being in the room for hours.
She, the maga, had missed it completely.
Jian was tacitly covering for her failure, so she wouldn't look incompetent. He even sounded happy again; perhaps because he was able to help someone.
Because he was helping *her.*

Don't you understand I can't be trusted?!! she screamed in her mind.

Why not choose to live up to his expectations instead? asked the quieter voice. You *do* have the choice . . .
If *he* cannot trust *you* with his heart, then why should *you* trust him with *yours?* asked the other voice.

She thrust both questions away, and walked back into the laboratory, taking the mirror with her—it wasn't heavy, as if its only weight was in its golden filigree.

Certainly magical, then; but she would have to study it later. There were other things worth doing now, with this portal—things that could possibly help them to survive.

She found a place to lay the mirror down, near her books and scrolls; and turning back, to close the tesser . . .

Jian was in the cavern.

Puttering round, in one of the casks; and as she watched, he pulled out . . .
. . . a towel.

He walked back into the laboratory, wiping his hands.
"I'm glad I saw those in there earlier! In fact," he grinned, "I think I'll get some water from the well downstairs, to clean myself up better." And nodding briskly, he left the room.

A towel.
She wouldn't trust him with her life, to get a thing she only suspected the worth of, and didn't even remotely know how to use.
He was willing to trust her with his life—simply to get a towel to clean his hands, so that he wouldn't annoy any others—no, so *she* would not be annoyed— with a stink.

She refused to watch him leave.
Instead she stood, watching the portal, for half a minute.
The half became one.

Then Gaekwar spoke.
"Y'know," he drawled. "I've been thinking about that bird of his. The one he wouldn't dream of treating like a pet. The one he wouldn't be enemies with, even if he had to fight her; the one he's willing to love, 'cause she and he both share a love for something. The one he's willing to risk his own life for. And I think I've figured out what they both love.
"He and she, both love *her*."

His drawl had disappeared, replaced by diamond-cutting hardness. "Excuse me," he said, uncoiling from his lounge against the wall. "I'm gonna go downstairs and get some hot spiced mead. Got a bad taste in my mouth."

He left, without looking back.

CHAPTER 46

All was in order.

And yet, Artabanus still felt . . .

. . . nervous.

Not frightened. Not unsure. Just on edge.

As if someone he wasn't accounting for, was watching him.

Not enemy scouts, exactly. They might or might not have penetrated his pickets; but he couldn't be everywhere at once—subordinate incompetence simply was a fact of life. He had learned to compensate.

Besides, he'd also learned that scouts were more effective at night, which only *now* was falling. He could see his first of aides returning from overseeing the evening scouting arrangements, exactly on time. So, no; probably there were no enemy scouts nearby. Not yet, at least. And even if there were—Artabanus put his trust in his own destiny.

No; *this* edginess clearly was something . . . else . . .

Lieutenant Noth arrived, saluting crisply—with a touch of nervousness himself. "Midomo! I have something to report." He meant to wait until given permission.

Artabanus snapped his attention to Noth at once.

"From the scouts. They have news." This was not a question.

"Yes," Noth missed a beat; his Domo knew already—? "A deputation approaches from the north."

"Interesting. Tell me what I wish to know."

Now Noth smiled a little—he enjoyed foreguessing his Domo's wishes, proving his right to serve this man. "Their style of armor partly confirms the story told, by the two deserters captured in mid-afternoon."

"Lieutenants from a western brigade." Odd; but not enough to make him edgy . . .

"Midomo, they are not alone: a slight man, richly robed, apparently leads them."

Artabanus paused—a reflection of shock, Noth recognized.

One moment only—then the tall magus strode, straighter than lightning, northward. Noth fell into step behind and to the side.

"Perhaps their leader *is* insane," Artabanus murmured. His gaze now rapidly shifted, searching among his brigade. "The surviving traitor's story becomes more credible . . . did you order the pickets to watch and not repel? I would prefer not to lose experienced troops for nothing. Ah!" He snapped his fingers, a lightning crack. Every head in sight turned instantly toward him; but, he pointed to only one, "You. Here!"—and so continued his march away without even missing a beat.

The others retained their attention on him for many moments more, ensuring that they themselves weren't *also* being called to serve.

Ensuring that they would live to serve him later.

The deadly man to whom he gestured, fell into step nearby.

"Alt—tell me what I wish to know," Artabanus commanded.

"Midomo," saluted the officer, equal in rank to Noth. "I see from your gait and bearing that we should expect an attack—from the north! Our brigade is prepared to receive your orders!"

"I do expect trouble, Alt; perhaps an attack. You and Noth shall stand with me."

"All power to you, Misire," his men saluted; then loosened their swords in their sheaths.

"Midomo," Alt continued, "the prisoner freely spoke about his former brigade, without coercion. Under coercion, he only insists increasingly that he is telling the truth. He and his slain companion were caught while coming south from this direction."

"According to Noth's report just now, a man who matches the traitor's stories about his former liege approaches, along with a small but armored escort."

"Sire . . ." Alt paused, though not in his march. "Based on what the prisoner says, which hasn't changed since first you heard it yourself . . . only *you* can preserve our brigade from destruction!"

"That may be," agreed Artabanus. *They* might worry; he was enjoying the challenge already. "However, you and Noth shall strike at the magus, should a battle begin—even if his men do flay the skin from your bones—even if you are broiled in the fire that I shall ignite in his lungs. I will *not* leave his life to the smallest possible chance."

"Clearly," they agreed, "he must die." Neither one considered disobeying this command, even for a moment. No matter how small their chances of survival, they preferred those odds to disobeying *him.*

The rise of Artabanus, was inevitable. They would dare any danger to prove that they were worthy to rule in his shadow.

As they reached the edge of camp, the magus attended to the forest. Some of the slaves were clearing away the underbrush, to provide the least concealment for an enemy, and to keep from hindering defensive fire. Even his arrival couldn't galvanize them to be striving any harder. Excellent.

"We shall meet our opponent here, for now, to insulate my brigade from harm, if possible."

"Shall I bring in the slaves, Midomo?" Noth inquired. "The sun has set already." Dusklight still remained, and the stars were shining fiercely through a clearing in the branches now above; but the canopy of the forest over where the slaves were laboring only filtered through a fraction of the brilliance of those lights. And the slaves would need to eat and sleep, eventually.

"They may run, if or when the fighting starts. Meanwhile they shall work," Artabanus judged. "They shall help us to know the approach of our enemies, where and when."

"We don't *already* know this? Midomo?"

"The basic direction, yes," Artabanus answered Alt's surprise, while scrutinizing the forest past his laborers. "But, *not* the angle. Hmm . . ." he pondered a moment. Then he snapped his fingers once again.

All the slaves stopped working—peering toward the clearing where their dreaded master stood.

"You. Here." Artabanus pointed. Seven men and a woman staggered forward from the treeline. "No. You men return to work. The rest do likewise," clarified Artabanus. The one young woman still remaining fell into a kneeling heap, at his feet.

"All . . . power . . . to . . ." she gasped, head bowed down.

"Return to camp, slave; to the interrogation tent. Tell the guards to bring to me the prisoner caught this afternoon. Lead them here. Save your breath for running. Go, now."

She went, running well, despite exhaustion; and had also borne her labors well. Perhaps he would assign her to another task, more suitable for her.

If he survived . . . ? The magus easily swatted the question away from his mind, as if it was an ash-punkie. He, and *only* he, chose whether he lived, or died; served, or ruled.

He chose to rule. Everything else amounted to details of history—which would be his.

Yet . . . there was that itching feeling again, at the edges of his perception . . .

"We are being watched." Then he added, "By someone hostile to me." For of course the slaves still worked nearby, and his brigade's encampment also wasn't far away.

Alt and Noth drew their swords. A corner of the magus' attention prepared to jott two shields of Silverphyre, which though permeable to swords, still would likely cause his men to hesitate before they struck him. After that hesitation, either they would be dead or wishing they were.

Artabanus had chosen—weeded, pruned—his officers well: they didn't strike at him. But for him, the fact of all reality was that every power strove against all other powers. He trusted his lieutenants only as far as he trusted his soldiers and his slaves: as far as he had power, fear or force, upon them. And no further.

Fortunately, he had plenty of fear and force to spare. Yet, he would draw more power—*every* power—into his hands, to be directed and dispersed at his command.

This, was his choice.

"May we have some light beneath the trees to see the threat, Midomo?" asked Lieutenant Noth.

"No, you may not. I myself cannot see who is watching us; and it would be worse than useless for me to reveal my presence to enemies *you* will *also* not be able to see. My slaves shall provide us adequate warning, if we are approached."

"Then none of you shall have adequate warning it seems."

One slave screamed, and scrambled away from a nearby bush.

A tall limber form rose out of the bush—blacker than the fallen night beyond the stars above; darker than the darkness underneath the nearby trees.

The other slaves scattered in all directions, quailing.

Noth and Alt paused only for a moment, discerning the figure in the gloom, hearing the deepness of his chuckle—then recalling a standing order of their liege, they leaped to attack.

They shouted no battle cry; war for them was a business, not an art. Two flanking attacks, together in the quiet darkness, should have meant an immediate victory over their target.

Artabanus knew better—knew that the man, who had crept so closely, could see in this pitchiness almost as well as the magus himself.

And as for fighting in the dark—

—seeming not even to tense, seeming not even to look, the man of the dark raised both his arms to catch the falling blades.

Steel rang on steel—shrugging, the dark man twisted his arms and hands, linking the blades of Noth and Alt, meshing, entrapping—inextricably twining their swords together, within the curving talons of steel above one hand.

The other set of talons rested gently, pointed up beneath the throat of Alt. The casualness of the gesture showed it might have been Noth as easily.

"I come to you, Artabanus, in peace," the man proclaimed; deeply, precisely. "To show you this, I give you back the lives of your guard." Two more twists—their swords flew into the shadows. "Although I think I shall keep their swords for now," he added—and whitened the darkening forest with his smile.

"Stay your hands," Artabanus ordered his men. "I accept your pledge of peace for now, juacuar. To show you this, I give you back *your* life—which I had been going to take."

A crackling hiss of a whistle—

—two smooth and perfect globes burst into existence, encasing within them an orange and reddish purpling swirl of vapor: elemental Phyre and traces of raw materia. They sank, down to the ground, guided by Artabanus. "Although I think my officers shall *now* retrieve their swords," the magus added.

His own smile was faint and cold.

The magus and the juacuar continued smiling in the dying sunglow of the plasmalights, taking measure of each other; Noth and Alt both stepped away from this unsettling man, whose arms now rested across his chest, claws of steel extruding the length of a hand beyond each hand, from steel-bound bracers of leather wrapped around his wrists.

The officers each walked over to a light; the juacuar released an appreciative chuckle, as they found their swords. "You pick subordinates well! Their minds do not lack honing, whatever might be said about their weapon-skill."

Artabanus continued smiling. "They serve me well; thus live to serve me, till they die. And I do not expect them to approach remotely to the skill of any juacuar that has survived the Culling."

One brief nod, acknowledging the compliment. Upon his brow the dark man wore a ring of polished wood—as if a crown.

"Tell me, juacuar," Artabanus said, "how you have heard my name. I know that it hasn't been spoken, in my hearing, since I came to where I stand." He let the globes dissolve; the treeline darkness under burning starlight seemed to pulse without the Phyre.

Alt and Noth stopped, where they were standing, till they could gain their bearings, flanking the confrontation at a distance.

"Your scouting pairs still speak to one another—though they *do* speak softly. Once or twice your name was mentioned. Bomas is my own name. And why do you restore the land to darkness—Artabanus?" He started pacing forward.

"On your next step you will die," Artabanus casually told the juacuar—who carefully set a bare black foot, back to a standing position. "As for why I choose the darkness, I remind you, who no doubt have already heard our conversation, that I expect a rival to soon arrive in the area. Light reveals its source much farther than it illuminates; as *you* must be well aware."

"It seems you need no light yourself in any event."

"Or, perhaps you shouldn't speak as you walk, providing a gauge to your distance and rate of approach." The juacuar had surely heard him reminding his men, implicitly, that he himself *could* see in the dark; however, Artabanus certainly wouldn't be giving a free confirmation of this, to any man who had managed to creep so close *despite* the magus' long-bound posiscrution . . . !

"So, do you wish for me to retreat a couple of steps, Artabanus?" Bomas slyly grinned.

"You may stay at that distance, if you feel more comfortable there," replied Artabanus, smiling his own oblique insult.

Granted, such a man might reach him in time to rip open fatal wounds, whatever Artabanus jotted. But, he refused to show concern—a casual bluff, if accepted, would serve for now as his first and most reliable shield from attack.

Still—*this* was why he intended to destroy *all* remnants of the Hunting Cry. Artabanus refused to let men live who could kill even faster than himself.

Yet, he was also enjoying this standoff, testing his wit and courage against this unfettered killer. How could he hope to reign, if he could not savor such a moment?

"You carry yourself very well, as appropriate for a man with the title given to you by one of your scouts, Artabanus—a title affirmed by the other man, and not denied."

"To which of my titles do you refer, juacuar?"

"Does *my* name frighten you so, that you cannot even dare to speak it . . . Arbiter?" His sly smile widened slightly.

"Whatever you call your name means nothing to me, juacuar," Artabanus smoothly retorted, "for I see only one of you, and so need not distinguish." *That* wiped the dark man's smile away, he noticed with satisfaction. "Furthermore, you err. No one *gives* me that title. I choose to take it for myself; and I choose for the world to acknowledge it. Thus it is fated, for I control fate."

"You dare great things, Artabanus," came the low reply. "I have heard of many Arbiters—but I have heard of none who seized that title by their wish."

"You have heard of many Arbiters; therefore you have heard of many who succeeded at seizing their title, juacuar. Of the ones who failed, you hear *nothing*. History swept them into the compost heap where they belong. The Arbiter of the recent Era, Anshu, chose the shape of his history, naming himself the Arbiter, and pronouncing the judgment of right and wrong."

Bomas shrugged. "Perhaps we have heard of different stories, Artabanus. Anshu claimed that Heaven granted to him the title and the authority. I have never heard he claimed it for himself."

"What is Heaven, but another name for fate? And what is fate, but the active choices of men? Anshu told the people what the people wanted to hear. Will you deny he gripped the intransigent necks of the magi who ruled their paltry territories—the ones whose independent wars had ignited a Culling? Will you deny he forced on them a fealty oath, to the Cadre he instituted, setting chains of convention upon them, thereby bringing law and stability into the land?

Have you ever heard of a single mage he allowed to live outside the Cadre? Or who, in violation of membership, escaped from Anshu's wrath? After his own death, Anshu's successors followed his steps. *That* is the power of *one* man, in and over history, juacuar. For this Era, *I* choose to be that man. *I* shall restore the stability. And *I* shall have all power over the present and over the future."

"*All* power?" Bomas emphasized. "I do not deny the sense of your reading of history; Anshu, however, did *not* consolidate Mikonese nations beneath himself."

Artabanus snorted. "Anshu had no need for what you call 'consolidation'. The Cadre had the power; and Anshu controlled the Cadre. Thus he controlled the actual power, letting the people imagine whatever they liked about their own freedoms."

"So you shall *also* follow in his footsteps—you who shall control and choose your path," retorted Bomas, an edge of mockery in his voice.

"Anshu erred, thus making another Culling inevitable. I shall not. There *shall not* be a Cadre, *no* more magi at all. Fate itself has shown us this, for haven't the Cadrists slain each other in yet another foolish war, ripping apart society? Anshu did not read the mandate of 'heaven'," the magus sneered, "for he let the magi live! I shall have *no* rivals, thus no repeat of that error. My peers shall *far* more easily die than his."

"Your strategy seems both sound and notable, I must admit," Bomas nodded, absently scratching the side of his neck with one deceptively delicate talon. "I salute your endeavor, Artabanus, and I wish you well. For," he viciously grinned, "I think you shall find your task more difficult than you expect. Or have you not heard of the man, approaching us through the forest now?"

One uneasiness slipped as a sliver through the heart of Artabanus. "I shall make my *own* estimation about his level of threat to me, juacuar."

"Of course," the dark man shrugged. "I would do the same, myself. Indeed, my reason for being here now, is that I seek a brigade to serve. And so I shall watch a meeting between the local captains."

"To serve?" Artabanus echoed. "And what of the Cry? Do you *not* serve it first? Or have you abandoned it?"

The magus found he couldn't read the smile he saw upon the face of Bomas.

"The Cry, has been Culled—as a man with *your* advantages must by *now* be aware, Artabanus. Only a scattering handful of the Guacu-ara now survive: there is no longer a Cry for me to serve. Thus, the fact I serve no Cry, does *not* mean I am a traitor, O Artabanus," Bomas chuckled. "Whether I will serve *you*, or not, remains to be seen."

"You may serve me, juacuar. Or you may die. I offer this choice to you—the choice I offer to all." Normally this was *not* a choice he would offer to a juacuar:

he very likely would kill the killer anyway, whatever the black man chose. As enjoyable as this conversation had been, while waiting for his proper peer, Artabanus had some other things to do in life than waiting to defend himself against a leap in the dark.

Bomas shrugged again. "Respectfully, I decline the choice, until I see more of the facts."

"To decline, is to choose."

"Perhaps . . ." And now the juacuar did tense himself. "My nose, however, tells me that your visitor shall be arriving momentarily." A northern breeze was certainly blowing through the trees, Artabanus noticed . . . "And so I regret that you must end our conversation so completely—for this man approaching must *himself* be of the caliber of the Arbiter! You seem to fear that I might choose to follow *him* instead of *you!*"

Now the magus heard feet, tromping through the forest underbrush, approaching from the north. "Very well, juacuar," he murmured. "Step aside, and watch, and make your choice."

The dark man moved to a side of the clearing, not quite under trees but against them. Artabanus motioned for both his men to quietly step back under the edge of the trees behind himself; as he also did—blending into the darkness instead of standing beneath the lights above.

The magus was more than a little annoyed at himself, however: this killer had managed to prick his pride, conniving a few more minutes of life!

But, he also had to admit, the game *was* growing more interesting.

Perhaps, he mused, the juacuar would serve as a useful demonstration, at an opportune moment.

And he smiled.

Yet . . . he wished that he could rid himself, of the feeling that someone else, someone he *still* had not accounted for . . .

was watching . . .

CHAPTER 47

Artabanus watched the figures approaching through the forest, limned in his sight by the energy binding the particles of the material world. In darkness, he lost only shadings of color: he could still see every leaf, every twig, every blade of grass.

To be seen by Artabanus, was to be a moment away from death.

His ears, on the other hand, were not thus amplified by the scrution he kept habitually bound on his eyes. But then again, no amplification was necessary.

"I hear . . . I hear voices . . . we heard them, over here . . ." A frantic mutter preceded the group.

A skinny young thin-haired man walked into the outlying clearing. He certainly wasn't using a posiscrution or similar jotting; his head was bobbing this way and that, in consternation.

"You Who Fill the Cavicorn, come out!" the robed man shouted, squinting in irritation under the misty colored suffusion of the heavens, while his servants—brutal men indeed, thus easy targets—shifted behind him uncomfortably.

A curious title, Artabanus thought. Was it supposed to refer to him? Was someone else expected? The itching suspicion remained in place, that someone else was watching—perhaps that explained it . . .

"I know you are here, for I have foreseen it!" Foreseen? Even more curious . . . "Show yourself, or commence your attack. We do have other things we wish to no, WE DON'T!!" he grated his voice in a shifted pitch. The Mad One began to bang his head against a tree, with steady increasing force; although at every bounce he would shake his head, muttering under his breath.

This was truly pathetic.

Artabanus chose to end this farce.

He jotted a catalyzt upon this "Praxiteles". The man would tremble and jerk, his blood boiling even in his brain, likely unable to jott an effective response; after some moments of this, the Mad One would burst like the bubbles upon his own lips, providing the brutes behind him an excellent object lesson. They might even swear an honest fealty to himself, after such a display—

"GAHH-AAHHHH!" Praxiteles spun in place.

Then he began to laugh.

Artabanus lost his grip, in shock, upon the catalyzt—and even on his scrution. Night descended on his eyes.

What he'd just seen was *impossible* . . . wasn't it??

"MONGREL!" shouted Praxiteles. "NOW I WILL GRANT WHAT *YOU* HAVE REFUSED TO *ME!*" Without semantics or percussives, and with only natural movements, the Mad One started throwing balls of fire, up and out in all directions. The streaking globes, smelling of burning pitch, careened into nearby trees, igniting them ablaze.

The men of the Mad One knelt in obeisance; avoiding one or two of the sizzling missiles. Noth and Alt instinctively threw themselves to the ground, scrambling to find a safety that might not exist.

Artabanus couldn't *decide* what to do, where to go . . . how *could* a jotting simply *fail* like that?! Could this man dissipate? But, no, that required a continuous upkeep: no one could possibly bind an intentive sphere impervious to intent! And this man . . .

. . . this man wasn't jotting *anything!* Not even the balls of searing fire . . . !

Off to the side, Bomas put his hands on his hips, his steel claws flaring out below, and boldly laughed.

Praxiteles shifted his glare between the laughing black-skinned man—who restrained his laughter long enough to helpfully point to Artabanus—and the tall magus.

"So, mongrel, you dare to strike at Gamin! I shall *crush* you like the rotten olive your skin resembles, wait no I won't," Praxiteles shifted his tone—or Gamin? How many mad magi now wandered these woods . . . ?!

Artabanus briefly considered begging forgiveness—then dismissed that cowardly notion.

"And why won't you kill me, stranger?" he brashly asked instead. Better to bluff, perhaps . . .

"Mmmm . . . that is for someone else, not I . . ." the thin magus mumbled, although he didn't sound afraid. "And, I had forgotten why I had come; not to slay you, no . . ." He snapped his mouth shut.

Well enough, decided Artabanus. "Then I welcome you, Gamin, to my camp, as I believe I heard you name yourself—"

"AACKKK!" The Mad One—surely there couldn't be *two* such men nearby!—violently waved his hands in front of his face. "I am Praxiteles, Praxiteles! You, however, may call me Sire . . ."

So, Praxiteles didn't want to be referred to, by this name that he himself had used.

Artabanus smiled. A little sliver of power, a subtle chink in the armor . . .

"Very well: I greet you, Praxiteles! Your reputation precedes you, and I can honestly say you are meeting it very adequately!" Not to be outdone, he added, "I am Artabanus. You, however, may call me—"

"ARRRRBITERRRR. . . ." the Mad One hissed, a vicious sparkle in his eyes, somehow crushing the 'r's into sibilants.

"Well . . ." Artabanus found himself taken aback, somewhat, by the manner of this interruption! "Yes, you may call me that, if you prefer. *I* have no objection in the least." He chuckled, flicking a glance toward the juacuar; who seemed to be merely enjoying the spectacle. "Would I, perchance, be also the One Who Fills the Cavicorn . . . whatever that means?"

"Oh, yes, you are that one . . ."

And Praxiteles began to chuckle, too.

Artabanus normally would have slain *anyone* who could laugh like *that!* However, he wasn't yet sure how to possibly slay this man. Perhaps the juacuar would have a use after all . . . ?

A falling branch from a burning tree nearby, reminded the magus of other priorities.

"If you will douse your lights," he offered, "I will gladly provide some less distracting illumination."

"*Why* should I?" the Mad One growled; his eyes drank in the glowings, giving nothing back. "Let it burn."

"Ah. Then I will do it myself." The tall magus walked from tree to tree, systematically jotting Phyrebelles; letting their surfaces redirect thermal energy out of the natural world and into the Puria, leaving a paradoxical sheen of frost behind; and then replacing the fires with plasmalights—which *still* could serve for attacking, in a pinch. He also reestablished his posiscrution, binding it into place.

Praxiteles only watched.

Their officers grimly eyed each other. Artabanus judged his two could take the three of Praxiteles, however.

Assuming the juacuar did *not* join the Mad One.

"So!—here we are, together, speaking as captains to each other," continued Artabanus, once he had order restored. "If you are not here to kill me, may I know why you have come?"

"No."

"Ah." Artabanus pondered how he should respond to this—until he heard a group from his camp approaching tentatively.

"Perhaps you are here to secure the release of the scout I have captured," suggested Artabanus—though he doubted it strenuously. "I return him to you as a sign of respect." He snapped his fingers.

Two burly soldiers, bearing a pole upon their shoulders, trotted into the plasma glares. The scout hung, slung from the pole, bound to it hand and foot, a sack pulled over his head, sporting cuts and burns from his interrogation. He had been offered no hope for anything better than a faster death.

And he was screaming and thrashing.

He had begun this on hearing the offer.

At their commander's gesture, the soldiers set their squirming load, and backed away again into the campward treeline.

"He was sufficiently helpful," explained Artabanus, "so we have no further use for him. Although we shall keep the collapsed-carbon axe he wore; we *do* have a use for that."

"No, Sire, please . . . ! I told them nothin', he lies . . . !"

Artabanus held his peace, and watched his foe.

Praxiteles stepped one pace at a time, half-circling the pole and his frantic minion—then in one movement he sank to a crouch, lanced his arm forward, and ripped the hood from the head of the scout: showing no concern at all that Artabanus *might* attempt an assault from the side.

"He lies, lies . . ." quivered the scout.

"I hunger," the Mad One stated, his voice inhuman.

The arm lashed out again; the thumb and fourth-finger pressed into the cheeks of the scout, who inhaled to scream; the first and third of his fingers touched the open eyes.

No scream—only a hiss of air emerged. The Mad One clenched his hand, and stood, and brought his fist to his mouth.

Praxiteles drank nothing, as far as Artabanus saw—but the scout, though twisting and twitching, now was dead.

"A little stronger Gamin grows, forcing other strengths to serve . . ." chanted the skinny magus. "Who shall be next, I wonder?"

And he turned his back on Artabanus. His three lieutenants prostrated themselves to him.

Desperate plans flashed through the mind of the Krygian magus: clearly, this man must die!—but how?! Not even one plan commended itself as feasible . . . he ground his teeth in frustration.

"Who shall serve Gamin next? Or, *shall* there be another? Who shall bring Gamin to nothing?" Praxiteles slyly mused. "*No* threats, here or there, to my left or to my right; not before me; not *behind* me . . ." Now he verged on laughter. "Not below me, for I am risen above the ones below . . . yes, *I* am the first, who once was the last, and of all who walk the face of the world, I, I, *I am* the worst!—

the *first* of the worst . . . and the skies have withdrawn, so my rede is complete. Let them watch, *let them watch the mother burn . . .*"

A knife, thought Artabanus. He did wear a knife, as every man who walked the woods, a long serrated knife. He *wouldn't* look weak in front of the damned juacuar! He would test his fate, seize his fate, *write* his fate, with one long *lunge* . . . let this maniac shrug away a wristlength worth of cold sharp steel . . . !

"Watch . . . watch . . ." teased whoever this Mad One was. Artabanus tensed himself to draw and to spring in one fluid movement . . .

"Watch . . . watch . . . watch watch watchingwatching—!" The other magus shifted from confident taunting to rising panic. His head was bobbing left and right . . . Artabanus *wanted* to strike—but . . .

he *was* afraid . . . afraid of what this man might do, if he sensed the incoming blow . . .

Artabanus thoroughly cursed himself, and gripped his fear, along with the pommel of—!

"WATCHING!!"

Praxiteles spun in evident fear to face his foe.

At first, Artabanus panicked—thinking the fear was of him.
Then he exulted and readied to strike—thinking the fear was of him!
but then—

"DON'T YOU FEEL THEM *WATCHING?!!*" the Mad One shrieked, lunging, grabbing Artabanus by the lapels of his field-jacket.

One part of the mind of the Krygian magus said:
now! plunge in the knife!
—but another part jumped to the front and shouted:
wait! *he feels it, too!*

"What . . . ?" he rasped to his rival. "Who . . . ?"

"THEM! *HIM!* THE *WORST!!* IT ISN'T *FAIR,* HE SHOULDN'T *BE* HERE!" The Mad One flapped the lapels so quickly, they seemed to buzz.

. . . . . . the *worst?*

Artabanus felt his flesh creep—a feeling new to him.

He hated that feeling.

He would *smite* whatever inspired that feeling!

Presently, that "whatever" seemed to be Praxiteles . . . !

Before he could strike, the Mad One flung his jacket wide, then turned to fretter away at an angle, muttering, "Where, wherewherewherewhere . . ."

The curiosity of Artabanus, fought against his practicality.

"*Where* are they, Praxiteles?" he softly asked, his eyes locked on the frantic magus. "*Who* is watching us—from where?"

"Not to the left or the right," the Mad One panted. "*Not* before—not behind . . . not below," he stopped in his tracks, "no, no, *not* below, but——

"ABOVE!!"

He pointed.

Artabanus squinted at the starry skies. With his scrution, he could see some distant drifting clouds—at night invisible normally.

Praxiteles wasn't pointing at clouds.

Many paces distantly high, there hung a scene—just like a long and frameless painting.

Lamp- and wisplight flowed from that frame. It seemed to face down at them—yet with a giddy disbalance, Artabanus saw the figures of people, standing along the edge . . .

Something smacked Artabanus on his bottom—his teeth clicked, narrowly missing his tongue.

"SLAY HIM NOW, OR ALL IS LOST!" The Mad One thrashed his head, his eyes squeezed shut, his jaw distended in his scream. *"DO IT, DO IT, DO IT!!"*

A cold wet hand was gripping the heart of the man who chose to be the Arbiter, squeezing, crushing.

when he had been very, very young . . .
    . . . he had imagined the Eye and His Agents watching the world like this . . .

But that was a story for children.

He threw every plasmalight, up toward the scene of impossible sanity; jotting more, and *more,* his concentration stretching past the breaking point—hurling the plasma, along with his hate, his hatred and fear—of being *watched* . . . !

Almost, it was out of range. Almost, but not quite.

Some of the plasma prematurely exploded, due to the fracturing stress of his concentration and also the distance involved. But, enough of them found their way into that place.

The window tilted, vanished—and only the stars remained.

Artabanus sat, where he had stumbled, panting.

Praxiteles merely stood, growling.

Artabanus gathered himself, rose to his feet, and jotted more plasmalights.

Praxiteles wiped his mouth, swallowed his growling, and straightened his robes.

Then the magi faced each other—though Praxiteles seemed distracted by something below Artabanus at a distance.

"So," Artabanus said. "Did I slay him? Whoever was watching?"

"Him . . . *him?*" the Mad One muttered. "No, not *him* . . . But . . . !"

The skinny magus then looked up, smiling the smile of a viperwyrm.

"But, you *shall!*" he hissed. "I surely see it! *You* shall slay him, You Who Fills the Cavicorn, *you* shall break his heart and slay him, pulverizing his body to atoms by the destruction you unleash! For this coming morning, I shall spare your life this evening."

Praxiteles bowed to Artabanus, laughing lowly. And, then turning west, the Mad One walked away. His minions picked themselves up and hurried to flank him.

"Yet," the strange man added, over his shoulder, as if in afterthought, "who holds the Tower of Qarfax shall slay *you*. This also is certain. Although," he granted, in that offhanded voice, "so long as you yourself are holding the Tower, all your plans and ambitions will surely succeed.

"Make your choice, maker of choices."

Artabanus heard the Mad One laughing, after the man had disappeared into the forest.

The Krygian magus stood for minutes, not exactly in thought, but in re-ordering his mind.

"Here, Bomas!" he called, turning to speak to the juacuar—using his name might *now* be somewhat worth— . . .

The black-skinned man was gone.

"Noth . . . Alt . . ." Artabanus breathed, "tell me what I wish to know."

"Sire," saluted Noth. "I would; but I cannot. I do not know when the juacuar departed, nor which way he went."

"Sire," saluted Alt. "I fear I must admit the same."

"Well," Artabanus said, at length. "Upon the path I choose, *many* threats will stand."

"All power to Artabanus," Noth sincerely replied.

"The power of right and wrong to the Arbiter," added Alt, no less sincere.

Within his heart, a flicker arose, a trickle of light—a feeling of gratitude. Almost Artabanus gave them, from his heart, his thanks for loyalty.

He killed the impulse.

He would not enslave himself to *any* ideals of others, striving to meet their expectations.

"Just so," he smiled to Noth, and watched his lieutenant's pleasure at hearing the simple reply, a favorite phrase of Noth's. Artabanus figured it served himself very well.

"You truly have seen the path that I shall follow," he answered Alt, who nodded once in satisfaction.

Then his lieutenants both looked west.

"Clearly," they said together, "he must die."

Artabanus wasn't about to tell them, that he had already failed to kill the Mad One at least twice this evening, once through sheer lack of nerve, and once through . . . what?

Why should jottings simply *fail* to affect that man?

Could a dissipation sphere be sigiltraced, thus carried on a person? *That* seemed no more possible as a theory—besides, Praxiteles had had no trouble in jotting his own effects . . .

But, no, he had never *once* jotted *any* effect—had he?

"Midomo!" Alt exclaimed. "I think I recognize an important weakness of that man."

"Speak on."

"I may be saying what you have already noticed, Midomo," Alt continued, "but, not only did this Praxiteles, or Gamin, seem to greatly fear whoever stood in the sky—"

"A fact that you may be able to turn to *your* advantage, Midomo," Noth interrupted, sagely nodding.

"But also," Alt continued, "I noticed: *he himself dared not attack!*"

"Ah," nodded Noth. "Or, possibly even *could not!*"

Artabanus gently exhaled, and pondered, pursing his lips. "You have rightly seen," he agreed.

"Midomo, consider!" Noth continued. "We know the damage your globes create whenever they detonate. Dangerous, yes," he added in haste, lest he be seeming to give offense, "and yet, to the same extent as *that* man's fire?" He didn't exactly dare to say it was less; but that didn't matter.

"So, here is a man," stated Alt, "greatly fearing the ones who watched, who should have been able to drown that . . . room . . . in *his* own fire; *but* who had to call on *you*—in desperation even!"

"What else *could* it mean, Misire?" Noth rhetorically asked in conclusion.

Artabanus mulled this over, however, sending his mind down other paths, just to be sure . . .

He found an alternative explanation.

He had followed this Mad One's direct command.

Praxiteles had *ordered* him to strike. And he had struck.

No!—he'd struck of his *own* accord, choosing the action which best advanced his *own* goals . . . !

And how, he forced himself to ask, did attacking those people best further his goals? Who were they, that he should attack them? Praxiteles hadn't said—only blathered some ominous drivel.

The magus cast his memory back . . . but not a single bit of useful information could be gleaned from Praxiteles' words, by which he could even imagine choosing such a response.

He simply and reflexively had *obeyed*.

One more reason to slay that man.

And *not* a reason that he would be sharing with Noth or Alt.

Those people in the window, though—who *were* they? Could *they*, perhaps, be set against the Mad One?

He focused his memory once again, their shapes distinct to his mind's eye, thanks to the posiscrution's clarity, even from that distance. Their shapes looked somehow familiar . . .

Yes! The brute in the background . . . larger even than Praxiteles' body-guards. Earlier in the day, he had been leaving Qarfax's Tower with the other juacuar, the one with the strange stick-weapon, along with two other men—a short man, and a Krygian such as Artabanus himself.

He didn't recall those other men or the juacuar at the gap in the sky; but, he *did* recognize the silhouette of that giantish man, especially with the framework worn on the back, rising above the head, which held the large man's weapon.

Furthermore—his first two scouts had reported in, not long ago, after being relieved of their watch at the edge of the dell. What had they said? A man who wore on his arm a metallic contraption, and also a leafcutter on his belt, had left the dell, walking south. Yes, possibly, possibly . . . the distance and lack of color made for problems; but, Artabanus trusted the discipline of his memory: that man might *also* have been at the window.

As well, the scouts had reported *another* man, unlike no other they ever had seen, with skin and hair the color of sand, who'd come to the door to draw in the dirt. So had a woman, to watch the man, with short thick hair pulled back from her face and ears.

He had seen a woman, too, above. The servant had who stood behind her *might* have been the sandish-colored man; that was much less certain. As for the woman . . .

The woman his scouts had seen, had walked and talked with an air of authority.

The woman *he* had seen, had stood at the edge of the gap, hands on her hips, as if looking down on insects under glass. Until the man who had stood in her shadow had pulled her away from the incoming plasma. She hadn't been wearing an obvious weapon.

A maga?

Artabanus fingered his chin—and crushed a sudden cascade of too many feelings, blurring his mind, confusing him . . .

Maga or not, the evidence showed that whoever controlled the Tower could make the effect that he had seen.

And what could be jotted *into* their . . . room . . . ? could also be jotted *out.* Or shot. Or marched.

They could attack with near impunity, pulling away from counterattack, reappearing anywhere else at will. Any number of troops could strike him *anywhere.*

And, what would happen to anything caught in the path of that window, when it opened?

Worse—what if Praxiteles, the rodent, seized this power first?!

"Noth, Alt. We will assault the Tower tomorrow morning."

"All power to Artabanus!" they saluted.

Yes, he thought, as he turned to return to camp. He *must* possess the Tower without delay. Praxiteles, it seemed, spoke truth in his riddles. Whoever held the Tower, could slay him. But, if *he* held the Tower . . . !

He halted in surprise.

"What, girl—*you* are still here??"

"Misire, I have done what you told me . . . but, you didn't give me leave to go." She shook in fear. "If I haven't pleased you, I beg you to let me try again! I didn't mean to fail you . . . !" She started to weep.

"Ha! Rise, girl!—I am not displeased at all! Rise—and cease your sniffling!" The girl now stood, unable to look at him, trying to wipe her nose on the sleeve of her single garment. "Cease, or I shall give you something to snivel about indeed," he smiled, as he looked her up and down. Releasing the binds, carefully, on the plasmalights, he saw the girl in the dark.

He focused upon her. Her hair began to float.

"No! Oh, *please,* Misire," she cried, "I am *trying* to cease, *please,* give me a chance . . . !"

"Noth, Alt—return to camp. Configure a plan of approach to the Tower. I shall meet you in an hour. Perhaps an hour and a half."

"Midomo!" they saluted, and immediately they marched away.

"Hush, girl," he ordered, for *still* she was begging, afraid of the suffering he had inflicted on others with this effect. "I do not intend to wipe your nose for an hour. Here . . ."

She sighed, as he focused further.

"Better. Now, walk in front of me. Go to my tent."

She turned and walked, as if in a dream, her hair floating.

He followed, enwrapping her in his power.

Every power would be his.

and yet . . .

He had done *exactly* what that "Praxiteles" had wanted. In virtually every instance.

It *grated* him—being forced, or tricked, or led, or pushed into being the tool of someone else. To live his life to serve their wishes; *their* plans, *their* gain. To be nothing more than a slave, just like . . . this girl, for instance, in front of him, who dared not rebel against him, who suffered whatever pleasures and pains he chose to give for his own sake.

And then, for a moment . . .

. . . for one bare instant . . .

. . . he knew, truly *knew*, what anguish this girl must feel.

This girl had always lived her life for someone else—certainly since his brigade had acquired her from . . . wherever.

What he resented and swore to prevent, with hope of success, this girl had always had to bear, with no escape. She would bear it tonight, and tomorrow, too, assuming she survived, and the day after that, forever—for he would *never* release her this side of death.

Not that the girl was unique—far from it. Others had been before her. But: she was here, right now, in his sight.

in that one moment . . . he sympathized with her.

it was horrible.

Two choices lay before him, each an escape from the horror.

He chose to kill his sympathy.

There. That was easy. The other choice had promised . . . something. It didn't matter anymore. Only *he,* Artabanus, mattered; and everything now was in order again, with himself at the center, where he should be.

except . . .

. . . he *still* felt watched, by someone he couldn't account for, looking even into his thoughts—and reviling him.

Artabanus, despite the filtered lens he chose to wear, could be remarkably perceptive, on occasion.

I assure you of this, beloved.

CHAPTER 48

"What'n th' flamin' *spew* are y' *doin'* down here?!"

The thug barreled round the doorframe of the laboratory, having charged down the narrow stairs. He skidded to a stop, avoiding various scattered burning books and scrolls. Seifas, following close behind, leapt past to the gap in the wall.

"Putting out fires!" answered Jian, with his usual cheerfulness. "Oh, they aren't big fires," he added, as if that wasn't obvious, "but . . . um . . . I guess we could use more help."

"And a shirt," Othon chuckled. Jian was smothering various flames with his new green shirt, which Othon tromped with his battle-boots.

"Jus' can't leave y' alone five minutes, without y'bringin' th' Tower down aroun' all our ears . . ." Pooralay muttered. But, with everyone helping—Seifas and Pooralay, Othon and Gaekwar, Portunista, Jian and even Dagon—the fires were soon extinguished.

"So, what happened?" Seifas asked, while they worked.

"Short version," Dagon replied, while carefully pouring some beakers of water on fires, them stamping the embers out.

"I wander up here, and find that we now can make holes in the wall over there, up high in the sky, by using a ball on this table, here, which serves as a map. I suggest that we use it to scout out the other brigades. Since I'm from the east myself, I start with the eastern one. It's certainly bigger than ours, and we can look *right* down at them from hundreds of paces up high in the sky, by rolling this ball on the map. A bunch of lights and explosions go off on the north side of camp; so, I twiddle the map in that direction. The fires are put out a minute later, and then some little orange wisplighty things—" "Plasmalights," the maga corrected him absently. "—little orange wisplighty things, pop up all over down below. Some guy starts screaming like a girl, then stops again. Another guy starts up instead, like he's angry or scared or both, and hugs another guy. Can't hardly hear them otherwise, 'cause the rotblooded window's too high in the sky, and Qarfax the Inimitable," Dagon sneered, "apparently didn't *complete* the table's controls, which means that we *can't* move the window up or down! Everyone's crowding right up to the edge of the window, discussing the matter, despite the

241

fact that I *TOLD* them not to," Dagon glared, "and as usual I was right, because the hugging guy hears us, or something, and throws some kind of fit, screaming 'Slay him, slay him, do it, do it,'" Dagon mocked in falsetto. "Then all the hells break loose, and fireballs start coming up in our direction, and lots get through before I can turn off the table. Then the thug jumps down the stairs and wants to know what in the flaming spew is going on. The end."

"You'll never be *quite* a bard!" Jian laughed, though not unkindly. "And I would-n't call *this* 'all the hells breaking loose,' exactly," he added, gesturing round.

"Oh, and how would *you* know what all the hells breaking loose looks like, sheepherder?" retorted Dagon; to which the fair man shrugged and smiled, "Good point!"

"Hells or not, I guess we were lucky that no one was hit directly," Gaekwar said.

"They only were plasmalights," Portunista muttered, flicking a glance at Jian. Seifas suddenly wondered whether the new green shirt had been ruined be-fore or after Jian had used it to smother fires . . .

"Why *didn't* they use something stronger?" wondered the juacuar, half to himself.

"Range problems, maybe," Portunista answered. "My *own* reach, in jotting, as you may have noticed by now, is rather limited. *Not* from lack of strength or training," she added defensively. "Even Cadrists don't—didn't—have much of a greater range than me. Remember Gaekwar saying, a week or so ago, that Qar-fax could have mulched an army, if he had wanted to? That's mostly bluff. Well," she granted, "not *entirely* bluff . . . but skill and ingenuity count the most for a mage in a fight. Some melémagi would specialize only in three, or even two jot-tings—*but,* they were deadly clever at how they used them."

"So, we can't just pop up ov'r an army and rain y'r pen-ta-darts on 'em?"

Portunista shook her head at Pooralay's question. "No, it just isn't feasible—not from the height the table's apparently locked at."

"Nor can we use it to run some soldiers behind their lines," Dagon groused. "It isn't even as good as the map upstairs for scouting. Not the way it currently is."

"Speaking of which . . ." Seifas heard a man running down the stairs outside the laboratory.

"Commander Seifas . . . Commanders!" exclaimed the watching-guard, see-ing all the officers in the room. "We're gonna have some company soon!"

A minute later, they all stood looking up at the map, in Qarfax's living-room.

"Five of 'em, headin' straight fer th' Tower. Too close t' in-ter-cept already," Pooralay mused. "I mean from ambush."

"Tell us about those people, soldier," Portunista ordered.

"Near as I can figure, Commander," he nervously answered—probably he had not *ever* been paid so much command attention, Seifas smiled to himself— "these are the ones that Jian had watched, approaching the eastern camp from the north, a little while back. Including that one trailing dot you saw, Comman—er, Jian," he stuttered.

"The one who followed the four?" Jian asked. The soldier nodded. Jian continued, "But now they're together, I see . . ." Jian rubbed his beard in thought.

"Yessir: he slipped around in front of that group, after they started moving west, and met 'em. Now they're all coming here."

Seifas went to the eastern window and looked out onto the dell. Minutes passed in silence at first; then Dagon started to argue with Pooralay whether the squad had been *really* too close to be intercepted.

"What's the point of setting an ambush anyway?" Gaekwar asked eventually, interrupting the escalating debate. "Obviously, they're coming to us already, right?"

"Cover *and* numbers," Othon agreed.

"Just as well we didn't send anyone anyway," murmured Jian. Seifas turned to look where Jian was pointing: the squad was slowly angling around the two eastern scouts. "I guess it also verifies the squad itself isn't eastern."

"How did they know those scouts were there, in the dark, from *that* far away?" Seifas wondered.

As the dots approached the rim of trees, the juacuar returned to the eastern window, leaning out to block the light behind him as much as he could, letting his eyes drink in the starry glory.

Shapes walked onto the sloping incline: three large men, a smaller one leading, and walking beside the smaller one . . .

Seifas heard a gasp.
Then he realized the gasp was his.

"What? What do you see?" Portunista and others crowded behind him, trying to look out the narrow window. This attempt, though doomed, ironically did help Seifas: now there was even less backlighting glare to interfere with what his eyes were reporting.

"I see . . ."—he stopped, hardly daring to hope.

Why not dare!? he commanded himself. Hadn't he learned to dare to hope, ever since midsummer?!

"I think . . ." but in fact he was certain, ". . . that one of my brothers is coming."

"You say that like it's *good* news—" But Dagon backed a step, as Seifas turned a glare on him.

"It is *wondrous* news, Krygian! Perhaps *your* friends and family mean so little to you—but you should rejoice that one of *my* brothers is still alive! Now we have a better chance to negotiate with the western brigade, if he is serving them. Unless you *really* want to fight three larger forces, as we stand," concluded Seifas, pushing past them all and striding to the door.

"Um . . . I guess we follow Seifas, hm?" Jian smiled.

And that is what he did.

"Well . . . maybe this will work," admitted Dagon. "Maybe we can kill off one of the captains, if he's dumb enough to come here."

"Sounds like a plan," Gaekwar drawled, as they left the window—no one else could sufficiently see the approaching figures anyway. "I volunteer *you* to attack the guy who might be hurling fireballs while protected by a juacuar who was tough enough to survive the Culling. I'll go take the other three . . ."

Down in the 'basement', Seifas' voice rang clear and strong: "Everyone not a commander, go upstairs!" The squads had brought supplies in casks and crates, scattering them in order to break up any incoming charge through the door— although not enough to provide an adequate cover for archers or even for cross-bowmen. "And free the stairs, for commanders are coming down," he added, somewhat in contradiction—but Seifas was more than a little distracted at the moment.

A brother . . . *another* of the Guacu-ara! Part of his mind had always insisted that he was the last, that all the others had died, because the others had all gone to fight, while he . . .

He shoved that thought away. It didn't help—and, it didn't matter now.

He watched the basement door, not even blinking, not wanting to miss the first clear sight of his brother. The others took up positions in a gently curving arc around him, paralleling the wall behind, centered on Portunista.

He and his brother could talk, just *talk* to each other; together, they would arrange a peace between the two brigades. That was how it had always been before—that was part of why the Hunting Cry existed at all. Why it *still* existed.

Except . . .

Seifas breathed, blinking back tears.

Except, at the end, it all had fallen apart.

Every action, and thus no action, had seemed to be justified.

And Seifas had fled.

He had fled from the fall and the failure of the Cry. Brother had fought against brother, thinking the other to be in the wrong, because they couldn't agree on what was right.

And he had been haunted, over those long slopings since—had he *himself* been the one to abandon the Cry? After all, his brothers had taken their stands, dying with honor. Hadn't they? But, how *could* there be honor, in brother slaying brother? Yet, was there *no* honor in putting one's life on the edge of the blade, defending what one believed was right?!

Whichever way he turned, thorns had torn at him.

But now—he had a chance. He could make it *right* again. He and his brother could show what the Guacu-ara *truly* stood for!

His ears caught the sound of the party's approach, drifting through the door, echoing off the wall of the room.

He smiled. No juacuar would approach like that! Surely, if these people meant them harm, his brother would caution for circumspection—or, at least advise this man, for only one of them seemed to be muttering: it seemed a reassuring and even cheerful sign, in *that* perspective . . .

A thin, greasy-haired man in dark purple robes, rounded the open door, head bowed down in thought. He was the one who was mumbling. Seifas was fond already, of this somewhat absentminded—

—man snapped up his head so sharply, his neck-tendons popped.

Seifas' candle of hope was *crushed* beneath a mountain of ice.

The scream of that man, *echoed* throughout the lines of his face—hateful, desperate, wretched, insane—

The juacuar struggled to keep himself from launching reflexively into an all-out attack. Darting his eyes left and right, he saw that even Jian looked grim, his own eyes shadowed by flickering wall-torches.

Oddly, however, despite such a maddened cry of fear and rage, his brother *hadn't* thrown himself between the leader he served and whatever threat would elicit such a cry. He hadn't even appeared at the door! Were such outbursts from this man a common occurrence?—and so too much should not be read into them . . . ?

This charitable suspicion seemed confirmed a moment later; for the gangly man recovered himself, vaguely blinking and looking around, like a sleepwalker waking to find himself in mildly curious circumstances.

"Ah," the man said calmly. "Yes. I see that I am expected here. Good." And yet, as he stepped through the doorway, he also was casting his eyes in all directions—as if *he* had been expecting someone, but couldn't find that person.

Ten paces into the room he stopped, shifting his robes around him. Three large men, nearly as large as Othon, armored in heavy banding, bustled inside behind him. But only one could fit through the door at a time, and Seifas had to swallow a smile as they jostled for position. Still, they looked brutish and violent; and Seifas could see, when their eyes swept the room, that all they saw were targets.

"This," acerbically muttered Poo, "does *not* bode well . . ."

And then, through the door, walked the man whom Seifas would gladly have died to see.

His brother—though he didn't personally know this man—wore wristbracer talons for weapons. He must be quick and limber, Seifas thought; and the fact that he had survived the Culling testified to his skill. He stood in the background, off to one side, watching every thing—but watching Seifas most of all, as Seifas was watching him.

Except—his brother wasn't smiling.

Well.

Following this example, Seifas restrained his obvious joy. His brother looked older than he, though not by much—no, older in his eyes: serious, competent, focused, professional. A man who *knew* what he was doing, confident in his thoughts, with plans and foresight reaching far and near.

So, Seifas also did his best to assume that air.

But, he felt ashamed; for he was trying to feign an image that wasn't true.

Still, he understood it had to be better than grinning like a schoolboy. So he did his best.

He opened his mouth to announce who they were—who *he* was—

His brother, whom he kept a constant eye upon, gestured flatly with a hand, scowling at him.

Seifas closed his mouth, even more ashamed. What was he doing?!—he was no arbitrator! The Cry had dissolved before he could have even decided to learn that role.

But, the Cry wasn't dead. He and his brother lived! Perhaps there were others. He would keep silent, and learn from this man, who must have indeed risen high in a corps: he wore a headring, such as Seifas had only seen Matrons wear . . .

"So," continued the man in the dark purple robe, calmly, fixing his attention on the maga. "You command this little group. I have . . . heard of you, woman. I have heard your name, once or twice. Portunista, is it not?" And he smiled.

It was not a good smile.

"So you have heard at least one thing correctly, then," she tensely replied. "I cannot say I recognize *you*—although perhaps I might the name . . . ?"

"I am . . . Praxiteles," he pronounced, as if giving them a gift.

Portunista made a show of searching her memory. Then: "No," she carelessly shrugged. "I never have heard of *you* at all."

Even Jian was smiling at this reply, Seifas saw. Still, she should have been more diplomatic, despite her rival's arrogance.

Praxiteles' own smile disappeared for a moment, although his eyes never changed—the eyes his smile had never reached at all.

Then the smile returned, without the veneer of benevolence.

"Well. You have heard it now. Perhaps you will often hear it again in the future."

"Anything *may* be possible, I suppose," Portunista allowed.

"I am here, for . . . . . . two reasons," Praxiteles continued, having apparently paused to tally them in his mind. "First, though not primarily, to see *you,* about whom I have heard a few . . . entertaining stories. Yes," and now he was grinning, as Portunista narrowed her eyes, "a few words mentioned here and there, and I have sometimes . . . thought . . . of meeting you myself." He sighed through his grin. "I'm *glad* I did . . . I *am* glad!" His voice took on a harsher edge, and he twitched.

But then he looked around, in growing confusion, as if he had been expecting a dispute . . .

"Possibly," answered Portunista in a harder voice, "you *won't* be so glad *later.*"

Praxiteles returned his focus to her. "Oh, I am altogether *certain* I am glad. As to whether I continue to be glad to see you, that depends upon the circumstances, does it not?" Now his grin showed teeth.

"Having fulfilled your first-although-the-secondary reason, then, perhaps we now may move along," said Portunista, "to your second-and-so-by-deduction-the-primary reason."

"*Very* glad to accommodate you," he chuckled. "Though later perhaps we'll return to the first-and-by-far-the-more-entertaining reason."

Seifas gripped the aasagai tightly, while he calculated exactly where its sharpened tips would pierce this lout. Brother's ward or not, he doubted he *ever* would come to like this man.

The smile of Jian had long since faded again as well; his hand was also gripping the pommel of his simple sword. Seifas took a moment to consider, with some satisfaction—mixed with an odd and unexpected pang—how well his plans involving Jian and Portunista seemed to be advancing . . .

The gaze of Praxiteles suddenly flew to Jian, his implicative grin dissolving. Well . . . perhaps this wasn't completely surprising. Even Seifas found that cold and narrowed glare unnerving—it was so uncharacteristic of Jian.

"The second reason!" Praxiteles announced, returning his attention to Portunista. "*I* now claim this Tower as *my* possession. I give permission for you to freely leave, you and your . . . men . . . although perhaps I may be persuaded later to let you return here to, hm, assist me." And he resumed that smile. "It depends on how much imagination you use to persuade me, of course."

"Claim this Tower, to your heart's content," replied Portunista. "I give my permission for you to return to your camp, claiming away all you wish, within the safety of your soldiers' embraces." Now Seifas was smiling, too, along with Jian—and diplomacy be damned . . . "I grant this to you, and to your men," continued his Commander, "because it *could* be argued that you have come here under a flag of truce. I suggest, however, you get yourself gone, before I imagine a way to persuade you out the door myself." Out the door, and two paces under the soon-to-be-utterly-blasted slope of the dell, her tone of voice completed for her.

Praxiteles' smile evaporated, like a final breath upon a mirror.

"You have *no* idea to whom you are speaking, wench—"

"As I recall I made that entirely clear when *you* began this meeting," interrupted Portunista. "Although perhaps you were dull enough to misunderstand me. Since our conversation has thus returned in a circle to where it began, I consider it useless and therefore concluded."

Praxiteles flexed his fingers, and ground his teeth. His minions loosened the swords within their sheaths. Seifas, looking left and right, saw his companions readying for the commencement of hostilities. Good—Gaekwar's disker was aimed directly at Praxiteles. Whether or not the man in the robes was a magus, those metal discs could split his throat in the blink of an eye; and *that* would be the end of Praxiteles as a threat.

Yet, his brother continued to lean against the wall. Why did he not intervene?! This was the time to protect his ward, if—

Ah, he was approaching now . . . ! His brother was whispering something into an ear of Praxiteles, who seemed . . . surprised the juacuar was speaking to him?

Seifas couldn't hear what was being said; nor could read the lips—his brother had prudently covered his speech with a hand. But now the leader whom he was advising looked shocked, nervous . . . the magus—*was* he a magus?—swallowed. And also began to sweat.

The other juacuar resumed his casual watching post.

"I . . . accept your terms," the robed man grated through the clenching of his jaws. "For now," he added, softly so that even Seifas could barely hear him.

Praxiteles backed away—his conventional bodyguards scrambled confusedly out of his path to the door. "Come along, Flooder, Stinger, Thunder . . ." Praxiteles instructed. "We shall spare them for the moment, and give them a chance to reconsider resisting me." Seifas nearly laughed aloud—what bodyguards with *any* dignity whatsoever would call themselves by *those* names?!

Then Seifas noticed his brother, the juacuar, had not been mentioned. Yet, after the other four men had left the room, his brother walked to the door as well.

He was *leaving?* Why could he not stay . . . ? *Ah!* Seifas chastised himself. Of course; his brother's first duty, as an induna, *must* be to protect his commander. He would be last from the room, to ensure that there would be no attack from behind. Then he must follow, or take the point, or perhaps he would serve his ward with further advice.

As his brother weighed him critically from across the room, Seifas realized with shame that he himself had totally failed to act in any benefit to the meeting.

Seifas had let his *own* commander provoke the conversation, nearly to the point of violence. The fact that he had agreed with everything Portunista had said, was no excuse. He should have been at her side, to counsel prudence, as his brother had done for *his* commander—as any good induna would have done.

No. As any true man of the Guacu-ara.

He had failed Portunista; and he had failed the Cry.

But—he would work to make it right. He *would* be better in the future. His brother would surely help him.

Now that his brother was here, there was hope.

As Seifas resolved himself to put his trust in his brother's wisdom, he saw the man across the room nod at him.

"I am glad to see you, brother," spoke the juacuar. "I hope that *you* will see me very soon." The man put his arms across his chest, the steel projecting past the shoulders, as he backed from the room.

But Seifas saw his brother's eyes flick leftward once; and though he held his left-hand talons steady, the right ones twitched—leftward past his shoulder.

Westward, where his brother's commander had walked.

Then his brother was gone.

A moment of silence passed.

"Impressive," Othon spoke.

"*That* was y'r impress'n of scream-boy?!" Pooralay exclaimed.

"*Re*-pressive," Othon added, with a furrowed smile.

"Now, unless my ears deceive me," Gaekwar mused, "*this* is the guy who was screeching 'slay him, slay him' earlier."

"Hmph. Those screams *did* sound a lot alike, didn't they?" Portunista smiled lopsidedly, hands on her hips.

"Hey, juacuar! Where are *you* going?" Dagon demanded.

"To speak with my brother," Seifas replied. "No one shall stop me."

And, no one did.

CHAPTER 49

Seifas loped up the dell's south slope. Praxiteles and the others were not yet far away, and Seifas hoped that they would figure that he had been sent with orders to Portunista's brigade encampment southward at the pass.

Rather, he hoped the other four men than his brother would believe this.

He didn't even know the name of his brother of the Cry. But soon this would change—he hoped. He *hoped.*

Not even three minutes later, the long-legged juacuar reached the edge of the dell. But even three minutes can feel like hours, when every moment is counted. Seifas truly hated being exposed for that expanse of time. But, nothing could be done about it; running east to put the Tower's bulk between himself and Praxiteles, still would leave him visible to the eastern scouts—and running right into their arms. For that matter, even running south—

—he plunged into the forest darkness, diving sharply to one side, flattening to the ground, arms and aasagai splayed, prepared to *kill* whatever might be waiting for him—

But nothing was there.

He spent a minute's half regaining control of his heart and lungs, so that he could properly hear and not give away his position with his breaths.

Then he moved, as only juacuara could.

This was his element.

. . . but he did not feel any better.

Something still was wrong.

Later, lying near the firepit on the Tower's second floor, Seifas would write in his journal—write with his shaking hand:

> "I am a man who is honest with himself.
> "But sometimes I wish I was not.
> "Life would be much simpler then . . .
> "But, no—that is a lie. I *am* a man who is honest with himself; and I refuse to justify a choice that closes my eyes to what I see around me.
> "This evening, though, I tried to lie to myself.

"As I moved beneath the forest patches of shadow and starlight, my heart was warning to *think* about something that I had seen minutes ago—during the meeting.

"I didn't *want* to think about it. My brother was here; one of my brothers lived. Everything *would* be now all right.

"Yet my reason, working habitually under my active perception, still continued to warn me:

"something was very, very wrong.

"I refused to listen. Every time my reason raised a picture of my brother, I thrust it away.

"I *did* want to think about him—on my own terms. I didn't want to acknowledge that itch of reason, like a scab on the back of my mind, like the scabs of shallow taloncuts across my back, demanding they be attended to, uncovered—removed.

"So I scratched my physical scars, instead.

"It didn't help. All that happened, was that I began to slightly bleed again.

"A man can train his mind to ignore a symptom far more serious than an itch. I have seen men collapse from wounds they'd long forgotten—their faces stunned by reality.

"Reality happens, whether or not we attend to it."

Seifas approached the circumference point where Praxiteles' group had been bound to enter the forest; and slowed to fully stalk.

If his brother had wanted to openly meet him, he would have *spoken* openly, Seifas reasoned. Therefore his brother would *not* be pleased, if Seifas made known his approach through carelessness.

Not that Praxiteles seemed to be paying attention. Seifas could clearly hear him marching at trot-speed westward through the trees, along with his three normal bodyguards; as if he hadn't a single worry of being attacked—although from his frantic muttering, Praxiteles *did* apparently have many worries.

Seifas wished that he had time to shadow the man, to try to hear the ravings more clearly. His brother, however, was more important.

Now: where would his brother be?

Seifas paused in silence to recall his scouting early this afternoon, as well as what he had seen of this side of the valley on the ceiling map.

Yes; a clearing—not too far off Praxiteles' line of travel. His brother would see a thinning in that direction, and know what it meant; so that would be a logical place to try to meet.

Seifas crept, toward the glade, enjoying his skill. *This* was where he belonged tonight—not in the Tower, and certainly not in that great open bowl of a dell . . .

Except, he reminded himself, he was also a subcommander for the brigade; and so he had obligations—including as an induna, representing the Hunting Cry.

He had avoided those obligations for so many weeks, while serving Portunista . . . Perhaps, in ways, he'd improved somewhat since Midsummer's Eve—ever since Jian had arrived.

But, tonight had clearly shown: he *still* was avoiding his duty.

Yet—didn't his duty, his training especially, also lie *here,* outside and alone in the night . . . ?

He put the debate aside for the moment. He was here, *now.*

So, he crept—fulfilling the duty at hand.

The glade was just ahead. His brother would likely be somewhere nearby. Up in a tree? Under the brush? Out in the glade—? No, too obvious. Up in a tree, at the edge of the glade, where he could see the best, both into the forest, and into the clearing; *that* would be where his brother would be.

Would his brother see *him?*

Well, he *could* just walk out into the glade, announcing his presence beneath the Eye and before the world . . .

. . . but *that* wouldn't be like one of the Guacu-ara!

Seifas would do his best to show that his brother could count on him to do *something* right.

Besides, he enjoyed the game.

Now, which of the clearing's sides would make the most sense for his brother to hide along . . . ?

Seifas froze.

There his brother sat, in the center, out in the open, facing east, resting his talons upon his shoulders.

He might as well have been wearing a sign in fire:

I AM WAITING FOR SOMEONE.

Also one saying: DISTURB ME, AND YOU WILL SUFFER GREATLY.

Seifas sighed, and felt paltry. Of course: his brother would want to be finished as quickly as possible—not to play hide and seek all night. He had a ward to protect and guide.

Seifas stood and walked directly into the glade.

"I see you, brother," he murmured, knowing the ears of a juacuar would hear him.

The man leapt up, tensed . . . then relaxed, and stood up straight.

"I see you as well, my brother," he answered, with more than a little force—perhaps to remind of his rank as an officer.

"I am Seifas." He offered his hand.

"I am Bomas." He took the hand. 'Thorns'; an appropriate name, fitting his choice of weapon.

Seifas could feel a tip of those talons upon his forearm, drawing a point of blood. He didn't complain. He would show strength to his brother.

He wouldn't show weakness by smiling, either; unless his brother confirmed by example, that *now* it was proper to smile.

"An auspicious meeting," Bomas pronounced, releasing Seifas' hand. "I have seen your name before. It holds a special place in certain lists."

"How so?" Seifas knew he was skilled, but also knew he was young. Many would vastly outclass him. Many had.

It hadn't saved them, in the end. Not all of them . . .

Bomas showed no inclination to take the conversation anywhere less exposed—shouldn't they sit on the grass at least, to minimize profiles under starlight? Was he supposed to wait for Bomas to seat himself? Or should he sit first, as the clear subordinate? Normally Guacu-aran officers indicated the protocol they each preferred, leading in example instead of waiting for their subordinates.

Bomas tilted his head, and used a talon to pick at his eyebrow—a habit that Seifas found disconcerting.

"You do not know of your special distinction, Seifas? Well, I suppose they would never have bothered to tell you."

"I am sure my Matron and other instructors must have had good reasons. Therefore, if you also know but have good reasons not to tell me, I am content." This seemed the proper reply to make, though Seifas was certainly curious.

"Yes, I think you should know—in the great plan of things," Bomas judiciously answered. Then he stated:

"You are the last."

Seifas' breath turned to ice in his lungs.

"The last . . . what?" he managed to rasp.

"The last of the Guacu-ara."

Now Seifas *heartily* wished his brother would seat himself . . . !

"There are no more? Just us two?" His voice sounded distant.

Bomas snorted. "Would I have discovered *that* in the lists? Listen, boy, and think." Seifas did not appreciate being called a boy, by a man who couldn't be older than five or six years—but, he had prerogative as the ranking officer, Seifas supposed . . .

A corner of his mind sought safety in thinking this, while he tried to imagine a resolution to the apparent contradictions.

"You and I are not the last of the juacuara," Bomas clarified. Seifas' heart leaped in hope—he must have misunderstood somehow . . .

"But you are the last, the *very* last, of the Guacu-ara, Seifas. At least, until the Culling. I have kept my ears to the ground and the wind, and I have heard of no others, but maybe . . . No," Bomas said, half to himself; his eyes were focused elsewhere. "I know in my heart there have been no others. The plan would deem it necessary."

"Inkoos . . ." Seifas still didn't know what Bomas' rank might be, but any man who deserved respect could be addressed as "chief" . . . "Please forgive me; I still do not understand."

"I see that I must explain it to you, as if you were a child. Well, I suppose that that is appropriate.

"You, Seifas, *are* the final child of the Guacu-ara."

Seifas shamed himself further, for he felt himself stumble backward to the ground, crushed beneath the weight of those words. Yet Bomas seemed not to take offense. Instead he advanced, as if pressing on into attack.

"*Think* of it, Seifas. For twenty years, *no* juacuaran child has been born. Even before you, we were rare in the world. But *after* you . . . pfft." He cut his hand across the air.

Seifas cast about in his memory, trying to find a piece of disproving evidence . . .

. . . he could remember no younger student at his chapter house. One or two of about the same age; and several not much older.

None younger.

He never had seen the implications of the fact, that he had *not* grown up while watching babies being brought to be nursed and cared for by the Matron and her adelphas.

It should have seemed strange . . . then increasingly ominous . . . then even frightening.

But for Seifas, only a student—that had been the normal way of life.

Every chapter house had existed more-or-less in separation from the others; and, as Bomas had said, juacuara had always been rare. Maybe his older brethren had simply concluded that their own chapter-houses had been unlucky.

But the Matrons, and the generals, *had* to have known—almost from the first.

They had kept it secret, through the discipline and the trust within the family of brothers.

Secret from a student such as Seifas anyway.

"Why?" he asked. He knew, intellectually, that he was sitting upon a spherical surface, spinning around the center of space—but till that moment, he never had felt to be spinning as if on the surface of such a sphere.

"If you mean, *why* did they keep it a secret . . . surely, Seifas, even *you* can guess. As to how *well* they kept it a secret . . . hm . . . did you hear *nothing* about it, during the wars of the Culling?"

"No, I . . . I . . ." Seifas couldn't bring himself to admit to this man, his brother, that he had fled the wars.

"You must have been slow as a pupil!" And yet, Seifas received the bizarre impression that Bomas was not chastising him. Instead, the man squatted down to Seifas' level, leaning slightly forward to balance upon the gentle curves of his steel. "Surely they taught you of how our race came into existence. Do you remember?"

Our *race* . . . ? Seifas had never once heard the Guacu-ara referred to as a separate race before, even back in the chapter-house. They were human . . . weren't they?

"In the Era before the Era of the Anshu Pax," recited Seifas—his voice was slightly shaking—"before the Arbiter Anshu bound all magi together; the juacuara were born—born of magic and natural philosophy, born to serve the world in peace and war, born to protect and advance the best of humanity—"

"Yes, yes; I also know the catechisms," Bomas muttered. "The short of it is: the magi made us, and somehow assigned a set of adelphas to keep us in place."

"Well . . . yes, I suppose the magi . . . but, I thought it had meant . . ." Seifas wished he didn't sound so ignorant, so much like a little child, in front of this man. He wished he was anywhere else, even talking to Dagon . . . "You mean we aren't human? We are a sort of . . . golem? Some . . . *magical* construct?"

"Hardly!" Now Bomas *did* sound insulted. "*Not* human? Seifas, we *are* the humans . . . the *real* humans! We are the *perfect* humans. The magi, or rather some group among them . . . they were distilling humanity's *essence*. We are that result. They were attempting to breed the perfect warrior—but the perfect human warrior is the perfect *human*. And they succeeded too well. They couldn't control us."

"So they . . . they sent the Agent Macumza to control us?! That makes no sense!"

"What 'Macumza'?" Bomas snorted. "Have *you* ever seen him? We were told of him by the Matrons, and also by others in authority—who were told of him by whom? The Matrons again. The Matrons with the skins of rotten olives, as I recently heard it described." Bomas chuckled. Seifas didn't understand the reference—although a corner of his mind decided 'normal' humans *could* be said to have a skin that color . . . except for Jian . . . what did *that* mean . . . ?

This scattered line of thought was quickly drowned by another—

"Macumza is a *lie* . . . ?" Now Seifas thought he might vomit. This had to be false . . . but here was a senior, an inkoos, a man in position to know . . .

"Perhaps Macumza exists; who can say?" Bomas shrugged. "The Matrons received their power from somewhere, and *not* by jotting. But that by itself doesn't mean that he really exists. He surely did *not* set the skies all aflame to protect us during the Culling, did he?"

"The Matrons . . . disappeared . . ."

"Oh, yes; and wasn't *that* suspicious, too? Right convenient, when you come to think of it. Where were they, when we needed them most? Well, I don't know the answer to *that;* but I know where they were when we needed them *least.* They were gathering us, *leashing* us, *preventing* us from breeding too often within the lesser humans . . ."

"That isn't *true!*" Seifas had now completely forgotten about discretion—about even being exposed in a meadow with rival brigades out scouting . . . "We were allowed to find wives, to marry—!"

"Pfft . . . of course we were. How else could more of us ever be made? Yet, how many of us ever *did* find a wife, Seifas? Were *you* encouraged to settle down, to raise a family? Or, were you encouraged to fight for the Cry, to live and to *die* for the betterment and the protection of humanity? And, who *exactly* benefited, Seifas? Was it us? Or the *olives?*" Bomas sneered. "No; they designed a way to keep us tight on the leash, our numbers thin—although we still played havoc with their petty national quarrels, didn't we? Even when leashed by convention and training, we *still* influenced the world—moreso even than the klerosa, didn't we? More than any other single group—but one. Our one true rival."

"The Cadre . . ."

Bomas nodded. "They had the *motive.* They certainly had the *ability,* clearly, to bring us into the world: it stands to reason, they had the ability also to take us *out.* As for the opportunity . . . well, they had whole centuries' worth. They could afford to be subtle."

"Inkoos . . . why *should* they be subtle? They are . . . were . . . magi! We wouldn't have been so difficult for them to slay—"

"*All* at once?" Bomas finished in interruption. "Maybe, if all the Cadrists acted together. I doubt that they all were acting together, though. Not at first. True, the Cadre was instituted to keep them from being too sequestered, too independent—to reduce the chance of cataclysmic infighting.

"But how effective would you say they *were* at that? Here we are, in the valley of a Cadrist's Tower," Bomas gestured. "Does *this* not look sequestered to you?!

"Besides, you surely must have noticed magi *cannot* simply blast wide acres of land to ash from any significant distance. Up close, yes, their power is vast. But: it only takes one arrow, Seifas, one *anything,* well-placed and quick—and then a magus, even a Cadrist, is only a corpse, like anyone else.

"And, would *you* have launched a series of destructive raids on chapter houses in every sizable city in the Nations? What would *that* have likely instigated, Seifas?"

"A Culling . . ."

"Exactly. Who wants *that?* Not the magi!—and certainly not the klerosa, hm? Or do you believe they disintegrate cheerfully when the time has come?" *Not* disintegrate, one tiny portion of Seifas' mind tried to calmly report: *Qarfax* disintegrated—but there were no piles of ash whenever klerosa vanished . . .

"And, besides, we aren't a major threat," continued Bomas, "as long as we're leashed, correct? So, what plan is best?

"To find a way to do it quietly. No risk. No fuss."

"No more children . . ."

"They outsmarted themselves, Seifas. They didn't think it through, far enough. Even with all our conditioning, we *still* were being trained to think—and we would figure it out eventually." Bomas leaned closer, balancing on those deadly claws. "We did, Seifas. We figured it out."

"And *that's* what started the Culling . . . ?"

"Who knows *what* started it? Well," he chuckled, "actually, I think *I* do. And I admit, it probably wasn't this—not exactly.

"But once it began, the Matrons disappeared, and we were left to sort things out for ourselves. That was our opportunity, the sieve through which we now would be sifted.

"But most of us failed, Seifas. Almost all of us. We couldn't get past the conditioning after all. We *wanted* there to *be* a right and a wrong—to fight *for,* to fight *against* and *with*. And so we were blinded, until too late. We should have chosen to fight for *ourselves*—to stand for *our* own rights, to *make* our own rights—*not* to seek to serve some outside concept of right and wrong! You *see* where that enslavement led, don't you Seifas?!"

"To brother fighting brother . . ."

Seifas wanted to weep, but refused to show this man such weakness . . .

"And where is the justice in that?" Bomas thinly grinned.

Only a breeze, hovering over the grass, answered him . . .

"So—the chapter houses, built of cards, collapsed on one another.

"And *now* the Cadrists acted all together in at least one thing: targeting *us* the first in any battles they were fighting. You were *there*, Seifas. Didn't you notice the pattern?!"

Bomas' eyes were blazing.

"The Culling was staged to exterminate *us!*"

No, Seifas had *not* been there . . . but it made no difference.

He could see the pattern as clearly as Bomas.

CHAPTER 50

"Culled, Seifas . . . we were Culled," Bomas continued, after a moment. "What does that mean?"

"To be . . . sifted, sorted . . ."

"To be weeded out, Seifas. But I agree; it *can* mean something else, in a way. After all, Cullings happen with some frequency, don't they? I mean the grand-scale Cullings, by which we mark the beginnings and endings of Eras. This wasn't merely some genocidal plan against our race, burning out of control. That is what I used to think—but lately I have become convinced of a deeper force involved."

"The Rogue Agents . . ."

"Possibly; but Seifas, I think that they are only tools themselves, for this principle."

Seifas blinked. "You mean . . . you think the *Eye* instigates the Cullings?"

"The Eye . . . the chief of the creatures we call the Agents . . . I think such creatures exist, but if the Eye is their chief, then he is reality's tool as well."

"That is blasphemy!" Whatever Seifas had heard up to now, there were some lines he wouldn't cross.

"Very well, you who know so much! *You* can tell me why the Cullings happen, then. I'm waiting. The Eye allows them to happen because . . . ?"

Seifas tried to find something to say—

but he could only answer, " . . . I don't know."

"If he lets the Cullings happen," Bomas persisted, "it is with his will, or without it, correct? He either wants it to happen, or not.

"If he *wants* it to happen . . . then he is no better than any of those creatures we were taught to call 'Rogue Agents,' is he? They are merely his rivals, for control of our lives.

"If he *doesn't* want it to happen, then he mustn't have the power to stop it—and so he is *not* the greatest power, and another power is greater. At best, he and the other 'Agents' exist within and under this greater power, and perhaps he succeeds in retaining some order—*his* order—for a while. But sooner or later the Rogues succeed in setting us at each other's throats, and so *they* win for a while.

"And so it bounces back and forth like that, order and chaos, forever. That is what it looks like, doesn't it?

"I am no sage, Seifas. But I can add the numbers up. I go with what I see—and what I see is a bunch of *things* fighting over us, unable to beat each other!

"And all of them must be fighting on a battlefield."

"That battlefield is the *real,* the *final* ground of existence: a neutral battle-field, with *no* opinion of what is going on; or else it would take a side, and what-ever side it took would win—for *it* is the ground that everyone else is standing on. If it *cared,* or *could* take actions, all it would have to do is cut off whatever support it is giving to one or another side, and pfft . . ." Bomas' claws snicked the base of some grasses.

"But, that doesn't happen, does it Seifas?

" *That* is what history tells us."

Seifas felt numb. He thought he might have tried to vomit once or twice, and had failed.

"I am a student of history, Seifas. And there is one pattern I always see, wher-ever I look.

"The strong survive; the weak perish.

"When wolves hunt deer, they take the sick and the old. Sometimes the young, if they can get it. But, the best of the young, the strongest, quietest, clever-est, fastest—*they* survive. They are not culled."

Do *I* hunt the sick and the old and the very young? Seifas asked himself . . . But Bomas continued.

"This principle happens so often, so pervasively, at so many levels, through-out all the world, that it might as well be a person, in some respects. You *could* even say it has goals, as well as predictable behaviors, and that what happens comes about because of its wishes.

"I don't believe that it's *really* a personality—although perhaps it takes a sort of shape from the shape of our minds, such as Aleza or the Eye . . . probably Aleza . . . But *that* is how I interpret history, and how I find the meaning in what has happened. It makes much better sense than anything else—such as kings in the sky who love us yet leave us to die.

"Doesn't it?" Bomas smiled.

Seifas couldn't answer. The shape of this was *so* horrid, and it was coming so quickly, that he couldn't decide what to think.

"But, as I said, I am glad to see *you,* Seifas. I think that you are a sign."

This ray of seeming hope pierced Seifas' mind.

"Why?!" cried the last of the Guacu-ara.

"Call it 'the shape of history'," Bomas shrugged. "We are the strongest, the smartest, the fastest . . . we *should have been* supplanting the weaker mass of humanity, bringing them up to our standards. But we weren't. History gave us our chance, eventually—and we failed ourselves. Yet the strongest survived, Seifas. You, me, a handful of others." Others . . . a handful of others . . . "The weakest and the weak-minded perished; but that was for the best. Now we can start again, here at the edge of history. We can be what we *should* have been: the kings and redeemers of all humanity! *We* are the ones who are fittest to rule and to guide humanity, Seifas. Look around you—tell me I am wrong!" Bomas laughed. "This is our purpose! This was *always* our purpose! The Cry itself, even in its diluted and muddied state, told us this over and over again. Now we can make things *right!*"

"How . . . ?" whispered Seifas.

"By taking our responsibility, where we should be, where we *should have been* all along. *This* was what we were trained for—even our strongest enemies could not successfully burn away the shape of destiny! It *continued,* pressing *onward*—in spite of their efforts to stop it!" exulted Bomas. "You *have* felt it, in your heart—haven't you, Seifas? The urge, the drive, to do your duty, to take responsibility, to guide, to *serve* humanity." Seifas nodded, unable to speak. "*We* are *the* humans!" Bomas reminded him. "We have a duty to guide the others who lack our advantages, helping *them* to become like *us.* It is far too late for those already born, of course," he shrugged. "But new generations arrive every day. Within three years, maybe less, we *can* assume our rightful destiny: as the kings we were born to be."

Bomas fingered the headring that he wore. "*We* shall rule as a unity, Seifas, with none of the olives above us to hold us, to hold *humanity,* back from our destiny! Not one juacuar was *ever* allowed to wear a headring, were we, Seifas? *Never* allowed to have the authority over our lives . . . But, that has changed." That was true, Seifas realized . . . only the Matrons had ever worn the headrings; the Matrons, who had held the highest authority over the Cry . . .

The Matrons, with the skins of rotten olives . . .

"And, we shall, we *must* do our part, to help the future generations become as we are. Don't you want a family, Seifas? A wife? Children? Grandchildren? We the first of kings will not be able to see the day when every human has shed his watered skin; but *we* can set the wheels in motion, by our actions here and now! Within a hundred years, or maybe two, *all* humanity shall be redeemed, risen to our standard!

"And we shall be blessed by countless generations—for finally doing our *duty!*"

"So . . ." Seifas felt dazed, as if in a dream where all his wishes and all his nightmares were coming true at once . . . "*We* should be the ones controlling brigades, after the Culling."

"Ah, yes! You *do* see! Exactly.

"The problem, is that the magi currently still have the power. And, Seifas . . ." Bomas lowered his voice, back to a murmur. "They *are* a greater threat than you have yet imagined. Or, perhaps you have seen the signs yourself . . . in your maga?"

"What do you mean, inkoos? How could they *be* any greater threat than they *already* were as the Cadre?"

"You have seen Praxiteles. Tell me what you think of him."

Seifas shrugged, confused by the change of topic. "I am surprised he has managed to hold his brigade together this long."

"So, why *has* he succeeded so far? I shall tell you—for *you* haven't seen the things I have seen, nor heard what I have heard, from him and from the men who serve him." Bomas lowered his voice again. "He has, for want of a better word, made a Compact."

Seifas hadn't thought his bones and blood could further chill. "What do you mean?"

"Tonight, you stood in the presence of one of the creatures we call Rogues."

Seifas wanted to laugh. "That shallow, witless, cowardly—?!"

"Had I not stopped him, Seifas . . . he would have destroyed you *all*. I have heard many tales, from his own scouts, when they were believing that they were alone. I watched him drink the soul of one of his own men. I watched him, in a fit of apparent irrationality, lever a cunning and powerful enemy, into doing whatever this Mad One wished. I heard the way he spoke of the future.

"I watched him throwing fire—*without jotting*, Seifas.

"And I am certain that the magus on your eastern flank already tried to kill him by jotting. It failed, Seifas. Utterly."

If Seifas hadn't been sitting already, he might have fallen again.

Praxiteles sounded like . . . Jian.

Except, Seifas had never seen Jian work magic of any sort.

Then again—without jotting, would he have recognized it?

"It won't stop here, Seifas. You and I both know that there are more than one of these creatures. And this is a *weaker* one, I think. What will occur, when its betters begin to arrive?

"The race for greatest power has already started, Seifas. Why bother to study and search for the keys to power, when all you desire can be given into your hand? Sooner or later, your maga will face that choice. And listening to her speak, back in the Tower—and hearing some of the things this man was saying, about the people in that room, including her—I *know* what choice she'll make, Seifas.

"Do *you* know what choice she will make? How well do you know your Portunista?"

Too well, Seifas thought . . . he wondered when last he had blinked . . . She would do it, she would do it in a heartbeat . . . She would give away her soul, and become a monster . . .

No, there was hope! Jian . . . he might restrain her, somehow . . . she might refuse such an offer out of . . . love for Jian?

He had hoped that Jian would be able to do for Portunista what Seifas did not believe that he himself was capable of. Things had seemed to be going as well as could be expected, given her character . . . but, was it quickly enough to make a difference?

And *this* assumed Jian wasn't part of the problem! . . . Seifas had *thought* he had hope . . . but then again, what he had heard tonight . . . and Jian *had* said and done some things which didn't seem altogether benevolent . . . especially in the terrifying light exposed by his brother. . . .

Even if Portunista refused, Seifas realized—even *if* she refused that power . . . it would leave her weak.

The strong survived. The weak perished.

"I can see by your face, you *do* know her mind on these matters, Seifas. So, what will you do?"

Seifas already knew the answer—didn't he? What he would do, if necessary, to keep her from becoming a monster . . .

"Well," Bomas nodded. "She and Praxiteles won't be the only ones. The only hope I have, is the Cry . . . the *true* Hunting Cry. And even then . . . I only can trust in the shape of history as it *has* unfolded, that we shall be enough," he gravely admitted. "But, we must be ready and in position, to do what we can. There are seven of us remaining, Seifas. Seven, and you, who now make eight—an even more important number. And you are the last of the Guacu-ara. These signs give me more hope!"

I will find the hope to have, or seek my death in finding it . . . Seifas remembered his vow, in his soul. *I will share the hope I find, or seek my death in sharing it* . . .

"Inkoos, I swear, I *shall* do whatever I can to help!"

"Then stay near your maga, as close as you can, whatever it takes. You *have* a good placement already, Seifas. The others also do—I alone am still wandering. But, I nearly have made up my mind while speaking to you . . . Yes, I think I will stay with Praxiteles. The risk is greater, in some ways; but when I strike, I shall strike to best effect . . ." Bomas murmured, deep in thought.

"When you strike, inkoos?"

Bomas looked to Seifas again. "Yes," he answered, as if to a fool, "when I strike off his head, to assume my role as the leader of that brigade! We ought to at least *at-*

tempt to deny these Rogues from holding influence within the world we are striving to save and inherit! I suspect that once they are junctioned, they shall not be finding new homes very easily after the deaths of their hosts: or else *this* one would have already been making plans, to transfer over to your eastern rival—who is clearly the stronger, stabler magus—rather than plotting to use him and then destroy him."

"But . . . what if Portunista *doesn't* accept such a compact?"

"Then she will most probably die. At least, she will certainly need every help she can get.

"And *then,* I suppose, you *might* succeed in convincing her, one way or another, to recognize your rightful power. You are fortunate, in that respect, my brother," Bomas smiled . . . Seifas didn't like that smile . . . "*You* have an option remaining the rest of us lack.

"And after all, we *do* need to breed descendants."

Bomas grinned.

Seifas stumbled to his feet . . .

"Inkoos . . ." Seifas tasted the word, and it tasted like ash . . . "I will do my best to serve the Cry, to serve justice, as always. And I *will* do my best to fight these Rogues, to the best of my ability. But I . . . I cannot . . ."

Bomas also stood. "Well. Let it be then, as history shall have it, Seifas. Think on what I have said; I trust that you will do the right thing. You may go now, my brother. Only, I do have this to say:

"Those who are not standing with us, stand against us.

"We are the strong, Seifas. I suggest you remember who you are, and where your loyalties finally lie."

And turning his back upon Seifas, Bomas, his brother, walked from the clearing, and into the forest—away.

A long minute later, Seifas turned, back to the Tower.

He walked alone, not trying to hide himself, unable to think of the duty at hand—unable to think of much at all.

He walked through the forest, alone—and perhaps it was just as well no scout did happen on him that night.

He walked, down the slope of the dell, alone.

He walked into the Tower.

Gaekwar was cleaning and oiling his disker; Dagon was fidgeting some of the casks around, unsatisfied with their current defensive positions; Othon was snoring, rumbling as much as when he was speaking; Pooralay was . . . somewhere, not in here . . . probably out in the woods, scouting . . .

Seifas looked at their skins.

He didn't speak to them; but went upstairs.

Here at the garrison level, the halls and the rooms were crowded with men—men with their skins the color of rotten olives. Men with faces and hair and eyes unlike his own.

More men here than in the 'basement' below; but they were not even his . . . friends?

Were *those* men, below, his friends?

These men were not. They respected him, feared him; perhaps looked up to him even—as if to a king?

But they were not his friends.

And even his friends were not his people.

He looked up the stairs—up to where they wound away out of sight. Jian and Portunista had not been down in the 'basement'; nor would they likely be here in the crowd for the night.

They would be up *there,* somewhere.

Together.

Seifas turned away, and walked down the hall, toward the firepit. He didn't look at any of the soliders.

He set himself, near the fire . . . and the other men pulled away, further crowding themselves, to give him room.

He looked, up at the ceiling—up to where Jian and Portunista were, together.

And, for one brief moment, Seifas hated every thing in the world, everywhere.

Including himself.

Then he turned over; from one rear short-trouser pocket, he drew a small journal. It wasn't his first—that book was safely packed, back at the basecamp. But, it was the current one.

Seifas opened it. And with the sharpened bone inside, and with the ink from a belt-pocket's bottle, and with a shaking hand—he started to write.

> "I am a man who is honest with himself . . ."

He wrote several lines and paragraphs more, trying to put his thoughts in order.

But, as he approached his meeting with his brother, his pen trailed ink into silence.

He couldn't bring himself to write of what his brother had told him.

Not yet.

Even though he *was* alone . . . those faces surrounded him, *watching* him.

He could have claimed a room for himself; but his soul felt trapped, and the thought of those cells was only crushing his soul still further—in more ways than one.

He could have gone upstairs and relieved whatever soldier was keeping watch on the map in the uppermost room; but then he might have passed, or stumbled upon, Portunista alone with Jian. And that particular room, though very much larger than any of these little cells, felt as though it might crush his soul even more—even if he was alone there.

Especially, alone there.

He could have gone back to the forest; but he knew that in his current condition he would have only been a target, not a hunter.

So he closed his book, and pillowed his head upon it, and tried to sleep.

And thanks his soul's exhaustion, he succeeded at this.

Eventually.

. . . but before his consciousness faded, Seifas wished.

He wished two things.

One of those wishes, I know—but, for his sake, I will not tell it, my beloved. Yet it did come true.

And Seifas would sooner have slain himself, when it did.

I also know the other wish. It never came true, but it was this:

Seifas wished he knew what Praxiteles and Bomas had said, that he hadn't been able to hear.

Seifas never learned this. Neither did Portunista. Nor did Khase Sage ever discover it.

But I, my beloved—I can look back, where they could not.

So I watch. And I listen.

I watch Praxiteles, as he leaves Artabanus. I watch as he starts to dispute within himself again. He pauses, alerting his henchmen about "the first of the seven" awaiting in their path, telling them that he may follow along. Minutes later, they do find Bomas waiting in their path; and he joins them, although the magus seems not to notice.

What is Praxiteles saying? That he wants to go—and yet he doesn't want to go. That he wants to see her—and yet he doesn't want to go.

He was pitiful, for he was miserable.

You would have pitied him; for in such things your heart is stronger than mine.

I tried to pity him.

I did not succeed.

As Praxiteles approached the Tower, he didn't seem to realize, consciously, where he was going. Yet his debate intensified, as he drew nearer to the door.

"Do you not understand??" he whispered to himself. "Do you not *see* who is waiting beyond that door!? Yes, *she* waits, whom I've wanted to meet, YOU FOOL!" He spat upon himself. "She who delivers the world to the paw of the panther is waiting beyond that door! Let her betray someone else, not us! And the bloody hand is there! And the son of the eldest! And the beast! And the slaughterer! And, worst of all—the . . . !"

But Praxiteles looked up at that moment and screamed; ending his dispute.

Minutes later, Bomas stepped to the ear of Praxiteles, having inferred an intriguing conclusion between the evidence of this meeting, compared to the one with Artabanus.

The juacuar put up his hand to the ear of the magus, and whispered respectfully:

"Perhaps, Uhlanya, you should show them mercy now and smite them later—

"for you are not all here, now . . . *are you* . . . "

CHAPTER 51

Portunista bent over the scroll, that she had unrolled on a laboratory desk, studying every scratch from Qarfax's pen . . .

—blink and a jump!—she pulled herself back to an upright position. Sighing, she rubbed her hands across her eyes. Instead of attending to clearly written entries, she had been staring at only the coded parts, as if she could learn their meaning through physically closer examination and force of will.

Besides, she felt as if her eyes were crossing every time she blinked. No wonder she'd had to bend down so far—she hardly could see the room *now* with her eyes almost closed!

The tip of her nose was itching, and she rubbed it while she yawned, her jawjoints popping; what really had happened, she now realized, was that she'd been literally falling to sleep.

This was getting her nowhere.

But, unless she discovered the secret defense—the one she was certain that Qarfax had hidden beneath the dell . . .

She sighed again. She was so *tired,* from everything that she had been through in the past two days . . . Yet neither could she stop, could she? No one else among them had the training to look for the answers that she—that *all* of them—needed.

She brushed away some tears, which to her exhausted annoyance were gathering in the corners of her eyes, clouding her vision further; drained the final dregs of lukewarm mead from the mug that stood near at hand; readjusted her slipping, cramping grip upon her concentration; and put the current scroll aside in order to work—

—then barely suppressed a sob, her patience splintering: she had gone through *all* the papers now . . . nothing remained to pin her hope upon . . .

Someone was coming nearer, humming a brisk but quiet march. She didn't have to look to know it was Jian.

She couldn't help but smile—and sigh, in worse frustration.

He would never give up, would he? He never gave up on *anything*. A snort of bitter laughter escaped her lips. She wished that he would at least give up implying that they were a married couple now—she didn't need to deal with . . .

. . . with *what?*

So *what,* if he wanted to think that?—*did* it make so much difference? Of course she knew better; but if it made him happy, so what?

Portunista refused to look up and acknowledge his presence; but listened while he walked in the room, deposited something, and then departed.

Because—resuming her previous line of thought—his claim was a claim upon *her,* along with implied obligations. She already *had* an entirely full plate of responsibilities, thank you *very* much, and didn't want more of them foisted upon her without her consent! Even denying their affirmation, still required energy she would prefer to be spending somewhere else.

Not that Jian had ever seemed to assert responsibilities—other than ones which were binding on him toward her. But *surely* he would claim them *from* her sooner or later. Especially since he was clearly determined to make their relationship into . . . well, something more than *she* would have it to be.

A claim *of* more was also a claim *for* more; for even his claim of more was more than *she* was willing to grant—or to believe.

And so his claim pressed down on her, even when unspoken.

Now that he had returned upstairs, she looked to see where he had walked, behind some tables and mid-floor shelves over there, to do . . . whatever it was he had done. She couldn't see, from where she sat, what that had been. Hadn't he left something there . . . ?

She debated within herself: stand, go and see, and fulfill at least *one* of her queries tonight; or stay at the desk and just stare at these rotblooded records some more.

It wasn't a long debate.

Standing—and wobbling more than a little—she walked to that side of the room. Why *here,* anyway? Not near the door, or the gap she had made in the wall. Not near the map-table. Not near the table where she had been studying—really, about as far away from *anything* in the room that she—

She stopped.

A stack of Qarfax's robes.

She couldn't help but smile again, remembering now the robe she'd worn the night before—and what that robe now meant to her . . .

Yes, she thought in amused surprise; it *did* mean something to her. She might even risk her life, just to save that *robe!*

And, in her memory, she heard Jian, saying:

"You will *never* convince me we wasted our time this morning."

She rubbed her eyes again. This was too unreal. She was so tired, it was making her sentimental—and maybe a minor fever . . . ? She didn't even know where the robe was at, aside from probably still upstairs! There, *that* showed exactly how much she cared for the wretched thing!

She turned around, looked up—

Jian was standing in front of her.

"Good evening, milady," he smiled, although he didn't 'loudly' smile—good for him; she might have been driven to murder by too much good-naturedness right that moment . . . "Pardon me; no need to move," he murmured, stepping around a midfloor shelf, to set another armload of robes on the ground behind her.

"Jian . . . what are you doing?" Portunista couldn't muster the energy even to curse.

The fair man stood, and walked to a panel on the wall; one that controlled the wisplight sigils.

"Jian!" she exclaimed—or rather she tried to exclaim: neither could she pull together the force for a proper upbraiding. He doused the wisps, leaving only the lamps on the wall to light the room—and some of *those* had already burned themselves out!

Actually . . .

Portunista blinked again, and looked around. Now that the wisps were doused, she saw that the only lamps still lit were flanking where Jian had placed the robes. And those had been turned down *very* low.

"Jian, there is no *light* in here!" That was a foolishly obvious thing to say, but it was the best she could do at the moment.

"I walked around the lab a while ago, to ensure the other lamps were safely out." Jian chuckled, wending back to her carefully. "Didn't even notice, did you?" There in the soft warm dimness, he seemed to shine in affection for her.

"That *wasn't* what I meant!" she retorted, trying to summon reserves of temper. "Now there isn't light enough to *work* by!"

"No one else will be using the tablemap tonight; unless the brigades decide to march before dawn," he shrugged.

After the meeting with Praxiteles, everyone—but for Seifas, who had gone out to meet his brother; and Pooralay, who had gone the-Eye-knew-where—had returned to the laboratory, to spy on the other brigades with the tesser-map.

The western brigade had been splayed in an almost random fashion, compared to the eastern brigade. But with the window so high in the air, at night, they hadn't seen anything very useful.

The northern brigade had been far more ominous. *Nothing* about their camp could be seen, even in the starlit darkness. Portunista hoped that Seifas and Pooralay had decided to scout to the north tonight to get some better information from ground-level.

Consequently, she had to admit that until the morning the ceiling map of the upper room *would* be a far more useful tool for information; and the guards could handle that.

She hadn't meant the tablemap, though.

"Jian, *I* won't have enough light," she told him, as he passed her again to kneel beside the pile of robes. "If *you* want to sleep up here, that's fine—I suppose that that's why you brought the robes," she rambled, "but . . ."

When he stood up, he was holding a robe.

Her robe. Their robe.

"This is a bed for you," he said.

Her exhaustion swamped her worse than ever.

"Jian, *please* try to understand . . ." *Blast* her eyes, she sounded as if she was *whining!* "I *have* to keep searching, tonight," she insisted, attempting a stronger voice, and mostly succeeding, "because tomorrow might be too late . . ."

"You've gone through every document in that stack already?"

"Yes!" she snapped defensively.

"But you didn't find it. *And* it's unlikely, in your condition, that you will find it tonight if you look again."

She felt her shoulders slumping . . . it even felt good, in a way . . . *Why* did he have to affirm what she had *already* decided she *had to* ignore . . . ?!

He walked to her, and softened his voice as he drew nearer . . .

"Here is the fact of the matter, Portunista. If you are not strong tomorrow, you will die. We *need* you to be strong for us." He stepped behind her, and settled her robe—*their* robe—upon her shoulders. The heavy felted fabric seemed to be pulling her down . . . "So. Let me take care of you, please, tonight," he murmured, wrapping his arms around her, supporting her as he stood behind her.

"my wife . . ."

He kissed her neck, beneath her ear.

And she found that she wasn't annoyed in the least by that word . . .

She was sinking, everything drifting, downward . . . *but* . . .

"Jian—wait . . ." she gasped; but this was important, *too* important . . . "The binding on . . . the maproom above . . . I can't . . . I don't believe that I can . . ."

"Shh . . ." he comforted her. "You're right—that mustn't fail." He laid her down, for now he was carrying her, down into the soft robe pile. "So don't fall asleep, just yet," she heard him smile. She wanted to laugh, in quietly failing desperation . . . sleep was the first and the *very* last thing on her mind . . . "I know you're tired," he continued, "so, concentrate *only* on that bind, just on it, not anything else. Let go of everything else; don't worry *any* more, tonight; don't even worry about the bind. Focus on that, just on that, and let go of everything else; and I promise you, I *promise* you, I will protect you, and hold you, and give you rest and strength."

She did.

It was the easiest thing in the world.

She let *go* of everything else, and . . . *poured* herself . . . a living fountain . . . up, and up, while the rest of her snuggled down into perfect safety. She felt him wrapping her into the robes, wrapping them both, securely and warmly and firmly, everything tucked into place, just where it should be . . . In total comfort, she poured herself upward, with more and more strength, yet with less and less effort; upward into the valley's heart, for she felt herself *one-ing*, spread out from the center in all directions; no longer sensing, nor even remembering, the ceiling and its mere artifice, for she was *far* beyond that, beyond and into the inner principles, of the land, of the *creation;* and she could *feel* it now, understanding it all, drinking it in, all together, giving her *self* completely; and she *loved* the land, and she *loved* what she had become, and she loved . . . she loved . . . !

She heard a sigh, close and far away; hers or Jian's or both together. It should have been in unity; and, it very nearly was . . .

But, there was a grain of sharp intransigence, blistering.

Again she received and again she gave, almost, *almost* everything. Everything almost was perfect . . . !!

except . . .

. . . she refused, feared, resented. She wanted everything, the all that was now being given to her; and also to hold her self in reserve, ungiving what she was receiving. She *wanted* this unity; yet, she wanted her self and only her self. The unity gave, *still* was giving, expanding, empowering, actualizing, making her *more* herself, more *distinctly* herself, far more than she had ever been—!!

—but, it *was* conditional.

It was conditional, on the unity.

It couldn't be otherwise. But she wanted it *to be* otherwise.

She wanted to have what she was being given; but she wanted not to need it, not to want it.

She wanted to be sufficient unto herself; and *also* to have the benefits of reciprocating love.

But only One could hold those places at once, only One of all realities.

And she, was only a creature.

She might partake of the unity, from the lowest to the highest; or, she might refuse that unity insofar as she was able.

But she, the creature, she the created, could not be the self-sufficient One.

She chose not to face that fact.

She wanted what she wanted; and she wanted both what she *could* have, could be—and also what she could *never* have, could never be.

In the moment of deepest consummation—at the moment of choice between aspiration and mere ambition—

she chose ambition.

But, grace allowed her to keep a portion of what had been willingly given to her.

And grace still kept whatever she had been willing to give, in the hope of a day to come when she might at last receive it back, this and ever more; to receive and give and receive again, in the rhythmic action of unity.

And grace decreed, that she should deeply drink of mere contentment; burying under the weight of a quiet ocean the memory of the aspiration she had refused.

So; she fell, back, but not into a pit; only back, gently, softly, into the warm and comforting darkness . . .

where there was only healing, and nothing that ever would hurt her.

"Shhh . . ." she felt someone say, someone she . . .

She felt the word, the words, upon her mouth; felt them rather than heard them. "Keep looking up, up, *breathe* upward, follow your breath, upward, follow, follow . . ."

She followed, with only the barest effort, as sharp and as bright as the tiniest star, as if her breath was a branching tree above her; the rest of her sighed, and curled up in the darkness, to heal.

And so she relaxed, spirit and mind and body; and she slept.

SECTION FIVE

WITHIN

CHAPTER 52

When Seifas awoke, he wanted to write in his journal.

But as he turned over to reach for the book beneath his head—he stopped. Nearby, Jian crouched.

Dawn must still be a few hours distant—Seifas could tell by the smell of the air through the windows; also, there would be rain today. The torches on the hallway walls were now burnt low, or had burnt out. Dew drifted in the Tower air. The firepit dully glowed with waves of warmth, but not much light. Down each hallway, and also in every small room, soldiers slept—as men will do, who understand they soon shall need all their strength.

They slept lightly, upon their swords.

Four crossbowmen stood their watch, one at every window—including the window inside a room at the end of the southern hall: the false door there was covering where a window would otherwise be.

Thus did Seifas take a habitual tally of the men's dispersion.

And having done this, he realized . . .

. . . he no longer felt alone.

Because of circumstances, even dangers, which he shared in common with these men?

Because, in sleep, the shared humanity settles in face and body, however different those might appear?

Perhaps because he had rested well himself; and so could think more rationally, in the predawn hour.

Perhaps because of the dream he had dreamed before waking.

And, perhaps because of Jian, drinking near the fire, suffused in its glow, his hair and skin and features as different from all the others as also from Seifas.

Jian seemed comfortable near them. He always seemed willing to treat them as people—even such people as Dagon. If, perhaps, he secretly saw them as being of another race, then still he behaved as though such a fact was only a fact—and not a fact remotely as important as the people themselves.

"How are you feeling this morning?" Jian asked softly; and rotated sticks upon which was toasting some meat within the coals.

"Well enough," Seifas murmured, truly, in reply.

"From what I hear, your meeting with your brother didn't go so well. I'm sorry."

. . . and Seifas felt the cuts upon his soul once more, throbbing dully in time with his heart. "Why do you say that?"

"I went downstairs to wash, when I awoke some minutes ago. Othon and Gaekwar both were awake already. Gaekwar said, that when you returned last night, you looked like Othon had punched you in the stomach with his mace." Then Jian smiled. "Othon said, 'Someone *else* needs punching,'" he grumbled in imitation.

Seifas felt his heart rise into his throat—and then he realized, that he could not imagine Bomas, his brother of the Guacu-ara, offering to stand up for him.

In a way, he had felt more alone with his fellow juacuar, than he had ever felt before. Now he understood, that he had carried that feeling with him, back to the Tower.

"If you would like to talk about it, we have a few minutes, I think. But if you would rather not, that's okay." Jian smiled in reassurance.

The loneliness given to Seifas by his brother, though, had not been what had cut into Seifas' soul.

"He told me . . . many things . . ." he muttered.

Jian settled, closer to the fire. "What were they about?"

—but Seifas found he couldn't speak. He *wasn't* alone; he knew that now. But if he spoke aloud what Bomas had said, where some of these men might hear—where Jian would hear . . .

. . . then he *would* be truly alone . . .

"I think that great injustices have been wrought, upon the Hunting Cry," was what he said, instead.

"Well . . ." Jian mused, as he watched the fire. "Maybe you'll be able to do something for it. I will help you as much as I can." And he nodded, with resolve.

But then his face turned grim. "Assuming, of course, I survive *today*."

Seifas wanted to laugh—surely Jian had a better chance of surviving the day than any man alive!

Then his skin chilled . . . he remembered what he had told Portunista . . .

But before he could fully grasp this implication, Jian had continued on.

"Would it help if you told me about the injustices? The more who know about them, the more you may receive of help in correcting them."

But Seifas shook his head, feeling despair welling up within him again—his friend couldn't possibly understand . . . "No one else will want to help correct these injustices, Jian."

"That, Seifas, is total bosh!"

Seifas blinked—Jian had *never* looked at him like *that* before . . . "Any good man should want to help to correct an injustice, my friend! And there are *many* good men, and women, in the world."

"Jian . . . I don't know that anyone else would think what happened was unjust."

"Why?" Jian narrowed his eyes—they seemed only black and white in the reddish light—like eyes of one of the Guacu-ara . . . "*You* believe an injustice *has* been done—don't you?!"

"Yes . . . I *think* so . . ." The juacuar sighed.

"So, if you think it over, and decide an injustice has truly been done; then *why* would you think most people would disagree?"

"I *think* most people will tend to put their *own* interests first!" retorted Seifas.

"So . . ." Jian turned back to the cooking meat. "To correct this injustice, will put so many people into a fundamental danger . . . you cannot expect their support."

He began to chuckle, darkly.

Seifas' skin was creeping, and he nervously eyed the sleeping—or possibly only resting—soldiers. This conversation was veering into the hopeless void that he had feared . . . !

"Well . . ." Jian sighed. "I suppose there might be injustices of that sort." He looked back up, to the juacuar. "I know how much you *care,* to do the right thing, Seifas. And I know very well: you *can* tell right from wrong. *I* trust you, to do the right thing. And as long as you willingly try to do what is right—then I promise, I *promise:* you *shall* have help."

Some of the men around them shifted. How much had they heard—? How many of them had heard—?!

Then Seifas' panic scattered away like mist before a rising mountain breeze.

Whatever else they had heard, they would remember Jian, pledging his trust in Seifas, as a man who was worthy to help.

yet . . .

Seifas remembered what Bomas had said:

"We *wanted* there to *be* a right and a wrong—to fight *for,* to fight *against* and *with.* And so we were blinded, until too late. We should have chosen to fight for *ourselves*—to stand for *our* own rights, to *make* our own rights—*not* to seek to serve some outside concept of right and wrong! You *see* where that enslavement led, don't you Seifas?!"

"Jian . . ." Everything Bomas had said, smashed into Seifas' soul all at once like a hammer—
"what if . . ." he whispered in misery, and stepped into the void
" . . . *there is no right and wrong . . . ?*"

A smothering silence descended within the garrison halls.
Jian pursed his lips in thought.

Then he removed the toasted meat from the fire and set the sticks upon the rocks to cool, before turning back to Seifas.
"You wouldn't have asked me this question, after the compliment I just gave to you," he answered, low and soft and strong, "unless you were an honest man, honestly facing your doubts, unwilling for credit that you do not think you deserve.
"You will *never* convince me that right and wrong are illusionary, with such replies as *that!*"
He laughed again, softly, richly. "You testify to the truth of my description of you, without even knowing it! And so my trust in you is *very* well-placed.
"Other than that—I have this to say."
And now his voice rang hard and bright, a well-kept sword, like the gleam of his eyes . . .
"If there is no such thing as right and wrong; then so much for claiming a real *injustice* has taken place, that *ought to be* put right!"
Seifas jerked, as if he'd been lightly slapped across the face, or as if water had briskly splashed him while he was sleeping on watch.
"Do you, or do you not, believe that injustices *have* been done, which *shouldn't* have been done, and so for which an action *should be* taken?!" the fair man demanded to know.
"Yes! Of course I believe that!"
"Good. So do I. *All* men do, who are men." Jian gestured widely to all the soldiers around them. "They even do when the only injustice they care to admit, is against *themselves*.
"You, Seifas, I trust and respect. But the man who claims there *is no* right and wrong, and then who expects me to act on the claim of a *duty* or else an *injustice* . . .
"*This* is what I think of that man!!"

And Jian thrust a raw bit of meat on a stick, into the heart of the glowing pit. Sparks erupted. Sizzling smoke arose.

Somewhere nearby, a soldier softly coughed—it sounded much like a satisfied chuckle . . .

"Now then," Jian continued, his voice like tempered steel, "because *you*, Seifas, are *not* that man, I am entrusting to you the treasure I value the most in the world. Up those stairs, is the woman I love. If I should die today, then *you* are the man to whom I now turn, to ensure that she is protected from *all* her enemies, without and within."

Seifas had thought the halls were silent before, but the silence now seemed intensely alive—alive, and not dead.

"Jian . . . you say that I am an honest man, so please understand why I ask you . . ." Seifas swallowed. "If, to protect her from herself, I must . . . slay her . . ."

"I forbid it!"

Thunder shook the clouds outside, with power and weight, as if a volcano stirred. Now Seifas *did* recoil, in shame, as Jian leaned forward, the fireglow hiding his eyes in shadow:

"You *are* an honest man, my friend; who *does* care what is right and wrong; and so I understand why you would ask me this. However, my life is given to be *protecting* that woman—for if she dies—!"

crack!

Seifas jumped.

Jian had broken a toasting stick. He tossed the pieces into the fire.

"I do not say there would be no hope . . . but . . ." Jian settled back, and sighed . . .

For the first time ever, Seifas saw worry upon Jian's face.

"Things have *not* gone as well as they could. Perhaps I have acted too cautiously . . ." Jian shook his head, distantly gazing away and down in thought. "No . . . I don't know . . ." he admitted. "I just don't know. I *do* know that Portunista has only herself to blame for some of the things that must now take place. But, that water is down the drain." And he laughed, softly, briefly, hardly. "It is taking too long. Events are coming too quickly, and I don't . . . I don't believe she is ready. I *know* she isn't ready. She is not *ready*, for all that must happen!" The fair man pounded his fist on the firepit's edge, his eyes brimming worry; he turned toward the juacuar:

"I may have to die today—and *Portunista is not ready!*"

Seifas had never before seen Jian plead with *anyone*, for *any* reason.

It frightened him.

"So . . ." Jian took deep breaths, not calming but reining emotions which Seifas now realized threatened to drown him . . . reining them back, and banking them, like a deep river . . . "My duty is to protect her. I love her, Seifas. And that is why I am asking *you,* to watch over her, if I should fall. *She must live.* She must *grow.* And I believe I can trust you to help her—through the sacrifice of *your* own life, if necessary."

"Jian—why me? Why not Gaekwar, or Othon . . . ?"

"I have my reasons; one of which is that I think this duty will be for *your* benefit, as well." That made Seifas blink . . . "You also must choose a successor, to be ready in case you should fall in your turn. Gaekwar would be my own next choice; but people change and grow, and I am entrusting you to make your own choice."

Jian paused; and in the fireglow, Seifas saw beads of sweat on his skin. "I do not lay this duty upon you, Seifas. I only ask you if you will receive it. If you do not truly want it . . . I promise, I know how painful this could be; and I promise, I will *not* hold refusal against you.

"But, if you will tell me you *will* accept this duty—I will believe you."

Seifas breathed once; then breathed again.

"I will . . . if you should fall, I will give my own life, if necessary, to keep alive your hope for Portunista."

" . . . thank you."

Taking up the cooled cooked meat, as well as a loaf and two mugs of water already drawn from the well below—Jian bowed gravely to the man of the Guacu-ara.

"And, Seifas," he quietly added, turning to leave,

"whatever choices you make . . . remember *all* the implications of what it means . . . to believe in justice."

Gently picking his way around the sleeping—or only resting—soldiers, the fair man walked away; down the hall, and up the stairs.

Seifas found he was hungry.

So he absently picked the cooking stick from the coals.

The meat had been rendered tasty, salted by fire. He nibbled while he opened his current journal, back to his very first entries. He always copied those entries, so that he would never forget them.

Except, he realized . . . he had, in a sense, forgotten them already.

So, instead of writing, he fed.

And as he read, he remembered the dream from which he had awakened, minutes ago.

It had been a very simple dream.

He had been a child again.

and his Matron, Cami, had held him in her arms,
rocking him, and comforting him with her love.

Chapter 53

Portunista blinked in the darkness; then she warmly sighed.

Jian wasn't with her now; but, she felt that he had left her only moments ago, having tucked her comfortably under the robes.

She breathed in deeply, smelling cool air of early morning.

Then, with a gasp, she inhaled again:

Morning—!

She rose, up, stretching and yawning, flushed with the rising strength within her, as though she was drinking new wine.

Soon she would fight, for her life and her future, against greater odds than she ever had faced.

With that thought, she felt a falling mist; cool and invigorating, even with fear—but not with panic.

Well.

They might crush her beneath their weights, perhaps . . .

. . . but they would find her no easy prey!

She stretched again, pulling oxygen into her body—and also feeling more than a little tacky.

She wryly smiled—and decided her first defiant act today, against her enemies and their threats, would be *quite* appropriate.

She spun herself out of the pile of robes; her bare feet landed on two smaller piles.

One was *her* robe; *their* robe.

The other, was her clothes.

Both of the piles had been neatly folded, waiting for her, along with her boots.

Yes, Jian most *certainly* made for an excellent . . .

. . . consort!—her mind stumbled, having caught herself in the nick of time.

Consort, she firmly reminded herself, throwing the robe around her, grabbing the clothes and boots, and striding out of the laboratory.

"Report!—anything useful?" she brusquely asked as she padded into the upper room. After a glance at the wide-eyed soldiers, gaping at her from where they sat around a table playing cards, she breezed on past; and with a dismissing wave she told them, "Never mind; that was a foolish question, I know: you would have told us so already. You are relieved of your watch."

"Uh . . . Commander . . ." one of the archers managed to say, despite a slackened jaw. Portunista was busy with studying dots on the ceiling map—some milling movements, no forward advances yet. Good. Slightly starting, she realized she must have succeeded in actively keeping the bind all night. She still retained some hazy recollection of how that had been, but the recollection was mixed with too many other impressions to be distinctive now this morning.

Although her memory *did* float up an association of Jian, chanting softly: "They remained awake to enjoy the duty of sleep."

Well; awake, or asleep, or *whatever* half-state she had rested in, it certainly *had* been enjoyable . . . !

"You, watchkeeper, go downstairs and get food for these men." She fixed the group from a corner of one of her eyes. "The rest of you, station yourselves in the laboratory. I know you'll be short a window, but it can't be helped; and you know quite well that we'll have plenty of warning anyway, thanks to the map," she pointed, "otherwise you would *not* be whiling away your time at gambling!" she archly smiled. "So, go, and take your cards somewhere else. Now!" She felt a fair mood for the morning, but that didn't mean that she had to be smiling *all* the time . . .

They went. Rapidly.

She started drawing a tub of water, not much more than barely warm. This was a time to be cleaned, not to relax. Placing her folded clothes to one side, she readied dry towels, and then disrobed, settling into the filling basin, sighing comfortably.

When she faced her doom this morning, at least she wouldn't look frazzled, she vowed to herself, and stared defiantly up at the forces arrayed against her.

She busily scrubbed her hair and her skin in the warm soapy water, while her mind chewed away at the problem of how to survive the day.

Whichever way she 'nibbled', though, she couldn't figure out how to swallow and then digest the situation. Which led to one uncomfortable, but unavoidable, conclusion . . .

She filled a nearby cup with colder water from the basin-tap, and having thoroughly sloshed its water around in her mouth with soda powder, she spit into her tub.

That's what happens, she thought with bitter humor, when I bite off more than I can chew . . .

A knock, discreetly, at the door, was followed by an equally quiet, "Milady?"

"Come in, Jian," she called, hoping he'd brought some food.

—a tug at her heart: she saw that he'd brought her some toasted quail on sticks, along with a loaf of longbread—connecting her feelings this morning, to the beginning that she herself had chosen one evening, weeks ago . . .

"No mead for us this morning," he brightly announced, and set the food and the drink on the platter from yesterday morning.

"I should hope *not*," she snorted. "We will save *that* for later this evening, hm?"

"I certainly hope so," he answered in turn, although he smiled instead of snorting. He didn't entirely sound as if he believed his own reply, however . . . Well, she supposed even Jian might be worried, today.

"Any new insights this morning?" he asked, as he pulled up a nearby foot-stool and sat himself next to the basin.

"Yes. I've lost." She sourly sighed, squinting up at the map. Still no forward movements yet.

Jian made no reply; she returned her attention to him.

He was watching her, with that smile.

"What!?" she demanded.

"I'm just proud for you, that's all."

She cocked an eyebrow. "You're *proud?!*—that I'm *not* strong enough to win this fight??"

"I'm proud that you're *strong* to face the facts and deal straightforwardly with them. Not everyone can do that. Besides, what did the *very* strongest one of us suggest we do, when *he* saw our situation?"

That was worth a laugh. "Run!" she growled in mimicry.

"Othon, as you may have noticed, has a brain that is bigger than any of ours," he grinned.

"Hmph . . ." Portunista plashed the basin water, in frustration though not in desperation. "Towel, please." She stood; Jian enwrapped her in the slightly musty cloth, softly woven of barbadense. She stepped out onto the furry rug, and reached for the smaller towel—then her eyes widened; she gasped.

"Jian!" she chided. "I am *entirely* able to dry myself!"

"I don't remotely doubt it," he answered. "I just enjoy doing it." She popped him with the smaller towel, her smile matching his.

"Well, then dry my hair. You can take your turn tonight in drying the rest of me," she suggested, dropping the smaller cloth on his head, while she firmly took control of her own drying.

"I most certainly hope so, milady," he breathed, kissing the back of her neck as he stood behind her.

But still he didn't sound confident of that outcome. The sight and sound of a worried Jian, was beginning to give her chillbumps . . .

"Once we finish drying me off," she continued, making the phrase a joke—trying to cheer up *Jian* felt intensely peculiar!—"we will break our evening's fast, and then call up our commanders. I have some ideas."

It was several minutes later before she realized what she had said; far too late to correct herself.

She hoped he hadn't noticed . . . how she had described *her* commanders . . .

❖ ❖ ❖

Praxiteles had *not* had a restful evening.

He had worn a small trench inside his tent, in pacing back and forth.

Admittedly, Praxiteles rarely had restful evenings, unless he doused himself past the point of dreams with hard plum liquor and women—and even then, the mornings seemed hardly worth rising to meet.

Tonight, however, Gamin had been especially restless.

And that made Praxiteles worried.

He had thought he would never be worried again.

Wasn't that the point of the Compact? He was the first, and thus was the worst . . . !

Except, he knew that this was only partly true. Gamin, he was learning, had a habit of seeing only part of the truths he saw: the parts he preferred to see.

It wasn't that those truths were any less clear than before—but, the magus had had his perception about them altered significantly over the course of the evening.

It made him want to kill someone—to kill *everyone!* Only in deaths could a life safely live. That was his goal, Gamin's goal.

Praxiteles wondered sometimes, if it was a mad goal.

He heard a soft polite scrape at the flap.

"Enter!" he snarled.

That black-skinned throwback, who seemed to know too much, stuck his head into the tent.

"Good morning to you, Uhlanya," the juacuar saluted the magus, grinning fiercely.

"*No* good mornings!" Praxiteles snapped. "No good days, no good evenings . . ."

"Come to think of it, I myself have recently come to much the same conclusion!" answered the juacuar with lethal cheer, as he entered the tent, and walked to the nearby table. "But after recognizing this, I realized that every day is much the same, and so no day was specially worthy of worrying much about." He poured himself a smallish cup of raki. "To the future, Uhlanya!" he grinned, saluting the magus again; then downed the plummy liquor in one quick swallow. "Pah!" he briskly expelled, as the fire of the drink drove away the cloudy chills of the predawn air.

"The future . . ." mumbled Praxiteles. "What do *you* know of the future, juacuar?"

"What do *you* know of the future, Uhlanya?" Bomas returned, cocking his head to one side, still wearing that devious smile.

"I know," the magus grated, in a different voice, "your split and severed barbarous tongue will strangle you, if *ever* you use it again to call me 'the Mad One' to my face."

That wiped Bomas' smile away.

"I beg for you to forgive my impertinent jest . . . Mikosi," Bomas bowed, most sincerely, using the plural term for "leader."

"I do not forgive," corrected Praxiteles, pointing a finger of warning at the juacuar. "But, this once, I will excuse you. And lest you misunderstand, I excuse you for my *own* convenience, not out of fear of your retribution nor of the treachery you are plotting. Be assured, O first of the seven, that you shall embrace the black eternal fires of death without having slain me. Ah!—you think I am bluffing!" The magus grinned, viperously, seeing the eyes of Bomas change upon hearing this proclamation. "So we will see. I, at least, am entirely willing to bet my life upon the *fact,* that you shall die without having murdered me. Test the future, to which you have saluted, and see for yourself." And now the Mad One's face seemed as a grinning skull.

"So you say, Mikosi," answered Bomas, setting down his empty cup, but never taking his eyes away from the figure in the robes. "And so, shall I conclude that you have worn a path in the yonder ground, in your joyous anticipation of this future?" He dared to smile with his eyes, if not with his mouth.

"Conclude what you like, it makes no difference to me." Praxiteles flicked his hand toward Bomas, resuming his pacing—though at a more stately pace. "Shall I be taking you into my confidence, traitor?" he mused. "How confident is my confidence, in what I have said—confident enough to speak of the limits of my confidence?" He laughed a sobbing laugh. "Nothing has changed—but *everything* has changed. There are holes, that I have not seen before, and the greatest of gulfs in the future gapes before me on this day. I SHALL BURY THE ONE I FEAR!" he shouted. "—and yet, the hole of the future lies before me . . . the hole, and not the whole . . ."

"*Some* holes can be jumped," Bomas offered, filling his cup again.

"Yes! No! Holes! *Out* of holes, out of the hole . . . it isn't *fair*, he shouldn't *be* here, how can it be *possible?*" whimpered Praxiteles.

"Who is 'he'?" Bomas asked, sipping the raki this time.

"He won't say . . . he doesn't know . . . or refuses to look . . . or having seen, he refuses to accept . . ." the magus groaned as he shook his head repeatedly.

"He doesn't sound very dangerous," Bomas prodded.

"Nnngg . . . he guards the most dangerous treasure . . ." the magus retorted. "*Show* me, damn your soul . . . !"

"A treasure might be stolen, or be taken by force." The juacuar sipped from his cup again.

"*Not* this treasure . . . and I don't want it anyway . . . nnnnnnNNNN!!!" Now the magus seemed verging on apoplexy.

"If *you* do not want it, perhaps I shall see if this treasure will be mine." Bomas wondered if goading Praxiteles to burst an artery in his head would count as murder. That might get around his unsettling prediction . . .

The Mad One snapped his gaze toward Bomas. "*That* treasure shall be given to another, for you constantly spit upon it!"

"That hardly seems likely," Bomas pointed out. "You haven't even told me what this treasure is, which you say is so dangerous yet you do not want yourself."

"Not that treasure . . . he can keep it . . . but—I will have *another* treasure of his, yes . . ." Praxiteles hissed, his attention wandering, his eyes sparkling. "I want *her*; and she shall come to *me*—of her own free will this day. She herself is saying I shall have her . . ." And Praxiteles almost began to dance.

"Hmph . . . a woman . . . perhaps you mean the one that we met this evening? Well, she *would* be quite a catch, Mikosi, but surely you have enough already in the breeding pen—or, perhaps you won't be sharing this one with your hanikim?" Bomas dared to smile. "They have finished relieving their tensions, by the way. I saw them as I walked here; they were reminding your people what fates await them if they do not fight for you with all their heart. The former scouts you impaled around your camp were not sufficient, I suppose . . ."

"They have no heart for me," the magus snarled. "As you are well aware, for that is why you are here. I only care that they fight and serve . . . indeed, if they struggle against me it makes their dissolution all the sweeter . . ." Now he was smiling again.

Bomas rolled his eyes in disgust, and set his drink aside. Killing this fool would not only be a pleasure, but a service to humanity, thought the juacuar to himself.

"And speaking of serving you, Mikosi," he bowed again, "may I be graced with the wisdom of your plans today, so that I may help to carry them forward?"

"Eh?" Praxiteles started, out of a daydream. "—you think that I would confide in a traitor like you?! You make me laugh . . ."

His laughter followed Bomas into the camp, as the dark man took himself away from that place.

❖ ❖ ❖

"Noth, Alt—tell me what I wish to know," Artabanus commanded, shrugging into his fighting jacket and pulling on his thin black gloves, leaving his dark command tent. He had returned to the slave girl that evening, after setting his plans of assault. She hadn't been nearly as strong as he'd thought, however: now she was twitching behind him in his tent. He would be curious whether she lived through the day; but only mildly so.

He expected to have a Cadrist Tower to occupy his attention by this evening.

"Midomo," Noth saluted, always alert and professional, even despite the late and early hours. "The troops have gathered in right good order, ready and willing to serve the rise of the Arbiter! All of the sergeants are briefed on their battle roles, including their alternate roles for changing circumstances. We all await your commands!" he bowed.

"Midomo," Alt saluted. "Our latest scouts report the northern horde of Ungulata hasn't yet departed from its position high in the mountain treeline. The horde is certainly sending southward more of its scouts this morning, though; they surely will see the fighting in the dell today! Whether or how they will join, themselves, is currently uncertain. Pickets and scouts took only few losses last night; but, they also estimate only a moderate interdiction of enemy scouts. They trust that you shall be merciful to them, as you well know the nature of—"

"Only the weak of heart give mercy, for the weak," pronounced Artabanus, seizing fruit and meat from off a nearby table set for his use. "But yes, I am quite aware of the limitations of counterscout missions; and so be assured on those grounds I will choose to excuse your moderate lack of success. Enemy scouts have been killed, and so to that extent my enemies must in the future rely upon fewer scouts—if *any* of them have a future, after today," he smiled.

"Sire," his lieutenant bowed. "What more is there to say? The future lies in your hand."

"The future is what I make of it, Alt," the magus agreed. "And today I will shape a sizable portion."

❖ ❖ ❖

"I wonder, Kambyses, if our tayasi will restrain the horde, until the proper moment," grunted an Ungulat scout, settling into concealment along the treeline.

"The shamen did seem agitated tonight," agreed his elder. "Likely all the tayasi will follow their lead today."

"Orgetorix must deeply desire the destruction of these clay-hearted murderers," grinned the younger scout, licking his sharpened teeth with his thick black tongue.

"Orgetorix must deeply desire the destruction of *something*," decided Kambyses. Although precisely what, remained to be seen.

❖ ❖ ❖

"I expect t'day'll be *interesting*," said one soldier to another, south at the camp of Portunista's brigade. He yawned as he watched for the first faint glow in the east.

"*You* hear somethin' just now?"

"Sounded like shoutin', off in the distance . . ."

"Hmph. Well, likely there'll be plenty of *that*. Let's get some breakf—"

A rock fell at their feet with a thunk.

"'ey!" another nearby soldier pointed. "That's a *rock!*"

Various soldiers sidled over around it.

"It's tied to some paper with string," observed another soldier, edging the rock with his toe.

"Wonder where it's—? GREAT EYE IN TH' SKY!" All the soldiers looked where this one pointed.

Hundreds of paces up high in the air, a rectangular window hung, streaming lamp-and-wisplight. Backlit figures stood at the window, waving—the faint but incoherent yelling seemed to be coming from them.

"*You* gonna touch that rock?"

"Not me. *You* touch it."

"Y'know, one of those guys up there looks kinda like, well, Commander Othon . . ."

"READ THE NOTE!!" came a roar from above, causing the steadily gathering cluster of soldiers to jump. "FOLLOW THE PLAN!!!"

"Ah, yep, that's Othon . . ."

"*You* gonna touch that rock?"

"Absolutely . . ."

"Here now, boys, *after* a count of three," a sergeant ordered, "like I just told ya . . . one, two, three . . ."

"WE UNDERSTAND!!" bellowed her squad in reply to the figures above, mostly together. The window disappeared.

"I expect t'day'll be *very* interesting," said one soldier to another, as the sergeants took the papers up to Portunista's vacant tent.

CHAPTER 54

"I guess we're committed *now*," Gaekwar drawled, as Portunista began to scroll the tablemap east. "Unless we drop 'em *another* rock and then have Othon yell 'Forget it!'"

"Explain to me again why we don't pack up all we can carry, and just *leave*," Dagon sighed.

"Because I refuse to simply run away!" the maga snarled. "And *I* am the one in command," she didn't add—she wasn't surprised that Jian looked no more happy than Dagon about this . . . "I'm not going to let them kill me, either," she said instead. "But *if* they want this tower, they'll have to fight me for it! These people are *not* best friends—we don't know what they'll do to each other, once the fur begins to fly. So, I *will* be holding this place for as long as I can before I tuck my tail and run!"

"Besides which," Seifas pointed out, "we'd better be willing to take any chance to keep them from using the tesser-window against us in our retreat."

"So, let 'ista *melt* the table," Dagon retorted, "or blast it into powder the way she did those generators!"

"It might still come to that," she agreed, fiddling with the controls. "But I will *not* destroy it *now*, before the fight has even begun! I *will* be keeping this Tower, if I can." She looked up glaring at Dagon. "So, *unless* you have something *useful* to contribute, I suggest you go downstairs and get the infantry ready to meet assaults."

Dagon dueled her eyes for only a moment; then he shrugged, and sauntered out of the room with an attitude of casualness.

Portunista squinted at her intransigent subcommander's back, and then returned her attention to the map. Soon she placed the sigilball on its variegated surface, snapping the tesser-window into operation. She rolled the ball; the view tipped over correspondingly.

"Bloody hell . . ." she muttered.

"Cloudy hell," Othon observed.

Pooralay softly whistled in disappointment. "So much f'r usin' th' window f'r scoutin'." A pearly mist, diffused with approaching sunrise, filled the tesser-wall; rotating the window only gave different views of low-riding overcast. "Lucky th' clouds weren't nearly so low t' th' south," he added.

"Bah!" The maga jerked the ball off the map, and slammed it into its holding niche. "The ceiling map upstairs will tell us enough. Let's go." She stomped from the room.

"Bristling like a cat in a storm raining dogs," Gaekwar said to Seifas and Othon. The three men chuckled affectionately, and followed after.

Jian stayed behind.

Pooralay noticed, and stayed as well.

The thug thought Jian looked small and alone, almost fretting, as if unsure where next to walk.

"Hey," Pooralay softly called, walking over to the sandy-haired man. "How'd th' talk with Seifas go?"

"Hm?" He sounded distracted. Now the thug was *certain* he needed something more useful to think about . . . !

"Oh," he blinked, and brought himself back from wherever his mind had been. "I think the talk went well," he answered, equally softly—the two men weren't alone in the room: an archer guarded every window, while a fourth was sitting at a study-table, waiting for someone to open the tesser-wall. "Thanks for letting me know, this morning, what you heard last night," he gravely nodded.

"Hmp! Rotblooded jaguar . . ." Pooralay spat on the floor. "Always kinda admired th' Cry, despite them bein' an oc-cu-pa-tion-al haz'rd, y'unnerstand. But— there I was, sneakin' along aft'r scream-boy an' th' three bears; had jus' picked up their trail—which wasn't hard, considerin' how much noise His Maj-es-ty was makin'," Pooralay grimaced in scorn, "an' damn, I hear *anoth'r* con-ver-sa-tion out in th' woods, jus' like a blasted tea party! Didn't hear all've it—but, I got close enough t' hear enough. Woulda killed claw-boy myself, jus' on gen'r'l principle— 'xcept I figur'd he might come in handy later, sorta. 'sides . . ." he lowered his eyes, and sighed. "I don't do that no more. Or, I'm tryin' not to as much."

"I know." Jian clasped the thug on the shoulder.

"Yeah—I reck'n y' prob'ly do." Pooralay looked up at Jian, with a bit of a knowing squint. "That's why I told *you* what I heard. Didn't 'xactly trust no one else, in a way; thought they might get, I dunno, mad 'r scared at Seifas. Woulda talked t' him myself; but, I figur'd y' might be a better choice, seein' as *you* got a skin probl'm, too. Not that it's slowin' y'down, s'far as I c'n see," he impishly chuckled.

. . . but Jian only sighed, and turned away slightly, resuming his moody musings.

"'Samatter? Trouble with th' missus? Y'let a viperwyrm crawl in y'r bed, y'only got y'rself to blame, if y'get bit, y'know."

"That isn't it," Jian shook his head. "I just need . . ." he turned back to the thug. "I'd like to have a place to be alone a few minutes. But . . ." he smiled and shrugged, gesturing at the Tower around them.

Pooralay rubbed his chin in thought. "All right. *That* I c'n fix. Hold still." And as Jian watched, Pooralay walked to the tablemap. "Made sure t' watch how this geegaw work'd," he explained, as he tapped the control sigils. Soon, he dropped the ball on the map; it whirled to a preset orientation.

Jian turned around, to see the storage cavern beyond the tesser-frame. "Ah . . ." he nodded.

"Figure, you c'n jus' walk in there, 'round th' corner—you y'rself told me last night that th' cave is a li'l bit bigger than how it looks fr'm here, right?—an', well, now you c'n be alone f'r a minute."

Jian turned back to regard the little man curiously—even with some suspicion.

"It's like this," said Pooralay, walking away from the table, back to where Jian was standing, " . . . an' I wouldn't tell this t' anyone else, but I got a feelin' that you'll un-nerstand. Fact is, *I'm* not a very good person. Never have been. But about a year ago—I was keepin' my profile low, what with th' Cullin' goin' on, an' all. Kinda depressed, didn't really feel like findin' work in all th' fightin' goin on. So I was sittin' and thinkin' a lot. And what I was thinkin', was that I'm near fifty years old, an' I ain't *ever* done nothin' worth bein' proud of. Done a lotta stuff, sure; stole a lotta things. Left some bodies behind. Got in an' outta a *lot* o' places, and made a whole lotta trouble. I did do *one* thing that mighta been good, long ago . . ." he sighed. "But, I messed it up. 'n now, it's one o' th' toughest mem'ries f'r me t' think about. If there c'd be *only* one thing that I could go back an' do over, that'd be th' one. But I can't. So—anyway," Pooralay brought himself back to the present, "I sat aroun' durin' th' fightin', keepin' outta th' way, drinkin' an' thinkin'. Maybe I drank too much, I dunno.

"But . . . I start'd havin' these dreams." His voice had sunk to nearly a whisper, and he pulled Jian farther away from any archers. "An' . . . it was like I was gettin' a chance t' *do* somethin'—somethin' worth *doin'!* T' make up for all th' chances I wasted before. Y'know? . . . You *do* know what I mean," he pleaded, " . . . don't you?"

"Yes," Jian answered, quietly. "I think I know."

Pooralay wiped his arm across his face. "Eyeblinkin' allergies . . . Well, see, I get a . . . a commission. Me! I'm a *thug,* an' I get a *commission!*" he marveled, lost again in the memory. "This man—this king—I ain't never been much f'r kings, but . . . this king, he tells me, in my dreams, t' go lookin' for th' Well at th' End of th' Wood.

An' . . . y'know," he shrugged uncomfortably. "I ain't got nothin' better t' do with m' life. So, I go. An', I end up here. An', well," he shrugged again, "I guess that hole in th' groun' below is it. But I was thinkin'—I mean last night, while I was scoutin' the grunts up north,"—Pooralay had told the others, during their strategy meeting, that he'd verified the northern brigade to be a horde of Ungulata—"I was thinkin' . . . it ain't all that much. Th' Well don't seem t'be all that import'nt; not enough f'r me t' risk m' life over. An' I was . . . I was tryin' t' decide . . . whether t' bother returnin' this mornin'," he quietly said.

"But I thought: it d'pended on whether I *really* believ'd what I saw in my dreams, those slopin's ago. Then I thought—maybe I was just wrong . . . wrong about th' dreams, 'r wrong about this bein' th' Well. But all th' signs were *seemin't'* fit. But th' Well didn't seem t' *do* anything!" Poo unconsciously balanced the different points, using his hands as a scale, watching it tip back and forth in his mind; Jian smiled, see-ing this. "So, I thought, okay—maybe I misunderstood th' commission. What *had* th' king said? An' then I remembered," Pooralay looked back up at Jian.

"He'd said to go *look for* th' Well."

"He didn't say nothin' else, 'bout it bein' important, or usin' or protectin' it, or nothin' like that. Just go *lookin'* for it. An' now that I'm here . . . th' fact is, *you* guys are more important than th' Well. I ain't had a thought about *it* since we got in here—before last night while scoutin', I mean.

"An' I see you, an' I know that *you're* important; an' I see Portunista, an' I c'n tell that *she's* important, too. An' I see you two t'gether . . . an' . . . ."

Tears were trickling down his face.

" . . . an' I think . . . this's my chance. I can't go back an' fix what I did wrong . . . not ever.

"But I can help you two."

He wiped his arm across his eyes again. "An' that's what I'm goin' t' do," he quietly finished.

"I ain't got anything else."

And having said that, Pooralay turned and walked away.

"Whatcha lookin' at, fletch-boy?" he snarled at one of the archers. "Go stick y'r head back out that window."

"All marching troops report in place, Midomo!" Alt saluted.

"All garrison troops report in place, Midomo!" Noth saluted.

Although he might be fighting three brigades today, Artabanus chose to keep a company here in reserve to guard his camp against the risk of flanking sallies—and to keep his noncombatants in their place.

His slaves had often demonstrated a definite lack of enthusiasm, for serving under the banner of the Arbiter for this Era. Despite some striking examples of punishment, hardly a week went by without another man or woman attempting to flee—to escape from serving the Arbiter! Some had even cursed him to his face—him and *every* Arbiter, and even the Eye Who sent them into the world.

It was as if they thought that such a defiance was worth being punished *for*, even when experience showed the defiance never succeeded.

Which, Artabanus noted, was only another way of saying irrationality thickly ran within humanity.

Which was why the Arbiters were needed.

"Your command, Midomo?" Noth inquired; his eyes were glinting eagerly, mirroring steel, the steel that encased the brigade . . . no, the *army* . . . the Army of the Arbiter.

"Advance," declared Artabanus, breathing in the moist air deeply, wondering whether a rain would fall today, wondering if the dripping forest would dampen the sound of his marching troops, maximizing any surprise he might achieve.

He himself stepped forward first, before his troops—around this corner of history's winding path: the path that he had chosen for himself.

❖ ❖ ❖

Praxiteles wrung his hands, with excitement, worrying.

"time . . ." he murmured, "time . . . the time . . . the promised time is coming . . ."

"How many troops should advance, Misire?" Ender asked.

"Send them all, all to the front, all to the edge . . . and have them wait."

"All, Misire?" Flooder asked. "We'll have no reserves to protect the camp from a flanking—"

"It doesn't *matter!!* The teeming multitudes . . . they . . . they *should* belong to me . . ." the Mad One whined.

Stinger caught Biter's eye, and raised a brow. Until this morning, the multitudes had belonged to Praxiteles—had belonged indeed to Gamin—without any question. But now . . .

The chill of morning clenched at Stinger's bones, through his armor. He knew that Gamin could see the future—

—and yet, how much of what they had heard had been true prophecy, he wondered—and what had been wishful thinking . . . ?

"Also, Misire," Swelter added, "some people may flee the area—"

"FLEE!!!" Praxiteles shrieked. "FLEE BEFORE ME!!"

Well, *that* was hardly the answer that Swelter expected . . . ! "I mean *our* people, Misire; not our enemies."

"Do any of you wish to flee?" Praxiteles calmly asked, holding high his head to look around him. "Now I give you the chance, so that I won't have to take the trouble of hunting you down and killing you later. Who wishes to save some time, hm?"

The people genuflected before him, bowing to the ground. Also he heard weeping.

"I think there is no problem," Praxiteles answered Swelter, with what was probably meant to be a reassuring smile. "And really, what does it matter?" he continued, turning his attention eastward, toward the dell beyond the forest. "Once the Tower is mine, then I shall possess the keys to our domains. Any Inheritors wishing to seize the Mother will seek my permission, and thus my patronage. This is how I shall quickly grow beyond all other powers and principalities. Yes," he muttered, "I *know* I have seen it . . . I *have* seen them coming . . . I *know* I have . . .

"Drive them," he grated to his lieutenants. "Drive them to the edge, and I shall follow after.

"Let us *meet* what awaits in the darkness around the corner!"

❖ ❖ ❖

Upstairs, the subcommanders of Portunista watched the ceiling map, along with an archery squad, while she pored again over scrolls and notebook codices: she *still* believed they held the secret to a mass defense of Qarfax Tower. She herself would bring these from the Tower, if she had to evacuate; and she had ordered all her soldiers to empty their knaps of supplies, so that she could quickly stuff them full with material, too.

It hadn't taken long. There weren't enough bags.

Portunista exhaled through gritted teeth. The fact of the matter, was that she would lose the Tower today; and she had *so* little clue of what she was looking at, she wasn't even studying during these final precious minutes, but merely letting her eyes wash over them uselessly—!

"They come." Othon rumbled like distant thunder, like hundreds of feet advancing.

Portunista looked. On the map, the eastern and western brigades were marching—marching to crush her.

The northern one at least was staying put; but Seifas had told her how fast the Ungulata could run over moderate distances, even in forests. If *they* decided to charge . . .

Well.
They would find her no easy prey, she reminded herself.
She had to remind herself.

"Archers; stand ready."
This is what she had meant to say—but her throat and mouth were far too dry, and only a quiet rasp escaped her lips. She wet her mouth, and managed to speak those words; and then continued on: "Fire at will; but listen for the bugle signal, for the retreat." One of the infantrymen downstairs was wearing the bugle. He had created and taught some new simple codes for the tower garrison, so that their brethren in the main brigade would not be led into faulty action by hearing similar signals.

"Subcommanders," Portunista said. "Let's go down and welcome our guests, shall we?" She hoped her smile looked jauntily confident enough.

"Midama!" they saluted: Seifas and Gaekwar and Othon, together.

She felt her lower lip quivering, at receiving this unexpected honor; but turned away so they wouldn't see if tears appeared in her eyes. Now she supposed she would have to promote them to Marshals . . . Dagon, too . . .

They trotted out ahead of her; limbering their weapons, stretching their limbs.

She paused to look around at this room—the water basin, the bed, the tables, the tray—she took the final longbread heel, and washed it down with water drawn from the basin into her mug . . . no, the mug was Jian's. She thought it was his, although she didn't know how she could possibly tell.

This room felt . . . like a home.
When had she last had a home?
When would she ever have one again?

She turned her back on those thoughts, and marched from the room. Out of the room, and down the stairs . . .
Here was the laboratory.
The archers stood on alert already; except for a fidgeting one, unable to find a window to shoot from. Well, she would activate the tesser, and give him . . .

Oh. It was *already* open.
Onto the storage cavern.

Pooralay guarded the tablemap, eyeing the agitated archer.
"Jian's in th' cave," the thug explained to Portunista. "He need'd some time alone. You go on downstairs; I'll go get 'im. Then I'll run th' window here f'r fletch-boy. For all th' good it'll do in th' clouds . . ." he grumbled.

Jian . . . alone in the cave . . .
Perfect, whispered a corner of her mind.
She could destroy the controls, and . . .

 . . . what in the world was she *thinking?!*
Do it, warned that voice which sounded suspiciously like her own. You know full well he'll only cause you trouble and grief. You've gotten your entertainment from him, but he has sunk his claws into *you.* He'll have you *dancing* around him to his tune in a few short weeks—and who will be whose consort then?
Nonsense! Portunista silently shouted. He believes I'm his *wife!* He *loves* me! I have him right where I want him!
Oh, do you, *wife?* You don't *want* to be a wife, and you know that he will insist upon it. He is playing you for the fool you are; and you are *letting* him do it— last night you were *very* willing to let him do whatever he wanted to you! Your people will soon follow *him,* instead—and soon you won't even care! Already you can see the signs around you. Do it *now!*—the cleanest break is best, and you're *already* so wrapped around his finger, you haven't the heart to slay him directly— which is what it shall come to, sooner or later, for you *know* he will always be striving to make you his property! Do you *want* to be his puppet for your life?!
The voice paused.

Portunista wavered.

Then the voice in sly triumphancy, asked:
 . . . is *that* the sort of person you are, to let your decisions be made by something other than you yourself . . . ?

Portunista remembered this question; a quieter voice had asked it before . . .
She also remembered how she had finally answered that quieter voice.
—and how she had afterward felt
—to be only a hole of a heart in a mountain of stone . . .

She made her choice.
Portunista openhandedly *smote* her thought, with all her anger's power, across the space of her mind.
It felt as though the voice smashed flat against the circular laboratory wall, leaving a smear on the stone as it fell.
That's *right!* she told it, reaching out to seize that thought, that voice, again— to rip it apart like a vicious cat killing a poisonous snake. I don't let *anything* make my own decisions—especially not some worthless little figment *of my imagination!!*
Coward! Slave! *Wife!* mewled the voice at her, seemingly through a bloody mouth of shattered teeth.

So she kicked it. It flew across her mind with a splattering thud. *Very satisfactory.*

So, she kicked it again.

She couldn't exactly get rid of the thought; but by the lords of above and below, it kept its mouth *shut* this time . . . !

Portunista opened her eyes, half expecting to see the lab more scarred than it already was.

All she saw was Pooralay and an archer, watching her.

"I *swear,*" Pooralay said, in a low, clear voice; "you had better *not* be thinking of breaking this table with Jian in there."

She blinked. "No . . . Pooralay, no—I wouldn't do that! He . . . matters to me."

And as embarrassed as she was, that the thug had guessed her original impulse, Portunista was also glad that she was able to tell him the truth.

"I'll be downstairs," she said, and turned away. It might be a good idea to stay away from this room for a while. She didn't have a history of behaving very rationally on this floor of the Tower. And she had *never* heard Pooralay speak like *that* before—it made her feel as if she was being targeted by those pentadart generators . . . "Send him down to me as soon as possible, and . . . give that archer somewhere useful to shoot from." She absently waved her hand in the soldier's direction as she left.

The thug didn't move until the maga had gone downstairs.

Still not trusting his speech, he *pointed* the archer, and then pointed somewhere else besides near the tablemap.

The soldier jumped over short free-standing shelves, in his haste to be 'somewhere else'.

Pooralay edged to the leftward side of the tesser, and carefully eased his head through its atomic membrane, peering as if around a doorway's corner.

There, on the other side, dimly lit by the backwash of light through the portal, Jian knelt, head bowed, resting against the natural wall of the cavern.

Pooralay wished he knew what Jian was thinking.

But even I, my beloved . . .

. . . even I do not know, what Jian was thinking.

Thirty years and more from that day, the outpost of Wye lay frosted beneath a late-autumn afternoon; its inhabitants bustling before the onset of winter.

Khase Sage was gamely picking his way through busy streets, dodging frozen puddles, attempting to figure if warmth and dignity outweighed prudence: should he throw out his arms to keep his balance, or rest his hands within the sleeves of his thick canary-yellow robes?

Either way, he was thoroughly loving his visit.

"Look at these building designs, Commander! I count at least seven distinct varieties; and I believe with some work I can date them in order of their assembly!"

"Not too surprisin', Exemplar, since Wye tends to catch th' worst of every war or invasion." The mercenary captain led his friend through the winding streets, using his baleful glare to warn: the man behind him was not to be touched.

Not that there was much need for worry, despite the city's rough appearance and nature. Strategically set up high in the only saddlepass between the Blackburn Range to the north and the Wynding Mountains southward, linking the narrow, fertile Blackburn Plain to the west with northern Lemalsamac portions to the east—perhaps also due to its reputation for trouble and for adventure—Wye was host to keeps belonging to Independent Knights, to the Order of Hand and Eye, *and* to the Kingsmen.

Trent doubted that *any* enemy ever would sack this town again.

Khase, though, had a different appreciation.

"I thank you again, for suggesting we winter here, Commander! I should find many new sources to check and compare!—especially with such important groups within . . . oh, pardon me, miss," the sage dodged past a well-armed woman. Not of the Oakroyds, Trent understood; they never wore steel outside of battle. A Paraplesia, on the other hand, never would clearly be standing on lookout for trouble. Probably not a Wyeian officer, then. Neither Kingsmen nor the Handsmen accepted women into their combat ranks. Maybe a Crier, one of the Independent Knights? A stiff breeze was blowing her cloak too closely around her—covering whatever swordpatch might have been sewn on her shirt above her heart . . .

But after all these years, Trent had an eye for people of her sort.

He made a mental note to check back later on this street, once he got his friend and charge well-situated. Khase would probably be there till late; and Trent himself had already heard the largest part of the stories that would be told. After all, this was why he'd brought the Exemplar to winter in Wye.

And maybe that lady would have some new stories worth sharing, over a drink or two . . .

Minutes later the captain announced, "Here we are, Exemplar," pointing to a tavern on the corner of two of the streets. "Kris told me he'd meet us at the Ice Berg." Trent pushed through the people near the door, making room for the sage to come in out of the high-mountain cold.

Two different fireplaces helped to warm the tavern; back in a corner of that warmth sat Kris—a man of much the same age and demeanor as Trent.

"Kris, Khase Sage Exemplar, Lifesearcher for the Rosatta Noi Orthogoni," Trent introduced the two men.

"Very pleased to meet you, sir," Khase said, offering Kris the customary right hand of greeting. Kris accepted—and shivered slightly, feeling the sigilscribed kran embedded into the flesh of the heel of Khase's hand.

"Never met a sage before. Hmph." Kris digested this moment, along with a piece of toasted quail, while Khase settled in.

"My friend Commander Trent, who has proven to be an experienced guide, tells me that I can trust you to be a reliable source of information for my research." While he spoke, Khase held his right hand up. A serving-girl appeared as if by magic, despite the crowded room. Kris decided that having a bonded Lifesearcher as a friend might be a good idea, and toasted Khase with his mug. Though personally, *he* wouldn't fuse a piece of silver into his hand, no matter if it *did* command an instant respect from even taverngirls!

Well . . . Kris corrected himself with a shrug and a smile—depending on the extent of respect . . .

"Yeah, I was there for a lot of Portunista's campaigning; saw lots of things—*survived* a lot of things," he chuckled. "You want good information, I got several mates around here who'd be happy to talk to you."

"Very good, since I shall be here all winter, I think." Khase pulled a carbon-stylus and a notebook from his pack. "Can *they* tell me some of the very same stories as you?"

"Eh? Well, some of 'em can, but don't worry, they got other stories, too." Kris shot a glance of confusion at Trent.

"That's how sages work," Trent nodded; he stood near the table, back to the wall, keeping an eye out for trouble. "It's like when you get reports from scouts: you want 'em each to tell you what they saw, so you can compare 'em later. People see diff'rent things, sometimes; sometimes extra things that others didn't notice."

"Oh. That makes sense." Kris had always thought of sages as people who didn't much fancy doing real work. But, though somewhat foolishly eager-looking, the man who sat before him also looked ready to chew through ore to get to a nugget of copper. Kris decided he'd rather be digging latrines, himself, than writing out the same story four or five times!

"Now," Khase began, "Commander Trent has mentioned your name, er . . . excuse me, you do have a rank do you not?"

"Yeah, but Kris'll do; right this moment I'm not at work," the mercenary winked.

"Ah. Then please, feel free to call me—"

"Th' Exemplar there is *always* workin', Kris." Trent glared at his friend for a moment. That meant Kris had better stay formal—anyway, wasn't an Exemplar like an ambassador? Always working . . . didn't this Khase fellow take any holidays?! Kris' *own* hand was cramping at simply the thought of writing all that stuff—which must be why the sigiled kran was fused into the *right* hand, he now realized, watching Khase scribble some preparatory notations with his left.

"You can call me Khase after our friend the Commander has gone," whispered the sage, loudly above the tavern babble, and winked in return.

"*All* right!" Trent groused. "I guess that's my cue. Kris, anything happens to him, it's *also* gonna happen to *you*, when I get back," he warned, only half-jokingly.

"Then I'll set him up with Iona over there!" Kris saluted his mug toward an especially dusky serving-girl.

"As I was saying," Khase began again, while Trent departed . . . old coot had probably lived in a library all of his life without even kissing a girl, Kris smiled into his mug . . . "Trent has mentioned that you were present, during the Battle of Qarfax Tower."

"Yep, you bet!" he nodded. "The Journal an' the Testimony both leave out some things I saw. Don't know why," he shrugged.

"No one is the All-Seeing," Khase answered. "That is why people like you are so important; to researchers, and to future generations. Which, in turn, is why I am spending my final years, helping to fill in some details of the history of the Emerald Empire."

"Huh . . ." Kris spent moments in chewing that over—he'd always enjoyed telling stories before, but never had thought of them being *that* important. Good for some laughs, some occasional yells; even a sniffled tear or two. Sure, he'd embellished some things, especially after a round of drinks . . .

. . . but, *this* guy was taking it seriously. Real people, decades or centuries down the line, would be reading this book.

And hearing Kris' stories.

Kris did have a rank, whenever he signed up for work. His rank was based on the trust of people who knew him—who knew they could trust him to be responsible. This would be like testifying to a court as an officer. Except even more important, perhaps.

And, he reminded himself, this fellow would hear the same stories from *other* people—for purposes of comparison.

Kris decided to stick to meaded water for a while.

"You gonna use my name in that report?" he asked.

"Absolutely," Khase answered absently. "Every source receives the proper credit." Then he looked up. "Assuming you want the credit, of course."

And Kris saw a very shrewd look in his eyes.

Kris' response to that, would make a difference in how this man would judge his reliability.

This was Khase's life's work. And he was prepared to give Kris the gift, of sharing in something important—*forever.*

But only if he could be trusted.

"Major Kris Vivitar," he replied, looking Khase Sage Exemplar steadily in the eyes—as a scout, to a Marshal.

CHAPTER 55

Portunista walked downstairs, into the ground-floor room which Qarfax once had called the basement. She would miss this place . . . miss *every* Tower level, in fact, she realized with a burst of surprise—why was that?! Something felt deeply in common among them within her . . .

oh.

She and Jian had loved each other, with each other, in all of them—even within the basement, in a way, the afternoon they had first arrived.

No wonder the Tower felt like a home . . .

"They can't be all that close already," Dagon muttered. "We *still* could make a run—"

"Go ahead and run," she told him flatly. "We don't need you." Maybe she *wouldn't* promote him to Marshal after all . . . ! He opened and closed his mouth some times, then shut it with a snap and looked somewhere else.

"Where is Jian?" Seifas asked.

See!? the bloody voice whined. She firmly backhanded it.

"He'll be along," she answered.

Minutes passed.

"I c'n almost feel their marchin' feet," one of the infantry mumbled. He had been assigned to carry out the Mirror of Qarfax; it lay on the floor nearby, face down.

"That's them gears in th' hole, you fool," another one ribbed him good-naturedly. The first one laughed at himself.

"Crossbowmen and archers are standing guard at all the windows; including upstairs in the ceiling-map room," the maga reminded everyone. "We can rely on them to let us know what's going on."

This eased the tension in the room.

Slightly.

Footfalls echoed above.

Down the stairs trotted Jian.

"Gentlemen!" he greeted, as cheerful as ever. "No word from the watchers, yet, but I must say: *I* wouldn't want to assault a basement held by you!" he grinned, receiving grim laughter in kind. Again the tension eased.

Slightly.

"Where should I take my place, Commander?" Jian asked Portunista.

She shrugged—and reminded the jealous voice that Jian hadn't been in the room for her 'promotion'. "Don't look at me," she answered him. "Dagon set up the defenses down here."

"You're over there—next to the door," the Krygian pointed.

"Ah." Jian gave a nod in a wry understanding; but he gamely took his place with a grin and a wink in Dagon's direction. "Wish I still had my red shirt . . ." he chuckled.

The other soldiers were waiting behind what barricades they could rig, prepared to leap on any enemies making their way inside. Dagon had set up a funnel of crates and casks, figuring that their foes would probably bring a battering ram. "Wait until they're about to shiver the door," he ordered Jian, who hadn't been downstairs for Dagon's original outlay of the plan, "then you unlatch it. They run through, you bar the door again to buy us a little more time—and we *stuff* down the well whoever made it in!"

"I like it!" Jian rubbed his hands in anticipation, grinning along with Dagon—who seemed a bit surprised at this agreement. "Count me in!"

Portunista shook her head, and wondered if Jian had ever really been in the thick of an all-out sword-to-the-liver battle.

Of course, he *had* beheaded that one fellow, or near enough, against Gemalfan back on Midsummer's Eve . . . And now she remembered Seifas' story about Jian's fight with Gemalfan's scouts, earlier on that day. But Jian had treated those fights like some kind of game—even though one those pigs had deserved to lose.

She didn't expect *this* fight would be much like a game.

Then again: neither had *she* ever fought in a battle this large . . .

Better to think about something else. Whistling up a wisp—steadier light than a torch on the wall—she opened her knap and pulled out one of Qarfax's notes. Who knew?—maybe, in the final minute, she would succeed in figuring *something* out . . .

The eldest infantryman—the one who had served as a cook the night before—nodded, as if remembering something, seeing the bluish strands of needle-thin Aire and raw materia. So, over he stepped to Jian.

"Jus' wanted t' let y'know: wasn't only Seifas who heard yeh this mornin'. *All* th' boys here are with yeh." A low-pitched growl of assent arose from the nearby infantry. Jian's smile changed; and he nodded his thanks, clapping the man on the shoulder. The man then squinted at Portunista, as he returned to his post.

The maga had *no* idea what any of *that* was supposed to mean!—but the bitter voice in her head piped up again:

See? Only a figment of your imagination, hm?

She didn't silence the voice this time.

But she *did* remind that corner of her mind: she *would* be dealing with this problem—in her *own* way. And this was neither the time nor the place—

—voices faintly rang, upstairs.

Tendons tightened from the tension.

"Maproom says th' eastern brigade will be at the edge of th' dell, within th' next minute!" called the crossbowman who was stationed at the garrison landing window. "Enemy combat strength is estimated as being about th' same as our full brigade including vendors, Midama. Th' good news is, they left behind a company guarding their rear. Th' bad news is, the western brigade isn't ten minutes more from *their* own edge of the dell; and it looks like they brought *all* their strength—no reserves!"

"Ouch," Othon rumbled.

"Maybe the grunts will do us a favor and attack Praxiteles up the rear," Gaekwar drawled. That earned some snickers.

"Any word about the horde?" Portunista called back up.

Moments later, the answer was relayed: "Not a change, although they *do* have some scouts in place to watch th' excitement!" That was about what she had thought—otherwise the watchmen would have told her—but she wanted it clearly confirmed, for the sake of the nerves of the others. "Our own brigade is still in transit; can't be sure they'll arrive in place before the fightin' starts," the crier continued; then he paused while he heard some more reporting. "Ceiling-map shows our dependents have finished retreating on back through th' valley's southern pass, according to th' plan—a couple of screening squads have taken positions inside the pass itself, t' give the vendors . . . wait . . . Maproom reports!—eastern elements now at the edge of the dell!"

"Hey, Jian!" called out one of the younger infantrymen, not much older than a boy. "Here!" The soldier pulled off his shirt, and tossed it to the fair-skinned man; who blinked in a bit of confusion. "It don't seem right you shouldn't have a shirt, bein' the front man near th' door, an' all," the soldier grinned. "B'sides, we're about th' same size, it looks like."

"Thanks!" Jian pulled the shirt down over his head, and tucked it into his trousers. "However, I've got to warn you, shirts don't always last too long around me, corporal . . . um?"

"Kris! You can sew it back up if you rip it!"

"Deal!"

Portunista clearly heard the next report, as it echoed all the way down the stairs in intensity; but she let the closest crossbowman call the report himself.

"Tally-ho!" he cried. "Archers and infantry, spotted by eye in the treeline to the east! Infantry *very* well-armored; they look like they mean business!"

"Well, I guess they aren't coming over for tea and biscuits," Dagon groused, slowly digging the falchion's tip into the sturdy oaken floor.

"Say . . . what *do* we know about them, or their leader?" Jian inquired. "Anyone here know anything?"

Silence followed.

"Um. No . . . ?" Othon answered, bemusedly.

"He runs a tight brigade, at least," Gaekwar offered. "I mean from what we saw last night, by looking at their campfire patterns. The heavy armor shouldn't surprise us; they're Easterners."

"Yeah, I guess it's too much to hope he'll be a punkie loser, like Praxiteles," Dagon sighed.

But Seifas remembered what Bomas had told him. It hadn't been much, but . . . "Let us hope they fight each other, and not against us," he murmured.

"*I'm* not holding my breath . . ." Dagon sighed again, this time along with a bit of ironic emphasis.

Portunista put away her book a final time, and doused the wisp.

They would learn that commander's intentions and skill soon enough.

Chapter 56

"Flanking scouts report the Ungulata still have not advanced, Midomo," Noth saluted. "But the southern brigade has marched. They won't arrive for another several minutes at least. They *will* be in a position to charge down onto us if we attempt to seize the Tower."

"Messy in any case," Artabanus said, scanning the dell with his piercing gaze. "I choose to let them come to *me*."

"Companies and squads are briefed and ready, Misire!" saluted Alt. "What will be your command?"

Artabanus paused a moment more. Above, the low clouds roiled, although no rain had fallen yet—as if the skies were saving tears until the deeds to come were done.

The sun, however, had risen behind him, far beyond the clouds; suffusing light, sufficient for the work of the day.

The condemned died at dawn, in the camp of Artabanus.

"Execute."

Ten heavily armored men rushed to take formation in front of the magus, raising large shields above their heads.

The man who chose to be the Arbiter stepped into their midst.

Then they were off, running, charging the Tower.

"Our leader goes, our leader paves the way!" cried a praise-chanter, properly on the cue Artabanus had instructed; cheers arose along the line, as in succession the eastern companies rapidly trotted down the slope to join their master.

"Ware the window in the sky!" Lieutenants Noth and Alt reminded every squad as it was charging into the open. Artabanus worried about it more than any other threat. Missileer squads readied crossbows along with some heavy recurves, scanning the skies for the window. Likewise, heavy infantry watched in all directions upon the empty plain of the dell: should the window appear down low, these had been instructed to force their way into the breach—thus to turn the Tower's advantage into a literal window of opportunity for Artabanus.

Yet, ahead of them all, the magus himself advanced at speed, protected by the siege-linked shields of his praetorians. Now within the formation came the clacking sound of a Dissipation: this was Artabanus, jotting an anti-magical field as wide as his skill and strength would allow. This wasn't altogether easy to do, while running down the slope of a dried-up lake.

Artabanus prided himself on his discipline, though.

The magus heard a single plink on the shields above him. Then another. So, the archers at the eastern windows were trying some opportunity fire. Let them waste their missiles on—!

"The window! The window!" Artabanus heard—distantly behind him, barely over the clanking rush. Now he would see how his plans would bear fruit regarding it.

"Sergeant: tell me what I wish to know!" Artabanus dared to stop his jotting long enough to demand.

"Midomo," reported the officer from behind him, where the lateral view was best. "I believe the window is high in the sky, within the overcast. One of the arrows just now . . . there!" Artabanus heard a plink again, as he resumed his Dissipation, listening to the praetorian sergeant's report. "It fell from the sky above—and seemed to be wobbling, so its force was useless!"

Artabanus didn't reply, preferring to keep his defensive jotting reestablished—no one could bind a Dissipation into place—but he furrowed his forehead in confusion. Was his rival trying to hide the window where it couldn't be counter-attacked effectively? At any rate, he—*she,* he reminded himself; their leader *must* be the woman—had clearly outwitted herself! Cowardly cow . . . He very nearly ruined his jotting by laughing at her incompetence!

This might be even easier than he had dared to hope.

❖ ❖ ❖

"I'm sorry . . . uh . . . sir," the archer shrugged. He figured this stranger, who *had* been sharing the Tower with his commanders, and who had dared to speak to Portunista so lethally, ranked a "sir" at least. "It's just too high. I can't see through the clouds to aim. Something seems to be pulling the shafts a little out of line, as well, whenever they go through the window. More of us might make a difference . . ." he shrugged in apology again. The short man *must* at least be a sergeant, the archer thought—he was cursing like one, as he frantically tapped the tablemap controls, trying to scroll the view to a decent shot.

Portunista trotted into the laboratory.

"Hmph," she snorted, glancing disapprovingly at the tesser-window. She started to demand that Pooralay lower the view, or rather that he jump aside and allow her to do it herself—but then she remembered the height was fixed, and couldn't be lowered. Worse, the portal was set in the eastern wall—no window was here on this level for her to watch the advance of the eastern brigade.

Sighing, she left the violently cursing thug and charged upstairs as fast as she dared.

Panting, she reached the ceiling-map room; and read the battle's opening moves.

"One side," she ordered an archer while striding across the room to the eastern window.

"Sorry, Commander . . . er, Midama . . ."—he had been present to hear the salute of the subcommanders—"I think those are Krygian guards down there. Maybe I'd be better off . . . oof!" Portunista shoved him out of the way. The shield-linked squad was angling toward the southeast corner of the Tower's outer wall; this would increase the difficulty of missile attack, even though also exposing the squad to double the number of windows.

As for the other enemy squads and companies . . . as she had seen on the ceiling map, they were spreading out, to repel an assault from any direction. Good. Praxiteles may have come from visiting this brigade last night; but he and its leader were clearly not allied.

And yet on the other hand, someone sounding much like Praxiteles had screamed for someone to "slay him," too; after which, "someone" had sent up and detonated those plasmalights. She wished she knew how to jott those balls of plasma, instead of her harmless little wisps . . .

"No apologies necessary," she absently told the archer, as she strode away from the window back to the door. "Find another target in range, if you can."

She checked the ceiling, a final time. Her own brigade would be in position soon. And then she would strike.

❖ ❖ ❖

"In the first position, Midomo!" announced the praetorian point man.

Artabanus ceased his chattering. This relieved him; disciplined or not, the effort was numbing his jaw, and that would make some jottings rather more difficult. Fortunately, the second stage of his plan would only require a purring hiss for the jotting semantic; after which he didn't expect to need to jott for a while.

Which was just as well—for he was about to tax himself to his limit.

But he was Artabanus. He chose *not* to fail.

"Open and give me a view!" he commanded.

❖ ❖ ❖

Should she wait till some eastern forces committed themselves to attacking her basement door? Portunista wondered as she navigated the narrow stairwell. On the other hand, their dispersion at the moment looked inviting in a way; maybe she should strike before they concentrated on breaching the Tower. Praxiteles wouldn't arrive at the western treeline for another few minutes; and she doubted the eastern brigade could know what *he* was doing anyway. Then again, she didn't want to commit her troops to where they might be speared on the flank by Praxiteles and his soldiers—

But *that* was likely to happen *anyway,* no matter *what* she did, she reminded herself—which had been a reason for why she *had* concluded she *wouldn't* be able to win this fight; only hit them hard and escape. All other things being equal then, she ought to hit them *now*—before the eastern commander pulled his scattered squads into a more cohesive front, arraigned against her, dividing her from her brigade.

Except—shouldn't she wait for Praxiteles to try his *own* attack upon the eastern brigade . . . ?

Now she was back in the laboratory; her hand was on her forehead . . . trying to second-guess everyone . . . feeling incompetent, useless . . .

"Praetorians opening rank!" the archery sergeant at the landing announced. "Here, snipe snipe snipe . . ." he muttered, drawing a bead on the opening; that was worth a smile, Portunista decided. Even from the difficult angle, archers stood a decent chance of impaling any unarmored foe who stepped from under those shields.

❖ ❖ ❖

The magus stepped from under those shields; imagining he could feel the eyes of archers, aiming their weapons . . .

Artabanus smiled. Let them look upon him. Soon, he would look on *them*— to see if *they* could stand.

He doubted that they would be able.

And if they did, then they would learn the price of intransigence . . .

Artabanus started jotting, quickly, precisely.

❖ ❖ ❖

"Ssssnipe . . . !" the sergeant hissed, grinning to himself. He saw two arrows flashing down from overhead; however, the missiles missed their mark, due to the difficult combination of upper and lateral angles—skipping shields instead. The man in the shadows beneath those shields never even flinched.

Cheeky fellow, brave or stupid . . . the sergeant would figure that later, once he had driven some fletches through that regal fighting-jacket. He heard some shouting down the stairs. What *were* those stuck-up crossbowmen doing? he wondered; he flexed and adjusted his aim through the window. They ought to have a *much* better shot than *he* did, and they thought their toys were so great—!

—shimmering flame popped into existence mere inches away from his face and hands.

"GAH!" he exclaimed, releasing the arrow by instinct, knowing his shot would be off the mark. He leaped away from the sheet, more than a little annoyed, but not greatly harmed.

"Commander!" he yelled.

Portunista had thought his first exclamation had been more fighting attitude; consequently, she was caught off guard, looking out the western window, pondering whether to call her brigade to attack, and also idly wondering if she would see the other forces when they arrived.

She turned; and saw the Silverphyre upon the southern window.

She raced to the landing; leaving behind the western archer with currently nothing to do.

He wondered whether this meant he never would.

❖ ❖ ❖

"Perfect," smiled Artabanus. Each of the Tower windows facing east and south had now been blocked with Silverphyre. He momentarily wondered why the third level had no eastern window; then decided he was just as glad it didn't. Keeping up binds on five of these sheets, was somewhat more difficult than he'd expected, especially at this distance.

How annoying to be reminded of his limitations.

But, he would grow. Greatness merely given was worthless.

And, once he held this Tower, all his victories would be assured . . .

"Closer in, praetorians!" ordered the man who chose to be the Arbiter. "Sergeant, signal: third phase *now!*"

❖ ❖ ❖

"Fire!" Portunista shouted.

"I can see that, Commander!" retorted the sergeant.

The maga growled. "I mean, shoot *through* it! It isn't solid!—your arrows will make it through!"

"I'll only be firing blind . . . !" But he saw the look on Portunista's face, and prudently ceased complaining.

"All right, snipe, let's see how you handle *this,*" he grunted instead. That fellow down there had worn no armor—he must have been a magus; probably who had jotted this thing in front of him! The archer knew something about their range limitations, having fought them, and among them, during the Culling. He speed-drew from his quiver, attempting to saturate the area where he had last been aiming. He *thought* he remembered the proper angle, but . . .

"Come on, snipe," he muttered, "hug an arrow." It only needed one; and he had plenty to spare.

"RAPID FIRE!" he heard his Commander shouting up and down the stairs. "SHOOT *THROUGH* THE FIRE, TRY TO HIT HIM! HURRY!"

❖ ❖ ❖

The magus had heard some shouting from the Tower windows when he'd sprung his little surprise; as expected. Now he could hear a woman's voice, shouting orders inside. A powerful voice: he could hear her over the racket, even though not what she was saying.

But, he smirked, a shrieking harridan wasn't the same as a good commander . . .

Missiles began to rain from the windows.

More impressive, Artabanus allowed. She must possess some presence of mind; as well as some will and command-charisma.

Not that it mattered: he'd already moved much closer, near to the edge of the southeast corner; and so the missiles were falling haphazardly in the wrong place.

Still, she had done the right thing, to encourage her soldiers to fire through the sheets.

Now, to make her react to him again; he diabolically smiled . . .

❖ ❖ ❖

The archery sergeant grimaced. "It just isn't working, Commander. He's either back beneath those guards, or else he's moved. *Or* he's stopping the arrows somehow. Any more guesses you want me to make?" he sourly asked.

Before Portunista could answer—

—the sergeant leaped back with a startled cry, shoving her from the window. The flame was pushing inward.

❖ ❖ ❖

"Far enough," Artabanus muttered. This simple maneuver would render the missileers even more helpless—without much risk of setting fire to the Tower which held the key to his ultimate victories! Of course, they *could* still shoot from the northern and western windows; maybe they'd have better luck in repelling his *other* rivals!

"Phase four: initiate," he ordered the sergeant nearby, who passed along the command with a shout. Squads of men started moving toward the southern end of the Tower, including his personal guard. This was a critical phase; partly because his rival in the Tower might take one of several options now.

The woman confused him. Based upon her first response to his Silverphyre, she didn't seem altogether incompetent; but the air-window hadn't yet made a significant contribution to her fight, and *he* could think of a *dozen* deadly ways to use it. Something about this didn't add up, he mused as he sidestepped with the praetorians. Maybe *two* commanders inside were quarreling over what to do against him.

Ah, well. At the moment, his ignorance couldn't be helped. But if the woman was truly as worthy as he was beginning to think, he *might* allow her to live long enough to explain how plans had proceeded inside the Tower.

It might even prove entertaining in *many* ways. Some experiments he had devised, required a woman of greater strength in mind and body than he had yet encountered . . .

❖ ❖ ❖

"It's *no* good, Commander—*blast* his flaming eyes!" The archery sergeant thought his curse especially apt, all things considered . . . "There's maybe an inch's worth of clearance now, around the edges; but I *can't* get close enough to the window anymore to be shooting *down!* Maybe the crossbowmen below will have a better shot," he grudgingly said.

"Okay . . ." Portunista sighed—and made a crucial decision. "Go and tell your missileers on the south and east, not to bother with their windows anymore. Then report back to me."

"Aye, Commander!" saluted the archer—and headed first upstairs. The crossbowmen on the garrison level could waste a few more quarrels, as far as he was concerned . . .

"Pooralay!" she next called out. "Move the tesser above our troops on the southern edge of the dell. I'll be back in a minute." She didn't wait to see if the thug would stop his cursing and kicking the table for long enough to follow her order; she dove down the narrow curving stairwell, almost barreling into the garrison landing's crossbowman—who also was muttering curses, though not as creatively as Poo.

"*Don't* bother shooting through it," she shouted to the crossbowmen, as she continued down to the 'basement'.

"Bugler! Up with me, on the double!" she pointed to the soldier as she cleared enough of the stairs to see into the lowest room. "Jian, open the door!"

"What?!" That was from several men, though Jian only looked as if he thought he had misunderstood her.

"We need to see out—I mean *really* see out, not just on the ceiling-map. I don't have time to explain! Just open the door, and get ready to meet an assault!" she commanded. "Come on, hurry," she told the bugle-soldier. "Follow me up to the laboratory . . ."

❖ ❖ ❖

Artabanus chuckled: the thick iron-banded Tower door was opening from the inside.

Exactly what he had hoped.

❖ ❖ ❖

"Pounce when the first one comes through the door, and hold the choke point!" Dagon commanded—

—arrows and quarrels deluged through the door instead!—

—"Back, get back!" Jian countermanded Dagon's order—the bushy-haired Krygian dove for the ground, narrowly missing the uncovered well. Jian was safe enough, behind the door that he had opened; he peered through the tiny gaps between the hinges.

"Casualties?" Seifas barked.

"Tim took a hit through the throat—he's a goner," one of the men reported. "Anyone else?"

"Nah . . ." another said. "Tim was always stickin' his neck where it didn't belong." Grim laughter followed this; along with a few farewells to their friend, and even some softer prayers for his soul, recited by rote but sincerely.

Seifas wondered who remained to pray to . . .

"Jian, you stinkin' sheepkisser!" Dagon roared. "Shut the rotblooded door!"

But Jian only rubbed his beard, deep in thought.

❖ ❖ ❖

"Go!—near the window," panted Portunista, dragging the bugler up the stairs. "Pooralay, is it ready?"

"Close as I c'n figure. Let 'er rip, horn-boy!"

❖ ❖ ❖

"*Told* ya it was goin' t' be an interestin' day," said a soldier to another; companies waited among the southern trees, resting from their march. "Those Easterners sure look like they know what they're doin'," another said. "Won't be pretty," said a third . . .

From the skies above, from out of the clouds—a faint but piercing trumpet-call.

Soldiers smiled, swallowing sudden lumps in their throat. "There's th' signal!" "Just like 'e said!" "That was a *fine* effect," said the first—

"Well, men!" a nearby sergeant cried. "What more d'y'need t' hear?!

"Let's go teach those boys how to play!!"

CHAPTER 57

"Hurry, hurry, drive them faster—*to the edge,*" Praxiteles muttered; he had been repeating this for minutes.

"Do you wish them driven *over* the edge, and into attack, Misire?" Ender asked. "The front of the . . . brigade . . ."—he'd almost said "mob"—"should be near the edge this very moment!"

"No! They must wait; wait on the edge. I must see for myself, and give the command . . ."

Praxiteles ceased his muttering; Ender roared the necessary orders.

Genuflecting, the crowd stepped back to let him pass. They parted for his lieutenants, too; but Praxiteles didn't care.

There, a thousand paces away, the Tower stood.

He would seize it. He would *jump* into the darkness of the future! This was all that was necessary.

This, and one other thing.

"Looks a right good time to attack, Misire," suggested Thunder. "Arty'll have his hands full soon. We could swing around a little left, then crush his rear when he turns to defend—"

"*Not* yet," Praxiteles proclaimed. "I will let you know when the time is right. Soon."

Thunder shrugged, and figured it made no difference.

He was safe. Nothing could ever defeat his Master . . .

"What of the woman, Mikosi?"

Praxiteles turned his head.

Bomas stood nearby, leaning casually on a tree; white teeth shone in his black face. "Will *she* be slain, or will you give orders to capture her?" he asked in clarification.

"There is no need to give either order." Praxiteles smiled benignly. "She will give herself to me, and I shall have her, very soon. I have foreseen it clearly. You shall see."

"I will believe when I *do* see that, Mikosi," bowed the juacuar respectfully, but also with humor in his voice.

315

"You shall see . . ." One thing Praxiteles remained completely certain of, encouraging him to leap into the darkness ahead:

the vision of that woman, coming to give herself to him, smiling with her anticipation.

Whatever holes he had recently . . . found . . . in Gamin's increasingly panicked communications to him, he would stake his future on that vision—the one he most eagerly waited for.

Only one thing must first be accomplished; and was it not equally sure?—for never once had his visions failed. They *all* had come true—every one! One thing only must be done, *would* be done, and then the woman would give herself, of her own free will—and since he foresaw *this* to happen, *that* one thing would also happen. Simple, irrefutable logic.

Praxiteles found himself in the pleasant position of trying to comfort Gamin about the future. He told his reasoning, over and over, glorying in its infallible strength.

"I will bury the one I fear!" he whispered.

Yet, Gamin remained afraid.

Artabanus watched the lateral hail of wooden shafts and razor-steel streaking through the door of the Tower. *That* should push away any defenders . . .

Very faintly behind him, he heard a clarion call.

"No more time to waste," he murmured.

"Praetorians, *assault!*"

Artabanus stayed behind, close to the Tower wall—out of range of any incoming fire that might be shot by the roaring multitude cascading down on the southern slope of the dell, and out of angle from any attempts to strike him through the door. His missileers would know to cease their attack at the proper moment. Then his heavy troops would storm the door, and establish a wedge, through which the other infantry soon would pour. He supposed he would have to be there, too; in case they met any magi. Besides, he wanted to see the woman . . . to see what she would do.

Artabanus edged along behind his praetorians; once again he began the clacking chatter of a dissipation sphere. This severed his binds on the Silverphyre above; but they had served his purpose. Now it was time to protect himself from any attacks that might be jotted from inside. And, of course, to protect his praetorians, too; although he didn't believe his sphere was deep enough to cover the front two men. Well, he would give their lives, for his sake.

"The judge of the world advances upon his enemies!" one of his chanters shouted behind him. Good; they had caught up, just in time. "Defend your right to serve him now!"

Artabanus' scattered squads were already running to form a unified front against the onrushing wave of southern soldiers.

Perfect.

❖ ❖ ❖

Jian was standing in the doorway's shadow, squinting through the gaps between the hinges. Three separate reinforced squads were spraying arcs of lethal missiles, forcing his comrades farther away from the door.

Seifas noticed that Jian had let impacting missiles push the door a little, gently back; he supposed that this was giving Jian some wider gaps to look through.

But it also seemed, as if he was *opening* the door . . .

in an invitation? in betrayal . . . ?

"Gaekwar!" Dagon shouted. "Go shoot Jian and close the door!"

"*You* want to go and close the door, then be my guest," retorted Gaekwar. Avoiding the incoming missiles wasn't difficult, of course.

It only involved not getting remotely anywhere near the door.

"Leave him be!" Seifas ordered; just in case someone decided to risk the attack. "He can see the outside better than us; and Portunista told us she couldn't do that anymore upstairs."

"Our friends are making contact with the enemy!" Jian reported. He stretched his neck in several directions, trying to get a better view. Then . . .

Jian snapped his head around.

"*Everyone, over here now!*" he thundered.

"You gotta be spewin' on me . . ." a soldier muttered, nicked by an arrow bouncing off the wall.

❖ ❖ ❖

"I am *not* looking out that window!" That's what the archery sergeant wanted to say. But he possessed a healthy allotment of prudence—explaining why he was reluctant to put his head out where a magus had recently jotted a sheet of streaming fire!

So, instead he said: "Commander, it's *got* to be a trap. He's waiting to roast whoever tries to look."

"I suppose you're right. But, who am I to disappoint him?" Portunista answered with a lopsided smile.

In the disciplex which she had recovered after her battle against Gemalfan, she had found a teaching for how to jott a dissipation sphere. However, she *still* hadn't made any progress in understanding it. Even simple jottings were only simple if you already understood the proper principles for interpreting them. She badly wished she could have deciphered enough to even try the jotting without any practice; it certainly could have made her life a whole lot easier recently.

But, she didn't know how to jott a Dissipation.

So she would have to make do.

She allowed herself to continue to smile: the shape of her lips wasn't all that important in jotting Silveraire.

She was *very* good at making do . . . !

Binding the mirrorlike surface into place—and wondering what would happen if the magus intersected the Silveraire with Silverphyre—she floated it out the window.

She couldn't see all that much besides straight down—

—her smile disappeared—

—seeing down was quite enough.

"Wait here!" she commanded, and then dashed downward to the garrison level; leaving the Silveraire to dispel behind her.

❖ ❖ ❖

Artabanus now was close enough; this volley would be the last. To his guards he shouted: "Go!"

The heavily armored soldiers leaped the last few paces along the wall of the Tower, toward the door—

—which was already closing??

Magic . . . ? No—the door would have already closed, during the missile volleys . . .

"Everyone!" called a man behind the door. "Over here, now!"

Artabanus snarled; he hadn't considered *that:* whoever did open the door could be safely protected behind it—watching through the gaps between the hinges!

"Push! Hard!" he told his troops. He would still win—this was *only* a small annoyance . . .

❖ ❖ ❖

Jian said nothing else; but gritted his teeth and pushed.

He almost made it shut.

"Oof!" he grunted—his forward progress checked—then his boots were skidding as he was pushed inexorably—

He could not possibly win.

But neither did he surrender.

Every half a moment he had bought, was buying now, *might* make the difference.

And, that was precisely what happened.

Only one man thought fast enough, to understand *why* the fair man had called for help.

And only one man was close enough to lend his strength to Jian in time.

❖ ❖ ❖

Excellent . . . Artabanus gave whoever was at the door some credit for trying. But, in another moment one of his heavy soldiers would squeeze inside, *cut* that one man down, and burst the Tower defenses wide.

And then . . .

"UGH!" grunted the soldiers in front—as if the door had been planted into the core of the world.

"What!?" demanded Artabanus . . . this was taking too long . . . !

"He must've . . . thrown a brace behind the door . . . Midomo . . ."

"He waited too late! It's wide enough!—go on through, before they think to bring up reinforcements!" Not that that would make much difference—his men could duck while he or the missileers—

Then the soldiers' eyes were popping; they and the door were shuddering *backward!*

"*That* ain't a brace," muttered one. "They must have a shoulderbeast in there . . ."

❖ ❖ ❖

"Come *on!*" Gaekwar commanded some nearby infantrymen. "Don't let 'em do it alone—let's go help!"

"No! Stay!" Seifas countered. "Jian is underneath, and isn't wearing *any* armor! He'll be crushed!"

❖ ❖ ❖

Artabanus heard that, faintly.

"All *ten* of you lean in!" he shouted. "Your armor will save you from being crushed! Do it!"

"We're . . . already doing it . . . Midomo!"

Artabanus blinked; it was true. His soldiers *had* formed a compression triangle, four on three on two on one, each one leaning upon the back of a one in front; the soldiers on the left were standing in the creek.

This should have worked.

And yet the door had budged no farther.

"You *heard* that fellow inside!" the magus verged on shrieking. "Only two men are on that door! *You* are ten praetorian guards!"

"Bring your ten praetorians!
"I have Othon—the Implacable!"

Artabanus blanched, slapped in the face by that glorious shout.

There *were* two commanders! The woman, and this man . . .

"O-thon! O-thon! O-thon!" The magus could hear the chanting cheers of soldiers inside the room . . . and then beneath the cheers, rose other men's voices in deep syncopation . . .

Artabanus stood, shocked by the surging morale.

If *this* man could inspire such loyalty . . .

what would the woman do when *she* arrived?!

❖ ❖ ❖

"What are you waiting for?!" Portunista called, racing down the halls of the garrison level. A crossbowman was standing by the southern 'door', staring uncertainly into the room with the offset window. "Lean yourself out and *shoot* whoever is *not* wearing armor down there!"

❖ ❖ ❖

Artabanus had to find a way to turn the tide, before the maga—surely the unarmed commanding woman *must* be a maga—factored into the fight again.

On impulse, he looked up, to where he last had heard her . . . she must still be up the stairs somewhere—her voice would've carried distinctly through the doorway gap, had she been below . . .

. . . What?

A man was leaning out the offset window one floor above—trying to aim a crossbow—

Aiming at *him*—!

Artabanus jotted Silverphyre into that window, and into the other two above it, binding the sheets into place.

❖ ❖ ❖

Portunista had been about to yank the man back through the window, to try a pentadart attack . . . *that* would be far more sensible—why *hadn't* she thought of that first . . . ?

But then the man thrashed and screamed, pierced within a plate of fire.

The maga gasped, and pulled him inside.

She was too late. The soldier flopped on the floor, his lungs seared together, smothering.

She did the only thing she could do for the man.

She backed a step, and launched a pentadart into his chest.

His heart exploded; the shock blew out his consciousness; he didn't suffer for even a few more moments.

Portunista stood above him. Her lower lip was trembling.

It should have been *her,* facing that fire. She might have had a chance. The archery sergeant had warned her.

Her arrogance and incompetence would destroy them all . . .

Why don't you go downstairs and cede the command to your *husband,* then? a corner snarled in her mind.

Her trembling lip curled back in a matching snarl, responding to that thought.

But as she backed from the room, she paused. Faintly, she could hear men chanting—Othon's name, and . . . and that stupid wordless rhythm Jian had taught them as a marching chant!

Did that mean Jian and Othon were holding the door? Against those men?

—against that magus?!

Portunista *raced* back up the hall; not realizing the snarl on her face had changed in texture—not thinking about *herself* at all . . .

"Crossbowmen!" she shouted to the missileers at other windows. "Go with me, up the stairs!—*run!*" She leaped the pit without a pause and barreled onward down the hall, hardly slowing as she peeled around the landing's corner, hurling herself up the winding stairs. She overtook the crossbowman who had been stationed at the garrison-landing window; the sergeant at the laboratory-landing had to throw himself backward to keep from being trampled by the pair.

"You!" she pointed at the archery sergeant, who blinked. "You were right! My apologies!" Oooo-kay, that was new, he blinked again in bemusement . . . "Now, run upstairs, and get the rest of the archers here! Go! *Go!*"

The sergeant was fourteen stairs up the flight before he even knew he had left the landing.

He burst into the upper room; most of the missileers were staring at the Silverphyre sheet pushed slightly through the southern window. One was valiantly trying to get himself and his bow outside the eastern window in order to shoot along the plane of the eastern wall. It wasn't working; he wasn't a crossbowman. "Let's get going!" the sergeant ordered. "Move it you mugs! The Commander has a plan!"

I hope, he silently added, as he stood aside to watch the squad run out the door.

None of the men had bothered to look at the ceiling map, during the past few minutes.

None of them looked before they left.

Consequently, no one remained to notice the northern brigade now surging southward at an inhuman speed through the forest . . .

❖ ❖ ❖

Artabanus felt the seconds slipping away.

He wasn't especially worried about repelling the southern brigade—assuming the captains here in the Tower didn't get *anywhere* near them . . . he didn't *even* want to think about the threat he'd face if the man behind the door could enhearten a whole brigade in the way those chants inside were indicating! But, that bloody Praxiteles was flaunting his own brigade along the western treeline. And, who knew when the Ungulata might appear?

"You on the right!" he shouted. "Draw your sword, reach around, and *kill* whoever you can hit!"

❖ ❖ ❖

"Careful!" Othon growled as he shifted position upon the door, letting his armor absorb the brunt of the slapping sword. Fortunately, the praetorian could only be mostly focused on pressing inward, and his striking angle was poor.

Nevertheless, his sword still nicked the cheek of the massive man from Manavilin Island.

Nor could Othon, shifting position, avoid a consequent shift in leverage.

The door edged open further again.

"Gaekwar!" Jian commanded. "Shoot those soldiers!"

❖ ❖ ❖

Artabanus heard that, too.

Not a bad idea, he admitted begrudgingly, while his mind was racing. For that matter, almost anyone in the room could strike through the gap with swords or axes—far more lethally than his breaching troops could currently strike in return.

Artabanus frantically tried to imagine a jotting option; such as igniting the lungs of that captain, or else this "Othon", in the same manner as he had slain that foolish crossbowman above. Most any jotting, however, required a line of sight—including all of the ones he knew. *So* far, he had had no targets.

Nor would he have any now, he suddenly understood. The contrast between the darkened interior and the natural light outside, despite and indeed combined with the dimness of early morning sunlight diffusing through the thick overcast above them all, kept him from seeing into the room beyond a couple of paces.

That must be why the captain behind the door had ordered somebody to *shoot* an attack—from further into the room than the magus could see!

Clever; damned clever.

But, *not* quite clever enough.

He might not be able to see a specific target—but he *still* had line of sight!

A plasmalight or two would grant him the light he needed to properly aim . . . No, he stopped himself, not that . . . that would only alert this "Gaekwar" that a magus was targeting him. He must strike *once,* and lethally; and quickly!—the man behind the door would only need a single missile to plow the praetorians; that would disrupt their efforts, allowing the door to be shut, trapping Artabanus *outside* the Tower . . . the sharp-edged fractions of moments were flickering by—ensuring failure *if he didn't*—!

He didn't wait. He jotted.

❖ ❖ ❖

Gaekwar was only a single step away from success, and running, his left arm stretched before him, pointing right . . . he needn't even aim, just release a barrage of the thin razored discs—

—a long thin plane of white-sheeting Phyre popped into existence in front eye-high—

—above his arm, and so missed the disker—

—he threw himself backward instinctively into a diving skid of a rightward roll, avoiding the sheet—

He didn't land on the disker this way.

He fell and rolled, hoping to hit the nearby wall with his back. Time seemed stretched in molasses as he fell . . . he would shoot when he next got a chance . . .

. . . another sheet forming above him . . . he had barely missed it . . .

Gaekwar did break momentum, colliding with the wall; and also he didn't break his back.

He continued rolling, leftward now that he was on his back more-or-less, over onto his stomach, stretching his arms and legs to conserve his momentum and free his disker, hoping to get off a shot . . . !

Thinking and acting as he was, on the bleeding edge of time, he found that he understood the intent of the magus outside the door.

A frustrated snarl—he sped his rolling, rightward now——he had to get away—!

The sheet of Phyre rotated, sparking against the wall.

Had it rotated one of two ways, its edge would have certainly caught him.

Gaekwar escaped.

He rolled to his feet, and *flicked* singed strands of hair from his eyes.

"Rotten blood," he rasped, as he watched the two sheets of Silverphyre rotating lengthwise in midair.

But, maybe—if he timed it right, he *still* could stick his left arm in line and get off a shot . . . no archer, probably even no crossbowman, would have had a chance.

Gaekwar smiled and absently tapped his fingers upon the disker frame, recovering from the dizziness of his spins.

❖ ❖ ❖

Silverphyre, despite its composition, didn't exude much heat, or even light. Even so, Artabanus saw he had narrowly missed some running man, who now had rolled away beyond his door-gap line of sight again . . . *what* had that been on his arm?!

The magus could only conclude the contraption had been the missile-thrower.

The point to revolving the sheets along their lateral axes, like long thin grinding blades, had been to prevent that man, or anyone else, from firing a bow or crossbow in that space.

That man, though, might *still* take the shot—with *that* unorthodox weapon he might *succeed*—as a follower of the man behind the door, he might *dare* to succeed . . . !

Artabanus ceased the rotation of the sheets—trying to keep them going while also holding their binds and the binds of the three other sheets above him, had all together been building up a headache anyway.

Instead, he turned them perpendicular to the floor, and pushed them into the room, away from the curve of the wall.

He couldn't push them much out of sight without him losing his bind on them, especially in these circumstances.

But, that was all right.

In many ways, Silverphyre was jotted similarly to plasmalights.

And Artabanus had just *now* realized the implication of this.

❖ ❖ ❖

Gaekwar was trying to time the sheet rotations; then they snapped to right-angles perpendicular with the floor.

He grinned, widely . . . *that* wouldn't stop him . . . !

First the bottom sheet, and then the top, pushed into the room toward him.

His grin disappeared . . . okay . . . *that* might stop him . . .

The lower sheet detonated.

Gaekwar flew—almost gently—backward, heaved as if by a sweltering cushion. Before he landed, the second sheet had *also* detonated; and a third was already moving inward.

The lanky man *skidded* upon his back, catching himself at the edge of the pit; his nose dripped blood; the constant chain of soft explosions assaulted his senses.

"Now . . ." he coughed and spit, and staggered to his feet

" . . . *now* I'm mad . . ."

❖ ❖ ❖

Too long . . . it was taking *too long* . . . Artabanus *needed* to be in that door!

The flashing explosions at least had disrupted the cheering chants within the room. He couldn't expect the sheets to do much more than that—although spread thin and thereby concentrated within the physical space they occupied, the sheets contained but *slightly* more detonation potential than a plasmalight. He couldn't push them any farther beyond his line of sight; and he *didn't* want to set fire to the Tower anyway!

Soon the two men behind the door would fail—the detonating sheets *would* be affecting *them*—but they might still hold out as long as a minute, or even two. And too much could happen within that time.

What else could he do? His men were already straining to their uttermost. Almost all his concentration was fixed not only on keeping the binds on the Silverphyre above him—which the foolish crossbowman had taught him *not* to drop—but also on jotting and detonating the rolling wave of sheets inside the room.

Another moment passed. If only he could *see* the men behind the door; if only there was something he could bind on his—

—wait—he *did* have one more card to play! One more jotting, always habitually kept in place, which he had forgotten—until now.

The man who chose to be the Arbiter turned his scrutiny—turned his bound posiscrution—upon the door itself, lacerating it with his intent, aligning his focus along the dancing electron web that rippled across the surface of all material . . .

. . . but especially through metal.

Such as the bindings of this door.

"Praetorians," he thundered, "cease, and stand away this instant!" He stepped away himself to give them some room.

The final sheet of rolling Silverphyre now detonated, without a new replacement, for he had stopped his jotting to warn his men.

But that did not remotely matter.

Now he would win.

"That's *it!*" the fair man's voice cut through the ringing in everyone's ears. "We've done it, Othon!" Almost shut, and then to bar it . . .

Othon blew backward, along with Jian's hair.

"*Now*, praetorians, *go! No one* could possibly stand after that!"

Indeed, the backwash had even dazed Artabanus' own soldiers! The ones behind had borne much less of the brunt than the ones in front, however; the ones in front needed only to fall where their comrades were pushing, from behind.

The door began to open.

"Something . . . is still in the way, Midomo!" gasped the one praetorian leaning directly on the door.

"An 'implacable' corpse, I expect!" Artabanus mockingly laughed. "Coordinate yourselves, and push, blast your souls!"

"That's it, doll, it's the best I c'n do!" Pooralay shouted.

Portunista had nearly chewed her lips to froth, hearing explosions below, imagining whom they were aimed at . . . but surely they couldn't hurt *him* . . . could they . . . ?

Then the explosions had stopped—with a heart-stopping crash.

And that, somehow, was *worse* . . .

"Ready, Midama!" declared her missileers in unison, drawing and aiming. The ones from the upper room had instructed the ones from below, that "Commander" was *not* her proper title anymore—and there had been *no* objections at all.

Portunista didn't notice. She wasn't thinking about her dignity. Or of her due. Or of her self.

"*Destroy them as they die.*"

At last . . . his soldiers' push was cohering . . . whatever was blocking the door lacked any more strength to stop them . . . *One more moment*—that was all he needed . . . !

He heard the whistlings half a moment before his men began screaming.

Quarrels and arrows slammed into the group like hail.

Artabanus leaped away, escaping without a scratch. The praetorians weren't so lucky.

Yet, the missiles were aimed at hazard, even wobbling, and the praetorian armor was thick. There still was a chance . . . but how could the archers be striking like this through—

The sky-window! *That's* where the bolts were falling from—down from the clouds above!

Furiously, he jotted and then hurled plasmalights. He couldn't throw many, while still retaining the binds upon the windows-sheets, and he didn't know how far up they needed to go, and the distance caused early or failed detonations . . .

. . . and Artabanus did not care.

❖ ❖ ❖

"Keep it goin', boys! We *nicked* the snipe!" The sergeant could hear a howl of rage, faintly through the window to the south, and felt like howling himself in glee. His bowmen were getting off five shots each, to every one of the crossbowmen . . . "*Faster,* boys! Go! Go! I *know* we can do it! This is our chance!!" His Dama had ordered a saturation with overkill—to destroy them as they died—and *that* was what he was going to do!

—but what were those flickering glows, below . . . ?

Portunista gasped; then—"Poo, roll the window, deactivate!"

She had seen this response to the tesser before.

Pooralay hadn't been there to see this response; he *had,* however, been there to see the results.

None of the lights made it through the window.

❖ ❖ ❖

"Activate the tesser-sigils!" roared the man behind the door. *"Shred the praetorians!—now!!"*

Artabanus felt his jaw drop open . . . it couldn't be . . . the captain *couldn't* still be conscious . . . there had been no dissipation jotting, he would have heard it . . . tesser-sigils . . .

This whole maneuver had been into a trap!

"Retreat!—*retreat from the door!*" he screamed.

Bloodied, exhausted and battered as they were, his proud praetorians, his loyal praetorians . . .

. . . were already way ahead of him.

They didn't know *what* a tesser was.

But neither were they going to stand and be shredded by it.

They dove to all sides, away from the door.

❖ ❖ ❖

Jian shoved home, and slammed the bar into place.
"Oh wait, that's right," he crowed:
"There are no tesser-sigils on this door!!"
And then he threw back his head and roared in laughter.

CHAPTER 58

Artabanus blinked. His jaw fell slack.

Through the door, he *still* could hear that piercing, blood-stirring voice—laughing.

Laughing at *him*.

He had been *bluffed!*

This captain had made him the butt of a joke! The fool of a simple jest! One that had capped the unraveling of his grand strategy!!

His praetorians wandered, confused, embarrassed, shamed by the cheers now rising inside the Tower, above and below.

The magus would gladly have roasted them all, right that moment.

But he had a better use for them.

"Pull yourselves together!—you spavined sons of goats! Redeem your sorry lives by slaying these peasants behind me!"

Then he turned away from them, dismissing their loyal salute, their shaky declarations of "All power to Artabanus . . ."

Now that he could pay more attention to the two or three battle lines to the south, he saw that his foes had enjoined a cunning stalemate. His men had superior armor and arms; in a straight-line fight, they should have already won.

But this more maneuverable rabble was . . . *playing* with him!

That's how it looked, for they would dash in close, in no fixed order, strike and retreat, all the while taunting and laughing at his soldiers.

This captain—these captains—had trained their peasants well. The lines of eastern infantry were dissolving to a chaotic muddle.

Maybe his failure was just as well. He couldn't afford to withhold his attention longer from this fight.

But he would expel his frustration upon the brigade of the Tower's captains.

"Midama; should we try again?" the archery sergeant asked.

"Honestly," muttered Portunista, "I don't know.

"We *can't* see through these wretched clouds; we *can't* get lower; he's *still* got the southern window blocked with that . . . Oh!" Struck by a thought, she raced across the room and out the door to the landing.

The magus, as before, had pushed his planes of Silverphyre into the room by only three or four inches. An archer would have to be closer than this, to shoot at any downward angle, much less let a crossbowman lean out to shoot for where the magus himself and any breaching soldiers would have to be—assuming they still remained near the door; and yet the flames were still close enough to the window to keep the resultant gap between the framing stone and the floating materia to a minimum—which kept *any* missileer from trying a long and mostly lateral shot onto enemy troops at a distance.

That narrow gap, however, might be all she needed, for the plan she now had devised.

"Careful, Midama . . ." the sergeant warned, as she eased beside the deceptively fragile-looking magical construct.

"I am *well* aware of what these things can do," she mumbled, flattening back against the wall and edging closer to the window. "I don't intend to fuse *my* lungs together . . ." The sergeant looked dubious, so she added, "Go downstairs and see if . . . anyone's hurt. Whoever. Just go."

"At once!" he saluted, descending the stairs nearby, though not without a worried glance behind him.

Portunista was glad her hair was cut so short; although she *had* been letting it grow out a little, since . . . well . . . since Jian had arrived, more than a sloping ago.

Her hair might have floated, otherwise, into the Phyre, hanging whitely a breath away from the side of her head.

If for some reason the magus decided to shift that sheet to the left by the width of a hand or two, her nose might be burnt off . . . if she was lucky . . .

Yet the sheet, despite its potential lethality, didn't exude as much energy into the atmosphere as its appearance would imply. Consequently, it almost was safe to touch.

Almost.

Portunista jotted, creating a plane of Silveraire within the window-frame—behind the Phyre.

Excellent . . . now with some slight rotations, she could see the reflecting surface—thus, the battle outside at a distance.

She studied her view as well as she could; this would give her far more information than any mere dots on a ceiling. The casualty rate appeared to be less than the frightful noise would indicate. Good: her troops were following orders, skirmish-harassing the heavily armored units.

Darting in a game of dare . . . That was worth a smile.

But, the dare could only last so long. Her troops, following orders, had brought no archers of their own—all those squads would now be guarding the vendors, on the other side of the pass; where, if things went badly here, at least they'd be able to help provide the non-combatants with food while they made their escape.

Eventually, then, the eastern missileers would pull back into ballistic range, and catch her troops between a rain of razors and a wall of steel—forcing her troops to commit to a full attack.

Against those heavy eastern lines, that would be suicide.

So, where was . . . *blast* that sheet!—she nearly swiped at the Phyre, in her frustration. She couldn't tilt her mirror enough to get a better view, without it risking interception with the plane of Silverphyre—something she certainly *wouldn't* be testing while standing so close to both the silvers!

If *only* she had more room to tilt the mirror properly . . .

Ah, of course! There was plenty of room *outside* the window.

And *she* knew how to take advantage of that!

She turned her Silveraire parallel with the Phyre, extending it to the size of the window. Then she pushed it out beyond her view. Not too far—she would lose the bind!— . . . enough. She concentrated upon the bind of the Silveraire, freezing the image upon its surface. The effort of doing this where she couldn't see it, on top of her recent exertions, was making the sweat roll down her face's left side. On her right, however, the Phyre was slowly evaporating the moisture from her skin! She swallowed, controlling her nervousness; then she carefully edged her plate of Aire back into the window, and then sideways through the gap between the weather-roughened window sash at her back and the Phyre.

At last it was done. Now she could see . . .

She dropped the mirror, dropped the bind; it shattered into nothingness.

"Everyone, listen to me!" she called, and strode into the laboratory. "The time has come for us to leave the Tower! Everyone take whatever you've been assigned, and come downstairs to the basement—now!"

She watched as the missileers grabbed up their gear and bags; probably full of Qarfax's worthless attempts at poetry, likely as not, but she hadn't had time to be more selective when cramming the knapsacks full. Every soldier saluted her while marching from the room and down the stairs—they would alert their sergeant to the change in order, when they met him either downstairs or on his way back up.

Pooralay sighed and picked the ball off the table, placing it into its niche, shutting the table and window down.

"Sorry, 'ista . . . I mean, Midama," he shook his head. "I did what I could."

"I know, it's okay; you did good. Thank you for being here to help." And Portunista smiled at him, watching his mood as he brightened. That felt good, to let him know how much his efforts meant to her—even if her defense finally failed. He snapped a quick salute to her, then raced to join the others.

Portunista looked around the laboratory one last time—feeling somehow this *would* be the last: never to see it again.

Even the sly, petty part of her mind had disappeared, as she slowly turned in place.

This *did* feel like a home.

never to see it again . . .

But she vowed: she *would* have a home again someday.

Not a cottage, not even a palace—but a *home.*

Yet . . . this *had* been someone else's home, once . . .

"Thank you, Qarfax," she whispered.

She hoped the Cadrist, wherever he was, had not been completely unpleased with her: the apprentice who had made his home, her home; defending their home in honor.

Except . . . she bit her lip, then added:

"I'm sorry I melted a hole in your wall . . ."

She turned away, and wiped her hand across her eyes. If anyone saw her apologizing to a dead old magus, she'd never survive the humiliation.

And yet before she left the laboratory, she seemed to hear a calm and quiet whisper in reply.

Go on, girl, it said in affection. Go on and escape while you can. *I* would have, if I had been able . . .

She snorted—or sniffled—as she bounded down the stairs a final time. One of these days she *badly* needed to get a grip on her imagination . . .

But, she did feel better.

❖ ❖ ❖

"They fight very well against each other, Kambyses."

"I think they also would fight very well *with* each other," the older scout replied. He even wondered if they would fight well alongside the Ungulata— there always was room for honoring any good fighters . . . though why was he thinking such things about clay-hearted murderers?!

"I wonder which force will prevail, to challenge us for the corpse of stone."

"Either would make for fine opponents, I think. I myself would prefer to fight the ones less armored," Kambyses mused. "They seem to enjoy their battle more. Though perhaps by the end of their fight, their attitude might be different," he allowed.

"I myself would prefer the powerful force with heavy armor. They surely would give us a chance to defiantly drink the fire!"

Kambyses didn't respond to this—partly because he had private misgivings concerning the Ungulata's duty within the river of fire; and partly because of the sound of racing feet behind them.

"Ours," his younger comrade decided, perking up his ears, twitching their tips to better catch the sounds.

"It is too soon," answered Kambyses in perplexity, turning to look for himself . . .

It *was* an Ungulat—a message-bearer.

And now, Kambyses thought he could feel a quivering in the ground, a trembling in awe of the coming horde: the servants of the Lord of Slaughter!

The messenger crashed to a halt in the brush where the scouts lay hidden—no subtlety at all, remarked the oldest scout to himself with professional scorn—and fell to his stomach, panting and grinning.

"It is too *soon*," repeated Kambyses, for the sake of the new arrival, injecting some dignity into his tone, and hoping the other would gather his own.

"No!—the time is just right!" The messenger fixed his sparkling eyes on the field of enemies. Kambyses raised a brushy brow to show his skepticism, but the gesture was wasted: the messenger never looked up from the dell. "Orgetorix has spoken!" The messenger managed to give *that* announcement some proper gravity—at which the other brow of Kambyses joined its mate. "Through all the shamen; especially through Nakhur. He tells us to charge—that by the time we arrive, we shall be where our Lord is wanting us!"

"Did Orgetorix give us special orders?" Kambyses asked.

Now the messenger *did* look at the older scout. "Yes, he did! *Your* soul must be close to our Lord, so that you know his mind!" Kambyses shrugged—he wasn't so sure of that himself . . . "We are to slay any clay-hearted who look especially distinctive."

"Hmph." Kambyses thoughtfully rolled his lower lip, returning his gaze to the dell. "'Strike off the heads of the Ydre, and the body shall thrash unguided,'" he chanted. "Although the body will *still* be dangerous for a time," he prudently added.

"'Any who look *especially* distinctive!'" snorted his scouting partner. "They *all* look different from one another, befitting 'a race with no single purpose,' 'ready to cheat each other, and even themselves betray!'" He spit on the ground in disdain, while also looking a little bit pleased with himself; as well he should, thought Kambyses, for having appended not one but two of the Declamara so effectively to his observation.

"Doubtless, this contributes to their perpetual bewilderment," Kambyses chuckled; as did the others at his joke.

"I suppose our Lord then means that we are to slay them all!" the messenger chortled, gripping the broadsword curved across his back in its holster.

This unseemly anticipation disgusted Kambyses, quenching his good humor. To grip the pommel in such a fashion, for some excitement *other* than courting a wife in a marriage thicket . . . ! The old ways were being eroded, little by little, with only crassness replacing them.

And deep in his heart, Kambyses knew at whose hooves the blame should be laid.

But he could do nothing about that.

So, tactfully he averted his eyes, sparing the new arrival's lack of shame as much as he could, flexing his fingers—far removed, of course, from his *own* pommel!—banking within himself the fires which comprised his immortal soul.

Maybe he couldn't strike, might not even dare to think himself right in striking, the deepest source of his discontent.

But plenty of other targets were fit to embrace his tusks and blade . . .

❖ ❖ ❖

"Midama!" saluted the missileers, watching for her descent down into the 'basement'.

Seifas and Gaekwar, Othon and Pooralay, instantly echoed, "Midama!"—also saluting.

After a moment of hesitation, the infantry looked at each other and shrugged, then affirmed the salute in rising cheer: "Midama!"

Jian did *not* join with them; but he *did* look intensely pleased with this turn of events—enough so that Portunista could easily squelch her suspicious voice, which was whispering . . . why didn't *he* salute me?

Besides, the wave of relief from discovering he was alive and safe and healthy, was driving most other concerns away.

For instance, she didn't notice that Dagon looked puzzled and spiteful, refusing to join the salute at any moment. Nor did she really register Othon was lying propped up against a cask on the floor.

She did, however, succeed in retaining some dignity in her advance as she walked to where she wanted to go—over to Jian.

"I . . ." She shut her mouth in time, before losing that dignity. "I am glad to see that you—you all—have successfully held the basement!" To cover her stuttering lapse, she turned to beam on the soldiers in the room.

They all were beaming back at her.

For some reason, this disturbed her—like they were sharing in some sort of joke.

She doused her smile, and glared at them instead, on general principle. This only widened their smiles . . . !

"Huzzah for our Dama and for her wrinkled brow!" shouted Jian beside and behind her; causing her to jump, and her eyes to pop wide open. "Let us *all* do our best to unwrinkle her brow for her, the way it should be!" he added.

She snapped her head *back* at him, too shocked at this . . . informality! . . . even to glare at him properly!

He pointed at her forehead, telling them: "See?" The common soldiers erupted in boisterous laughter; and then nearly rolled on the floor when she did succeed in fixing a properly furious glare upon the impossible man. "We *shall* do something about that, gentlemen!" Jian announced, as he walked to Othon, shaking his finger at her forehead, while shaking his own head and tsking.

"You do *your* part—we'll do *ours!*" the young man Kris replied, pumping his fist in the air and continuing: "Zah, Zah, Huzzah for Midama!" The others recovered amazingly fast from their mirth, to finish the custom, repeating the cheer twice more—

—then practically falling while laughing again, at Portunista's blush.

She decided that she would ignore them as much as possible. Not long ago, she'd have thought this to be only mockery—instead of affectionate loyalty.

Uncomfortably affectionate, true. Better than surly ambivalence, though.

"Was Othon badly hurt?" she asked, finally understanding the meaning of why he lay on the floor.

"Not too badly," Dagon admitted grudgingly from his squat beside the man. Dagon had joined neither cheers nor merriment. Portunista didn't care. Neither had Othon—but he was normally taciturn, and besides *he* hardly looked displeased with the situation.

"Only shocked," grumbled the giant man, flexing his hands and arms to restore circulation.

"Even a bolt of lightning cannot stop the Implacable One!" laughed the sandy-haired man. The infantry started to chant, inspiring the group with more delight: "One man, ten praetorians . . . one man, ten praetorians . . ." shifting their gazes from hand to hand as if weighing in equalities. "Why can I not open the *do-or?*" whined a soldier in mockery. "I have ten *prae-TOR-ians!*" The infantry deeply replied in their chant: "*One* man! *Ten* praetorians!" now repeatedly flashing the number of fingers.

Othon grimaced, though smiling too, leveraging off of the floor to his feet.

Portunista chewed her lip to keep from smiling herself—but someone had to retain decorum. Better strike now while the iron is hot, she prudently decided.

She raised her hands above her head, to draw attention.

"*If* they want this Tower so badly—they can *have* it!" she flung her arms *down* in dramatic disdain. "I am *quite* finished here, and they can play with the garbage we leave behind!" This inspired another brief cheer, along with a raising of knaps containing material from the laboratory. Very good, thought Portunista; always a good idea to call a retreat a 'strategic withdrawal' . . . No reason to let them know that for all *she* knew, they'd only be porting out garbage themselves.

"Now our brethren are fighting against our assailants outside!" the maga continued. "They *need* our help! I intend to punch through the backs of the enemy's defensive line, and lead all our people *away* from this place . . . and woe be to *anyone* in our path, or whoever dares to follow us!"

"Zhi! Zhi!" they hooted, rather than fully cheering—for they were drawing strength into themselves, banking their energies for an outburst, preparing themselves in mind and body to live and to die.

Portunista couldn't help but admire them. She wished, wistfully, wryly, that *she* had such a strength . . .

And then, in a blaze of surprise, she realized: somehow she *did!*

She didn't stop to ponder this revelation; years later, however, she would write:

> "Achieving that strength was difficult, yet also simple.
> "I only needed to turn my attention away from my self."

"We mustn't waste more time! I intend to leave on the minute!" That brought her speech to a fine conclusion, she thought.

She heartily hoped that she really did know what the hell she was doing . . . These soldiers were ready, eager, to lay down their lives for her . . .

For *her,* she understood with a start.

Not for her ambition.

The future that she had been choosing rose up before her: built on the bodies of some, maybe all, of these men.

She felt sick to her stomach.

She turned away from them; she had to look somewhere else; she couldn't bear to look upon them while holding such thoughts . . .

And so she came to understand, that as long as she thought and planned and acted to serve her ambition, she did not deserve the lives and the deaths of these men—and neither did they deserve her as their Dama.

They fought for her, not for what she wanted to be or to do—they fought for *her,* personally.

The way they would fight for Jian.

And if *these* men had claims upon her, for their loyalty—claims she couldn't deny without killing her soul—

then what did Jian deserve of her?

There he stood, watching them and smiling. She had seen that smile before—and realized now, with another small shock, that she was beginning to recognize his different smiles! She shook her head, amused in disgust at herself . . . but, she *had* seen that smile before . . .

. . . when Jian had told her, that he was proud for her.

She walked to where he had moved, out of the way of the marshaling of the troops into formation.

He turned his attention to her. She opened her mouth to tell him . . .

. . . but she couldn't do it.

There still was a hardness somewhere in her chest; a place in her mind and her soul that shrieked, like fingernails on slate, whenever she even vaguely approached what she knew to be the right thing to do, whether she liked it or not, with respect to Jian—with respect *for* Jian.

But she gave him the best that she could manage.

"I want you to know," she told him softly, " . . . I'm glad that you weren't hurt."

Well . . . ! He looked as if *he* was about to cry, despite his smile!

She felt so paltry, for not being able to give him more—for not *wanting* to give him more—for not *choosing*, she had to admit, to give him more.

"Listen to me, Portunista," he said; but she did not want to listen, for now he would surely press his claim, and this was not the time . . .

"I swear to you, and I swear to you, the truth that I am about to say," he formally pronounced—*that* was certainly odd enough to halt her silent petty evasions . . .

"There is nothing that ever will happen to me—there is nothing that *could* ever happen to me—

that I do not completely deserve."

Portunista blinked.

She didn't realize that he had been holding her shoulders, sharing this . . . comfort?? . . . with her alone, until he patted her gently and walked away.

Only after he went away, did she realize how much his touch indeed had comforted her while he had told her this. But now he was gone, and . . .

. . . and, what *did* that mean?!

She turned to see that her subcommanders—her marshals—had taken positions, around the column of men.

"Infantry!" Jian called out for their attention. "Once we commit to a charge, spread to a wedge. Men who are not directly engaged in fighting, be ready to parry for, or avenge, or otherwise help a fallen comrade. Missileers: wing *out* to the left and the right when we charge, and give us at least two volleys to soften any part of the line we hit on our way out. Then collapse back into two columned lines, and do what you can to protect our flanks and rear, after we punch on through. Our Dama," he gestured for her to approach, "will be in the *center* of our formation, where she can best protect us from any magical attack—and where *we* can best protect *her!*" he grimly emphasized.

"Zhi!" responded the men. Portunista stepped, as if in a dream—but *not* a dream in which she wanted to be. There was a panic beginning across the fringes of her mind; and not a panic for herself . . . The men enfolded her in their protection, settling around her as if they were liquefied diamond, in a communion of purpose, not one man of which would fail her for lack of trying.

"Once we reach our lines, Midama Portunista will have more orders, depending upon the situation," Jian concluded, and nodded . . . satisfied she *was* as protected as he could make her, she realized . . .

Why didn't he say that *he* would have further orders for them? demanded the spiteful side of her mind.

An obvious answer quelled her spite again, drawing the panic closer.

"Seifas and Pooralay, you are the best at working independently; you shall flank our group on either side, and take whatever action seems appropriate," Jian instructed. The little thug gamely twirled his daggers in his hands; the juacuar swirled his aasagai through a salute of acknowledgment. "Gaekwar will help the other missileers, providing command support at the rear." Portunista saw now that the lanky 'cowherd' looked more singed than when she last had seen him—also, dried blood was on his face. Jian's order of battle would keep him out of the thick of the fighting as long as possible. "Dagon and Othon, you are our two most imposing men, and so will be at the front to land the heaviest opening blows." Othon nodded and carefully drew his edged mace from out of its long wooden brace on his back.

"Uh-oh . . . better add in another five praetorians . . ." one of the infantry quipped to general chuckles, but the cheers were withheld. The time to shout would be soon enough.

"And where will *you* be, oh great leader?" Dagon nervously snapped.

"In front of you and Othon."

Dagon didn't quite know what to say about that.

Portunista had *plenty* that *she* was wanting to say about that . . . !

But she couldn't bring herself to do it. Events now seemed to be cascading, and all she could do was ride the crest.

The notion of praying, really *praying*, crossed her mind. But, she didn't know how.

Jian drew out his simple sword, and took the place he had set for himself.

Then he smiled again, and shook his head, and turned back to the company.

"Sorry. Um . . . would you all mind stepping back, about three paces?" he asked, with a touch of embarrassment. "There isn't room enough now to open the door . . ."

Praxiteles saw the opening door.

"The time is here," he calmly declared. Hearing the Mad One speaking sanely, shriveled Flooder's skin in bumps . . .

"You eight lieutenants shall stand by my side, as my hanikim—for the greatest danger of all my life is now approaching."

A fair-skinned man strode out the door.

Flooder didn't think he looked *that* imposing . . . had he been part of the woman's group, the night before? A military contingent followed the man, out in good order.

"Drive them over the edge . . ." Praxiteles hissed.

"The western brigade commits themselves," Kambyses noted.

He couldn't hear the charge of the screaming murderers, though.

The thunder-quaking behind him drowned all rivals.

The shaman Nakhur leaped running from the forest, onto the slope of the dell a score of paces leftward. The Ungulat, decorated with signs of slaughter, skidded, stopped, pointed his hand at the monsters in the dell, and raised his head to cry above the thunder:

"Drink your fill of the River of Fire!!"

The edge of the forest erupted.

SECTION SIX

WITHOUT

CHAPTER 59

The past two minutes or so had been amusing for Artabanus.

True, he lacked sufficient power for mass destruction; nor could he throw many jottings, while still protecting his back by maintaining those distant binds on the southern Tower windows.

Still he had wreaked some havoc among these peasants, from safely behind his defensive lines. Indeed, now he was strongly considering calling a general charge. He doubted the southern brigade would be able to scramble back up the side of the dell quickly enough to escape him!

Once the dell was secure, he would attend to the Tower.

So what if his first plan had failed?!—he growled as he wracked the limbs of another peasant, disjointing them from the stress, allowing his men to finish the kill with impunity.

He knew he was clever, persistent and patient. He would besiege the land about, and *starve* those cretins out of the Tower if necessary. He suspected he now understood the sky-window's limitations; it might be a source of irritation, but wouldn't be able to save the soldiers invested in the Tower.

Ironic . . . he had committed into this all-out attack, sooner than he would have otherwise preferred, based on that sky-window's threat. And yet, there hadn't been much to worry about after—

—wait . . .

he paused, neglecting to target another peasant, allowing his soldiers to do the work for which he had drawn them to himself . . .

That *wasn't* altogether the reason why he had chosen to fully attack immediately . . . Holding the Tower would guarantee the success of his ambitions, he had been told; but even *that* was not a proper reason to *rush* an attack . . . was it?

No—but, he had *also* been told: whoever held the Tower would be able . . . no, *would* . . . no, no wait . . .

The magus cast his memory back to that strangely panicked moment, as a faintly similar fear began to nibble at the edges of his composure . . . With his attention now withdrawn, the superior flexibility of the attackers achieved a temporary stalemate once again against his defenders—who dared not change the plans of Artabanus.

No, what he had been *told* was . . . that someone in the Tower would *certainly* . . .

He shook his head, trying to sort out the meanings of his memories. The words, exactly, had been:

"Who holds the Tower of Qarfax shall slay *you.*"

The blood of Artabanus chilled.

He had been told subsequently, that so long as *he* himself was holding the Tower, all his ambitions and plans would succeed. Artabanus planned to die at a ripe old age in bed—if ever he died at all! He *didn't* plan to be *slain!*

But *that* had been conditional: *if* he held the Tower . . .

—No! He would *never* get into the Tower!

He would fail, and be slain by whoever was holding the Tower, *at that moment* yesterday evening!

That was what he'd been told! . . . by—

"Praxiteles!"

Yes, by Praxiteles!—that little *rodent* . . . !

wait . . . that hadn't been *his* voice . . .

With a shock, Artabanus snapped from the haze in which he'd been dithering nearly for half a minute. He frantically looked around; Noth was standing nearby to his right.

Noth wasn't looking at him. Noth was looking westward.

And pointing.

"Praxiteles, Misire! That's his brigade rushing down upon us! I doubt he means to aid our cause, Midomo!"

"The Ungulata!" What . . . ?! Artabanus spun back around to his left, finding Alt behind him, looking north-northeast.

And pointing.

A wave of skins of greenish black was charging out of the northern treeline.

"Misire!" Alt and Noth together shouted . . . where to look . . . ??

In his confusion, Artabanus turned further leftward.

From directly north, up the floor of the valley, out of the Tower door, a company marched at a rapid clip.

The captains within had sortied, to aid their ailing brigade.

Yes, the woman was in their midst . . . her sharply vulpine features were focused in concentration. But . . .

where was her partner?

him, in the front?? That *feather* of a man, with a meager sword?? The huge armored man . . . no, that must be Othon, not the leader . . . perhaps the Krygian—*he* looked sufficiently lethal in his rage . . . or maybe the juacuar, tensed like a devil and ready to strike . . . *clearly* he must die! . . . *he* might be the leader . . . but then, why was—?

"LOOK, YOU MEN!" the pale man cried . . . and there was no mistaking that voice . . . "HERE ARE WRINKLES UPON THE BROW OF OUR FAIR DAMA! *THEY MUST BE SMOOTHED AWAY!*"

"ZHI! ZHI! ZHI! ZHI!" they called in return, the old agreement and affirmation, the ancient cry for justice!—and then they leaped into a lope, swinging out into a new and deadly formation.

Artabanus blinked and shook his head, trying to smother the growing fear that somehow, somehow . . .

. . . he would *not* be the Arbiter . . . !

. . . that all his choices, and all his plans, and all his assertions, were not enough, would *never* be enough, to make it so . . . !

"Slay him now, or all is lost!" The words that Praxiteles had spoken burned through the mind of the Krygian magus. The Mad One hadn't been faking that fear, had he?

No, he had not.

But . . . then again . . .

"Did I slay him? Whoever was watching?" "No, not *him* . . . But . . . But you *shall!* I surely see it! *You* shall slay him, You Who Fills the Cavicorn, *you* shall break his heart and slay him, pulverizing his body to atoms by the destruction you unleash! For this coming morning, I shall spare your life this evening."

Artabanus couldn't pulverize a body . . . not exactly, not just yet . . . but he could *burn* a dead man's body, till less than a memory even remained . . .

"Listen to me, my followers!" cried Artabanus, as they wavered, caught on four fell points. "I *command* you to slay these miscreants, who dare to oppose me!—for I promise you all a victory as complete . . ." he focused his lacerating scrutiny down on the body of that approaching *sheep* of a man . . . "as the destruction of this, the leader of our foes!"

Artabanus pointed at Jian.

"See! See!—the sign of our fate, from the author of fate!" called the nearby Krygian praise-chanter. *Do you see?!* the magus smiled to the fool who was rushing to death—even this ignorant wretch's own lieutenant could see what was going to happen, throwing his arms to slow the advance of the company . . .

The pale captain never slowed.

"Here," Artabanus screamed, "is how *I* give heart to *my* people!"

With all the force of his intent, dropping every bind, even sacrificing the posiscrution in a synaptic shock that lightly scorched the skin of his eyes— Artabanus hurled his hatred to the fair man.

The feather of a captain *exploded* with a sizzling pop.

"Hah!" Artabanus barked in satisfaction, hearing the gasps of awe around from friend and foe alike; he madly blinked, trying to clear the blurs away from his stinging eyes. The release of *that* much power, through the scrution, might have been a mistake . . . but, no, with *that* man dead, surely he himself would never lose, even with Praxiteles' mob *and* a horde of demimen still descending upon him.

He had defied and created his own fate . . . !

"Well!—*that* was certainly not impressive!"

. . . Artabanus felt his face falling.

Throwing his dignity to the winds, he tried to wipe his milky eyes clear.

He partially succeeded.

Through the filmy haze, he could see . . .

The man.

Standing unharmed, on a faintly smoking circle of grass.

Laughing at him.

"I truly shudder to think of the heart you put into *your* people, villain!" mocked the man in rich good humor. "But, as for the hearts of *my* people—they are *entirely* able to speak . . . *THEMSELVES!*" he roared, his hands thrown wide, as wide as his smile.

Artabanus stumbled, half-blind; a storm of steel engulfed him.

"Pull *back* the western line!" Noth shouted above the din. "Pull back, and protect the center!"

"We *still* can escape!" Alt savagely spit to the men around them. "Neither the rabble of Praxiteles nor the peasants of that fool, have *our* advantage in armor and weapons! Back, back to the east, in *order*, blast your eyes!"

Artabanus still could hear the pale man laughing . . . laughing . . . *laughing*, at the blasted eyes of Artabanus . . .

"Misire!" Alt grabbed the magus. "Come back this way! We haven't lost!"

"Alt speaks truly, Misire!" Noth panted, within the ferocious waves of clashing metal. "We are withdrawing well, and soon shall be in good defensive posture again. The mob of Praxiteles now takes up the attention of much of the southern foe, and as for the Ungulata . . . well . . ." Even Noth couldn't think of what to say about *that* development.

"Noth, Alt . . . you have told me what I . . ."

Artabanus choked.

" . . . what I need to know. Take us back east, as you say; but maneuver my troops between me and my retreat. I must be protected, for I cannot see to protect myself, and it may be some time before I . . ."

"At once, Misire!"

"All power to you, Misire!"

"No conqueror ever was utterly undefeated, Misire!"

"With this strategy, we shall still prevail, Misire!"

Artabanus wasn't so sure.

CHAPTER 60

"So, there Jian stood, laughing at this guy who looked a lot like Dagon—'xcept more arrogant," joked Kris Vivitar, to good effect among his listeners, all of whom were more-or-less familiar with the nearly proverbial character of the Krygian fighter.

Kris spoke clear and distinctly—between some occasional sips of meaded water—as if he was giving a testimony in court . . . which in a way he supposed he was . . . except, he *never* could have enjoyed any court-martial so immensely!

Over time, the tavern crowd had gathered round; and Kris had recognized an elderly man, who'd been the sergeant of archers for Portunista's Qarfax Tower garrison.

Khase would have preferred to interview this other man in private, in order to ensure a lack of collusion between the witnesses. But, no circumstance could be perfect. And with his years of experience guiding him, Khase did not detect, so far, significant marks of embellishment—indeed, the two men corrected each other on definite points.

Of course, the shape of much of this could have been easily borrowed from the Journal and the Testimony; perhaps from stories told by other men as well. But, the level of sober details—even ones which dared to correct the published accounts, though never in a flamboyant manner—was convincing the sage that he had found good sources.

Later, before his compilation, he would reprint his notes, working to faithfully reproduce in the written word the voices of the two witnesses.

❖ ❖ ❖

Yeah, I don't know what I'd expected to happen. We'd been marching up the dell, had gotten maybe a third of the way to the enemy line without being seen. Then, I dunno, all the mob of Praxiteles and the Ungulata coming up the rear—which we didn't know about ourselves, at the time, although we *could* see the mob, of course—it must've caught enough people's attention, to make this guy turn around and find us.

But Jian wasn't fazed by the loss of surprise. He shouted, "Look there, men! You see those men who are wrinkling the brow of our fair Dama? They must be smoothed away!" And by the sun and the stars, I was ready to *do* it! I mean, I *knew* I could do it! And the others with me, they knew it, too.

We all could see how much that Jian loved Portunista, and of course we'd heard, many of us, what he had said to Seifas that morning. ("And what Pooralay also said to Jian! We third-floor archers heard some of that!") And, well, we'd seen how he looked at her, like she was just made of diamond, or something, worth that much or more. She didn't hardly give him the time of the day, but when she came down the stairs and smiled at him that one time . . . well, then we knew how she felt inside.

Okay, we're all tough guys. But, y'know, there's something about real love . . . and some of us'd lost our loves like that, in the fighting of the Culling; and some of us wished we knew where our loves were . . . Some of us wished we *had* had loves like that, instead of . . . well . . . the kind that soldiers tend to have, whenever we're bored and got nothing to do . . . Couple of us even had some loves out fighting right that moment outside, waiting for us to help . . . ("I did! One of the toughest sergeants you no-good infantry had! But give her a little daisy you plucked in a field, and . . . whew! I'd've crawled into a *furnace* for her! No . . . she's been dead for years . . . But, I'd *still* crawl into a furnace for her today!"—scattered cheers and toasts)

I guess those two were like symbols, representing something worth our fighting for. And, because we could see they loved each other . . . well, we'd always thought of Jian as a person, 'cause he was one of *us* . . . sort of . . . but Portunista, well . . . she was our Commander! Y'know, most officers just aren't people. (general laughter) The good ones are; and some of the others are more like Agents, I guess . . . ("Like Seifas!") Yeah, or Othon. They can do things you can't, and so they get respect and maybe fear. But they don't usually seem like people. Some of them . . . well, they seem like Roguents instead! ("Like Dagon!") Nah, he was just annoying. Not till later, anyway. But, there *had* been times when Portunista looked like a Roguent, up there in her tent, plotting and scheming to get ahead. She was ruthless enough . . . ("Showed *that* enough times afterward, too!"—a spit. "Sorry.") Yeah . . . (an unhappy pause) But anyway, *that* day, we could see her as someone worth loving: worth Jian's time and effort to love, maybe even worth Jian's *life* to love. And more important, we could see she loved him back. Not altogether as much as we would have liked . . . ("We wanted to see them *kiss!*"—rousing cheers) Well, yeah, if we'd've seen *that*, we might've torn up those *other* brigades by ourselves! (general laughter) No, I'm serious! *Some* of you guys have to know what I mean, right? (scattered chorus of affirmation, some jubilant, some half-ashamed)

So anyway, when Jian said that, that was our cue. We got into our positions, and started charging. Then this eastern fellow gets an attitude all of a sudden . . . ("First he got scared—and damned skippy for him! *Then* he got an attitude!") Yeah, true . . . should've *stayed* more scared of us, or we wouldn't have had more trouble from him later! (general laughter) But he must have thought he was awesome, like Gaekwar once told . . . what was his name? ("Carl . . . Gimpy Carl."—general laughter)

Yeah, Carl had thought he was pretty awesome, till Gaekwar showed him otherwise. Well, *this* guy clearly had a high opinion of himself. So basically, he tries to use Jian as a sacrifice, to get the morale of his people back in line. "I promise you, we're gonna beat all these people the way that I'm fixing to beat *this* guy!" That sort of thing. Gotta admit, that was pretty intimidating . . . seemed like, I dunno, history itself was pressing down on us . . . we all slowed down . . . ("I saw Dagon holding you back!") You couldn't've seen that, you were back—! ("Flung out wide on the side, when we started the charge. Believe me, I saw it!") Okay, anyway, we slowed down. But Jian didn't. It was like he was daring this guy to do his worst. And I guess this magus *did* try his worst . . . but it looked more like he burst a bubble of spit! (general laughter) I still don't know how Jian beat that; but then, there's a *lot* about him I still don't know . . .

Anyway, we all just sort of stopped what we were doing . . . yeah, with the Mad One's mob *and* the unks still on their way to kick our heads . . . and *stared.* Just couldn't believe it. And this flake, who thought he was awesome . . . ("Like Gimpy Carl!") He's the only one who doesn't see it! Guess he popped an eyeball or something, from staring too hard! (general sustained laughter) He's blinking there, thinking that he's accomplished something—and then, Jian starts laughing at him! And his face does this . . . (more sustained laughter) And Jian says . . . ("Wait, you forgot something! The flake had called out to Jian, saying, 'Look how I'm gonna put heart into *my* people!'") Oh, yeah, good point . . . Wow, did *that* not work . . . ! (more general laughter and scattered cheers) So Jian says, "*That* was certainly unimpressive! If that shows the sort of heart you put into *your* people, here's what *mine* can do!" ("He said, '*You* speak of what you put in the heart of *your* people—but *my* people speak for *themselves!*'"—cheers and cries of "Hear! hear!")

And damn, did we speak—'cause we weren't only speaking for *us,* we were speaking for Jian! He was *trusting* us to back him up, so his word wouldn't be worth nothing: and did we let those guys have it! (more cheers)

Now, the problem was—we didn't want to *escape* anymore! We wanted to fight, and *win!* And, I dunno, maybe that wasn't so smart. At the time, it seemed like a good idea . . . ("Yeah, right up to the point when the mob arrived!"—laughter, and groans of sympathy)

Yeah, *those* poor guys. Not that we thought of *them* like *that* at the time. We thought they were crazy!—and, I guess by then they mostly were, they were so scared of Prax, and what he might do to them for failing. Anyway, suddenly *they're* on top of us, fighting just as hard as us, almost. ("Sure took the starch out of *our* carrots . . ."—scattered laughter) And meanwhile this guy is pulling his men back into a good retreat. And let me say, those guys were tough! I'm glad things turned out the way they did, in the end, because I gotta say: after banging on plated steel for a while, your hand starts to hurt! (general laughter, some cheers for the Easterners) Yeah, we got some Krygians in here tonight, I see . . . well, fellows, you'd have been proud. *Damn* proud. Damned embarrassed for following a flake . . . (sustained laughter) Seriously, though, your guys fought good . . . any of you in here tonight? Nah, don't see any . . . Oh, put your hand down, punkie whippersnapper, you're too young . . . ! (good-natured ribbing) We learned a lot from those guys, just by watching them . . .

So, there we were, in the thick of things, Seifas poking that swordspear of his, Howclear, up, right and every which way—real useful for poking through chinks in armor plating, too. The Easterners learned to stay away from *him,* double quick! (cheers for Seifas and for the Cry) Othon—hah! He had three or four infantrymen behind him on either side, guarding his flanks, and they were chanting all the time . . . "*One* man! *Ten* praetorians!" (the crowd takes up this chant, for a few moments; it is extended by the modification 'One *King's* Man! Ten praetorians!') Portunista, *she* looked kind of lost. Well, she had her moments—but she wasn't doing so much right then. Oh, just you wait! *You* know how the Journal and the Testimony end the fight of Qarfax Tower! (rousing cheers for the late Empress) Gaekwar might have been having trouble the most. He was a plenty good fighter, but you could tell he was trying to not run out of those discs, being thrifty with them. And that leafcutter *was* an okay weapon, 'specially when he extended it out for two hands, but . . . any of you in here got one? Okay, there. Look, there ain't any *leading* edges, only *drawing* edges. You have to land a hit, *then* make a draw-cut with it. Damned screwy weapon, made for special Barodian blood-duels, I think; not for all-out brawls midfield. Yeah, yeah, I know why *you* wear it, browncoat! And here's a salute to you! You got more guts than I do—I'd rather stick to my sword! (general sustained laughter, and a salute to the Handsmen in general) Most of your brethren agree with me, I notice, by the way . . . I mean about swords being better . . . Now, don't get all annoyed with me, take it up with them!

I happened to still be running a screen for Midama Portunista . . . But she wasn't going much of anywhere, just looking around at the general muddle, throwing a pentadart or two. So I had time to fight, as much as I wanted, taking on guys who made it past the others. Hey, you Krygians! Did you know I punched out more of you, than I killed? Whole lot easier to hit a man's face, than chop through armor with a sword! (general laughter) That was pretty normal, by the way, which helps explain some other things later, in case you all had ever wondered . . .

Now, Jian . . . he was doing okay. Kind of helping out, here and there, mostly with parry work. Don't get me wrong, he was in the thick of things. But on his side of the field there were mostly armored Easterners, and all he had was his sword. Yeah, it was *that* sword . . . I'm telling you, I was there! ("Me too! Same sword, just like Kris is saying!")

That little sword . . . don't look at me like that, you weren't there! You think I'd make this up? If I were making it up, I'd make it six wrisths long and full of jewels . . . no, it *wasn't* that long, less than two, rather. Just like the ones that most of you're wearing, for walking around in town. No, the *sheath* had jewels all over it, sapphires and emeralds, that kind of thing. Not then, *later!* (general breakdown for several minutes, while the properties of Jian's sword are discussed) Anyway! It was a *short sword;* and he couldn't do much with that against the Krygians. Yeah, I *know* they weren't all Krygians; but they were all outfitted and trained that way, because the flake was Krygian, I guess . . .

But Jian was in there, hopping around, getting in his licks, helping as best he could. Just watching him made me think, y'know, if *he* can do that, *I* can do that. Except better, 'cause I got a better sword . . . (chaos comes close to engulfing the audience) Whatever! Surely *some* of you guys know what I'm talking about, don't you? I mean, even some of you youngsters have to have gotten *that* from reading the books . . . about how even Seifas and Portunista thought that Jian never did a thing the rest of us couldn't do ourselves if we tried. Didn't you *believe* them when they said that? Okay, so, I'm saying, it's the same way. ("Yep, Kris is right! When I was out of arrows, all I had was a sword, not even as good as Jian's, and I didn't care, I just ran around doing like he was doing . . . helping out other people who could do the job better!")

Well, Jian was really good at parrying, and not getting hit. I think it was because he was short . . . Of course he was short! You don't believe me, go read the books! And meanwhile, the Krygians . . . I mean the Easterners . . . they're still in a fighting retreat, and doing a bang-up job. Except that the unks are all over them now, and about to be all over us! *Whew,* was *that* fight ever a mess!

Then . . . I see these seven guys . . . they were some of the eastern praetorians . . . Now, hold up before you think I'm going to bad-mouth them, because I'm not! This is really important, so hush and just listen.

These guys are real heroes, because they put themselves right in line between us and where the flake was retreating to, just a straight line, and you could see in their eyes they *wouldn't* be budging. I don't know where the flake got 'em, but he didn't deserve them. He didn't deserve *none* of those guys, out there dying for him . . .

Shut up! I know I'm sniffling—you think I don't know? That could've been *me* out there, fighting for Prax or the flake—it could've been *me* just as easy. Times were tough back then, just as tough or tougher than later. And we *all* were looking around for something or someone to put our lives back together, and if I hadn't found Portunista's brigade . . . well, it could've been me . . .

I didn't think any of *that* at the time, of course. I sort of admired those seven guys for taking their stand, but mainly I thought: *those* are about to be trouble! And, they must've been *real* Krygians, because they gave that salute you guys have, all of them together . . . damned impressive looking. And then they shout out, completely in union, so that you can *hear* them over all the racket.

And what they say is: "We give our lives for the Arbiter of justice!"

No, I'm not making this up! You guys must only thumb through the books, looking for the parts that . . . ! I dunno . . . obviously, you guys don't read close enough. This cowardly little flake, who thinks he's so awesome, has convinced all these people that *he* is the Arbiter!

So then they charge, right at us, like they're going to push us back—for *that* guy! And Jian, he isn't doing a thing . . . he's only standing there, kinda in shock, like someone has slapped him about seven times across the face. Me, I don't care—*anyone* can call themselves the Arbiter, it don't mean nothing unless you show it, like Lestestauros has. But I can see, Jian *cares* . . . and I think, does he *believe* these clowns? But, lemme say: they weren't clowns. That's not right. They were deadly serious.

I think Jian actually might have let them run him over—except, suddenly Othon is there crunching them up like lobsters with that edged mace, and Seifas runs over from nowhere and sticks another two, and one of them sprouts a disc in his face from nowhere . . . ! And *I* got one. I killed him, dead as a doornail. Oh, and didn't *I* feel good about that . . . Seven of these praetorian guys, and me and Othon and Seifas . . . together . . . well, and Gaekwar, but anyway . . . *we* take 'em out! It was like, I was a hero like them!

Oh wait—you think I'm puffing *my* head up, don't you? But listen . . .

I'm standing there, feeling great, and the others are gone, and there's sort of a lull, 'cause the battle is still going on all over the place, but it ain't *there* for a moment. And Jian, he's still standing there, holding his sword, kinda loose, just looking down at those guys. And then . . . he kneels down next to one of them . . . Seifas had got him, through a rib-joint, and he was bleeding to death on the inside. And I think, well, Jian must have taken a hit on the head when I wasn't looking—I better go over and stand nearby and make sure someone don't take him by surprise.

So, I hear what happens.

Yeah, Jian talked to that guy. Or rather, the guy talks to Jian . . . he thinks *Jian* is the *flake!* Or something . . . because he says: "Misire Artabanus . . . I'm sorry . . . I failed you . . ."

Yeah, I've known the flake's name all this time. You'd know it, too, if you'd read more than just a few chapters in the books, here and there. I just don't care to say his name. Stupid punkie flake don't deserve to have *anyone* say his name, ever again. Ask these guys . . . ("Yep. The eastern leader's name was Artabanus, and he claimed to be the Arbiter, and he was the rottenest son of a bitch who ever lived, and I hope that he's burning in hell.") See? You don't believe him? Ask this guy, Khase Sage Exemplar. I'll bet *he* knows. (The author vouches for this fact.) See? He swore by that thing in his hand. You guys know *anything* about a sage, you know that he'd rather cut *off* that hand than tell you something untrue after swearing it. That's his *life,* to know these sorts of things.

Well . . . now . . . now I'm kind of wishing I could cut off *my* hand . . . because *Jian* is crying, and this guy is in total despair about how he's failed the Arbiter . . . and Jian is crying, and he isn't smiling anymore . . . and he says . . . he leans over and kisses the guy on the forehead, and he says . . .

"No, no, you *haven't* failed him. I promise."

damn . . .

I never saw *anything* like that before. I never saw anyone *do* that for an enemy before. And the man died, choking on his blood. But he was smiling.

Because Jian had made it all right.

It was the damnedest thing I ever saw.

No . . . that's not right. That isn't right, to say that. That wasn't the damnedest thing I ever saw. What I saw happen there was something . . . something completely, totally different.

Then I looked at Jian's face; except I couldn't see it very well, 'cause now I was crying, too. And his face . . . his eyes . . . I was glad he wasn't looking at *me* like that.

And he stood up, after closing the eyes of that man with his hand . . . he stood up, and looked out over to where the flake had gone off to. And he didn't say anything: not to Seifas, or Portunista, or Othon, or me, or anybody.

He just started walking that way.

And I decided I'd follow behind. 'Cause I didn't know right *then* who this Artabanus was.

But I *did* know he was about to be the damnedest thing I ever saw . . .

CHAPTER 61

The crowd in the tavern is silent—aside from some quiet sniffles—as they listen to the story being told by Major Kris Vivitar, veteran of the Battle of Qarfax Tower. Kris needs several swallows from his mug, before he can bring himself to continue: "So, I started following Jian . . ."

❖ ❖ ❖

I don't know whether he saw me or not. And I can't see how I made any difference, really . . . but, it made a difference to *me,* to be there.

Now, Jian is walking forward, each step just like a ticking clock, not even slowing or stopping for *anything*. But, he isn't fighting much, either. In fact, he doesn't even have his sword up to attack anyone. He has to parry sometimes, but every time he does, he asks the guy attacking him, "Where is Artabanus?" And the guy tells him, and points, and they go their separate ways. It's like, Jian ain't a threat to these guys anymore, so except by accident they don't try to attack him. And he's weaving back and forth . . . no, that's not right, it wasn't like weaving . . . he'd walk a few paces in one direction, then shift real sharply right or left, and go another few paces, and then strike off at another angle. It was like . . . like how it would be to see lightning going down the sky, real slow.

Any of you ever read the part in the Journal, where Seifas talks about Jian sort of finding the path of least attention . . . ? Pah! You guys are going to have to go back and read those books all the way through . . . just read them like they were books, not like they were important or anything. I mean, yeah, they *are* important, but if you read them like that, and not like books, then it's like you're making them *more* important than the things that happened. You think that Seifas or Portunista wanted that? You ask this guy, here . . . You want *your* book to be treated like that? (the author strongly denies this) See? Didn't think so. That's just wrong, making the books to be more important than the things that happened . . .

Anyway, I realized later, several years ago: *that's* what Jian was doing here: following out a path of least attention. But, I got a problem—'cause *I* don't know how to do that! (general laughter) And I told you how tough those Krygians were . . . They'd see me, and want to fight, and if I'd've fought them, well, I wouldn't be here now.

So, I put my sword in its sheath, and then I just follow Jian as straight as I can, and I keep saying, really obvious, "Where's the Arbiter? Where's the Arbiter? I want to see him!" Nearly made me sick to say that, because there was no *way* that flake could have been the Arbiter! But it did the trick, 'cause as far as the Easterners now were concerned, I *also* wasn't a threat anymore! See, they weren't like murdering hooligans. They were just people, trying to do the best they could. That's what made me so mad, because it wasn't fair to *them*.

Well, I was mad, and getting madder all the time, but not at the Easterners. And yet, I was also . . . happy . . . no, that isn't good enough . . . it was better than happy. No one could be mad and happy at the same time, and getting madder and happier. But, that's what this felt like.

When I had killed that one of the seven, I know I'd felt happy, and *really* proud . . . 'cause I had thought I'd done a thing like some real hero, like Seifas and Othon. But then . . . Jian did what he did for the dying guy . . . and I realized that what I felt was really shabby. And it was like, out of *that* feeling, this completely *new* feeling was coming up, and growing. But it felt good, like it was really *right* to be this mad. I wasn't killing anyone, wasn't even fighting anyone, but I felt . . . I felt *more* than a hero. Like something was pouring into me . . . and, it didn't matter anything what might happen to me; but, whatever happened to the people around me mattered *everything*. I know, that sounds stupid. Maybe some of you felt that, too, once or twice, though.

Now I'm going to tell you something that'll sound even *more* stupid. I wouldn't even say it, except to be honest here, for the Exemplar. One time . . . at least one time . . . I told an Easterner, "I'm trying to *follow* the Arbiter."

And then I realized what I'd said. And at first I wanted to puke, 'cause I thought, there's no *way* I'd follow that flake! I'm *lying* to these people, the way *he's* lying to them! And then, to take my mind off that, and also to make sure I didn't say that anymore, I told myself: "No, I'm following Jian instead."

And then I thought: "Yeah—*Jian* should be the Arbiter, not that guy."

All right, all right . . . I know that Lestestauros is the Arbiter, I'm not saying *any-thing* against him. But some of you *must* have thought about Jian like that yourselves, sometimes. And you think about Lestestauros, and you remember how he got to be where he is . . . I mean, if the Eye decided we *needed* two Arbiters, for some reason, *I'm* not gonna complain! And *I* know Jian never claimed to be the Arbiter—but you think about it . . . neither has Lestestauros, has he? No, think about it . . . I bet he's *never* said it once, not him himself, not on his documents neither, or anything. Exemplar, *you* ever seen him claim that? (the author, after some consideration, replies in the negative) And *this* guy is trained to remember things, for later. Lestestauros doesn't call himself *anything*—he never takes *any* title. He gave up his old name and titles al-together, didn't he? He uses an anvil as his symbol. You guys from Lemalsamac call him the Anvil sometimes, right? But he doesn't even call himself the Anvil.

I'm not saying that means he *isn't* the Arbiter. All I'm saying is, you look at this guy, who we all agree *is* the Arbiter—and he doesn't call himself that. I bet there were plenty of people who thought of Jian as the Arbiter for a while. You guys know as much about him as I do, in some ways. Don't *you* believe he would have been a good Arbiter?

Well, maybe I felt that way too, following Jian, because I really *was* on the path to seeing the Arbiter—except I guess it was Lestestauros, and Jian was forging the path for him, and I was just along behind. It was like . . . we were in a river, out there in the fight-ing, and Jian was going against the current, and making a *new* current as he went.

Now, I was so busy *not* being killed by the Easterners, and trying to keep an eye on Jian, that I completely forgot: where *we* were going, the Easterners weren't fighting *us!* All of a sudden, this river of people around us pushes and shifts . . . and I've still got my eyes on Jian, and I see him look surprised, like he'd *also* forgotten what was going on around him . . . And these unks come breaking through the line!

That was when I realized just how far I'd actually gotten into the Easterners. And here we were, all of us, together, fighting grunts! Now, unks have armor and weapons; but they ain't as good as those Krygians! (cheers for the Easterners) But, on the other hand, there *is* a lot more unks! And some of you know how good a grunt can fight. So now, I'm fighting side by side with these Easterners, and . . . that was okay . . . I didn't feel too bad in fighting the grunts, because . . . it was more honest, or something . . . I didn't hate them or anything; I just didn't want to be killed.

But now, remember, I don't have as good a protection as those Easterners do. And the fact of the matter is, we're about to be overrun, and I'm probably going to be the first to die. But you know, that didn't bother me. I was fighting *with* those guys, instead of *against* them. And I thought—I'm gonna *show* these guys something . . . something that's *worth* their being loyal to. Only, it wasn't to *me,* you understand. That never occurred to me. It was like, I was representing something else.

Then . . . bam! Jian's in there with us, slicing and stabbing and parrying, and shouting to the Krygians, and cheering them on! Now, these were the people *we* were supposed to be fighting, remember! But it seemed the right thing to do . . . maybe because I was already doing it . . . And the Easterners now are taunting the unks, and they're saying, "Even our peasants fight like demons! You can't win!" And we're holding the line. Didn't occur to me that we were also protecting the flake! If I could've opened a line up directly to *him,* I'd've let those unks go run him down, and cheered *them* on! But I didn't think about that; I was just trying to help those guys.

Now, there were some of the unks who were dressed in skulls and bones and pelts; and they were yelling and driving the other grunts on. Then one of these unks—they were the shamen—one of the shamen sees Jian. And he yells, real loud: "Slay the worm! Slay the worm! The white worm! Orgetorix commands it!"

Well, we just *thought* that river of unks was hot before! Now it's like every single one of them is pressing down on us . . . they can't even swing at us right for crowding in . . . And we can't hold the line anymore, we're being pushed, back and back, and can't hardly get in good strokes ourselves, only some parries . . . and my arm's getting tired . . . and some of the Krygians now go down, because they're too slow and get mashed . . . and I look over there and I see Jian . . . and he's got this look on his face . . . like he's seen this coming, and he's near the end of his rope . . . sweat's all running down his face, and it's red and flushed, and he's breathing hard . . . and he's not cheering on our guys—I mean the Easterners—anymore . . .

And right that moment, I figure: this is it. This is the end. We're gonna be drowned in this river of Ungulata.

And then, from somewhere on my right . . . that was east, toward the treeline, which we were much nearer by *that* time . . .

. . . I hear this *sound*—like a mountain-horn, but a hundred or maybe a thousand times louder. But, it's *not* a horn, it doesn't *sound* like something a human made . . . You know how any horn, no matter how good it sounds, sounds like it's living and dead? The living, us, lending our life for a moment to something that doesn't have life?

Well, *that* wasn't what this sounded like! It was *alive,* through and through.

And it was *mad!*

Then I hear this funny screaming, like "Baluk! Baluk!" And the big hooting roar is getting closer. And the unks in front of us get this *really* weird look on their faces, almost like kids who've been caught doing something—like *this* . . . (general laughter and scattered cheers) And we're so beat up we can't even hit them back; I mean while they're confused. So we all just stand there looking east, trying to figure out what's going on.

Then I see the Krygians—who all're taller than me, I can't see over them—their jaws drop down; and then I see unks flying up in the air, screaming, and the flying unks are getting closer, if you know what I mean . . . and then I can see something that looks like . . .

. . . well, don't *anything* look quite like what was coming *our* way!

Somehow this got left *out* of the Journal *and* the Testimony, but I'm here to tell you . . . ("I saw him too, I saw him too!") Yeah, anyone far enough back or tall enough could see who was coming, kicking those unks all over creation and scaring them to pieces.

It was Tumblecrumble!
(roaring cheers and scattered laughter)

Yeah, some of you probably grew up singing songs about him, eh? Well, us old-timers actually *saw* him! I just about busted a gut, laughing. 'Cause those grunts were *scared!* None of them would *touch* him! They couldn't even get *away* from him fast enough—but they sure were trying!

Jian is waving his sword in the air, and laughing, and calling out to the shoulderbeast; and I guess Tumblecrumble sees him, because he makes a beeline straight over to him.

Now, this shaman who'd been yelling out "Kill the worm!", he sees the unks all crumbling—and being *crumbled!* (more cheers)—and I guess there must be some rules about unks fighting shoulderbeasts. 'Cause none of them wants to fight him, except for this shaman, who yells: "The Baluk is demented! He has become diseased!"

Well, *that* made a difference, I could tell. They still weren't all that keen on the notion, but fighting a crazy shoulderbeast was legal I guess, or something. So I can see them getting their nerve back up—and to be honest, if all of them had gotten together, *that* would have been the end of us and of Tumblecrumble, too.

But the shoulderbeast just trots on over to Jian, and turns and roars at the unks, and Jian is patting him on the leg. Then Tumblecrumble looks back at Jian, and kneels down low, and Jian climbs up behind the shoulderbeast's head, which was the only place that Jian could hold on anyway.

Well, *damn!* You could hear this great big *gasp*, going up out of the unks, and the shaman just sort of chokes himself off in mid-rant. I guess it was pretty obvious that Tumblecrumble might be *mad*, but he wasn't *crazy!* (more cheers) Jian is smiling that big old smile of his, and patting Tumblecrumble's head, and the shoulderbeast starts to roar at the unks again.

And *that* was pretty much the end of *that!* (laughter and cheers)

The unks start backing up, real confused . . . not retreating, exactly. The Easterners have gotten their breath back now, and want to charge; but Jian shouts out, almost as loud as Tumblecrumble, not to harm even one more hair on their heads—I mean on the grunts!

Now, there's still a lot of fighting going on, of course—the Praxi-mob don't care about any of this, and the Easterners still are fighting everyone everywhere else. Things had come to a sort of standstill here, at this one corner, but where it's going to go from here, *I* don't have a clue. *Now* what are we supposed to do? Who are we supposed to fight??

And that was the point when the dell just sort of exploded . . .

CHAPTER 62

A man screamed, pitifully, swatted aside, knocked to the ground with the shaft of Seifas' aasagai.

Fighting the armored Easterners was one thing—but, *these* poor wretches . . .

Seifas remembered his conversation with Bomas. Killing these men might in fact be a blessing to them.

Yet he recoiled, from what he had to do.

They had no hope. Whether they won or lost this battle, they had completely despaired.

And that was breaking Seifas' heart, to see it.

They deserved better than this.

Still . . . there was nothing that Seifas could do for them now, except to show as much mercy as they would allow him to give, either by rendering them unconscious—or else by slaying with utmost speed.

With every kill, however, the anger burned more brightly in the heart of the man of the Guacu-ara.

"The strong survive. The weak perish," Bomas had said. And that, admittedly, *was* the natural way of things.

And Seifas, with his skill and endurance and knowledge and speed and strength, was proving, with every twist, parry, thrust and death, that he was the stronger.

The anger boiling within him, however, wasn't directed at these people.

They ought *not* to have been here, fighting him. It *shouldn't* have been necessary, for him to kill them.

It was unjust—that he and they had been put into this situation.

He wanted to give them hope. He wanted to make them strong—to give these people, themselves, the hope they deserved—*not* to write them off as losses.

But how could he do that? Ripping the head off the fiend who had driven them *to* this, would be satisfying; but, would that help them? It might stop further damage, and so it might be well worth doing—but would it be helping *them?*

Seifas did not know. And so he wept as he slew.

as if he had joined the wars of the Culling after all . . .

. . . No! He might not know how to help these people, who didn't deserve to die by his hand; but he was protecting one who would know how to help—who at least *represented* something worth protecting!

Yet, Bomas also offered hope—didn't he?

—but, hope for whom?

Hope for future generations, at the expense of the present. Hope for himself and a chosen few—at the expense of the present.

Would Bomas pity these people? No . . . Seifas was morally certain that Bomas would not. He either would never have pity for them; or else he wouldn't prefer to see them as people.

They would be only rotten olives, to him. His pity would only amount to throwing them onto the burning garbage heap, as worthless.

Bomas would *never* attempt to save these people, his enemies.

But Jian . . .

but *was* Jian any better? Wasn't he leading the fight even now, helping the slaughter?

Seifas could feel his mind shutting down, beneath the strain of conscience; could feel an animal prudence, that his reserves of endurance were not infinite—that he *could not* afford to waste his strength and attention on anything but the immediate threat.

. . . . . . Seifas chose to fight this inclination—

the inclination to smother, for his own self-preservation, the cry in his heart.

The cry that kept him from being a monster.

—find *something* specific to do, he told himself, particular actions to take, goals to reach, *anything* however small worth *doing* . . .

Seifas saw Portunista, bent on one knee, pressing one hand upon the ground; her eyes were closed, her brow was furrowed in concentration, in desperation.

Some of the Ungulata had seen her, too.

So had some of the mob.

Seifas dove forward, acting to *save* at least one life.

The four Ungulata were closest to his Commander—his Dama.

Their broad curved swords, crudely smelted, raised up beyond their heads together to cleave the maga in pieces . . .

One black spike, collapsed carbon, five wristlengths, stabbed across the sky—driven by hands as black.

It stabbed across their hilts, from their right, above their heads, pressing down upon the cutting edges—barring them from their strike.

Seifas twisted his aasagai, aligning one sharp quillion with the skull of an Ungulat. Then he redoubled his lunge.

His shaft *slid* unimpeded upon the edges of the swords he'd blocked—although the skull of the Ungulat *did* resist somewhat.

Some. Not much.

They staggered left, off balance—their rightward soldier dead with a spike to the brain.

Seifas yanked his weapon free of the skull as he leapt behind the squad, rotating himself to whirl the shaft away from their hilts above their heads—a full spin on his shifting heels, bringing himself around to rest in a forward lunge—

—bringing around the aasagai to plunge the pommel-spike with magnified force, utterly piercing the primitive armor and skin of the farthest Ungulat, as well as the artery left of the spine.

One dead soldier pushed on the line of grunts from the right. A thrashing and dying soldier flopped on the line of grunts from the left.

The middle two Ungulata struggled, shocked and trapped between them, panicking, trying to turn.

Seifas let them turn—having drawn their attention away from the kneeling maga.

The six raving soldiers of Praxiteles bearing down on Portunista, didn't worry him. They would be dealt with, too . . .

The bestial demimen finished their turn, bringing their weapons to bear. Their eyes widened—they inhaled—

—Seifas fixed them with his glare, with his smile.

"One of the olden murderers . . ." rasped the one on Seifas' right.

"A hunter of the darkness . . ." gurgled the one on Seifas' left—as he disentangled himself from his comrade's final throes.

"I *do* hunt darkness, Ungulata," Seifas answered them. "Now we face each other as soldiers—*not* as those who slay the distracted and helpless." His eyes flicked, briefly left and right—the two slain squad-members finally slid to the ground. "It is better this way—don't you agree?

"Come! Come!" he demanded, seeing their hesitation. "I offer a death or a victory of honor! You *do* believe in what you are doing, do you not? Then come!—drink of your river of fire!"

That helped to decide the matter, for them. "I," cried one, "shall tell of my victory over the hunter of darkness! Thus will I find a mate, who shall bear the children to whom I shall also tell the tale!"

"Come here then, and secure your future, brave one!" Seifas crooked his finger in invitation. "Slay me fairly, and fairly tell the tale, and I shall be as one of your own nekais wakani unto your children. Here is a witness," Seifas gestured, to the other Ungulat.

"Dark one—I shall eat of your flesh!" the Ungulat declared. "As shall I!" the other promised.

"Then *both* of you come and share the honor!" laughed the juacuar. "For I can find no honor in slaying one lone Ungulat!"

"He has said it!" cried the one on the right.

"We shall drink of the fire!" the left one cried.

They leapt together, forward, swinging their scimitars, high to low, from right to left and from left to right, outsides in, aiming to meet together in the heart of the juacuar.

To parry one, would leave the other unchecked.

In both hands Seifas gripped his aasagai, raising it as a horizontal bar—the blades crunched down, rending a cry from his heart—

—they couldn't shatter the weapon of the Cry.

He slid the shaft a handwidth or so to the left—rotated it one-quarter-turn, bringing a quillion perpendicular to the parried blades—a heaving stretch, he *slid* the shaft back rightward, collecting and trapping both the scimitar blades between the quillion and the aasagai shaft—pulling forward both the Ungulata, marginally to his right, off balance.

Then he stepped, *forward* a lunge to the left, shoving the sharpened pommel with all of his weight and power directly into the foreskull of that Ungulat.

Punching through the throat *would* have been *much* less difficult; but Seifas didn't want this demiman to suffer more than necessary.

Nor *did* he suffer more than surprise of shock, before his spirit joined his ancestors in the river of fire.

This lunge had freed the scimitars from the quillion. It had also freed the quillion from the scimitars.

A difficult shaft rotation, with the pommel-spike still in the skull of the dead Ungulat—but the fine-grained crisscrossing channels running the length of the aasagai helped for Seifas to keep his grip. Besides, he still had time for one more strike—

—the strike did land, quillion to temple, before the final Ungulat of the squad could recognize his peril and respond.

"I am glad I haven't taken a father from your children, Ungulat," murmured the juacuar to the one on the left, as he knelt to wipe his weapon upon a patch of short autumned grass. "Drink of the fire with your brother, as you would wish to do," he murmured as well to the one on the right; and then he stood again.

The six maddened fighters had not even reached the kneeling maga, as Seifas had thought, had *trusted,* they wouldn't. He'd kept an eye upon them, just in case, of course—and now was watching to see if Gaekwar required his aid.

One of the fighters had already fallen, a disc in his throat; but the lanky commander was keeping his disker reserved for thornier circumstances—throwing himself into the group instead, his leafcutter flashing in arcs through the air.

"Stop! Stop it!" Gaekwar cried, to the soldiers. "There isn't any *point* in what you're doing—don't you see?! Why are you wasting your *lives* for that cretin?!"

They only moaned, miserably, and did not listen.

Seifas blinked—Gaekwar was thrusting and punching between his parries, striking the Praxitelians with the dulled fore-edges of his leafcutter.

He was trying to spare their lives.

"You *idiots!*" Gaekwar flatted a forehead. "He isn't worth dying for! Open your eyes!—look around you!"

They only picked themselves off the ground with growls, and did not listen.

"You are *men,* not animals! *Think* about what you are doing!" Gaekwar's breathing was coming in spurts—he flung his axe from hand to hand, sending it through rotations and revolutions—spinning, diving, striving . . .

Seifas prepared himself to help. Although he certainly sympathized with Gaekwar, he wasn't about to let his peer—his *friend*—be killed; and he could see that Gaekwar's exertions were burning him out.

Indeed—

—no! He had waited too late!—Gaekwar had stumbled—could only escape with a nick to his arm—the others were lunging, now crying their answer to him:

"We give ourselves to the storm, *rather than be swept away!*"

—but a splinter of storm, a cyclone's eddy, dove into their midst, hacking artlessly, driving them back through fury.

It was Meg—the least of Gaekwar's company, driven past the point of panic herself; but, responding to the peril of her commander.

Seifas watched in amazement, as she *leaped* back and forth—a candle burning as bright as the sun!—pushing the soldiers away with what seemed to be *one* continuous ring of steel!

For five whole moments she held off five armed men.

On the sixth moment—

—*flogged*—

—by the edge of a sword, upon her side.

On the seventh moment, as she gasped on the ground to which that blow had thrown her

she was stabbed below the navel of her belly.

On the eighth moment, a boot was placed on her neck, and one voice said, "Let us take her to the master! He shall be pleased with us!"

They would have been dead already—at the hands of Seifas.
But he could see their deaths were now ordained.

The leg of the boot on her neck was *struck*—struck by a leafcutter, *far* behind the axe's leading edge—
—an artery sprayed Meg's face, after the weapon's vicious slice.
With tendons severed, the soldier fell away from her.
"You . . . you're all *alike!*"
Gaekwar panted, stretching forward, pressing one hand upon the ground, shielding over Meg—his face now twisted like a snarling lion.
"You spend your lives, doing what anyone tells you . . . ! You follow blindly, anywhere anyone leads you . . . ! You *never* think about the consequences to other people . . . ! Whatever wind is blowing, *that* is the way you go . . . ! You are nothing but cattle! *Cattle!*" he screamed at them, spittle flying from his mouth. "You are only fit to be butchered!!"
A soldier dared to strike at him—from behind.
Gaekwar threw his leafcutter up above his neck to catch the blade. Flinging himself off the ground with his braced left hand, he pitched around in a twisting spin, revolving the leafcutter free of the parry, coiling right arm and *releasing*—
—striking the right leg *off* the soldier below the knee.
Rolling forward, through the crimson shower, Portunista's furious western commander gathered his feet beneath him, converting his roll to a leap—flinging his right arm *out* to slice across the neck of a Praxitelian soldier—left arm tracking another inerrantly, plunging a disc through sternum into heart.
The fifth man fell to his knees, weeping, as yet untouched.
"Butchered!" Gaekwar smashed the face of the legless man with the edge of his axe. *"Butchered!"* He did the same to the man who had placed his boot on the neck of Meg. "And shall I leave *you* alive, to be a usurper's tool, you traitorous dog?! You faithless sheep?!" The fifth man quaked beneath the eye of the raging commander. *"Here are the wages you have earned!"*
Gaekwar smote, his axe plunging down—
—sparking against a collapsed-carbon spike, shooting beneath it, barring its bloody edge—!
"Traitor!!" Gaekwar screamed without looking, spinning left three-quarters a turn, and punching his left arm forward to fire—
—the springs cycled forward and back, a puffing explosion—
—the disc cut air as bone and skin, faster than eye could follow—!
—CRACK!!—as lightning!—

—driving Gaekwar back—shocking sweat off his face in mist—

The disc shrieked away, wildly angling into the sky, far beyond the battlefield.

Seifas—anticipating that Gaekwar, lost in some tragic delusion, might respond in such a manner, and seeing the 'cowherd' rotating left—had rotated to the right upon his heel, putting his body out of the path to be chosen for the disc.

But Seifas had thought it imprudent to let the disc, about to be released at such hazard, continue its course.

So he had finished the spin by sweeping his aasagai, snapping steeply, arcing from high to low and low to high again—avoiding the grieving Gaekwar . . .

. . . but intersecting the flight of the flashing disc, batting it into the sky.

"*I* am not *our* enemy, Gaekwar," stated the man of the Guacu-ara as he pointed his left first finger toward the 'cowherd' standing stunned—Gaekwar's face was falling, as he realized what he had almost done.

"And, neither is *he*," Seifas added—and pointed his aasagai toward the quivering soldier.

Gaekwar's lungs were heaving—he looked down to his left, where the man of the mob of Praxiteles sobbed:

"please, he is coming, he hurts, no hope . . . why have the lords *abandoned* us . . . ?"

"Thank you," Gaekwar rasped, to the juacuar.

Then he turned his attention to Meg.

She still lived.

"Commander . . . I tried . . . I really did try . . ." she wept as she gasped.

"I know, Meg. You did just fine." He tried to wipe the droplets of blood upon her face away. "You *did* learn well."

"I was scared . . . . . . I'm. . . so *scared* . . . "

"It's okay to be scared. It really is okay. You don't have to be scared, anymore . . ."

"I'm so tired . . . I'm so *tired* . . . of being scared . . ." breathing rapid and shallowly, like a bird slapped down from the sky by hail.

"Then go to sleep. Go on, Meg—it's okay. When you wake up . . . things will be better . . ." Gaekwar choked.

The young woman's breath diminished, her energy spent to the uttermost end, the candle guttering, her chest only twitching up and down. Her eyelids drooped.

Gaekwar leaned in closer, so she could hear him. Seifas loomed above them, his eyes and body promising death to any enemies even daring to turn in their direction.

"Meg . . . Thank you for saving my life. I'm proud for you . . ."
And then he kissed her forehead.

She gasped, but couldn't keep her eyes from closing.
"Comman . . . der . . . !" her voice floated up to him. "There are . . . things . . . coming . . . horrible . . . wonderful . . . I'm not . . . tired . . ."
Then her eyelids also floated up; gently; half-open.

Meg slept.

Gaekwar stood.
His long thin strands of hair were plastered in shards across his face. He looked around at other people, people just like Meg, mostly.
Falling, to sleep, like her.
"There is no justice, Seifas," said the 'cowherd'.

Seifas would have replied that he had hope.
He didn't.
Such words seemed emptier, meaning less, than all the screams around them.
Even to him—hope felt like some random letters written faintly long ago on burning paper.

and then—
—when hope and justice seemed to have vanished away from the face of the earth . . .

     . . . things got worse.

CHAPTER 63

Portunista stumbled through a nightmare landscape—guided, escorted, engulfed—entrapped.

The men assigned to protect her, seemed to be dragging her; as ruthlessly and as inexorably, as she herself had dragged them to this place.

She had dragged them here for her own purposes; they, in turn, now carried her with them—almost unconscious of her presence, as if she was vapor pulled helplessly into their wake—they carried her as they rushed to fight—to kill for her, to die for her.

Above, below, behind all this, a different tension also grated her soul—a dread—a portent.

When she had seen the magus threaten Jian, as a sign of destruction—her heart had stopped.

Fate had descended to crush the fair man.

—and fate had bounced off Jian again; and he had laughed.

Then she had only felt foolish, for thinking an obvious jotting would kill him. Hadn't she learned any better from her *own* experience? Had she *not* seen hundreds of pentadarts merely blast the shirt from his back?!

This Eyeforsaken apprentice couldn't even destroy Jian's *shirt* . . . !

But, *she* hadn't been the *only* one to see this sign: and so her brigade, before and behind her enemy, surged to drive her rival to ruin.

Which, in principle, *hadn't* been such a bad thing. Except, that she had then been carried by the wave into the heart of the storm.

And except that even in fighting retreat, these armored eastern soldiers were tougher than stones to crack.

And except that moments later, a desperate mob had engulfed them all from the right.

too many things, to concentrate on—

—where to turn, where to act, what to *do?*—

366

She stumbled across the battle-field that she had helped to sow—watching men and even women kill and die.

Then the Ungulata arrived.

Now the mob had swallowed all the western side of battle, fore and rear; the horde was doing much the same from eastward; pressing her forces into the ar-mored Easterners swinging at *everyone's* throats in the middle.

She wanted to help.

She didn't know what to do.

This was *so* very different from every other skirmish in which she had fought, guiding her men from behind, jotting simple effects in their support. Here . . . where could she jott without striking down two or three of her own soldiers?— men she couldn't afford to waste?

Men who had *trusted* her?

She didn't even dare release her pentadarts. People were running and diving and leaping back and forth so quickly—she narrowly missed her own troops twice, the times she tried—

She *wouldn't* ever slay her own men again—she'd *vowed* it in the Tower! She *wouldn't* take their lives again upon her incompetence . . . !

—yet, wasn't that happening now? Her continuing failure to act, to help, might be killing them all . . .

She had thought herself so clever—but even *Dagon* had been right, damn his bones . . . ! She should have *run*—she should have taken them all to *safety*, when she had had the chance!

Jian's quiet smile, full of love for her, was haunting her—his smile when he had told her this morning:

"I'm just proud for you, that's all . . . I'm proud you're *strong* to face the facts and deal straightforwardly with them. Not everyone can do that."

And yet, not even an hour later, her pride in herself had insisted she stay.

She had nearly killed him once, with her pride, her refusal to listen to any good sense, her resentment that anyone—even Dagon!—might advise some-thing better than her own wishes.

And now her pride had put them all in danger again, the men who had cho-sen to follow her.

and she couldn't get them out.

Once again, as in the fight against the aasvogels, the despair of what she had done was flooding her.

Once again—other people were risking their lives, giving their lives, for the sake of *her* life.

Once again—she had never done *anything* for them, to be worth their willing sacrifice.

Once again—she feared to live with the guilt that she had heaped upon herself.

Once again—she feared to die, crushed by her guilt forever.

They were dying; for her—for *nothing.*

. . . she was not worthy to be their Dama.

and with that realization, a fatal conviction gripped her.

she had faced the truth.

And now she could—she *would*—deal with the consequences.

She couldn't save them all. But whom could she save? In all that teeming mass of chaos, *whom could she save?*

One man deserved, if any one did, to be saved by her.

She would start with him. And then, if she could, she would save one more. And then one more.

And she would keep on, saving one more. Until she couldn't save one more. but . . .

. . . but where *was* he?

She couldn't see him!

Why couldn't she *see* him?! She could hear no one man in that maelstrom, and she couldn't find him. She could feel him, in her memory; she could even taste his smell, the smell that was *him* and no one else. Why couldn't she see him? She wanted to see him!

"Why can't I see you?!"—the security of her hoped redemption, evaporating . . . !

if she couldn't save *him* . . . then nothing would ever matter for her again.

something was wrong

something *terrible* was going to *happen*

The clouds loomed above, pressing down on the valley, closing off all in the dell from the sky.

hope was about to die—if someone did not do *something*

She could think of only one thing to try.

She knelt on the churned bloody earth, closing her eyes, pressing a palm against the ground so tightly her knuckles grew pale, as pale as Jian's skin.

—and in her desperation, without even realizing it—

—she did what she *would* have said, was impossible.

She had forgotten, was *still* forgetting, partly because of familiar effort, partly through her unfamiliarity with the lack of side effects: she still held a bind on an Yrthescrution.

Had she not been *so* completely swamped by the battle's confusion, had she had the presence of mind to try more than a pentadart or two, she would have inadvertently snapped that bind, still working up and away, in the living room of Qarfax—

—the man who had claimed to have four faces guarding him, so that he would *never* be taken by surprise . . .

Now, with that binding held though forgotten, she closed her eyes to receive the skim of elemental Yrthe—and jotted a *second* Yrthescrution, sending it into the ground of the dell.

Even then, she didn't recognize that in her desperation she held *two* scrutions now—focused in different ways, through different media, on the same object:

the magus-shaped land of the dell.

She sent her intention pouring downward, searching for the ball-shaped object that she had believed to be the control for a mass defense of Qarfax Tower.

Portunista had been entirely correct.

The stone responded at once to the first caress of her coming intent—for *now* she was carrying with her a link, to the incomprehensibly complicated sigil scribed into the highest ceiling of Qarfax Tower.

But—

her delighted shock devolved into consternation . . .

and then into terror . . .

the stone was doing *so many* things, everywhere, under the dell—she couldn't keep track of its operations—

Only a Cadrist, with decades of disciplined training, could have hoped to control all the forces released on those preprogrammed plans of reaction.

Only a Cadrist . . . or something even more powerful.

❖ ❖ ❖

"Yes, yes, things are progressing *very* well . . ."

"A shoulderbeast is arriving, Misire!" Swelter exclaimed.

"True. And interesting. Ultimately, though, irrelevant . . ."

By now the Mad One had almost regained his former blasé composure. As far as his hanikim cared, that was a welcome sign.

Another lieutenant, of sorts, had other opinions . . .

"If your mob is consumed by the cauldron of yonder steel—would *that* be relevant to you?" Bomas asked.

"Not especially, no," the magus shrugged, not even looking at the juacuar. "They could all be consumed—so long as *he* is consumed. And . . ." he smiled, his voice changing pitch, " . . . I *live* by consuming, as do all creatures. Sooner or later, sooner or later, they *all* will be consumed for my benefit, for my *pleasure* . . . "

Bomas continued to lounge nearby against a tree; but inwardly he was debating if now might not, after all, be the best time to strike. To waste those forces in one unguided thrust would be a shame: Bomas wished to appropriate *some* appreciable remnant of a murdered mage's army.

Yet, what would attempting a coup serve now? The mob had not yet recognized his authority—and he could hardly frighten hundreds of soldiers into submission by himself. Slay them piecemeal here and there, certainly!—but, not cow them.

And he didn't expect to receive support from the hanikim. Not that their presence around the magus meant much to the former Guacu-aran soldier. The magus would die whole instants before they'd be able to act in response, and then maybe two or three of *them* as well before he disappeared into the forest. If they wished to hunt him there, all the better! Otherwise, he could stalk them at his leisure, over whole slopings if necessary.

Except—he didn't think he had whole slopings remaining to him. Not if he wished to ascend to his rightful place as Inheritor of Mikon.

And so, Bomas reached a conclusion: one way or another, he would be better served to be finding *another* mage to serve as induna. Even though he believed he soon would be very hard-pressed to find any mage less inherently lethal than *this* one. The Process would weed out the weak, leaving increasingly more formidable targets, even for a juacuar.

Targets most likely possessed by powers beyond the world.

But—at least he might spare the world, *his* world, the attentions of *this* one . . . !

"Wait . . . wait . . . waitwaitwaitwait . . ." Praxiteles began to mutter, "something is *happening* . . . " Yes, Bomas thought, tensing his muscles to spring—your doom approaches. Let us see how safe you *truly* are from my talons . . .

The earth quaked.

"Oooooo-*ooooo* . . ." The Mad One's eyes were widening, almost in child-like wonder—the ground began boiling within the four dell quadrants: the spaces bound by the running brooks.

Curiosity held the juacuar back from striking.

Consequently, Bomas still was standing next to his tree, when it fell over on him.

Not that the agile juacuar was caught completely unaware. He leapt away from being smashed by the old, root-worn trunk.

The place his foot first landed, however, collapsed beneath his weight, spilling him into a roll.

Consequently, he rolled directly beneath the falling branches of *another* tree . . .

Praxiteles ignored the distress of his treacherous ally.

"Come, my loyal hanikim," he calmly said, to his somewhat-less-than-calm lieutenants. "The forest isn't safe right now. But *you* shall be safe, within my shadow." And so he stepped out into the dell, focusing on the four creations rising from the ground.

Praxiteles had never witnessed animated plateaus—seventy paces across, or otherwise.

Gamin, however, had seen many things, both above and below.

"Yrthementals . . ." he hissed, and grinned. "Ah, no, *better* even!—someone has linked them together, in one control. It is *one* Yrthemental—four completely separate faces—with every face *also* having four faces! Hah!" he clapped his hands. "Who could have done this?! The One Who Fills the Cavicorn? No, he hasn't the strength, and this would lie outside his realm of interest anyway. The woman? Her nascent strength, one day, one day . . . but no, that day isn't here; it cannot be her. And *his* strength," spat the magus, "rests outside such things altogether. Hmmm, yes, altogether outside . . ."

And Praxiteles, or Gamin, or both, grinned more widely.

"So the dead magus!—this is *his* handiwork! *He* had the strength, the skill, the desire . . . But now he is gone, reduced to remains—so . . . So *no one* remains, to operate this charming toy!"

Praxiteles began to bounce on the balls of his feet, rubbing his hands in gleeful anticipation.

"Yes, yes!—I shall *slay* him, and be *sure!*—not leave it to others, I myself . . . !— but *not* myself! That is the *best:* I can be here and not there! Ha!"

"erm . . . Misire . . ." Stinger nervously ventured. The facets of the corporate construct, having raised themselves on long thick columns of earth, were now beginning to blunder around—only, half-aimlessly. The swaths of former dell-floor had no need to turn themselves; instead they thrust out new appendages from their bulk, driving them into the bowl of the dell, then lurching their weights upon them, retrieving 'legs' no longer necessary.

The nearest one, to the northwest, even though only half-aimlessly, was piledriving toward them.

The Mad One absently hummed to himself, as Gamin sent forth his own intent, scanning the artificial creatures.

"*Let's* see, let us see . . . he would have had a control-focus somewhere . . . probably buried deep in a middle . . ."

"Misire!" The unliving creature advancing upon them was not *exactly* gaining speed, but its movements were steadily growing more precise.

"Not there . . . not *there* . . . well!—not there or there either . . . surely he wouldn't have put it up *there* . . . unless—someone has moved it perhaps?—— Ah . . . !" he sighed. "And whom do I find at the leash!?—being taken for a drag, as it were!" he giggled. "I am impressed, my dear, that you have managed even this much," he murmured; the mass of earth began to shadow the clouded sun. "But I have my *own* desires to fulfill; so, here," he flicked his finger and snickered. "Wait for me in the avalanche, won't you?"

"Lord!—save us!" Rester cried, though even now he dared not touch his master. The creature towered above them, striking *down* at their group with its next appendage—!

"Hush!" Praxiteles raised a finger, looking at neither his minions nor the construct.

The swirling concentration of earth ground to a halt, hung in the air one moment . . . and then with a crash, the pillar surrendered to gravity.

What did that matter?—the towering table drew more material from its mother earth, to replenish its mass.

"Now . . ." the magus rubbed his hands. "Let us go hunting for sheep, shall we?"

CHAPTER 64

Seifas had wondered at first if the tremoring indicated another horde's approach. Why not? he sighed to himself. Another five hundred demimen, more or less, would make little difference at this point . . .

But then, the ground began to boil.

"Hey!" exclaimed a familiar voice, nearby.

Pooralay perched atop the back of an armored Easterner, a long knife resting across the throat of the man, yet undrawn as the thug shifted focus away to the strange effect. The Easterner, understandably far more concerned about the fight in progress, continued attending to Pooralay—although this didn't amount to much, for the soldier's armor prevented him getting an arm or a sword in proper position to scrape the thug from his back.

"Seifas, look! It's a gem o' some sort!" Pooralay pointed with the knife. Seifas could hardly decide which scene to pay more attention to!—he managed, by rapid shifts of his head, to keep the thug and the boiling earth *both* in view and in mind.

"He's right," Gaekwar mused. "There . . . do you see? A blue sort of *stone*, in the center of . . . that . . . fountain? Pool?" No word seemed to fit.

And now the sharp-eyed thug saw something else; he rang the pommel of his knife upon the helmet of his current not-quite-victim, shouting in his ear: "Hey! Chrome-boy! Truce, okay? Somethin' *weird* is goin' on, all ov'r th' dell, an' I wanna see, an' I'm short, an' you're tall. So jus' hold still, an' lemme use yeh t' look around f'r a minute or two, an' I promise I won't hurt yeh!"

The Easterner didn't understand, or possibly didn't believe his erstwhile tormentor; so he threw himself backward to the ground, instead.

His attempt to crush the short man failed—the thug was far too nimble to be caught by such a ruse, and easily spun himself to safety—but the Easterner did succeed in knocking himself unconscious thereby, allowing Pooralay to spare his life.

"*All* right, I guess *you'll* do," Pooralay muttered, half to himself and half to Seifas. "Hold still." Before Seifas could open his mouth to protest, the thug had swarmed up his back, and now was perched on the juacuar's shoulders, holding his hand above his eyes, trying to focus far afield.

"Right smack *dead* in th' middle o' three o' th' quarters of th' dell," reported the thug for his friends. "I think I c'n see it up over on th' slope behind th' Tower, too! . . . wonder what it means . . . wha-hoah!!"—the tremors became more violent—Seifas, already unbalanced by such an unaccustomed load, nearly snapped his neck while keeping from tumbling.

"Get . . . *down* . . . " gritted the juacuar. "I cannot *breathe* . . . "

"Yo! Doll!" Poo was already halfway to the ground, having leapt toward the still-kneeling maga. "That's a great effect, but whatcha doin'? You *are* th' one doin' it . . . . . . right?" he nervously amended; Seifas and Gaekwar approached Portunista, too—

—a grating *crunch!*—

—a section of grassy dell surged up to rest upon columns of earth, thicker than any tree of the valley.

Three more entities also heaved up into obvious view, from the quadrant centers.

Three of the sides of the dell were most or entirely clear of fighters; most of the fighting on *this* side, where Portunista knelt, was south of the new plateau, arrayed in an arc between it and the forest.

Most, not all. A few of the men were caught by the edge of the rising earth, and thrown to land with broken bones.

A squad of Ungulata found themselves now standing atop the table of earth; about as high as the third Tower floor. Their confusion quickly evaporated, and they started celebrating—maybe for having survived a potential disaster; or maybe in victory for securing, as they saw it, a prime advantage over their enemies—

—*BOOM!*—

—a new appendage *punched* from the top of the table, beneath the grunts at an angle, hurling them far beyond the edge of the dell into the forest.

"Oooo-kay . . . " Pooralay arched his head to watch the flying grunts. "That could be good . . . I guess . . ." He looked back down at the maga—but Portunista was swaying on her knees, like a young and vulnerable tree beneath a sharpening gale, groaning faintly. "Um . . . yeah . . . don't pay no mind t' me, doll. You just . . . um . . . keep y'r mind on what y're tryin' t' do, there . . . don't worry," he patted her shoulder. "We'll protect ya. Me an' Seifas an' Gaekwar're here . . . ain't no one gettin' near ya . . . EYEBLINME!"—another appendage crashed from the bulk of the entity, thudding the ground. The thing *heaved* its bulk in its new leg's direction; then shifted back; then it leaned in *another* direction. The other three plateaus were also clearly wavering.

"Heh . . . heh-heh . . ." Pooralay nervously grinned. "Man-o-man, if she ever gets th' hang of these things, she's gonna walk all *over* th' bad-guys by herself . . . um . . ." He looked behind, to where the mass of soldiers stood agape, unsure of what these things might mean. "Hey, doll . . . I hate t' bother yeh, but . . . maybe these things ain't such a good idea . . . we're all, um, kinda smooshed t'gether here," he observed.

"I mean, y're likely t' wipe us *all* off th' map, tryin' t' get . . . um . . . *can* y'hear me? . . . . . . 'ista?"

She had begun to sweat, and to gnaw her lips.

❖ ❖ ❖

"Noth, Alt—tell me what I want to know!" Artabanus rasped.

"Yes, Misire . . . um . . ." Alt had no idea what he should be telling first, nor what it meant.

Noth decided to stick to the facts, in order of sense importance.

"Four . . . *tables* of land, scores of paces across, have pushed up into the sky, each of them standing more or less at the center of every section of dell defined by the brooks, Midomo. They attack, and presumably move, by smashing immense new appendages out from their bulk—those were the sounds we now just heard. They aren't, however, doing much yet . . ." he squinted his eyes in thought. "The general melee now has halted, thanks to their advent, and . . . wait . . . That distant booming sound you hear is the entity on the other side of the Tower from us, walking . . . westward, not toward us. I do not yet know why, Misire."

"I . . . see . . ." Artabanus muttered, the irony of his acknowledgment hardly lost on the half-blinded magus. "And the shoulderbeast?"

"Still there, Midomo, watching these new developments, much like the rest of us. The southern captain rides upon its neck, but seems as unsure of what is happening as . . . . . . well," he shrugged, "as the rest of us."

The shoulderbeast . . . the scouts of Artabanus *had* reported a shoulderbeast roaming the valley; but they had also been clear the animal wore no harness or tackle, and that it had only seemed shy of them—certainly, they had been shy of it! So, aside from idly wondering whether it might be captured and tamed to serve him, the magus had instantly set it aside as irrelevant.

Another rude surprise of misjudgment! When the thing had burst from the forest, the shock had been *so* total, Artabanus nearly had utterly shamed himself before his own lieutenants! True, the creature's arrival and actions seemed to have saved this corner of his brigade—the corner he currently occupied, thus the corner he cared most about—from being overrun by a fanatical rush of Ungulata.

On the other hand . . .

Several disparate pieces of information suddenly fell into place in the mind of the magus.

"Noth, Alt . . . now we are leaving. Take me away from this valley."

"Misire?"

"I don't control those tables of earth," he bitterly reminded them, "and I do *not* know how to stop them—consequently they are my enemies; ones I cannot defeat. Furthermore . . . I . . ."

"I am afraid of that man. He is chasing me."

"Midomo," Alt hesitated. "The captain?—he is simply sitting on the shoulderbeast, staring at the—"

"Yes!" the magus spat. "*Sitting*, on a wild *shoulderbeast*—deep in the midst of foes who should have *killed* him forty times over! How did he *get* there, dullards?! And why would he *be* there at all? You've told me that none of his people are with him . . . !"

"Well, perhaps one infantryman," Alt added, tentatively—

"He is *chasing* me!"—the voice of Artabanus cracked—"*That* is why he is here! I cannot *stop* him and none of my *men* can stop him and *I* cannot see and all these giant things will grind me to *powder!*" He managed to gain some control, and then continued. "You say he looks confused? Fine; that means those things don't serve him either, probably. Let *him* deal with them. Between these threats and me, I place my army—to insulate me until I have safely escaped. We shall retreat to the camp; we left a company guarding there, large enough to keep my slaves in check, and we shall leave this area. My soldiers *here* might just as well be dead already, so let them buffer me. Well?—why are you *hesitating?!*"

Then he lowered his voice, and reminded them: "When I ascend to my authority, my revenge shall make the *stars* to weep. And you two, my lieutenants, shall be my agents under me. But if you abandon me now—what shall you gain? *Nothing!* You will be mere slaves—assuming you aren't simply slain out of hand as untrustworthy traitors, having betrayed *one* master already. Now, save yourselves, and secure your own future, and *take me away from here!*" he demanded—

—punctuated by a thunder strike—an appendage crashing into a cluster of soldiers.

They went.

Alt led the way; Artabanus walked directly behind, his hands being placed on the shoulders of Alt; Noth was guarding the rear.

They soon arrived at the edge of the dell in this fashion, and shuffled into the woods—

—and after them echoed the sounds of giants slaughtering men.

❖ ❖ ❖

"Portunista, stop!"

Seifas bent above the maga, shaking her by the shoulders.

Then he recoiled—for she had opened her eyes—eyes still thinly layered by Yrthe.

She opened her eyes, unable to see, and faintly screamed—breathlessly—the scream choked off—Yrthe frothed from her mouth.

"Rotten blood . . ." Gaekwar cursed; the nearby Yrthemental continued its systematic attack on the massed brigades—the other three creatures advanced upon them as well.

Pushing away the stunned juacuar, Gaekwar knelt beside the woman, who writhed in a fit. She did not, *could* not resist him, as he gently clasped her face in his hands, his thumbs moving in toward her eyes—

—he hesitated, seeing, in his imagination, his own grimy thumbs pressed clumsily onto her eyes, as she shook in convulsions. No, there *had* to be a better way, a safer way . . . !

An almost unnoticeable smile of relief, twitched the corner of his mouth.

he bent his mouth down to her face, cradling her gently
and carefully licked the materia from her eyes.

"Hmf!" he spit to the side, although with the binding broken thus, the Yrthe now was dissolving. "somehow . . . that doesn't taste right anymore . . ." he mused; wistfully, quietly.

Portunista closed her eyes, and weakly retched on the ground, clearing her passages of the materia.

"Jian . . . ?" she quavered.

. . . the smile of Gaekwar also quavered—but did not disappear.

"No," he told her. "He's off to your left somewhere."

"He's doing something good, though. You can bet on it."

And as the cataclysm increased around them, Gaekwar stood, and walked back over to kneel beside the body of Meg.

"Doll, c'mon! We gotta *go!*" Pooralay dragged her to her feet. "Whatever you did, we'll *all* be squashed if we stay here!"

Seifas, though, had followed Gaekwar.

"Come, cowherd. If you stay . . . you will die."

Gaekwar sighed; and laid a hand upon Meg's brow.

"Yeah," he grated. "Guess there's nothing to stay here for. Might as well save myself, hm?"

He stood, and turned his gaunt face to the trees.

❖ ❖ ❖

"Down, down . . . !" Jian was patting Tumblecrumble's head, trying to get the excited animal low enough to keep a leap from breaking a leg. The Ungulata and Easterners swirled around them like debris in a flood. The southeast Yrthemental, the one in their own quadrant, was punching appendages one at a time in various directions—not needing yet to truly move. But, its two western 'brothers' soon would be joining it; its eastern 'brother' had almost arrived already, driving the Ungulata before it.

Jian now leaped from the shoulderbeast's neck, hitting the ground on all fours, then rising to his feet among the trample of panicked soldiers.

"Everyone, out of the dell!—into the trees!" he trumpeted. "It isn't safe to run in circles . . . ! This way, there, come on!" he waved, redirecting the nearest soldiers, Ungulat and Easterner alike. The general movement toward the trees that Jian was engendering spread in all directions; many more soldiers were rushing to relative safety—the fair man darted here and there, waving and pushing to show the way.

A short young infantryman, however, followed Jian at a distance, instead of running with the crowds.

"I mean . . ." Kris Vivitar later would tell the story, "I had gotten *that* far alive by following *him*. And after all, he *was* my commander . . . sort of . . . so, I had a duty to try and help. Though really, all I could do was watch. Anyway—diving into that treeline along with a bunch of unks and Easterners didn't seem like a great idea . . ."

"No!—don't clump together! *Spread*—spread *out!*" Jian shouted. "*Watch* these things: they're targeting larger clusters first—!"

—a new appendage *smashed* a scrambling mix of soldiers, reducing them to smears.

For a moment Jian hesitated, watching the flow of the crowds—then he dashed ahead again. Another knot of soldiers coalesced along the path he'd chosen; Jian threw himself among them, waving his arms and shouting, "Go! Go on!—get *away* from each other! You're only making yourselves a target . . . !" Jian continued his charge, through them and out the other side, having gotten some soldiers to scatter—

—only some soldiers to scatter—

—an appendage blasted them down—

—narrowly missing Jian—

—a body tripped him—

—he fell to the ground—

❖ ❖ ❖

Praxiteles hummed a tuneless tune, casually strolling across the dell, not going much of anywhere other than nearer to the carnage. "She escaped my trap . . ." he hissed; and then, "No matter," he calmly replied. "Trapped or not—she will come to *me*. I have foreseen it. Meanwhile . . .

"AH! *There* he is! The little palefaced *sheep!*"

His hanikim warily shifted their gazes in all directions; their quadrant of dell, however, still was clear of foes—assuming towering Yrthementals no longer counted as enemies.

"Now . . . !" the Mad One giggled, clapping his hands . . .

❖ ❖ ❖

Jian was stumbling to his feet, off his balance from falling, the near-miss blast, the constant undershaking—

Many paces above him, the ground was quivering, gathering like a tornado about to strike from a thundercloud—

—the appendage erupted downward—

—streaking from earth to earth—

—directly toward the dazed fair man—

but

intercepted!—

a leaping shoulderbeast blasted through the appendage, his own hulking mass disrupting the energies binding together the leg of the Yrthemental!

Jian dove aside to avoid the crash of Tumblecrumble amid a ruin of rock and earth.

"Oh, *no* . . . "
the dirt-streaked man ran back to the animal.

Tumblecrumble lay on the ground, coughing
and what he coughed, was blood.

Above them, another appendage began to form.

Jian looked up at it—his lips trembling, curling

Then he ran away
to where *another* appendage already rested—the one from which he'd tried to save the group of soldiers, moments ago.

He drew his simple sword,
and began to hack the massive earthen leg.

He might as well have pounded an oak with a twig.

But Jian didn't stop.
"Hey!" he shouted upward. "Hey, look here! *I'm* a threat! Try *me*, if you want a fight!—down here!!"

"Ow . . ." Praxiteles unconsciously wrung a hand. "I didn't know shoulder-beasts could do that . . . I didn't know a shoulderbeast *would* do that . . . stupid animal . . . well, we'll finish it off—Hm? What's this? Oh *there* he is!" the Mad One happily sighed. "I *won't* have to find him again after all! Eh . . . ?" His face clouded—

—then he began to laugh, in disbelief.

"Oh, *this* is rich! He's threatening *my* big toy, with a little *sword?!*"

He threw back his head and cackled; then:

"Die!" he commanded.

The appendage shot—
but Jian leaped away
and it *crashed* into the Yrthemental's other leg!

The magical construct wobbled beneath its self-inflicted assault; and at first, Kris thought Jian might only have doomed himself and the shoulderbeast to burial.

But the unliving creature had been well-programmed; throwing forth another appendage to balance itself, it then drew back the fractured legs.

"That was *pitiful!*" Jian shouted up. "Let's see if you can kill a little punkie gnat like *me!* Come on!" he waved to the unliving monster, glancing rapidly round to find a place to draw it away from the injured mammal and also away from escaping soldiers. "Crush *me* if you can! One on one!—you and me, let's go—!"

—jinked *backward*—

—another column plowed where Jian had been standing.

Then the fair man sheathed his sword, put his hands on his hips—and *laughed* at the creature looming above him.

The Ungulata spread in splintered groups, upon the grass and in the trees; where members of the horde dashed northward along the edge of the dell instead of fighting with the Easterners also escaping—pouring back out behind the advancing northeastern Yrthemental, where other companies of the demimen now were regrouping.

"Behold!" Nakhur pointed. "The earth itself is rising to smash our enemies for us! Truly, this is a glorious day!"

That, Kambyses thought as he panted nearby, must mean that *we* are our own worst enemies!—fully half the horde had been crushed by the two plateaus under which they had scampered retreating.

"Then why did one of the holy beasts smite the earth?" a braver soldier ventured to ask.

Before Nakhur, or one of his peers, could think of a plausible answer—

A tayas, arrayed in royal colors, pointed his own talon.

"Look!—*the white worm!* The one the baluk protected as a cub! He wars against the tables of earth—alone!"

This engendered appreciative murmurs.

"He is protecting the holy beast, who protected *him!*" Kambyses took his courage in both his hands, and dared to proclaim: "I see it with my eyes! Tell me, O Ungulata!" he turned, and shouted to the survivors. "Why do *we* stand here ashamed—

—while *that* one worm of a clay-hearted murderer sells his *own* worthless life *for the life of a holy beast!?*"

❖ ❖ ❖

"*Now* I've got you . . ." Praxiteles mumbled. "Caught between two hammers, heh—a hammer and anvil shall be your death—and *here!*" he shouted between his teeth:

"Here I am—with hammers and anvil for you!!"

. . . but then his eyes snapped open wide

a deep-throated roar *smote* the trees, the dell, the Tower, the low-flowing clouds of the mountain valley—a roar that rent the tears from the sky.

"What . . . ?" the magus squeaked. "But you . . . you were running *away* . . ."

The Mad One began to shake, as the living mass of the Ungulata horde immersed the legs of the northeastern Yrthemental, passing on to also strike at the nearest parts of its southeastern 'brother'.

"Aggh! You *dare!*" the magus frothed. "You *dare* to defy me . . . you dare to . . . to hide the worm! I cannot find him among you all! All of you ants look alike!

"So I will crush you *all!!*"

And the two tablelands pressed close together, reinforcing one another as a mighty rain of hammers *destroyed* the ground beneath the stony clouds.

But the Ungulata chanted, as they pummeled the Yrthementals.
They chanted, as they died:

"THE FIRE . . . ! THE FIRE . . . ! THE BALUK AND THE FIRE . . . !"

CHAPTER 65

"Well—so much for *that* threat," Dagon grimaced.

From the southern edge of the forest, Portunista and her marshals watched as the Ungulata were ground to bloody pulp.

"Least th' should'rbeast got away." Pooralay sighed as he watched the slaughter. "Now, tell me again where *he* came from . . . ?"

"We'd better be getting away *ourselves,* while the getting is good," retorted Dagon. "Those other two whatchamacallems . . . Yrthementals . . . *might* not be doing much, right this moment, but I bet they *all* come chasing us through the trees, after the unks get squashed. And then won't *that* be fun . . ." the Krygian groused.

"Where is Jian?" Othon had arrived, only moments ago.

"In the trees," Seifas said. "I think. He led the shoulderbeast off the field, sheltering under him, while the Yrthementals were being . . . distracted." Seifas held no particular fondness for Ungulata; but he didn't believe they deserved to die like this. Did they?

or, maybe they did—not, he thought, for such a reason as Bomas would offer—but because they had *chosen* to give their lives: for something other and higher than themselves.

"So let's go," suggested Gaekwar, dully. "Jian'll know where to look for us, back at camp. We need to get our people away from here before the fighting breaks out again." But he said it by rote; no spirit, no heart.

"Yeah . . . not a bad idea t' be gone b'fore scream-boy over there gets into th' Tower," Pooralay muttered, pointing down toward Praxiteles and his guard.

"*He* doesn't look too worried," Dagon mused. "Madder than all the hells, but not too worried."

"*That* might change, soon," Seifas smiled. His own sharp ears heard cries of surprise, of greeting and admiration, along the treeline to their right.

The soliders of the southern brigade had not been the *only* ones to witness Jian defying the Yrthementals.

"Oh, hey, *there* you all are!" Jian skidded into a stop, and panted. "Does anyone here have something to drink? I'm a little . . . tired . . ." he weakly laughed; sweat was dripping from him.

"There's a brook: knock yourself out," Dagon grunted.

"Good idea! Thanks!" said Jian sincerely; and he walked to their left where the rippling stream, unaware of all the events of the past quarter-hour, blithely gushed through the woods and into the dell.

The Krygian rolled his eyes, and sighed. "You're going to just lie down and drink, with those monsters standing over there, ready to crunch us up like *pinenuts??*"

"Yep!" Jian sighed, in gratitude; then he slowly drank from the clear running water. "Ah, that's good . . ." Nearby, other soldiers were also refreshing themselves, while they waited for their commanders to leave the area.

Seifas thought it was interesting: members of all three human brigades were gathering at the brook, slaking their thirsts. But no one was fighting each other. And no one seemed to want to.

Even more interesting . . . Jian was greeted not only by Portunista's brigadiers, who cheered considerably when they saw him; but also by heavily armored Krygians, who grudgingly, or with formality, or politely wished for him "good day." Two or three of them bowed and saluted, the Krygian way—being true people of Krygy.

The soldiers of Praxiteles stood, listlessly, dejected and destitute—*Dagon* could have probably slain them all, by himself, Seifas thought!

But even *they* perked up, when they saw that Jian had returned.

Some of them asked their enemies who the pale man was. The soldiers of Portunista were glad to tell; the Easterners also listened.

But Jian, after waving a friendly greeting to them, almost shyly, walked back over among the southern commanders.

"The reason, Dagon, that *I'm* not worried," he smiled, in answer to the Krygian marshal's implicit question, "*is* because I have every confidence: Portunista will figure something out. She's the maga." And he settled himself to lean against a tree, turning his smile upon their Dama.

She slumped, breathing hard.

silence for a few moments . . . silence, except for the final remnants of Ungulata scattering under the legs of the Yrthementals.

Then she said:

"I don't know what to do . . ."

"Hey, uh—'ista!" Pooralay offered. "Me an' Seifas an' Gaekwar saw this blue-kinda stone, comin' up outta th' ground—had li'l squigglies 'nscribed all over it. Would *that* be, y'know, th' control box, or somethin'?" he hopefully asked.

She snorted. "Yes, Poo; that's the 'control box,'" her mouth twisted bitterly, "—but *I can't* control it. I'm not even sure how it activated. I tried to bring it up to the surface, hoping that *that* would help, but I . . ." Her eyes unfocused; she swallowed as she remembered: ". . . . . . like floating deep in a storm, trying to follow *all* the blowing drops of rain. While also hurtling through the air just over a mudslide stretching forever. All I could do . . . my . . . my mind was pulled into pieces—*four* pieces; and I couldn't see *anything* that I understood . . . except for some dots, like on Qarfax's ceiling map. Not exactly, but similar . . . and I didn't want to try attacking a group, because we were all mixed up . . ."

"Good thinkin'!" the thug agreed.

"No," she snarled. "If I had been *thinking*, I wouldn't have *gotten* us into this mess! Dagon was right: we should have just run, earlier when we had the chance."

"Dagon!?" Gaekwar sounded as if Portunista had proven the sky was red instead of blue . . .

"Anyway," the maga sighed, "I saw a ten-dot cluster over westward. I figured that *that* was Praxiteles watching the fight; so I tried to get one of the Yrthementals to crush him . . ."

"*Good* thinking!" Othon pronounced, in a tone that discouraged denial.

"Well . . . maybe . . ." she allowed; her lips twitched faintly upward—though still she couldn't bring herself to look at anyone. "but . . ." she shuddered, her dusky skin paling in memory,

" . . . something . . . happened." She stopped; then started again:

"Trying to herd even one of those things to where I wanted, was like . . . standing in front of an avalanche, trying to change its course with my bare hands.

"Then . . ." she whispered, "something picked me up, without any effort at all—and threw me *into* the avalanche."

A tear trickled down her cheek.

"I was drowning—and still alive—and battered and pounded—and—I couldn't do *anything*—only be carried along with the storm, and that *hand* controlled the storm, and I could *feel* what he felt about me . . ."

"It's okay," she heard, as she bent over retching. "Gaekwar saved you," Jian said; "and I . . . we're *all* here now; and he *won't* get you. I promise."

"I can't do that again," she shook her head. "He took control from me, and . . . and . . ."

"Shhh . . ." Jian placed a warm, cool hand on the side of her shoulder; letting her keep some insulating distance, but also letting her know that someone cared.

Letting her know she mattered.

"Yeah . . . well . . ." Dagon shifted uncomfortably. "So, does that mean we run?"

❖ ❖ ❖

"Not here . . . not here . . . he's gone . . . he escaped . . ." Praxiteles mumbled.

And with that realization, and with his anger against the horde expended, all four Yrthementals ceased to move, waiting instead for his next command. "But . . . but he *must* be nearby. Somewhere. And I must kill him. Here, in safety, I will kill him. There, in fear and pain, he must die. Yes, before he runs too far, *I must strike . . . !*"

"Misire . . ." came a tentative voice.

"*What,* Biter!?"

"We . . . we're nearer the Tower now . . . *that* is good, isn't it?" Biter sincerely hoped that this was good. His master's vexation felt highly unpleasant.

The magus blinked, and recalled his focus briefly, looking around and up. "Why, yes!" he calmly exclaimed. "Yes, we are! It *is* good, Biter—very good! Let us enter our new home, and have a bite to eat, while we crush our enemies down before us! Shall we?" invited the Mad One; and he turned, north to the door, less than three hundred paces away.

❖ ❖ ❖

All four Yrthementals lurched, swayed—

—then pounded forward, southward, eastward; heading for the forests.

"*NOW* can we run?!" demanded Dagon, edging away.

"Are you so eager to surely be *crushed?!*" Seifas snapped at the bushy-haired man. "I don't believe that any trees will slow these things—but they *will* slow *us!* And flatten us, too, for the falling trees will extend their reach!"

"Yeah," Pooralay groaned, as the unliving constructions continued approaching. "From what 'ista said, *and* what I'm seein', I'm bettin' Praxy over there is controllin' 'em—an' he *won't* have any trouble spottin' us, no more'n *she* did spottin' *him* in th' trees! An' out in th' open, we *might* could run faster—but in this undergrowth—with somethin' like ten klips to th' pass leadin' outta here?" He shook his head in fatalism. "We'll be lucky if any *one* of us makes it out of th' valley alive . . ."

"Yeah, well, *I'm* feeling lucky . . . so I'll be taking my chances, thug!" And Dagon turned to flee.

But Seifas was watching Jian—

—as the fair man looked from place to place . . .

from Portunista, to the Yrthementals, to the marshals, to the men on the edge of another panic, to the Tower, to Praxiteles advancing unhindered . . .

back to Portunista . . .

And then Jian smiled, as if a path had been cleared
but also wistfully, as if in resignation.

And he sighed.
And Seifas watched him whisper . . .
"oh, well . . ."

This sight awakened a dread in the juacuar.

The fair man patted the maga's shoulder a final time . . .
Then, steeling his face in resolve, Jian raised his hands and clapped them together loudly.
"All right!" he shouted. "*I* will end these things!"
This got the attention of everyone, even Dagon.
"All of you—keep back; don't draw their attention! Once I've destroyed them . . . well, then decide for the best what to do!"
Portunista now looked up, dumbfounded as every other face along the treeline. "You . . . you're going to *what* . . . ?!"
But Jian knelt down in front of her.
"I'm sorry, my . . . my lady . . ."—Seifas wondered what Jian had been going to say instead—"but I don't have time to explain. Here . . ." Jian unbelted his sheath, and drawing from it his common sword, he held the soft empty leather out to Portunista. "Keep this for me . . . or give it away . . . whichever you choose," he told her. She took it, uncomprehendingly. "Thank you for giving this to me; and as for my sword . . . if you happen to find it out on the field somewhere, then have it repolished and sharpened so some other soldier can use it."
The approaching Yrthementals sounded to Seifas like the pounding of a giant's heart—like *two* hearts beating, almost together, almost in time . . .
"Jian . . . ?" The maga's voice was as small as a little girl's.
"Be good, Portunista . . . please . . ." He put his hand over hers for one more moment.

Then he turned away, and strode to the edge of the dell.
"I ask for one other man to help me! Only one! Who will go with me?—to fight these things and win!"

No one stepped forward—they only stared.
"He's daft . . ." "Not I . . ." "He wants to go wrestle those things, he can have at it . . ."

Seifas heard the murmurs around them—and anger boiled inside him at their lack of trust and loyalty for this man. From the enemies, he could understand; after all, why should *they* know *him?!* But from men who *should* know Jian already—who should *know* why he was willing to do this . . . !

Then, his anger was doused beneath a burning icy fountain—how *dared* he judge these soldiers, when he himself was not standing forward?!

But this was clearly a suicidal mission . . . !

. . . it *couldn't* be hopeless—Jian believed he could win . . .

Did *he* not trust Jian? Seifas berated himself through his mounting fear. After all he had seen, all he had thought—

Jian turned, regarding them all; his face, clouded.

"Is there not even one?" His heart was breaking in his voice. "Is there not even one who will stand with me . . . ?"

"Here is a sword!"

Seifas held his aasagai high in the air, proclaiming his choice above the mountainous thunder.

And he stepped forward—trodding down his fear.

Jian nodded, once—a grim smile broke the cloud of his face.

"It is enough," he said. "Let us go."

CHAPTER 66

The two men stood together, facing the oncoming storms of rock and stone.

"Seifas—listen to me," said Jian . . . and Seifas listened. "You *must* survive, for *she* must be protected—and I entrust her to you. These things cannot hurt you, as long as you keep your head; so, *don't* stop running, don't stand still. I only need a distraction at first, and then . . . you must hold the field alone. I do not know how long. Keep them in the dell as long as you can. Don't you *dare*," his voice was shaking, "let them get. . . near. . . *her!*"

"They won't, so long as I live. And should I fall, I *know* another will gladly take my place—to give his life in turn, for the one you cherish most."

"Well," said Jian—and sighed as he settled himself.

"Well," Seifas said—the first of the Yrthementals reached the trees, left and right of their position, scattering panicking soldiers.

"And all manner of things shall be well—my friend."

The two men smiled.

"Now," said Jian, "we will go."

"Where *is* he . . . ?" Praxiteles muttered, absently wandering toward the Tower door. "Perhaps I have already buried him under a tree, or under the stone. So many targets left to kill . . . so many . . . but I have time . . . and soon," he tittered, dancing a little jig, "very soon now, she will come to *me*. So, his death must *also* be—AH!" he halted and spun on his heel, his mouth pulled wide in unholy satisfaction. "THERE HE IS!"

From out of the forest, beneath the leading legs of the southernmost Yrthemental

came running the white man and the black—together.

"Leave all the others!—come get him my pets! There he is! *There* he is!" Praxiteles hopped in excitement.

"Split—go left!" shouted Jian to Seifas. "Draw them back into the dell, away from our men!"

Seifas didn't bother to ask what "our men" meant; for he remembered—

—the courtly if cautious way, that Jian had been greeted by the Easterners—

—how he himself had wished that he could give hope to the Westerners—

And he was content with his choice:

to come out onto the dell, with Jian, to die.

❖ ❖ ❖

"What is he doing?!" "He's gone insane!" "He doesn't stand a chance!"

Portunista, still holding the empty sheath in a daze, heard the soldiers around her decrying the choice of . . .

. . . of her love.

She lifted her face and lifted her voice:

"He is drawing your deaths away from you, *and down on his own head!*"

There was stunned silence.

Then, there were cheers.

Portunista didn't join them.

It wasn't fair . . . this shouldn't have been necessary . . . !

"There is nothing that ever will happen to me," Jian's voice rose up from her memory, "there is nothing that *could* ever happen to me—"

—was *this* what Jian deserved . . . ?

This was what he had freely chosen, she realized.

As for what he deserved . . .

"We *will* help him," declared Portunista. " . . . somehow," she added, watching the men, the black and the white, darting in front of, under, among, around the crashing legs, drawing the Yrthementals from the forest.

Yes—that was what he deserved.

And she would see that he got it.

But, *how* to help . . . ?

She knelt to the ground.

and bit back nauseous fear . . .

her failure in the sigilstone, even merely *thinking* of jotting an Yrthescrution again, was making her soul and body shiver . . .

Jian deserved *help*.

She jotted.
The Yrthe formed beneath her closed eyelids.

. . . only their usual minor annoyance.

She sighed in relief—compared to what she had dreaded, they almost felt like kisses . . . !

So!—Now she needed knowledge, more than what she had, to decide how best to help.

Still, she sent the scrution delicately—fearing with every step of her intent, that she would be swept again—into that hell from which she would never—

. . . *stupid* cowardly snip of a *cow!* she cursed herself. Gaekwar had helped her escape before—he remained nearby to do it again. Grow a spine, she commanded herself, *and trust your own men for once!*

"Seifas!" Jian called breathlessly. The juacuar dared not reply: *all* the Yrthe-mentals now had entered the dell again, and Seifas was far too busy in trying to keep their attention—and in trying to stay alive.

"Trust me!—*hold the field!!*"

To Seifas, it wasn't a question of trust anymore, but of *being* trustworthy himself: for he had promised to give his life to protect the hope for Portunista—a promise worth giving a hundred times over. So, unless . . . *until* . . . these creatures were finished, *no* other options remained!—between abandoning her, whom he had been entrusted with and for—

or else to war against avalanches.

But, for what it was worth, Seifas also trusted Jian.

He seized his fear in both his hands, and slew, moment by moment, all temptation to disgrace.

"Wait, Alt . . ." Artabanus gripped the shoulders of his guide. "What . . . what do I hear behind me??"

"The mightiest battle ever." The officer's voice was tinged with awe. "And . . . and *cheers.*"

"cheers . . . ?" The face of the magus twisted, in fear and confusion.

"Do you wish to return, Misire?"

"back *there?*" Artabanus whispered. He paused, with drooping head, hoping for some alternative . . .

"Midomo, look! Oh, I mean—" Alt corrected himself. "I see someone approaching."

"from behind?!" the magus rasped.

"No, Misire," Noth attempted to reassure him. "From ahead. Two of our scouts, it seems, are coming to us!"

Moments later, the brothers-in-arms fetched up beside their leader.

"Why do you stare?!" demanded Alt; although in truth he knew they must look foolish—as well as completely defeated.

"ah . . . that is . . . All power to Artabanus!" one of the scouts saluted—although the magus detected less than usual enthusiasm. The other man may have saluted, but he didn't echo the proclamation.

"Noth!" Artabanus pulled himself upright, resuming some measure of dignity. "Take these brave and loyal men!—return to the battle! I must continue to camp, to ensure its . . . security . . . and to heal my eyes. Whether the battle goes irretrievably ill, against the capable hands of the sergeants in whom I have placed my trust; or if, as I fully expect, we have carried the day—for do I not hear cheering?!—then come and report to me. Assuming," he added regally, "I have not already gathered my strength and wrath, to arrive myself at the line of battle, turning the tide and securing our victory!"

Total silence greeted this stirring speech—which, Artabanus had to admit, he frankly had expected. Unlike the minions of Praxiteles, *his* men were not fools.

"At once, Midomo!" Noth stepped back, saluting with a professional, serious snap. "Come along you two—let us discover what our leader wishes to know!"

Artabanus decided Noth would need rewarding, somehow—assuming his lieutenant survived this debacle—for that reply had been altogether free of ironic tone, filled with confidence in the magus, and in his fated mission.

On the other hand, he *might* need to slay those two scouts: they simply walked off, leading Noth back to the front.

The man who chose to be the Arbiter resumed his blind degrading struggle eastward.

❖ ❖ ❖

"Ah!—what an amusing game!" Praxiteles sighed in contentment; his arms were folded across his chest. "I had worried he might escape me after all—but look!" he pointed for his subordinates. "There he is!—practically *begging* for me to kill him!"

. . . but then his evil smile deflated.

"There . . . there he is . . . he is . . ."

Jian had dashed away—

"he is . . . he is coming *here!*"

—north, to where the gasping demon stood.

"Agh! No, back up, back up!!" The Mad One stumbled into his hanikim.

"Misire!" Swelter exclaimed, and tried to give a comforting laugh, "surely he will never make it to us, and even if he did . . ."

But then he realized:

this man had already fought against the killing plateaus for several minutes, escaping completely unscathed—

and then: if even Gamin feared this man, then very possibly neither Gamin nor Praxiteles could stop him—

and then: if even his master couldn't stop this man . . .

"Back up! Back up!!" Swelter added his urgency, too.

❖ ❖ ❖

"Look at him! He defies the stony death and laughs! Look at him! Even the mighty Praxiteles cannot bear to stand before him!"

Portunista decided to post this Krygian praise-chanter into the kitchens, or maybe the cattle-pens—or *anywhere,* so long as he shut his mouth with his stupid poetry . . . !

It didn't occur to her, till later, how easily she had assumed: the Krygians now would be working for *her* . . .

A soul-filled roar of rage erupted around her, stronger than the cheers for the battle against the Yrthementals.

It frightened her, reflexively; yet somehow, she wasn't worried.

"What is this?" she asked her officers, raising her voice to be heard, but not in a panic.

"Prax's soldiers," Gaekwar told her, kneeling by her side.

"I think they're servin' scream-boy notice," Pooralay chuckled behind her—Portunista could hear his wicked grin.

"Serving notice?" she asked, echoing the smile she heard.

Othon clarified: "'We quit!'"

The maga had been lightly scanning the energy flows beneath the ground—well away from where she had left the sigilstone!—searching for an exploitable vulnerability; now she took a moment, to send her intention upward . . .

There: *those* two feet belonged to Jian . . .

Was he charging Praxiteles alone?!

Her smile disappeared; she furrowed her brow. She didn't expect the magus could hurt him—not hurt *Jian* of all people—but:

Eight strong, well-armored men were guarding the frantically back-stepping magus. Jian could not defeat them all. Could he . . . ??

Where was Seifas?! They *should* have been charging together . . . ! *There* he was . . . Hadn't he noticed that Jian was charging? What was the damn-fool juacuar still *doing* there?!!

oh . . . he had to be holding the Yrthementals' attention.

But—Seifas would tire, eventually! She *knew* these things would not! What in the pit below were they trying to—?!

Wait . . . the maga told herself, as lights linked up within her mind. Wait, wait wait . . .

. . . *how* did she know these Yrthementals would never tire?

and . . . why—another part of her mind reported—

why was Jian not angling straight for Praxiteles anymore?

The four Yrthementals had not been kept at bay, exactly, by the lone juacuar. True, so long as the dance was a game, the hostile unliving entities played their part, according to how their master commanded.

Now their commander had new commands, and new concerns.

Seifas halfheartedly dodged a final appendage; then bent down to catch his breath, dipping his hand within the cool of the burbling stream nearby, bringing water to his mouth. Not much: he couldn't risk a stitch in his side; then he would die, if—when—those things returned.

The Guacu-ara, the Hunting Cry, *still* had a duty: to live as well as to die.

Praxiteles flustered to a halt—watching the path of the running man who careened down the slope, chased by four plateaus.

"He . . . he isn't coming after *me* . . ." the Mad One exhaled in relief. "Hah . . . He's only . . . only . . . ARH!" he gritted his teeth. "He's only running toward the Tower door! Faster, *faster* my pets!" He clenched his hands at his sides, and willed the Yrthementals to a new extreme of speed.

—which, for them, could not be much more extreme than one running man . . .

Portunista sent her intent below again, avoiding the cascading energies of the marching Yrthementals, orienting herself at safer distance. She had no clue why Jian was running toward the Tower; but she was working out a plan of her own.

She traced the shape of the mind-crushing energies, skirting them carefully, staying away—but following down their shape within the deepness of the earth.

As she had inferred: they branched from an energy ring.

A ring that flowed from beneath the Tower.

She laughed in triumph, having confirmed her plan would work, and stood to her feet, blinking away the flecks of Yrthe under her eyes.

"Well, *you're* in a better mood about this than the Praxitelians," Gaekwar muttered, looking around them nervously.

Portunista could also feel their shifting tide of opinion: the western mob had clearly been hoping for this impossible man to challenge their tormentor.

Instead, he raced into the Tower through the open door.

"Hmph!" she snorted—leave it to Jian to do something that made no sense at all . . .

"*I* will stop those things," she announced.

" . . . you *also* gonna run inside th' Tower, leavin' Seifas alone outside?!" Pooralay asked in perplexity.

"No." Portunista smiled, anticipating her coming victory. "But neither will anything *else* be running into that Tower!"

Leaving that promise to hang in the air mysteriously, she studied the situation a moment longer, contemplating how best to achieve her goal . . .

❖ ❖ ❖

"BAH!" the Mad One snarled, and slammed his bony fist into his palm. "He means to *escape* from me!"

Ender laughed. "Not by running in *there,* he can't! The idiot! Why, you can just have those table-creatures reduce those walls to powder—and *then* where will he be?!"

"The *Tower* . . . " Praxiteles explained, " . . . is what . . . I have *come* for . . . and is the *KEY* . . . to my ultimate *VICTORY!!*" he sprayed his spittle upon the quailing soldier. "I *won't* dismantle it, even for *him!* Surely he knows that! In fact, I see: he's *counting* on it! *That* is why he is safe in there!"

"So? We camp outside after killing off everyone else, until he gets hungry enough to make a break for it . . . Or!" suggested Flooder: "You can send *us,* Misire! He is a bare little *sheep* of a man! We can take *him,* I think!"

"Yes, I agree completely!" Rester enjoined. "Please, Misire, have *no* more worries about this man! I beg you: give to *me* the honor of killing him for you, personally!"

Swelter, recalling his previous thoughts on this matter, decided, as far as *he* was concerned, that Rester and Flooder were altogether welcome to go first . . .

"Yes . . . maybe . . ." Praxiteles reined his temper. "Maybe . . . the eight of you hanikim *might* be able to kill him . . ." Well, Swelter dryly thought, *that* was reassuring news . . . ! "But not today. He knows he is trapped, you see? That *I* have trapped him!" the Mad One continued, working out the implications to his satisfaction. "Yes, like a rat in a hole—my faithful cats outside preparing to spring on him . . . and so he will leave . . . through the *window!*" he foamed at the mouth. "The hole in the air, you fools! *That* is where he has gone! I see it, I know it! He will escape far away, and then . . . no . . . that doesn't make sense . . ." He absently wiped the foam from his chin, his temper shifting again. "I also have clearly foreseen his woman giving herself to me instead. Which, I also know, *can't* happen, unless I have already buried him; for, why would she do *that*, so long as he lives? And this shall happen *very* soon—I am certain of *that* . . . so . . ." he pondered. "No, wait . . . perhaps he need not die . . . she will see his coward's retreat, perhaps, and then . . . she will cast away the gown that he has woven around her: *rejecting* him . . . so . . . I will have buried his reputation and memory!"

But Swelter thought that Praxiteles hardly sounded certain of *this* interpretation.

"Only . . . except . . . yes; there is another; *more* than one . . . the ones I have seen before!" The Mad One began to froth again. "Yes! No! They *all* are my rivals, every one! So long as even one of them lives, she *never* can be mine! Therefore, *all* must die!! Starting with . . . *that one* . . . " he hissed, and turned his narrowed hatred upon the juacuar. "The servant of the Watcher!—and of the One Who watched the Watcher!! The final one . . . I will begin by slaying him first . . ."

❖ ❖ ❖

"He's trying to bloody *escape*, I tell you!" Dagon shouted; much to the consternation of the crowd who'd gathered around the edge of the dell—the crowd who was already disappointed by Jian's refusal to fight the Mad One. "He's leaving us here to *rot!!*"

"Doll-boy," Pooralay answered with straining patience, "it's a tower. With only one door. And with big hulkin' dirt thingies *outside* th' door."

"And a big wide *tesser-window* upstairs, you imbecile!" retorted Dagon.

"And he's just gonna jump on outta it, hunnerds o' paces up high in th' *air?*" Pooralay counter-retorted, his face turning livid. "Why not just stand'n one place an' let one-a those thingies squash him flat?!"

"Why not just roll the map to a *mountain*—like to those *peaks* over there?" the bushy-haired man mocked the little thug's tone of voice—he pointed toward the northern end of the valley; the low clouds shrouded the mountaintops.

Pooralay started to counter-counter-retort—
his face fell, as he considered Dagon's idea.

"The ball," responded Othon, confidently.
"Huh?" Dagon was thrown off-stride.
"Yes, of course, the roller-ball, you gnat-wit!" Gaekwar explained—much to
his own relief. "Jian *can't* be planning that," he laughed—nervously—"because
he *has* to know that none of *us* would be stupid enough to simply *leave* that ball
in a room we figured was probably going to be . . . overrun . . . um . . ."
Gaekwar noticed Pooralay, holding his hand up like a penitent schoolboy.
"Sorry, guys," he rasped. "I . . . I don't know what I was thinkin' . . . I *wasn't*
thinkin' . . ." he berated himself. "I just was *doin'*, not thinkin'. I . . . I'm pretty
sure I left th' ball . . . It ain't in one my pockets," he patted them in futility, "an',
'ista and I were the last ones out, an' I was th' one at th' table . . . Hey, I'm older
'n *two* o' you kids put t'gether at least!!" he exploded. "One-a these days the ol'
squash is goin' t' go," he beat his head with his fist, "an' it might be startin'
today . . . ! B'sides, maybe 'ista has it . . . um . . . Midama?" he asked, hesitantly.
"No, Poo," she absently answered, "I don't have it." She wasn't paying more
than half-attention to the conversation, having discarded several plans to achieve
her goal.
"oy . . ." The thug put his hand across his eyes, muttering curses against
himself.
"This is a *stupid* debate!" insisted Gaekwar, trying to take the initiative back
from the smirking Dagon. "We *all* know Jian won't just run away: because he
loves Portunista, who—"
"—who is a *bitch*," Dagon coldly finished.

That got Portunista's full attention.
Dagon ignored her shocked glare. "That's what she does. She *collects* men,
like you and me and Othon over there. Who *cares* if she's slept with him? You
think that makes a difference to *her?*" he asked, witheringly. "She treats him like
something she scraped off her boot!—and you expect him to just throw his *life*
away for that?! His little speeches before were fine and dandy, but face it: he was
caught in a crack, and needed us pumped up and ready to fight our way out.
Then he heard the thug and Seifas saying that no one would probably make it
out of the forest alive with *those* things chasing us; so, he heads for the only *other*
way out of the valley. Out the tesser-window. Pulling the wool over *your* eyes, 'my
lady'—the way you've been trying to do to him; making you think that he's going
to try something that's *obviously* impossible, so *you'll* stay here and watch . . . and
then get munched, when he doesn't come back.

"That's his 'nifty' little slap in the face, back at you, babe. Hope you had a good time."

No one said anything.

Portunista wanted to flay the skin off Dagon's bones—something she now could easily do—but . . .

. . . but that voice of hers, in the back of her head, was *laughing* . . .

All four of the Yrthementals shuddered, and lurched away from the Tower.

Down below in the dell, Seifas straightened, then tensed himself, ready to face them again.

Alone.

"I'm gone," the Krygian said with finality. "Looks like the cry-baby down there is going to go another round with those things, doing what Jian decided *not* to do: buy enough time for whoever might actually *care* about living to leave. Huzzah for the old Hunting Cry," he declared acidically. "Come on, 'ista, let's go."

She blinked at him.
"No."

Dagon's mouth twisted at the taste of that flat refusal.

"No? Y'know, sometimes I've thought you were crazy, 'ista. I didn't think you *wanted* to die. There are easier ways, if you really want to. However: all these guys around you currently have a high opinion of you—not knowing you as *I* do," he grated, "so if you leave, then *they'll* leave, too, and follow *you*. We take the brigade, with anyone wanting to follow, and we pick up the vendors outside the valley, and we bring along all those notebooks you had us pack from the Tower, and we go off and do something else—maybe find a town to sponge off of, over the winter. The 'jaguar'," he sneered, "down there *is* probably stupid enough to keep on hopping around in front of those things, long enough for us to get away before he zigs instead of zags."

The maga could hear the frantic game of dare crescendoing once again behind her.

The soldiers along the edge were not cheering anymore. They were standing, confused . . . leaderless . . . waiting for someone to tell them where to go, what to do . . .

waiting for someone to save them . . .

"I doubt that Praxiteles will chase us very far outside the valley with those things," continued Dagon. "Not with that *other* guy, who tried to pop Jian, still hanging around. So, let's go; while the getting is good."

He held out his hand.

"No."

Now it was Dagon's turn to blink. "I swear . . . 'ista, sometimes you don't have the sense of a brain-hammered mule," he growled, striding over to her. "I don't have the time anymore to be reasonable with you," he seized her upper arm, "so now . . . !"

His voice choked off.

"Now," said Portunista, barely audible over the ruthless thundering, "*you* will remove your hand from my arm, Commander. Since I *do* in fact understand, that in your own way you are trying to help, I will forgive you, and spare your life. For another count of three. Three . . ."

She didn't even need to make it to two.

Possibly, the fact that one blunt spike from an edged mace, one sharp tip of a knife, and a disker, all were pressed against Dagon's head, had something to do with that.

But Dagon didn't even seem to notice them, as he backed away from Portunista's leveled stare.

"You know what, Dagon?" she said. "Maybe you're right. Maybe Jian has tricked me somehow. And maybe I do deserve to be treated the way you said. But this is *my* brigade," she gritted through her teeth. "And *that*," she pointed behind, "is still *my* Tower. And these are *my* people, Seifas included, risking their lives for *me*. So, I am going to stay here, and take the chance that Seifas is buying for me, and play my final card. You can run if you want; or you can stay. If you stay, you will do what *I* tell *you*, without another *peep* from you, until this is through! If you run . . . you'll do a whole lot more than peep, if ever you even *dare* to show your face around me again."

She turned her back on Dagon.

She heard some scattered clapping, but she ignored it.

Now it was time to see if she could save Seifas, and maybe the rest of the soldiers in the valley.

She knelt, and closed her eyes, and jotted, binding an Yrthescrution into place. Then—she jotted again.

❖ ❖ ❖

"These . . ." Praxiteles sighed. "These things just aren't any use at *all*. We could do this another half-hour, before he trips and falls, the stinking polecat. Ah!" he slapped his forehead, shaking his head and laughing at himself. "What am I thinking?! I don't need *those* to kill *him!*"

He started walking toward the lone juacuar.

❖ ❖ ❖

" . . . uh, Midama . . ." Portunista didn't have time to listen to Pooralay—although she did smile grimly at the respect in his voice . . . "That Praxy guy is headin' for Seifas."

"Actually," she did take time to respond, "I think his name is mud . . ."

❖ ❖ ❖

"So many ways to skin a cat," the Mad One mumbled happily to himself. "Even from a nice safe distance . . . eh? *Now* what?"

An Yrthemental shuddered to a stop, tottering on its legs.

"Oh . . . oh-oh . . ." Praxiteles shuddered to a stop himself. "What's happening here? What, what what . . . ah!" he smiled. "Well; clever girl! um, whoops . . ." he lost his grip on his facile appreciation.

❖ ❖ ❖

"Just as I thought!" the maga grinned in relief; she opened her eyes and batted away the flecks of Yrthe.

"Mud?" Othon asked, in confusion.

"Specifically, vitalized mud," she replied. "More specifically: vitalized then *de*vitalized mud. Look out onto the dell, and tell me what you see."

"Aside fr'm the jaguar fightin' only *three* big flat earth thingies now . . . um . . . th' Tower . . . th' river . . ." Pooralay squinted.

"A *dam!*" Gaekwar pointed for his companions.

"Not just a dam." Portunista proudly folded her arms in satisfaction. "I've rerouted the stream! Look!"

The brook's new channel now led to the feet of the enemy magus.

"*That's* what our Dama thinks of Praxiteles!" shouted a nearby soldier; inciting a wave of laughter, cheers, and gestures of rude defiance to the magus, who was daintily hopping out of the stream's new course.

"I cut the Yrthementals' power off at the source," the maga smiled.

"The wheels!" Othon exclaimed in understanding.

"Only one of them, at the moment," Portunista nodded. "The water *still* will seep into the sluices, of course; but those wheels require the streams to be hitting with force *applied*—*not* to be only dribbling down the opening. I can't reach the other streams yet. But now it's a whole new game!" she loudly proclaimed, for the sake of the nearby soldiers, receiving some hopeful cheers in return. "So, let's go put a cork in those other streams before . . . !

"before. . . ."

Portunista's jubilation faded away.

The halted Yrthemental was moving again.

❖ ❖ ❖

"Very clever girl," the Mad One gritted through his teeth, fastidiously avoiding the stream, and glaring up at all the defiance hurling at him from the treeline. "Yesss . . ." he hissed. "I will enjoy consuming your mind and body both . . . But," he shifted tones again, "I know someone cleverer than *you-oo!*" he sang.

Dismissing her with his own rude gesture, the magus resumed his march, toward the straining juacuar.

❖ ❖ ❖

"'ista . . . Midama . . ."

"I *know,* Poo, I *know!*" She knelt once more to scrutinize the energy flows. "I *know* I was right," she continued, half to herself. "Why is it still . . . ? *Scourge* his bones!" she pounded her fist upon the ground, releasing her Yrthescrution bind and standing up again. "It's Qarfax!"

"The dead magus . . . ?" Othon attempted to clarify.

"Qarfax—who *designed* this defense," she retorted. "Qarfax!—who wasn't *stupid* enough to leave such an obvious way to halt it! He's probably got capacitors all around inside the Tower, or even under it, storing excess energy from the wheels as they power the sigiltracings . . ."

" . . . building up a charge for slopings," Gaekwar finished hopelessly. "Maybe for *years.*"

"Y'mean . . . y'can't stop . . ." Pooralay looked back to Seifas.

"Peep," Dagon sighed.

❖ ❖ ❖

Seifas spun away again, rapping a nearby appendage with his aasagai, his chest on fire, legs wobbling, brain reeling.

Dodging one of these Yrthementals was taxing enough, if not especially difficult.

Dodging four, surrounding him, boxing him in—

He wouldn't surrender . . . *refused* despair . . . !

he had to make sure they wouldn't—

he had to give Jian a chance to—!

Seifas struck with his swordspear, leaping and twisting beneath the looming monstrosities, making himself a threat, forcing their programmed reactions to counter-attack him, rather than moving onward.

At least they were hampering one another, in their close proximity. but he wished that Jian would hurry . . .

Fire and earth tossed him backward in mid-leap.

❖ ❖ ❖

"Aw, damn an' blast-it!" Pooralay hopped up and down, as Praxiteles saturated the area under the Yrthementals, with balls of fire. "We gotta do *somethin'!*"

"I . . . I'm sorry . . ." Portunista watched in shock, racking her brains. "Pooling their legs??—that wouldn't do any good; they'd only draw up more—"

"And Jian isn't back yet, either," noted Dagon, with a touch of self-satisfaction.

"He might have left *me* here to die!" Portunista rounded on the Krygian in frustration. "But Jian would *never* abandon Seifas! Not *Seifas!*"

"Well . . . Seifas *did* volunteer . . ." Dagon hunched, and backed a prudent step in the face of her baffled fury. "It wasn't like Jian *elected* him to go down there and be an idiot. But, whatever," he fatalistically sighed. "No one ever listens to me."

No one, Portunista thought, except the soldiers around them:
edging away from the dell again, watching each other suspiciously, fingering swords . . .

❖ ❖ ❖

"About *time,*" Praxiteles sighed. "Die, last of the first . . ."

❖ ❖ ❖

Seifas gasped on the ground, unable to move . . . even his lungs seemed bruised . . . they didn't seem to be working right . . .

He rolled on his back to fix the Yrthemental with his eyes—
"I promised— I *kept*—!"
—facing his death straightforward—

❖ ❖ ❖

Then
from high in the clouds

an inhuman scream

answered the Guacu-ara.

CHAPTER 67

The paralyzing cry *shrieked* out of the clouds above.
The bony magus blinked.
Beads of sweat coldly popped on his skin.
His eyes were starting out of his face.
He tilted back his head.
"No . . ." he rasped. "No no nonononoooo. . . ." he whined.

❖ ❖ ❖

The soldiers stopped their retreat from the edge of the dell. They stopped, but only could stare.
Othon, Gaekwar, Dagon and Portunista also stared, mouths falling open.
It seemed the only fitting, the only possible, response.
Pooralay was staring, too.
But *he* found something to say.

"Th' reason that no one *ever* listens t' *you,* doll-boy,
is b'cause *you* are a punkie-brained idjit . . ."

Out of the clouds above, plummeted Jian.
He was grinning, drinking the blood of the wind.
For he was riding the back of an aasvogel.

The bird of death streaked down the sky; its hunting cry *rang* Tower stones and towering earth.
Praxiteles fell, backward, to the ground, still whining.
His hanikim dutifully drew their swords . . .

But Jian wasn't diving on *them.*

One in the unity, man and beast knifed down, the avian spreading her wings with the sound of silk catching wind, pulling her dive to a final moment's hover, the trapped air buffeting on an Yrthemental-top.

From her back, Jian *leaped*—landing with both feet and one hand, his blade stretched safely behind him in the other.

Scrambling forward as the avian flapped away, Jian gripped his sword with both his hands, and plunged it at an angle into the top of the Yrthemental.

"STOP HIM! CRUSH HIM!" the Mad One demanded—although his scream seemed only like a whimper compared to the hunting cry which rang again above the valley.

Jian pressed down with all his kneeling strength upon his shortsword's pommel.

It wouldn't be enough.

Still he grinned in expectation.

"What . . ." Portunista distantly heard a person asking—perhaps herself— "does he think he is *doing?*"

"An', why is he lookin' hunched?" Pooralay pondered, stroking his chin in professional curiosity.

Under Jian the earth began to swirl and boil.

"Run!" "Get away!" "You'll be killed!" the crowd at the treeline shouted.

"Too late," Dagon said.

"NOW!!" Praxiteles smote his hand on the ground.

A mighty appendage cannoned from the plateau—
—heaving Jian with monstrous speed and force—
—and in opposite reaction
heaving Jian *down* upon his pommel with an equally monstrous force—
—enough, even to snap the short sturdy blade—

Except:

the object beneath its wedge, loosened by the shifting consistency necessary for making the appendage, and now subjected to the terrible power thus transmitted by leverage . . .

. . . *popped* out of the ground.

The appendage reached its full extension, throwing Jian high in the air.
Along with his sword, still intact.
And also the blue sigilstone.

"AAAIIEEE!!" The Mad One clutched at his face, as if the sword had scooped into one of his sockets.

In between moments, a time measured only in stress, all could see Jian give up his sword, reaching instead, striving, twisting, as he rose through his arc— until as he cleared the balance of gravity

further upward, soared the lighter stone . . .
. . . into his hands.

The crowd would have shouted!—but couldn't force the breath from their lungs—
—for now the fair man fell
—fell from a height which no man could hope to survive
—curling the stone up under his chest
—his face to the ground, his back to the sky . . .

He shouted a cry—
not in fear, not in anger, not in sorrow;
but in exultation
and in hope.

And with the eruption of another cry—
a cry that completed his own,
but which apart from such a unity
never could have meant any more
than violence and hunger—
his cry of hope became something else.

It became a cry of justice.

Eight sharp talons struck down
out of a streaking feathered cloud
piercing the shoulders and back of the falling man
and granting to him the gift of mighty wings.

Jian touched ground, upon the southeastern slope of the dell
delivered by the wings of death
now the wings of victory.

"Lammefange! Lammefange!" shouted the Krygian praise-chanter—the avian *soared* back into her skies, buoyed by the cheers of hundreds of men!—
and so the adolescent aasvogel was named: the Lamb-lifter.
Jian threw down the stone, which bounced and rolled away as he bent over laughing.
Portunista felt the earth and the trees themselves, *shaking* with cheers; saw the stream-water dancing and *leaping* with cheers!

The cheers smothered, moments later.

The shaking and thundering, though, did not abate.

"You . . . *cretins!*" Praxiteles frothed, shaking his fist at the men who dared to defy him—a fist which, one small part of him saw with relief, wasn't bloodied.

It only had *felt* as if his eye had been ripped out.

"You truly believe that *this* will stop me?! . . . Behold!"

All four Yrthementals started marching forward
targeted on the one fair man.

The Mad One cackled.

"Qarfax wasn't a fool! He programmed these to retrieve the guiding eye, *relentlessly,* should it be lost!

"You haven't won!—*you've only assured your death!*"

But Jian laughed harder;
laughed until the tears ran down his cheeks . . .

Then he bent, and seized the stone in his hands again
and holding it over his head,
he turned to the crowd and roared:
"LISTEN! LISTEN TO ME!
"WHAT I DO NOW, I GLADLY DO
"FOR THE SAKE OF OUR LADY, *DAMA PORTUNISTA!!*"

And spinning upon his heel, he turned and charged back down the dell alone—into the faces of the oncoming storm.

Before him waves of stone arose, straining to crush him.
Behind him waves of sound arose,
straining to push him to victory.

Some of Portunista's brigade began to chant the deep syncopation.
Others were punctuating the chant with cries of "Zhi! Zhi! Zhi!"
Soon the ones who had come from the east and the west were joining in.

"What an idiot!" Praxiteles marveled. "I *cannot* believe I was *ever* afraid of this man!" And he tried to laugh.

But, he *was* afraid.

"Seifas!" shouted Jian, as he charged once more beneath the frantic poundings of the Yrthementals. The juacuar, now somewhat recovered, was trying again to attract the things' attention—though to no avail.

"Go on, my friend, go on!" Jian waved. "Hurry!—go back to *her!*

"I am counting on *you!*"

Seifas stood in place, no longer the target of earthen wrath, watching as Jian dashed by.

The man of the Guacu-ara saluted his friend, with the aasagai, bowing low. Then he loped away with tears in his eyes.

As Jian passed under the midpoint of the cluster of plateaus, the final dregs of blood all drained from the face of Praxiteles.

"No . . ." he shook his head. "That . . . that *cannot* be what he will do . . ."

But Jian laughed out in joy to his enemies: "COME AND CATCH ME IF YOU CAN! *OH, DO I HAVE SOMETHING FOR YOU NOW!!*"

"Catch him!" shrilled the Mad One weakly. "Catch him, you lumbering useless clods of earth!"

But even with all his effort pushing them on,

the Yrthementals *still* couldn't move very much faster than a single running man.

"Stop trying to *smash* him!—just go *block* him!" Praxiteles demanded.

But with the sigilstone in peril, even Gamin through Praxiteles couldn't effectively guide the bounding destruction.

"Go!—block him, you hanikim! Go, or I will feed you your own peeled skins!!"

But they were backing away, as Praxiteles himself was backing away, their faces as ashen as his.

"Stop! Stop! Go back!" the Mad One plaintively cried.

But neither Jian nor the Yrthementals heeded his wishes,

and from the edge of the dell was rolling a swelling roar of imminent victory.

With long leaping strides, Jian crossed over the final score of paces . . .

. . . straight for the door of the Tower.

Behind him, the furious earth surged on . . .

. . . straight for the walls of the Tower.

The Mad One wordlessly shrilled—the pale man *threw* himself in a leap toward the door, an appendage rushing behind him, unable to catch the one lone man;

and Jian rotated in midair, to cradle the stone, so that he would land upon his back—

—fixing Praxiteles with a hard dark smile, a smile that promised him *total* defeat—

—and the final sight the Mad One had of Jian, was of a pointed finger, pointing at *him!*—singling him out!—

and Gamin wailed within Praxiteles as the magus fell away . . .

. . . but then the appendage smashed the ground outside the Tower door.

—and Gamin saw Jian no more.

The magus cringed, unable to watch.

The Yrthementals lurched to the walls of the Tower . . .

But, the cheering died, along with the plateaus' thundering.

The Yrthementals only stood there, each beyond the size of the Tower itself, as if guarding the walls and the door from an army of armies.

Praxiteles opened an eye.

Then he opened the other.

Then he began to giggle.

Then he stood, and began to cackle.

"Hah!" he pointed toward the Tower, and toward his vanished foe. "You *failed!* You failed after all!" He began to dance. "Qarfax wasn't a fool! He commanded his creatures: the Tower should *never* be harmed under *any* circumstances! Ha! ha-*hah!* Your noble run was completely useless! *Now* what will you do!?"

The answer came from within the Tower,

from high in the Tower,

from under the Tower.

The earth began to shake so violently, Praxiteles stumbled backward to the ground *again;* along with all his hanikim.

The Yrthementals placidly stood.

Carven stones began to fall, from the nearby Tower walls.

The Tower imploded.

It caved upon itself, *all* its floors, Qarfax's wheels and spindles and gears and machinery snapping and shredding, spears of wood exploding, hulks of hard heavy stone bespattering grass and water across the dell in all directions, ricocheting off Yrthen legs, piercing out of the billowing dust.

Then, just as the Tower began to settle within the floor of the dried-up lake,

its thousands and thousands of stones in rubble floated gently upward, shivering, humming

a star appeared to burst within the Tower

a cosmic tower unto itself, punching past the crumbled corpse to flower into the clouds above,

the mists departing, rushing away at its touch,

and then, as the magical energy flickered and died,

slowing to fall as rain.

All four Yrthementals collapsed in an arc, south of the corpse of the Tower of Qarfax, burying it with a muted *thoom.*

For the first time in half an hour,
silence fell in the dell

silence fell with rain.

CHAPTER 68

Silence fell with the gentle rain, into the dell.

The silence wasn't broken for minutes;

except by the sounds of birds and other small animals in the forest, coming out from their storm-safe holes.

The fight's survivors, combined, stood along the rim, still; soaking in the sight, along with the misting rain.

No cheer, word, or proclamation, seemed appropriate to the moment.

Though Dagon *did* dare to mutter: *"finally . . ."*

Seifas stood with Portunista's officers, protectively towering over the maga. He no longer wept; he felt the skies wept adequately for him. Indeed, his heart wasn't grieved.

For Jian had done what he had said he would.

Portunista also stood; and also didn't weep.

But she was left with a vacant hole in her heart.

Jian was gone . . . utterly gone.

So now, she wondered, what was she supposed to feel? She ought to feel something.

This, she decided, must be how it feels, to lose an arm—or shatter a spine.

It hurt too badly to hurt.

The pain, she thought—she knew—would come to her later.

As for now . . . she had already wept more than once for Jian, over the past few days.

And so she wouldn't lose herself here, at this crucial point in time,

in front of soldiers poised on the edge of the future.

The misting rain quickly settled the dust, and Praxiteles stared at ruin.

"He did it . . . *How* did he do it? He *couldn't* have done it. He did it anyway.

"And now . . . now my key is gone . . . and they will come, in their own time, they who are stronger . . . stronger than me . . .

"They won't need me . . ."

and the Mad One sighed

for he saw only darkness ahead of him.

. . . darkness—and one other thing.

He sniffled.

Then he snorted.

Then he giggled a giggle, as if in a burp.

Then he stood and began to laugh—pointing at the ruin, and dancing.

"He's gone! He's *gone!* I did it! I *buried* him; just as I foresaw! Just as I foresaw would be *necessary!* HAAAA!!"

His eight lieutenants picked themselves off the ground, and looked around nervously; they were the only ones standing alive, upon the slope of the dell.

Yet, up in the treeline . . .

"Misire . . ." Flooder dared to say. "Misire—what should we do?"

"I suppose," Thunder muttered to the others, as he watched his master, "—this means it'll all work out for us after all . . . ?"

The other seven soldiers shrugged.

"Misire," Rester inquired, tentatively. "*Have* we won?"

"We have won the *prize!* The prize I wanted more than anything else! No, I wanted the *Tower* more than anything! No, I wanted *this!* At least we wanted him to *die*—and there we have *buried* him!!" The magus clicked his heels, spitting in the direction of the cairn. "But . . . the Tower was the key . . ." he mourned. "Yet, think, think and look ahead—what do you see?" he answered himself with a grin. "*She* will come, come to us now, to give herself freely to us; and look further! I cannot!" he rasped in fear. "Then, look at *her!*" he self-insisted. "Look and see what having her will mean! Treachery!—betrayal! So? Are we not equal to that risk? Do you not see that she herself will be holding the key to ultimate victory, over all our rivals . . . even . . ." he hissed, " . . . even over the plans of the greatest Enemy . . . Think of it . . . *His* plans, which we ruin in defiance of His tyranny, all undone, and His world swept away, given over to our control . . . It can happen . . . It *shall* happen!!" he frothed. "And so, to be possessing her shall be the defeat of *all!* And mark, now that *he* is buried, she will come as we have foreseen—to give herself to us!

"*Victory!!*"

The Mad One pumped his fists into the air—defying the hidden light and weeping skies.

" . . . *that* guy . . . he just spit on Jian's *grave* . . . !" Pooralay stated this, first in amazement; then with a rising growl.

"I," Gaekwar said, fixing the distant magus with a stare that promised pain and indignity, "am just about tired . . . of *that* man . . . !"

Othon tightened his gauntlets around his edged mace.
"His time has come," he pronounced as immutable law.

Some of the heavily armored Easterners stood nearby, watching the celebration of the distant magus.
"Clearly," they muttered, "he must die."

But Seifas was silent; for he remembered the words of Bomas, concerning this man.

"All of you stay here," said Portunista.
"I will go down, and have a word with him."

They turned to regard her.
Her face was unreadable.

"I promise," she said, not looking at anyone but the distant magus—she said, not blinking,
"I promise that when we have finished speaking, he shall no longer be a threat."

Over the edge of the rim she stepped, onto the short dell-grass.

An army also stepped, with her.

But . . .
"ALONE!" she commanded, not looking at them, only raising her hand.

She stepped again.

Her command was obeyed . . .

. . . by all, save one.

She stopped again, and sighed, not turning, not blinking. "Alone, I said, Seifas."
"Midama . . . I promised . . . I promised to protect you . . ."
"You cannot protect me from this. For what I am going to do, you would only be in the way."
"Midama . . . Portunista . . . listen . . . this man is not a normal magus. Look!" There was no need to say this: everyone could easily see the Mad One gleefully pounding ball after ball of fire into the Tower's corpse. "He isn't jotting."

But she did not turn; and she did not blink. She only growled:
"He will stop that, and soon."

"Portunista," Seifas tried again. "I know from one whom I trust on . . . on
this fact . . . Your magic will have no effect on him. He won't even let you get
near him, before he strikes you down!"
Now she turned, though still she did not blink. She looked up, at Seifas,
and her face changed,
and she said,
"Oh, I think *my* magic will affect him well enough.
"And I think he *will* let *me* get near to him!"

Her voice had dropped to a purr.
Her smile had become . . . inviting.

And with that smile, she turned back to the distant magus.
And now as she walked, she did not merely walk.
She sauntered.

She left them all behind her.
They stared at her bold departure; as if they had all been slapped.

Seifas watched her go.
. . . and in his mind, he heard Bomas, asking:
"How well do you know your Portunista?"
And he remembered Bomas' plan, for such magi.
And he remembered the day, when he had realized
he himself would slay Portunista, rather than see her become a monster . . .

. . . and then he heard Jian saying, in his memory:
"I forbid it!"
Once again, deep within the clouds, a bolt of thunder rumbled, rising and
falling and pounding the earth and air.

And *that,* as far as Seifas was concerned, was the end of the matter.
He had promised Jian: to protect her life, from threats without and within.
If somehow now she fell . . . he would protect her, and try to bring her back.

And with that resolution, another memory, much more recent, came to
Seifas' mind.
He remembered the eyes of Portunista, above that smile and walk.

Whatever else her body might be saying,
those eyes had been the reverse of inviting.
Seifas stayed where he was, and resolved to trust the eyes of Portunista.

❖ ❖ ❖

"Misire!" Biter addressed his master in awe. "Look! She comes . . ."

"And why do you sound so surprised? After all this time, do you not even *yet* believe that I can *see?* Here is the consummation of victory, coming to give herself!"

The magus gave an expectant sigh, and stately paced back down the slope of the pile of an Yrthemental, from where he had been conveniently perched for pounding the corpse of the Tower with his spiteful glee. Advancing onto the slope of the dell again, he found a suitable place to wait, and settled back, arms folded, to watch the approach of Portunista.

Over minutes they watched her, those above and those below. They watched her walk the distance down to him.

Nearing him, she whistled; wisps appeared, floating along with her, caressing.

"Ah!" the Mad One sighed in satisfaction, as the maga arrived before him.

"You wanted me, Praxiteles," Portunista told him in that purr. "And now you are going to get me."

"See? See?!" he exulted. "She even has said it herself!" He hopped up and down. "YOU IDIOT! LOOK AT HER EYES!" he shouted. "SHE WILL BE-TRAY YOU! BEWARE! BEWARE!! Beware . . ." he hissed at Portunista. "Beware of the wolf who comes dressed as a shepherd; the hope of the future to death he betrays!"

"I think," she replied after briefly considering this, "that we have other interests to discuss." The weaving wisps continued to dance on her in curves. One of them floated over to the magus, tracing a matching pattern across his robes.

But Portunista rubbed the tip of her nose, as if it itched her.

"You sotted fool!" Gamin hissed again, as he batted away the sensuous wisp. "She loves *him,* and seeks our complete destruction, and the pit . . . !—the pit of the future now gapes before us . . . ! *Strike her down!* Ha, tra-la," Praxiteles said in answer, as he watched her delicate finger tracing down from her nose to her mouth.

And as he resumed his confident air of slightly nonchalant boredom, he said: "Come, now, and believe in yourself.

"What do *her* wishes mean, compared to our own? What do they matter? What does *anything* matter? Don't you see? You see," he said to Portunista, gravely smiling, while his eyes both danced and burned in time with the wisps.

"*Nothing* matters, you see."

She pursed her lips, in thought.
"Nothing matters . . ." she agreed.
" . . . to *you*."

Underneath, within her purring voice, lay a gurgling hidden.

Praxiteles was given a single blink to see
her face convert to complete rejection—
matching the eyes that he had refused to see,
the undercurrent in her voice that he had refused to hear

a single moment to feel his own face fall, to feel his own eyes bulge in fear.
Then beneath him
opened the pit.

More precisely:
a rectangular prism of earth, four square paces in area, fourteen wristlengths
deep, became like water.
Praxiteles sank like a stone with a plop.

Portunista sauntered backward, step by step, having released the Yrthepool,
entombing the Mad One hard within the ground.
"Resistant to magic, hm?" she mused. "Not too resistant to mud, I see. But
just in case . . ."
her voice froze diamond-edged in hate
she *pounded* her fist into her palm, again and again.

The nearby hanikim, shocked, fell, unable to keep their feet—the ground
beneath them supersaturating with seismic ripples.
Portunista struck her hand, and deep inside she struck her self, until she felt
something break.
Then she struck no more.

Where the Mad One last had stood, his blood began to seep from the
ground—then to spurt in burbles, driven upward by the pressure of the earth.

The maga curled her lip, and wiped her nose again.
Then she turned her attention to the hanikim.

She walked to stand upon the blood of Praxiteles, wisplights floating free
around the area.

First the eight men scrambled back away from her.

Then they pulled themselves together, standing to their feet, leveling their swords at her, encircling her at distance, warily, making sure she'd have nowhere to run—nowhere to retreat.

Portunista had no smile for them.
But, she did have a message.

"When you see your master, in the consuming fires below, tell him I said . . . . . . something matters to *me*."

They raised their swords, as she spun in a pirouette, her arms thrown wide.
They advanced one step as she sunk in a bow to the ground.
They halted—overcome by beauty
or by weight of doom.

She fountained up from the ground, stretching all her length, face and arms raised high, eyes squeezed shut in anguish, screaming her rage and her sorrow.
There absolutely was no sound, however.
Until the wisps exploded.

each needled sliver of Aire combined with raw materia
lancing outward many times the speed of sound
thousands and thousands, all together . . .

Their range, admittedly, wasn't that impressive.
Their effect on anything *in* that range, however, was most impressive.
The eight lieutenants of Praxiteles dissolved, shredded by bluish needles piercing skin and bone, leather and steel, in all directions.

Portunista opened her eyes and lowered her arms, as she felt their drenching blood.
But she didn't feel a single needle.

For not even one single needle could pass the Airebelle surrounding her.

Then she walked away, releasing the deadly vacuum, heedless of the liquefied remains of the men whom she had slain in half a moment.
Their blood was falling off of her in sheets.

Staring at this gruesome sight, Gaekwar said:
" . . . I *seriously* suggest you shut up now, Dagon."

"yeah . . ." the Krygian rasped. "that . . . might be a good idea . . ."

CHAPTER 69

On another gray day, high in her upper room, the long hair of the Empress seems the color of rust, instead of autumn leaves; the color of ugly death, instead of vibrant celebration: no less drenched than her dark black hair had been that day long past.

Into the clay she draws her words, words the color of rust, carefully, quickly, one small letter flowing into the next.

❖ ❖ ❖

I alone remained upon the field of battle.

Even when all the soldiers released a mighty cheer, and poured down over the rim toward me—I remained, alone.

I turned to look at the cairn of stone, partly buried beneath the Yrthen foes that Jian had defeated, smoldering in the misty rain that now abated as the clouds raced low above the valley; a shrouded rent allowed a lance of morning light to fall upon the stones from east in the heavens. It still was morning—early morning even.

I seem to remember the battle as lasting for hours.

It only had lasted less than one.

I looked at the light on the stones. And I heard above the clouds the cry of the avian.

She did not sound grievous.

She sounded victorious.

I looked at the stones.

And I thought of all I knew of the man beneath them.

And, at that moment—I resolved.

I resolved to believe what I could not see.

And I resolved to act on that belief.

Shaking, and with my final strength, I carefully pooled the Yrthen remains, creating a wide and sloping trench leading up from the valley's floor to the stones of the Tower. I had no way to effectively move the vitalized ground, other than simply to let it follow the gravity of the world from which it was made; and so I didn't pool the stones of the Tower in turn.

I turned away, minutes later, to face the onrushing remnants of the three brigades. Despite my complete exhaustion, I commanded myself to stand.

They saw me; they must have seen my face; they saw my enemies' blood, of which I did not care one drop.

They steadily ceased to gladly shout and leap, becoming solemn—although they still advanced.

When they were close enough that I did not have to shout, I spoke to them.

"Go; dig him out," I told them, pointing behind me, where I had no need to look.

"He isn't dead," I told them; blood ran down my face, serving perhaps for tears I was not crying.

"Go!" I said again, more loudly; still I did not shout.

"He waits in there! He did that for you! Get him out!"

Then I turned away from them, back to the ruin behind me.

Finding a place to watch, I stood, still, still not blinking.

At the periphery of my vision, I saw soldiers approaching hesitantly—toward the Tower, not toward me. They looked at me, but did not come to me.

That was fine. They went where I wanted.

I had to briefly look at some of them—a flicking glance between them and the Tower. I never had to look at anyone twice.

They went.

My soldiers, and the Easterners, and also the rabble of Praxiteles; they went.

They didn't all go, for some of them turned to the west to find the camp of Praxiteles; in order to tell the people there that they were free. And that was fine.

Some of them told me that they would go to where I had ordered our vendors' retreat, south beyond the southern pass, to bring them here. And that was fine.

None of the Easterners went to the east, to their own camp—and that was also fine: Artabanus waited there, and I could understand their reluctance to go.

I stood, and watched, not blinking, as surviving men and women started climbing the cairn. I watched, as they began to move the rubble, little by little.

Someone told me they were sorry Jian had died.

I said he was alive.

Someone, sometime later, carefully ventured to tell me: *no one* could have survived in this.

I said he was alive.

Someone, sometime after that, quietly explained to me, that even if he wasn't crushed, he *would* have been cooked by all the magical energy.

I think I laughed; one laugh.

And said he was alive.

Someone brought me a towel, and some water. A few minutes later someone helped me clean myself off.

I said he was alive.

And so I stood, not blinking.

I stood, watching clouds move away, watching, like the sun flowing over the sky, watching shadows shift on the ground.

A time came; the world tilted, I felt an impact; and my teeth clicked together.

I think, that sometime after that, I began to blink every once in a while.

But still I watched.

Someone, Gaekwar I think, suggested I try an Yrthescrution, to help them to know where to dig. I answered I already had, and that the stones were jumbled and fused together too much for me to locate anything in them.

But I lied.

I lied, because it was simpler than simply saying, that deep inside myself I believed the Yrthescrution wouldn't be necessary.

I didn't know what to think about that belief.

I didn't want to think about that belief.

I tried to remember all that I knew about him.

I watched; they brought out the basin we had bathed in.

I watched; they brought out the sheets in which we had never slept, in which we had loved instead.

Someone, hesitating, tentatively, brought me his sword, laying it at my feet.

I said to take it away. I said to give it to him when they saw him again. And so it was taken away.

At the time, I didn't realize: I had *never* let go of the sheath, after he had given it to me—after he had given it *back* to me. When I had been pounding my fist into my palm, destroying Praxiteles, I had been crushing the simple sheath around its single metal bracing—the hardness for meeting the edge of the sword, the softness for wrapping around the blade as a home.

My left hand had been broken while crushing the sheath in my right, as I crushed the one who had buried Jian—who hadn't broken Jian. I was trying to believe.

I didn't know my left was broken yet; any more than I knew I still held the sheath in my right.

Some time, after noon, Seifas sat beside me.

"He will be at the bottom," he said.

"Very likely," I replied. I didn't look at him, because I didn't have to.

"Any other man would have been crushed by thousands of stones."

"He is alive."

"Any other man would have been cooked by residual heat."

I remembered Praxiteles, dying in mud.

"He is alive."

"Very likely no fresh air can reach him. He was at the bottom. It may be tomorrow before we find him."

"He is alive."

"Portunista . . . he may not be alive."

"He is an errant. You said it yourself. He *must* accomplish what he was sent to do."

"I also said I have never heard of an errant who didn't die accomplishing what he was sent to do."

"He hasn't."

"Portunista . . . how do you know that?"

Moments passed.

I couldn't answer.

"Portunista . . . you will have a *true* army, now. One that will be true to *you*. One inspired by Jian's example to similar feats, in hope that you are worth living and dying for—as Jian believed you were.

"You have this now; and now you will have commanders newly committed to you as well; and you will have what you wanted from the Tower, too—for you have preserved the knowledge of Qarfax, for your study and use. And . . . I believe that you yourself have become a better person, Midama. I told you once, I did not believe that you were ready—not to receive the power you wished to have. But now, I know there is hope.

"Jian has accomplished all of this," he said.

I put my face into my arms upon my knees.
I looked at the Tower no more.

Seifas left; to dig, up on the Tower, I think.
It seemed that shortly afterward I heard even more digging than ever before upon the corpse of the Tower; stones being frantically pulled and tossed away, wood being chopped at speed with axes.
I didn't bother to look.

Some time later, a child and mother passed nearby.
"Look," I heard the mother softly say. "That is Dama Portunista. She is the one who freed us."
"Mother, why is she crying?"
"She loved Jian very much."
"Mother . . . Praxiteles never loved anyone . . . did he?"
"No, dear, he didn't."
"Dama Portunista is a *good* lady . . . isn't she?"
"Yes . . . I think she is."
"I'm glad we are going to live with her. Will she love us?"
"I hope so, dear. Come along; we shouldn't disturb her."
"She's crying harder, Mother. I think she's hurt!"
"Yes, dear, I think so, too."
"I'll pray for her. Then she'll get better."
They faded away, into the distance.

The girl was right. I was hurt.
And I didn't know if I would ever get better.

Yes, a voice within me said. You will get better. But only if Jian's dead body is pulled from that cairn.
Why?! I whispered within my self.
Because, he will continue to be a bleeding wound upon your soul; a weakness, through which you can be struck. If he is still alive, do you believe you will die in bed together?! No; you will suffer this pain again, and then again, and then *again*, until it happens for the final time. Until your heart breaks *utterly*.
Is that what you want? No man is worth this pain, is he?
Furthermore: consider your army—*your* army. Now you have what you wanted, what he has died to give you. Just as Seifas was trying to tell you. But if he isn't dead,

shall it be *your* army then? You are deceiving yourself. He will do everything in his power to draw your power to himself. Isn't that what it means for you to be a *wife?* Ah!—you had forgotten that! Is *that* what you want? To serve his dinner quietly, while *he* discusses important matters with the other *men;* to be a trophy like a breeding mare; to show off *his* importance? Then shall you retire to wait on him every night, willing and suppliant?

He *never* would treat me that way . . . he *loves* me!

Yes, agreed the hateful voice; and your father always said he loved your mother, too. I gagged.

There can never be peace between a woman and a man, the voice continued. The only natural balance is competition; the only safety is domination. Either you have power over them, or else you will have *nothing*—nothing but a master, who at best will treat you like a pet.

"Of course she isn't a pet," I heard Jian say, in my memory. "I would be insulting her, to treat her like that! . . . I am learning from her, and she is learning from me, and so we are communicating . . . I want the love we share to grow."

Very well, shrugged the voice—*my* voice. Don't say I didn't warn you. Won't these soldiers now be willing to follow him, far more so than to follow *you?* You know quite well how power corrupts—*don't* you, former apprentice to the Cadre? *Maybe* he would be as you say; but he is naive, as you well know. He will not resist them, but *embrace* them—as he embraced *you,* that first night. Even *if* he does it with good intentions, the damage will still be done.
It is better for everyone—even for Jian himself—that he be dead.

Yes; I am the one who thought these things.
I thought these things, and hurt.
I hurt.
And Jian was why I hurt.

So, I hardened my heart.

Far back at the edge of the forest, I faintly heard that rhythmic chant the men enjoyed in singing—the chant that Jian had taught them, which they now applied to him. The vendors, I supposed, must now be cheering on the diggers, having been told I expected to find him alive.
I heard their hope.

And screamed in pain, inside my self; forever and forever.

I didn't let their hope inside again.

I stood, and sighed, and wiped my eyes, and wiped my nose—a Dama of an army shouldn't have a runny nose—
I would *end* that stupid chant.
Let them chant it when they died for me, perhaps.
Let them bury him in silence—piling stones to crush my pain.
Let his memory be entombed away from me. Forever.

I lifted up my head. I saw the workers on the mound, drenched in sweat and afternoon light.

I opened my mouth, to tell them to stop.

But they had already stopped their working.
They were looking.

not at me.

CHAPTER 70

From the treeline, Noth watched Seifas warring with the Yrthementals. The eastern scouts assigned to him—two brothers—told him they had been stationed here the day before for most of the afternoon; but that they had *never* had a clue, of any guards like *this*.

Noth explained the previous battle-flow to them, as much as he knew.

Well . . . not *quite* that much.

He left out bits he deemed the scouts were better off not knowing.

"I am surprised," said one of the scouts, "that none of our men are here along the eastern edge. They all still seem to be southeast instead."

"Maybe even farther south than that, along the edge," agreed the second scout.

"Perhaps," Noth mused, "our men have conquered; and now are guarding prisoners while they watch this final enemy die, trapped by rampaging weapons meant originally to slaughter *us*. Artabanus did declare the juacuar must die, remember."

Noth received some dubious looks.

None of these three men had seen, when Jian first left the valley.

All three men could see when Jian returned, however—on wings.

"Great lords of the *sky!*" murmured a scout, watching as Jian assaulted four Yrthementals—with the help of one large bird.

"Who *is* that man, Commander Noth? Do you know?!" the other scout inquired, watching as Jian escaped with his life from four Yrthementals—with the help of one large bird.

"Ah . . . well, he is a worthless enemy of our Domo Artabanus, the . . . um . . . Arbiter . . ." Noth trailed off, as soldiers from all three forces gave the fair-skinned man a roaring ovation.

Noth received dubious looks in response.

All three men heard Jian devote his defiance of the Yrthementals to a woman, whom he called "Dama" and his Lady.

"Who *is* this 'Portunista'?" asked the first of the scouts.

" . . . Well, she is a foul and faithless rival of our leader Artabanus: a woman, low of character, worthy only of . . . scorn . . ." Noth trailed off again, as *all* the soldiers cheered the fair man's race beneath the ground of death, for the sake of Portunista.

"The pale man didn't *seem* to be a fool," mused the second scout, dubiously.

All three men watched Jian somehow succeed in pulverizing the Yrthemen-tals, destroying the Tower—and burying himself.

"Ah! Good. One rival dead," said Noth in satisfaction. "Artabanus will be *pleased* with this report!"

"A shame he didn't think to lead those creatures over the top of the capering imbecile yonder," said the first scout.

"Maybe he thought the Tower's destruction or else the fall of the killing plateaus would slay that man," the second scout suggested. "I am more than a little surprised he lived at all, in such proximity. Also, simply running over that fellow . . . who is he?"

"Praxiteles," answered Noth. "An enemy of our Domo Artabanus, the—"

"Perhaps if he had only run over this Praxiteles with the walking plateaus," the second scout continued, to his brother, "that would *not* have served to end the plateaus *themselves;* which," he added, watching the fool, dancing down below, "frankly seem to *me* to have been the greater of the threats."

"I am glad that *we* did not have to fight against the pale-skinned man," the first scout said in some relief.

"It is your—!" Noth interjected; "I mean, *our* honor and privilege, to fight whomever our Domo decides must die!"

But in response, he only received some dubious looks.

All three men watched Portunista walk out onto the grassy dell.

All three men watched every soldier along the treeline step to join her in her march.

All three men watched Portunista order the soldiers to stay.

All three men watched all the soldiers stay where she had told them.

"Perhaps she has ensorceled them somehow," suggested Noth.

"Perhaps," allowed the first scout . . . dubiously.

They watched her resume her walk—her very alluring walk!—down to Praxiteles.

"There! See?!" Noth exclaimed. "A woman of *very* low character!"

"Perhaps," allowed the second scout . . . dejectedly.

"Then again," the first scout mused, with a lopsided smile, "I *can* see why that other man might have been so willing to die for her."

The brothers chuckled at this, good-naturedly.

Noth, however, didn't chuckle.

"Obviously," he said, "she has decided to align herself with the wretch, down below—perhaps because the other man is dead, and so she needs a tool. The empty sheath she carries must be symbolizing the sort of alliance she wishes to forge . . . as if that wasn't *completely* apparent already," he added in scorn.

"Perhaps," the first scout said, judiciously.

All three men watched Portunista thoroughly slay the magus and his minions in the space of half a minute.

"Perhaps not," said the second scout, also judiciously.

All three men watched Portunista return like a queen, drenched in the blood of her foes.

All three men watched *all* surviving soldiers, from the three brigades, rushing down to greet her.

All three men watched Portunista awe them into silence with a grim and royal stare. Then they watched her point, to the ruin.

From *all* three camps, soldiers helped each other to dig.

"She must be retrieving any treasures which might have survived the Tower's destruction," Noth explained.

He received only dubious looks in response.

"Well!" Noth stood and stretched. "It seems the battle is over, and we . . . mmm . . . well, frankly . . ."

"We have won," the first scout said.

"Artabanus did not win," his brother clarified.

"And yet it hardly looks as though we lost."

They nodded to each other, as they watched the stream of morning sunlight falling on the cairn.

"What do you say?" the first one asked his brother. "Shall we go down yonder, to discover *why* they are digging through the ruin?"

"We are scouts," his brother answered. "Two more Krygians should be safe among that group."

"And if we find that she is seeking for her fair-skinned man?"

"Then, perhaps I will stay and help our men in looking, too."

"I think perhaps that I will join you then, on the cairn."

"No!" Noth demanded. "You *both* shall come with me, this instant, back to—!"

He received a final set of dubious looks.

—emphasized by steel at his throat.

❖ ❖ ❖

Artabanus paced in his camp.

He wasn't pacing far: he still couldn't see well at all; and so he stayed within a now-worn track in front of his tent.

He didn't go into his tent, to blindly pace, for he could hear some faint confusing sounds from westward, and he wished to hear them better.

Also, there was a dead girl in his tent. And right that moment he did not consider it prudent to assign a slave to carry her out in broad daylight.

At first he tried to *slowly* pace: a stately step and then another. Soon, however, he discovered that he was rapidly striding along his chosen path.

He forcibly slowed, and told himself that he should be—he *was*—a pacing lion!

Then he avoided *that* analogy: for it brought to mind the picture of a crippled, captured beast, miserably going nowhere.

He tried to jott a posiscrution once; but that had been like throwing salt into his eyes.

So, he only paced; and made some fanciful guesses as to what the sounds could mean.

Artabanus was *so* intent, on ignoring his situation, and on pondering all those western noises instead, he totally failed to notice Noth's return.

"Ahem . . . Midomo . . ." Noth discreetly coughed. Artabanus spun to face his blurred lieutenant.

"Noth!" The magus restrained himself from grabbing the shoulders of the other man. "Tell me what I wish to know!"

Noth decided a simple straight account of what he had seen, would be sufficient.

Artabanus listened, without a comment, until his lieutenant ceased.

"Well . . ." Artabanus sighed. "At least that captain died. And I will surely *not* be weeping for the rodent Praxiteles. As for our brigade . . . hm. I must consider how we may remove the sorcery placed upon them. Perhaps," he mused, "if we slay the woman . . . or, if she could be *leashed* somehow . . . The sheep will follow the bell: if she was solidly under my thumb, I would then have every opportunity to unravel her magic—while taking my own advantage of her."

Having formed a plan, of sorts, Artabanus clapped his hands together firmly. Yes, everything soon would be in its proper place again. Surely his lieutenants had been right—sagas often were sung of how a captain's great defeat helped make the subsequent victory even greater. And, after all, *this* defeat had hardly been *his* fault . . .

"Tell your scouts to find some food—I cannot offer them rest, for we must break our camp and leave this valley at once. I may assign them, however, to stay behind and scout for us. Yes," he nodded, "that will be entirely satisfactory. You may leave to give the orders, Noth." And so, dismissing his lieutenant, Artabanus turned to enter his tent.

Then he remembered he still was more than a little blind, and that he didn't want to stumble around inside, perhaps to trip on the body of that girl . . .

"Ahem . . . Midomo . . ."

Artabanus blinked. Noth was still here?

"Yes?"

"The scouts, who accompanied me . . . they . . . mmm . . ."

"Well? Spit it out, man!"

" . . . they decided to stay behind. Already."

Artabanus nodded, and thoughtfully rubbed his chin. "Foresighted. Impertinent, maybe, but certainly I will remember them—for when I draw all power to me, you and Alt shall need your own lieutenants—"

"They decided to stay behind, permanently . . . Midomo . . ."

Whole moments passed. Noth fidgeted miserably.

"What?" the magus eventually asked. "I didn't gather, from your report, that any of you went anywhere near the enchantress."

"I do not believe they fell beneath an enchantment, Midomo."

Artabanus swallowed his fear, focusing on fury.

"And did those traitors die by your sword?"

"They drew upon me, Midomo, before I knew the extent of their treachery."

"And yet, here you stand before me," growled the magus, "instead of having given your life in attempting to stop them."

"They spared my life, Misire, so that I might bring you a message." Noth now sounded as if he wanted to weep.

"And what . . ." Artabanus breathed, " . . . did these . . . quislings . . . *dare* to say to me?"

More moments passed.

"Well?!" Artabanus thundered. "Shall *you* fail *them* as you have failed *me?*"

"I . . . it . . . I do not . . . . . . It was a private message, to be delivered to you alone, Midomo."

"Everything considered," declared the magus, frostily, "I prefer to hear it now and in the open—*not* alone with *you,* the message-bearer of traitors."

He heard Noth swallow; but couldn't make anything out of the following mumbles.

"Speak up, man!!" Artabanus roared. *"Tell me what I wish to know!!"*

Noth took a breath—and loudly proclaimed:

"This is what your scouts told me to say to you, Artabanus!" Noth could see, all over the camp, that heads had turned toward them; but, he plunged ahead perversely.

"You, Artabanus, *claim* your titles for yourself! The pale man *receives* his ac-claim from others, freely given! *You* treat us as slaves! The pale man treats his *en-emies* as his brothers! *You* give only fear and defeat! The pale man inspires both love and victory! *You* sacrifice your allies to save yourself! The pale man sacrifices *himself,* even for his enemies! We choose to follow *him,* therefore, though he be dead, rather than spend another single moment in following *you*—even if you are the king of the world—*which you shall never be!!*"

Noth stood, panting—finished.

Now *every* head in camp had turned their way. In the distance, he could see, though not yet hear, the murmurs now beginning.

A corner of the mind of Noth was laughing in hysteria at the thought, that aside from his bushy hair, Artabanus *now* looked like a pale man *himself*—pale, down to his lips!

"Misire," Noth trembled, "I . . . still stand by you. These traitors are . . . they are . . . *I* stand by you, my Lord!"

"Call in all the scouts and pickets, Noth. *Immediately,*" Artabanus rasped. "Surround the slaves with continuous supervision, until we break from camp . . . YOU, THERE!" the magus pointed toward a menial. "STOP!"

The menial only pushed his wagon faster, to the west.

That man was close nearby, for the magus was able to see him. Noth, how-ever, could see a similar exodus starting in *every* portion of camp.

"Shall . . . . . . " Noth swallowed. "Shall I give orders to the pickets, to slay these treacherous slaves, Midomo?" From what he could see, they *all* would have to be slain!

"At once!" Artabanus opened his mouth to say.

But then he closed his mouth again, and thought. The pickets had probably *not* heard Noth's report, of the traitors' declaration. But, if they were ordered to slay these slaves—*then* they might hear.

And if his final soldiers rebelled—

"You are to *run,* Noth, to the western pickets, and tell them to let these dogs go through. The pickets are not to even get within hearing distance—do you un-derstand?!"

"Implicitly, Misire!" Noth saluted, happy that he could do *something.* "If they ask . . . ?"

"Tell them that *my* command alone should be enough; but that if they dare approach any *one* of these people, then they shall share the fate of the army to which I am sending them. Yes . . . let my final company think that I have infected these rats with *plague,* which I will be spreading amongst my enemy."

Noth again saluted, and ran away.

The magus stood, still—and he waited.

A plague, in truth, *had* been spread—but not by him.

The dead, pale man had spread the plague.

Artabanus couldn't compete against . . . *this* . . . with *any* mere fear of death. Or, perhaps he could—but then, the pale man *still* would win. Artabanus needed to find some way to regain the hearts and minds of soldiers and slaves alike.

The scouts had delivered a personal challenge—not from themselves, but from *him.*

And the magus refused
to be haunted the rest of his life
by a dead pale man

Hours later, deep in the afternoon, Artabanus struggled, along with the last of his soldiers, back up and over the valley's eastern ridge—the only point of exit they dared attempt.

And as the soldiers grimly pushed and pulled the few remaining supply-carts over the ridge, Artabanus paused and turned to stare behind him, through the cloudy haze of his eyes.

Westward—where a joyous victory faintly chanted through the trees.

❖ ❖ ❖

Two more eyes had watched; along the western rim.

A simple falling tree was only an inconvenience, to a juacuar.

Although, it *was* entirely sufficient to trap him there for half an hour or so.

Bomas had spun beneath the falling tree, dodging here and there, severing smaller branches with his wristbracer talons.

The talons, however, had not been nearly as useful in trying to cut through some of the tree limbs; necessary for the disgruntled juacuar to extricate himself from the trap of fate.

By *that* time, Praxiteles was already far in the dell, clean out of Bomas' reach. So, the juacuar had crouched at the edge of the dell instead, where he had been able to clearly observe the final moments of the Mad One.

Bomas had been impressed.

In fact, he then had spent the next few hours, pondering whether he ought to slay his brother in secret, and then to offer himself—a few weeks later, of course—to this Portunista, as her new induna. The advantages of that, from what he could see, would certainly seem to be numerous and considerable.

This opinion only increased in strength, as he watched throughout the morning and noon; meanwhile, he easily dodged discovery by the former minions of Praxiteles as they traveled back and forth across the valley's western half.

Around midafternoon, however—

—Bomas decided it might be better to try another plan.

Stifling his disappointment—and the fear he refused to acknowledge—he quietly worked his way around the encircling forest, north then east, avoiding the few surviving Ungulata, making their own way north back over the mountains and into the Middlelands after their strange foray.

Bomas told himself he wasn't bitter—this was even true, to a real degree. Seifas was a brother, now in place. Bomas remembered their meeting the night before—remembered how Seifas had been affected by his revelations. When the proper time approached, Bomas would visit his brother again, to impress upon him—using whatever necessary means—the *importance* of the Plan.

Bomas doubted Seifas would be spurning his final brothers; but even if he did . . .

Well. Bomas knew what seven juacuara could do.
And so would Seifas.

As for the woman . . . ?
That was no great loss, in the end. He had seen her demeanor, had heard her voice—and he had seen the eyes of Seifas.

That woman would certainly make her choice; and Seifas then would kill her.

Besides, there were plenty of women with skins of rotten olives. And he would be choosing plenty, in years to come, to help redeem humanity.

Meanwhile, Bomas knew of a magus who now would be *glad* to accept the aid of a juacuar . . .

CHAPTER 71

Seifas lay within his tent once more, late at night, the lantern burning low, but still sufficient for his deep dark eyes, the eyes of a juacuar—penning entries into his latest journal.

So the soldiers started digging through the ruin; a dangerous work: the heavy stones would shift and settle further as we moved upon the surface.

Portunista stood and watched us.

I, in turn, watched her from an edge of the pile, where I could aid in removing stones while also directing newcomers where to dig.

I do not think I ever saw her blink, while she stood.

She made no effort to clean herself.

I quietly sent a worker to find some linen and water.

The worker brought it, and left it for her.

Still she made no effort to clean herself.

So I dispatched another runner to find some women to help.

She accepted the cleaning in silence.

Gaekwar told me, that she had tried an Yrthescrution; but that she could not find a body due to the jumbled mess. I doubted this at the time—I hadn't seen her doing anything of the sort.

Some of the soldiers of Praxiteles journeyed west, to bring their people here. I watched their dull and dispirited faces; watched, as they saw the cooperation among the former enemies. I watched their faces, as people told them the story, again and again.

And I was glad. My wish, my prayer, was coming true.

I watched their hope awakening.

But most of all I watched a face in quiet desperation.

I watched her, stepping as slow as the sun in the sky, up the concourse she had made for us; she stepped, minutes apart, as if unconscious of her movement. Eventually she stood near the edge—stood near me. Together we watched them digging down into the ruin.

I was so glad to be able to serve her in something.

About three hours into the dig I heard a peculiar sound nearby.

Portunista had fallen.

It would have been funny in other circumstances: she looked *so* surprised and perturbed, to be so suddenly sitting on the ground! But still she scowled at the stones, unblinking, resting her arms upon her knees.

And still she held the sheath.

Not long after this, dozens of haggard civilians began to arrive, from the east. They had fled Artabanus. Gaekwar welcomed them in, and bade them set up their wares nearby; for we would soon be needing food and drink, to buy from them.

I watched their faces, too. And I was glad.

At noon I began to organize lunch, for the workers. Some of them wouldn't stop digging. So, I let them dig, but emphasized that they must be relieved when the others returned. I explained that they would only hurt themselves and others, if they persisted without any food. Some of them didn't care—until I reminded them, that they could dig more quickly, and more effectively, once they had eaten. They accepted that.

Leaving Othon to guide the dig, I went to find some food myself. Our vendors now had returned from having retreated beyond the southern pass; although they still were mainly busy in setting up camp along the southern side of the dell, up into the treeline. The eastern and western civilians—now our vendors, too—invited us to sit to meat and bread. I thanked them, gratefully—and I enjoyed their faces when I did, and when I paid.

No one, however, would sell me meat and drink for Portunista; instead, they nearly crippled me trying to thrust it into my hands! I came away with food enough for three burly men, which I gave away as I saw fit, mainly to western and eastern children.

I brought the rest to our Dama.

I sat down next to her.

I don't believe she ever saw the food.

Whether Jian was alive or dead within the pile, I didn't know. But, I thought I ought to prepare her for the real possibility: that we would find him dead.

He had, after all, accomplished many things: giving to her a loyal army, and helping to make her worthy of it—certainly worthier than she had been, before we came to Qarfax Valley.

Those were goals worth dying for, I believed.

Consequently, I wouldn't be surprised to find Jian dead.

I fully expected that he would be smiling, too.

but then . . .

. . . I sooner would have killed myself

she put her face into her arms and wept

I did that to her
I only had wanted to help her
I only had hurt her more

That, I told myself, was *exactly* why Jian should be *alive*.

I strode past Othon, down and onto the pile.

Men looked at me. I started to throw the stones away, prying them free with my aasagai. They looked up, above us, at our Dama—who could no longer bear to look in hope. They watched her weep.

Soon, I wasn't the only man rolling the stones more recklessly from the tomb.

We worked together, all of us. We didn't care what happened to us. Broken bones, broken necks—miraculously we were spared these things; but we didn't care for ourselves. We only cared that *she* was hurting. That she, who all these hours had been our anchor of faith . . .

—what did it matter, if *I* had died on that cairn?! I deserved a greater condemnation! I deserved to be burning to ash *forever!*

I had slain her hope.

when I would gladly give my life to find and share the hope for her . . .

We worked together, mostly; though only hours earlier we had been trying to kill each other.

Once, I did see two tired men: one an Easterner, one from my own company. They had begun to dispute as to how to remove a set of stones. Soon their dispute was edging toward insult and threat.

They stopped—my shadow had fallen on them.

They looked up at me.

I said nothing.

I only pointed behind me: to her.

They swore an oath to help each other; together we three, along with my aasagai, removed the stones.

We did very well, I think, all of us together; we men who strove on the hill of stones. By midafternoon, we started finding many pieces of wrecked equipment and shelves from the laboratory. I just had been called to look at the ruined and still half-buried tablemap . . .

when from the south I heard the sound of chanting.

It was the syncopation; the one our people used when singing of Jian.

It stirred my heart, and I smiled; wondering if, wherever he was, Jian could hear it, too.

But on the edge above us, I saw Portunista tensing. I imagined what she, with her moods, must think of the song.

I even thought I heard her screaming quietly.

No—the song would not be good, for her. Not yet.

So I began to pick my way down the other side the pile, careful now of slipping with my sweaty feet, preparing to run around the ruin and back up the slope to the south, in order put a stop to the song. I wasn't sure how best to stop it; I hoped that I could explain to them *why* the song might not be appropriate now. I certainly didn't want them to *forget* the song. I *wanted* to hear it often.

I hoped to hear it, and to remember, as we entered the battles we would fight—together for her.

For her, as *he* had been.

Then I realized
along with the chant
cheering.

That was sufficiently odd.

Perhaps, I thought, they were cheering the singers?? I never had heard the men give so much gusto into the chant, not even when Jian had made his final run against the Yrthementals.

Then the cheering, chanting crowd strode out the southern treeline.

They were following Jian.

I blinked several times, and wiped my eyes.

I *had* told myself, I *would not* be surprised if Jian had lived after all. But . . . why would Jian be *there??*

Yet, *there* he was.

Even at that distance, I could see his smile.

I told the others to look as well; and then we scrambled down the empty tomb as rapidly as we dared. Some of the workers *now* sprained ankles, I think!—but they hobbled on anyway.

Men and women and little children were rushing from all directions; running toward the center of the slope; *running!*—forming lines on either side of his path! They swelled the chant to heart-bursting.

I took myself to where I knew he must be going, and awaited him there.

Portunista rose, and turned; and found herself at the end of a path of joy.

The people knew as well as I where Jian should go.

"You were *right!*" I exulted, watching as he walked along the living hall to her. "Portunista, you were right! *He is alive!*"

"Of course he is," she said.
She said it bitterly.

I looked at her in shock
my smile was smashed from my face
her face

she looked as though a sword was piercing her gut

"Of *course* he is alive," she muttered.
"He hasn't finished what he came to accomplish."

Cold sweat broke on me, hearing the shards of her voice.

I wasn't the only one who noticed.

The people wanted to drink their fill of looking back and forth, between the man and the woman he loved, living a story, taking their part in a legend—expecting a happy ending.

Portunista's attitude was *not* fulfilling their expectations.

The cheering and chanting progressively died away, like cold air sinking down from a mountain during sunset—except the chill was flowing from Portunista, up the valley.

Jian could see that something was wrong; he softened his smile, to something like wry pity.

By the time the two were standing face to face, an arm away, at the edge of the ruin where he was supposed to be buried, his smile was the only light in the sunlit valley.

The man and the woman watched each other.

The rest of us watched *them*—wishing, hoping, silently pleading for love to enfold us warmly, as it should have been doing.

"Hello, milady," said Jian—an edge of hope in his voice.

"Hello, Jian," said Portunista—dulling the edge.

"I brought you something." He offered his hand.

He held the sigilstone.

Portunista looked at the stone; then took it and put it beneath her arm. "I thank you," she formally answered, "although I suppose it is useless now."

The fair man's smile almost vanished.

It did disappear from his eyes for a moment.

Then both were replaced by another smile.

The smile of a man who believes an opponent worthwhile.

Not the smile of a man expecting a welcome from his love.

"I see that *you* have something for me, as well," he brightly announced, that edge of wit alight in his eyes. He refused to give up trying, but I could see that he had resigned himself to struggle longer than he had hoped.

"And what would that be?" replied Portunista; the only hope I could glean from her answer, rested in the sound of her acceptance of the duel.

"Well," he said with that secret smile, "I had lost my sword in the fight"—indeed he had given it up to secure the stone for her—"but when I walked into the camp, some worthy fellow returned it to me." And he flourished the simple, common blade, which he had casually carried close beside and behind. From a place far up in line, there drifted a lone "Halloooo!"; which Jian acknowledged, turning and bowing, saluting with the sword. "Already well on the way to being re-sharpened, for which I thank you!" he declared. Then he returned his attention to Portunista.

"So . . ."—his eyes were twinkling—

"may I be sheathed?"

This brought a start from her.

She opened her mouth to tell him . . . what?—then closed it again with a snap, and a look of further surprise, as she glanced to her right and downward.

She must have forgotten:

she still held the sheath, which he had returned to her.

She looked at it. She looked at him.

I think she made her decision, though, when she happened to look at the crowd.

They would demand a resolution: why had she held the sheath so long—*through so much*—if not for *him?*

Grudgingly, yet with some matching of Jian's flair,
she held it out to him.

"Here is your sheath," she told him.
He reverently received it.

Then she added, as she walked past him:
"If you insist on having that sheath,
don't expect a better sword."

"No matter," he said as he carefully put the blade in its home, and bowed to her back.
"No matter.
Any sword will do."

She froze, and grimaced, as if she'd been tapped on the top of her head by Othon and his edged mace.
But the crowd was cheering; and so she walked away.

CHAPTER 72

I do not believe Jian willingly parted from Portunista, my beloved; but the crowd was pressing closely round him.

"I wanna know—!" Pooralay started—but Dagon interrupted:

"I want to know," he demanded, almost accusingly, "how you survived!"

Jian shrugged. "It wasn't all that difficult, really. All I did was jump down the well."

Dagon blinked.

"The well," the fair man reminded him with an ingenious grin, "which has—or had—a tesser at the bottom, leading to a fast-running stream. Oh, and by the way—who was in charge of the Mirror?" he asked the crowd with teasing humor.

" . . . Tim!" a soldier answered, after some moments of general talk. "oh . . . *spew* . . . "

Jian only laughed. "Then *that* explains it: he couldn't hold onto the Mirror along with a shaft in his throat!

"Really, though, it's *my* fault; I mean if it's anyone's. It was *my* responsibility, to be paying more attention. Especially since he died defending the Mirror . . . Thank you, Tim," he quietly said. "You did a better job than me . . .

"Anyway, so: when I ran into the Tower—surprise! There's the Mirror, lying on the ground; with Tim nearby, now that I recall.

"My first time through, I didn't do anything with it, because I believed we still had a chance to keep the Tower after all—*if* I could get that stone from the top of the Yrthemental. But on the second run, I took a moment to chunk the Mirror down the Well and into the tesser.

"I couldn't be sure where the stream would go. But, there wasn't much point for Qarfax to put a tesser there, unless the stream went *somewhere*. Why go through all that trouble to scribe a tesser-ring to reach a stream that was farther down the well—and one that from its description had to be a *different* stream—instead of buying an extra hundred wrisths of rope?" he asked rhetorically. Now that Seifas looked more closely, he could see Jian's back—his strangely hunched back—still seemed damp. The juacuar would have asked of this, but Jian continued with bardish panache: "The stream was frightfully cold, but also running *very* fast; so, before I 'ran' out of air," he grinned, "pop! There I was, hurtling downriver, out in the morning! I pulled myself to the shore, and lay for a while in the sun, resting—and thanking Qarfax," Jian saluted the sky, "for devising such an easy way to escape! Then I spent some time in trying to find the Mirror—but I guess it washed downstream. And *then* I hiked back *here;* which took *quite* a while, and . . . well . . . . . . I got lost," he admitted in wry embarrassment. The crowd laughed and cheered anyway.

"I wanna know—!" Pooralay started again; but Gaekwar insistently interrupted:

"I want to know how you flattened those walking plateaus!"

Jian modestly shrugged again. "I heard our Dama talking about the sigil-stone; and I could just barely make out, from our vantage point at the top of the dell, that Praxiteles hadn't bothered to pull the stone underground again; *and* I figured that getting it either would stop those things outright, or else there'd be a safety-feature designed for retrieving the stone. I expected the latter, though, for I've been very impressed with Qarfax's cleverness over the last few days— sometimes impressed rather *forcibly,*" he winked. "So, I wasn't surprised when they started up after me. Nor did I doubt that I could stop them. I *knew* already they couldn't stop *me*—or, for that matter, stop *any* one who kept his head and feet together!" He bowed to Seifas; who bowed in return, during the cheering applause. "I would have simply blocked the water running down to the wheels beneath the Tower, but I didn't know how—and anyway," he shrugged again, "I suspect that Qarfax planned for *that* possibility, too."

"He had," the juacuar confirmed. "Portunista said there must have been *many* capacitors inside the Tower, building excess energy up, in order to power those plateaus if water was ever lost."

"Which seems pretty likely anyway, should the Tower be sieged by *armies,*" Jian pointed out. "It would be awfully silly to go to the trouble to make a system of mass-defense, powered directly by something an army would likely have stopped already, even if only in passing!

"So, if nabbing the stone didn't work, the only thing remaining to try, as far as I knew—and what I knew I could *do*—was to destroy the *Tower:* and that, I figured, would certainly stop the Tower from *generating* the Yrthementals. I guess when the Tower imploded," he mused, shaking his head at the mess, "it also destroyed the capacitors. Glad I wasn't there for *that* . . . "

"Boom!" Othon rumbled, gravely nodding.

"Why did Qarfax even *have* that lever?!" Jian inquired of Dagon with a jaunty grin—the Krygian blinked. "In the Tower, next to the door," explained the fair man for the sake of the crowd, "a bracing lever was mounted on the wall, which, when pushed, released a rope. Releasing that rope, however, caused some serious problems with the machinery in the Tower—as we discovered a couple of days ago," he wryly added; Dagon glowered. "Eventually I decided this was Qarfax's way of destroying the Tower in case of last resort: something easy to use, that wouldn't require an exhausted, defeated magus to do any jotting while on his way to his route of escape."

"*That* seems stupid!" Dagon snorted. "*Anyone* could have walked right in the Tower door, and thrown the switch!"

"Exactly right!" Jian pointed his finger in the air; Dagon slightly jumped at this unexpected compliment. "Not only that, but Qarfax would have been alto-gether aware, that *however* well he defended his Tower against a magical strike, and *however* well those giant tables on legs might *smush* a couple of armies,"—Jian stomped the ground dramatically, as he was walking uphill—"the Tower would *still* be vulnerable to an attack by single adversaries: whoever might dare to run the gauntlet, under the shadow of death, and into the Tower. Probably, Qar-fax feared a rival Cadrist would attempt it—someone who might be able to blast a door to bits despite its bar: but, who *then* would have found himself, *not* in the so-called 'basement' . . . but *up* one floor: dashing *into the garrison halls*," Jian an-nounced in triumph, "defended very easily, even against a Cadrist, by hiring nine expendable mercenaries, along with one *extremely* deadly juacuar!"

"There *had* been a tesser bound to that door!" Seifas confirmed for the fol-lowing crowd. "I was the one whom Qarfax hired, back at the end of the Culling, to guard his garrison."

"But, the tesser had only been *bound*, not *scribed* into the door," Jian re-minded him. "Either Qarfax, as we know from the tablemap, had not had time before he died to do all the scribing he wished; or perhaps he foresaw a possible need to be doing battle himself, out in the open, and in a retreat from the field would want to escape as soon as possible. And, it takes a lot less time to drop a bind and throw a lever while running through a door; than to run *into* a Tower, *down* two halls, *down* some narrow stairs—and then *back* across a half a floor again!" Jian described this with his hands for the crowd.

"But," Dagon added—caught up in the explanation in spite of himself—"the moment he died, the bind that was linking the two doors together, the real and the false, *failed* automatically!"

"Right again," nodded Jian. "And now, as you also rightly said, anyone *could* get into the 'basement' easily, *and* to that lever, the natural, old-fashioned way: straight through the only door."

"You figured all that out," Gaekwar suspiciously drawled, "in only a couple of moments, before you made the run?"

"Well, no," Jian admitted. "I figured it out in bits and pieces across the past few days. I only put the final couple of pieces together, back when we were standing along the edge of the dell. And then I certainly didn't have time to explain it," he smiled in apology. "Sorry. Giant killer tablelands, remember?"

"I don't suppose you know how Qarfax died, or why," Dagon squinted at him.

"Ah . . . um . . ." Jian considered this for half a minute; then, "Nope!" he shrugged, brightly smiling. "Haven't a clue. Not remotely. Now I wonder whether we'll *ever* find out," he mused, as he looked back at the crumbled ruin.

The crowd had been making their way upslope, following Portunista to some extent; and soon after this, they reached some vendor stalls. The background was suffused by a general shuffle, men and women buying food and drink—often on credit, or else on barter, as neither the Easterners nor the Westerners had much money yet. *That,* Seifas thought to himself, might soon prove to be a problem: *lots* of things might soon be proving problematic, with an army—not only a small brigade—to feed and warm. Autumn had not yet reached its peak, but winter would follow behind . . .

"There's somethin' *I* wanna know!!" demanded Pooralay—once he had slaked his thirst.

"All right, *what?!*" responded Jian, with a good-humored grin.

"I wanna know . . . why in th' flamin' *spew* are y'r shoulders all hunch'd!!"

"Oh!—right!" Jian slapped his forehead. "I'd gotten so used to having it there, I had forgotten all about it!" And he laughed at himself. After the wide-spread merriment settled down from this, he continued:

"I fully expected the sigilstone wouldn't be easy to pop from the ground. Still, I figured from watching the way those tables attacked, that I could use their own appendages, in order to help me remove the stone.

"So, I had two problems: how to get up there to it; and how to survive when the Yrthemental popped the stone, and *me,* into the air!

"Well, over the past two nights, I'd made an acquaintance I hoped would be helpful—that young aasvogel. I believe I heard . . . one of you named her Lammefange? I . . . mmm . . ." Jian thought for a moment, his eyes glinting secrets; meanwhile the Krygian praise-chanter told the crowd *exactly* who had named the avian . . . "I get along well with animals," Jian mysteriously smiled, "and, I'd already ridden upon her once. So, after spending some time in helping her get to know me better last night, I was reasonably sure I could count on her, to carry me once again. It *was* a risk . . . the greatest one I took," he soberly said—his eyes lost distant in memory; of his fall perhaps. ". . . . . . *But:* I'm also someone who has a *lot* of hope," he smiled again. "And I try to plan ahead for consummation. In this case, I *hoped* that Lammefange would be catching me, once I was catapulted. However: aasvogels, as you saw, are rather like giant falcons; so, she would *catch* me," he emphasized, "the way that *her* kind catches *anything:* not on her back, but with her talons!

"And I did *not* intend to go through all of that, just to have my shoulders ripped to shreds. So . . . !"

Jian—with a bit of struggling!—whipped his borrowed shirt off over his head; a wadded lump fell onto the ground behind him. After carefully throwing the shirt across his shoulder, Jian retrieved the lump and shook it out.

The lump was a robe—thick, sodden and torn.

"This," he announced with a flourish, "is a robe I borrowed from the tall and portly magus: Qarfax!!"

In the midst of the cheers and laughter, someone shouted: "Apparently *you* won't be using it much yourself, anymore!"

"I think you have a point!" Jian called out. "Perhaps I will give it to Portunista, then!"

And as the laughter swelled again, the fair man smiled an impish, wistful smile—and reverently, he rolled up the robe.

Seifas lay in his tent, later that night, having written the gist—though hardly all the words—of Jian's explanation.

But, you, my wife, will know very well: I have my ways of finding out what was said . . .

"That meant something—although I don't know what," the juacuar was writing, thinking of Jian's affectionate smile and of the robe of Qarfax. "But," he continued, unconsciously shrugging his shoulders, "I still wonder many *other* things, as well . . ."

❖ ❖ ❖

I wonder what we shall do now—where we will go.

I wonder if we shall be hearing again from Artabanus.

I wonder what killed Qarfax; and whether we, who spent two nights in his tower, have now been marked to face a similar fate.

I wonder to what extent my brother, Bomas, was correct about Praxiteles—and what that portends.

I wonder to what extent he was right about many things . . .

I wonder what we shall do about the lone Ungulat we found unconscious on the field, suffering from a concussion. Ungulata have thick skulls; soon enough, he will awaken. We have tied him with rope; and I hear talk of chains.

From talk I have heard, I am glad that I am not him.

For his sake, I hope he never awakes . . .

I wonder what happened with Gaekwar today in the fight; why did he go berserk?—and shall he do so again? He seems to be taking the death of Meg very easily, now; so, I doubt that his fury sprang from him having had a liaison with her—although, perhaps he did realize she might have deserved such attention from him . . .

No—something else came to the surface. Something from the past of this 'cowherd'; whom, after all, we know so little about.

Jian spent the rest of the day, in helping the army settle for the night, spread out along the upper expanse of the southern rim of the dell.

I wonder: was this truly the Well at the End of the Wood?

If so—did it "deliver both evil and good"? Jian, certainly, seemed to make good choices, as he "leapt into strife." But if he learned any "prices of death and of life," they remain his secrets.

I wonder what sort of prices the Well could teach him, that he doesn't already know.

I wonder how Portunista *now* will behave.

I watched as the sun fell into the night, and the sleeping tents were set. Portunista's tent was among the first to be moved, and she ordered all the scrolls and codices and notes which she had rescued from the Tower, to be brought to her. She spent the rest of the day in study, out in the light, where she could keep an eye on her new army's efforts at organization.

I wonder what she found to be worth learning; I saw her concentrating on a scroll, practicing movements along with percussive semantics. Whatever it is, it mustn't require both hands: her left, still swollen and blue, has now been bandaged to set and heal.

She sat outside, even after sunset, in the light of wisps: studying, practicing, watching. She did this till Jian arrived, with food and drink for her.

I wonder if she would have even deigned to notice him, had he not brought her something she needed.

I wonder why her face changed, to something unreadable, when he showed her the carefully folded, and newly repaired, robe of Qarfax.

She seemed to deflate; and didn't watch when he entered her tent.

Not long afterward, Portunista also went inside.

I didn't see them emerge, before I went to my own small tent.

Instead I watched the sky, and the autumn trees at night, and the stars above and below.

And I wondered where the Agents are, and what the Rogues are planning.

And I wondered what the Eye is planning;

for, there *is* an old saying:

"The enemies of the Lord Above plot deeply and plot well,
but the Lord Above plots, too—
and He is the best of plotters."

I suppose this means, that whatever Bomas might have said to me, however much of the truth may have been in his words—

I still will trust in the hope for justice.

And now let us see what the future will bring.

❖ ❖ ❖

Seifas closed his journal, closed the stopper on his ink-bottle, doused the lantern, pillowed his head . . .

and went to sleep.

CHAPTER 73

Nine years later, my beloved, the Empress also looks at what she has written.

Wind and rain and brilliant shafts of sunlight strike the upper room, where she sits and writes; mirroring feelings within her heart—she pours her mind, back to that day.

"Yes," she writes, "I said those things . . ."

❖ ❖ ❖

. . . which shouldn't be a surprise: I had *thought worse* things, only minutes before. After all that I had gone through, at the unseen edge of hope's consummation—I had abandoned hope, to try to stop my pain.

And so when hope arrived, I wasn't ready.

What I said, I said in accord with the path I had already made—and according to how I chose to follow that path.

This is important to understand. I *could* have chosen, even then, to say and do things differently. I could have thrown my arms around him, kissing him near to an inch of our lives! That *wasn't* something I normally would have done; but I *could* have.

I could have done what he deserved. Something. Anything.

I know what he said—I still remember; but even if he also deserved what I *did* do instead . . . I didn't have to give him that.

I could have given him something better. Anything better.

But, I didn't.

Our choices affect the momentum of our minds—and I had chosen wrongly; and so my pride was once again at stake: my pride in my present, and in my future, and in myself.

I had convinced myself, once more, that Jian was a threat.

And, indeed, he was. He was a threat to my self—the most dangerous threat one's self can face.

What I didn't understand—what I *refused* to understand—but what I understand now, is this:

There *is* a threat that enslaves the self, to another self. And this, I still believe, should be resisted, to the very blood.

But, there *is* another threat.

It takes away the food of the self, gnawing upon the self,
and gives to the self . . .
everything else.

The first, the hideous threat, resembles the other; making the hideous threat more hideous.

But—the second threat should be accepted, when it is given, if it is given, if *ever* it is perceived: for much the same reason a mouth and teeth and tongue should eat, ideally, of anything—
except themselves.

How is *that* a threat?! Is it not glorious?!

Yes; it is glorious.
But, it means one's self must be dependent, after all,
on something other than one's self.

And I, my self, refused to accept that truth—that threat.

So, I imagined that threat to be the other threat. The hideous threat.

I imagined it, I say; for I know, I admit, I *testify:*
I could have made other choices.
I knew different, even then—I knew better.

But I, my self, did not want to make those better choices.
So, I chose for the worse.
And how I wish . . .

. . . Lord Above,
how I wish I had chosen something else . . .

I had, in fact, been given all I wanted.
Yes, I had fought for some of it; but I had been *given* my opportunities even to fight, to make my contributions.
Given opportunities, given gifts—given *everything*.

And I still wanted to *take.*

So, over the next few days, I grew; becoming more and more aware of all that I had been given—and of my dependencies.
Was I grateful? Did I receive my new opportunities, acting upon them?

No.
I was resentful.
And I took those new opportunities, acting upon them.
And that makes all the difference.

I intentionally trod the sharp cliff's path; the path that I had been forging—off of which I could have stepped, had occasionally stepped, might *still* have stepped.

But off of which I did not step.

I will, however, say this, too—in memory of the girl who prayed for me, and who may one day read my testimony.

Thank you.

And do not despair. Your prayers *were* answered.

I did get better.

But I got worse before I got better.

And that was my own fault.

The Empress weeps, as she often does when she writes her Testimony. Silently, she cries—hearing the cry of justice.

But, she reads again what she has written,
and reminds herself: the little girl's prayers *were* answered.

And so, she rises to her feet, carefully, unable to bend very far; and taking the tablet of reinforced clay from its stand, she lets it drop to the floor, in the center, above where a column stands solidly deep, down into the heart of the city itself.

And in the sunlight striking through the clouds, she glides across the floor, to the window above the palace garden; out the window, and gently down the wall— not to sleep; but to act on what she has learned about herself and others over the years.

She goes, to act upon the opportunities she has been given.

The sun slowly washes the room of rain,
till only the chair and the stand remain.